# CINDER[...]
# THE P[...]

LOIS FAYE DYER

AND

# THE TEXAN'S HAPPILY-EVER-AFTER

BY
KAREN ROSE SMITH

MILLS
BOON

Dear Reader,

I was intrigued when my editor asked me to be a part of THE BABY CHASE series. First, because fertility clinics can be beacons of hope for couples with fertility issues. And second, because I was charmed by the prospect of writing a hero who loves women and balances a playboy personality with a passionate commitment to his patients. And third, because I've never been able to resist a romance novel about a rake falling in love at last, especially when the woman who owns his heart is an independent, wary career woman and single mother of an adorable little girl.

I had so much fun watching Dr. Chance Demetrios meet his fate in beautiful Jennifer Labeaux. And to add icing on this particular cake, Chance finds himself feeling ferociously parental and protective toward Annie, Jennifer's adorable little girl. How can you not love a guy who is charmed and enchanted by a red-haired sweetly precocious child? And how can you not cheer for Jennifer, a woman who's strong enough and wise enough to choose a mate like Chance?

I hope you enjoy reading *Cinderella and the Playboy*—I thoroughly loved writing Jennifer and Chance's story.

Warmly,

*Lois Faye Dyer*

# CINDERELLA AND
# THE PLAYBOY

BY
LOIS FAYE DYER

First published in Great Britain 2011
by Mills & Boon, an imprint of Harlequin (UK) Limited,
Eton House, 18-24 Paradise Road, Richmond, Surrey TW9 1SR

© Harlequin Books S.A. 2010

ISBN: 978 0 263 88876 8

23-0411

Harlequin (UK) policy is to use papers that are natural, renewable and
recyclable products and made from wood grown in sustainable forests. The
logging and manufacturing processes conform to the legal environmental
regulations of the country of origin.

Printed and bound in Spain
by Blackprint CPI, Barcelona

**Lois Faye Dyer** lives in a small town on the shore of beautiful Puget Sound in the Pacific Northwest with her two eccentric and lovable cats, Chloe and Evie. She loves to hear from readers. You can write to her c/o Paperbacks Plus, 1618 Bay Street, Port Orchard, WA 98366, USA. Visit her on the web at www.LoisDyer.com.

With my heartfelt thanks to Karen Edgel,
hospice nurse, in Republic, Washington

# *Chapter One*

"Hey, Jennifer—Dr. Demetrios just walked in."

Jennifer Labeaux noted her friend Yolanda's mischievous grin before she glanced over her shoulder. As usual, her heartbeat sped up at the sight of the tall, dark-haired male striding toward her section of the Coach House Diner.

Dr. Chance Demetrios was easily six feet four inches tall and built like a linebacker. He wore his black hair a shade long and his eyes were a deep chocolate brown—eyes that twinkled, charmed and seduced Jennifer with each conversation they shared.

She watched him slide into his usual booth, third from the back, with a view of the Cambridge, Massachusetts, street outside. He always sat in her section. Jennifer was torn between being flattered and wishing he wouldn't single her out. Not that she disliked him—quite the contrary. He made her yearn for things she knew she couldn't have and she was far too attracted to him for her own good. No doubt about it, Chance was too sexy, too rich and too high-octane for a waitress whose most sophisticated night out was visiting her neighborhood ice-cream shop with her five-year-old daughter.

Over the past six months, she'd seen Chance nearly every morning. There was no mistaking the male interest in his eyes but his persistent friendliness and good-natured acceptance of her refusals when he had asked her out had slowly but surely eased, and then erased, her natural wariness. The conversations she'd overheard between him and other customers only increased his appeal. He appeared to be genuinely interested in the lives of the diner regulars.

Even if dating were possible in her life at the moment, she'd never date Chance Demetrios, she thought with regret. Rumor had it that he loved women and went through girlfriends like a PMSing woman went through chocolate bars. Despite being power-fully attracted to him, Jennifer knew he was out of her league. If she ever became involved with a man again, he wouldn't be someone with a stable of women.

She tucked a menu under her arm, picked up a glass of ice water and a fresh pot of coffee and walked to the booth.

"Good morning, Dr. Demetrios," she said with a bright smile. "What can I get you?"

"Morning, Jennifer."

His deep voice seemed to linger over her name, sending shivers up her spine and heat curling through her belly.

Determined to ignore her rebellious body's reaction, Jennifer kept her gaze on the thick coffee mug as she poured. She steeled herself, setting down the pot and taking out her pad and pen. Despite preparing herself, however, meeting his gaze was a jolt. His dark eyes were warm, appreciative and filled with male interest.

And then he smiled. Jennifer had to fight to keep from melting into a pool of overheated hormones.

"The usual?" Thank goodness her voice didn't reflect her inner turmoil, she thought with relief and not a little surprise.

"Yeah, please," he said, his smile wry. "And maybe you can just hook up an IV with black coffee."

"Late night?" she asked with sympathy. Her gaze moved over his face, noting the lines of weariness she'd been too preoccupied to notice earlier. His dark eyes were heavy lidded and his jaw shadowed with beard stubble. He looked as if he'd either just rolled out of bed—or hadn't gone to bed at all. "Did you work all night?"

He shrugged. "Back-to-back emergency calls."

"You work too hard," she commented.

"All part of being a doctor." He smiled at her. "I knew the job had lousy hours when I signed on."

She lifted an eyebrow at his reasoning. "Maybe so, but if you don't sleep, how are you going to function?"

He glanced at the Rolex on his wrist. "Maybe I'll catch a nap on my office sofa before my first appointment."

"Good plan." Jennifer heard the cook call her name and realized she'd been chatting too long. "I have to go. I'll tell the other waitresses you need your coffee topped often this morning."

"Thanks."

Taken in by his appreciative smile, Jenny forced herself to nod pleasantly and turn to her next customer.

Through half-lowered lashes, Chance sipped the hot black coffee and watched her walk away. He suspected the employees and regulars in the diner weren't fooled by his attempts to play down his interest but he couldn't summon up the energy to care if they knew he loved looking at her. She wore the same attire as the rest of the waitresses—black slacks and white shirt under a black vest. But with her long legs, lush curls and graceful carriage, the clothes took on a different vibe on Jennifer. The diner's owner might think the uniform made his waitresses blend together, but she stood out like a long-stemmed rose in a bouquet of daisies.

He'd been asking her out for months now and each time, she'd turned him down. Six months earlier, he would have shrugged and moved on to the next beautiful woman. But for some reason that he couldn't begin to understand, he'd lost the urge to pursue other women since meeting Jennifer.

He couldn't accept that she wouldn't go out with him. He knew damn well she was attracted to him. Despite her never-wavering, cool-yet-friendly reserve, he felt the strong tug of sexual chemistry between them every time he saw her. He'd dated a lot of women over the years. He knew he hadn't misread the faint flush of color over the high arch of her cheekbones when they talked, nor the way she shielded her gaze with lowered lashes when he teased her.

No, Jennifer was definitely interested. But he'd asked her out at least a dozen times, probably more. She'd always refused, saying she didn't date customers.

From the snippets of conversation he'd overheard from the other waitresses, Chance didn't think she dated anyone at all.

Which only made him more intrigued and determined to spend time with her, away from the diner.

He rolled his shoulders to relieve the ache of muscles too long without rest and stretched his long legs out beneath the table. The red, vinyl-covered bench seat was comfortably padded and, like everything else in the Coach House Diner, reflected the 1950s theme. The effect was cheerful and welcoming. Chance had felt at home here from the first moment he'd stepped over the threshold six months earlier. Since the diner was only a short walk from the Armstrong Fertility Institute where he worked, it had quickly become his favorite place to have coffee, breakfast, lunch or grab a quick dinner if he'd worked late.

He glanced around the room, nodding at Fred, an elderly gentleman seated on a stool and eating his breakfast at the end of the long counter. Fred was a retired railroad engineer and, despite his advanced age of ninety-five, still woke early. Chance had spent more than one morning next to Fred on the round seats at the counter between 5:00 a.m. and 6:00.

He took another long sip of coffee and rubbed his eyes. It had been one hell of a week. After long hours of hard, frustrating work, he and his research partner Ted Bonner had finally disproved allegations that their work was questionable.

In the midst of proving the funding was legally and morally ethical, Chance had also watched as Ted fell in love and got married over the past several months. Chance would never admit it aloud, but observing his best friend's happiness had raised questions for Chance about his own lifestyle. Did he want to meet a woman who could make him settle down? Could he be monogamous?

Given his relationship history, Chance doubted it. He loved women—their smiles, their silky hair and skin, the way their eyes lit with pleasure when they made love.

No, he couldn't imagine ever settling down with one woman.

Which made him wonder why he hadn't dated anyone over the past six months.

Unconsciously, his gaze sought out Jennifer, locating her at the other end of the room. Her laughter pealed musically as she took an order from two women in business suits.

He muffled a groan and swigged down the rest of his coffee. He knew damn well Jennifer was the reason he hadn't dated anyone in months.

*Or maybe I'm just too busy with work,* he thought, unwilling to accept that the beautiful blonde was to blame for his nonexistent love life.

Midweek, he'd spent two long nights in the operating room. His volunteer work at a free clinic in a low-income Boston neighborhood often expanded to include surgery during emergency situations. This week, those emergencies seemed to roll in almost on each other's heels.

*I'm too damn tired,* he told himself. *That's why I'm being introspective. A solid eight hours of sleep and life will look normal again.*

He frowned at his empty coffee mug. He hated examining his feelings and no matter how he sliced it, he couldn't deny that he'd been spending too much time lately considering his life. And for a man who was rarely alone, he could swear he sometimes felt lonely.

"More coffee?"

Chance looked up. The red-haired waitress he often noticed talking with Jennifer stood next to his booth.

"Thanks."

She quickly filled his mug and left, letting Chance return to his brooding.

He'd had plenty of affairs, but none of his relationships with women could qualify as meaningful.

*And that's the way I like it,* he thought. *So why am I wondering if there ought to have been more?*

He dragged his hand over his face and rubbed his eyes. He reached into his jacket pocket but the tiny vial of nonprescription eyedrops he kept there was missing. Instead, he found a note he didn't remember putting there.

He scanned it and felt like groaning. The 3x5 card from his secretary was a reminder that the institute's annual Founder's Ball was the coming weekend.

And he didn't have a date. He frowned and tapped the card on the tabletop.

The prospect of going alone held no appeal. Attending the event was mandatory, and he'd *never* attend without a date.

*What the hell,* he thought. Given that the only pretty woman he wanted to date was Jennifer, he might as well bite the bullet and ask her to go with him.

*She'll probably say no. She's never said yes any of the other times I've asked her out.*

But just talking to her always made him smile— and he could use a smile this morning.

"Here you are—eggs over medium, French toast and bacon." Jennifer slid the plate onto the tabletop in front of him.

*Perfect timing,* he thought.

"Would you like me to bring you some aspirin?" she asked, glancing down sideways at him.

Her comment was so far from his thoughts that he blinked in confusion. "What? Why?"

"You were frowning as if your head hurt. I thought you might have a headache."

"Oh. No, I don't have a headache. Not yet, anyway." He held out the card. "I was reading this."

She glanced at the note, her eyes scanning the black type. "The Founder's Ball? It sounds very glamorous."

"It's black tie." His shrug spoke volumes about his lack of interest in whether the event was sophisticated. "The institute holds the ball every year. The band is supposed to be excellent and I hear the food's worth putting on a tux and tie—but it's no fun to go alone. Which is why you should take pity on me and be my date."

Jennifer brushed a strand of blond hair from her temple and fought the temptation to accept. The diner was located only a few blocks from the institute and many of its customers worked at the medical center.

The women employees had been buzzing about the Founder's Ball for weeks, discussing gowns, shoes, jewelry and hairstyles.

Enticing as it was to think about donning a glamorous dress to go dancing with Chance, however, she knew she couldn't.

"I'm sorry, but I can't." She slipped the card onto the table next to his hand, taking care not to let her fingers touch his. She'd made that mistake once and the shock of awareness that hit her when she'd brushed against him had rocked her. "Thank you for asking me, though."

"Don't thank me." His deep voice was almost a growl, although his dark eyes were rueful. "Just say yes."

She shook her head. "I told you. I never date customers."

He leaned back against the padded vinyl leather and tipped his head to the side, eyes narrowing consideringly over her. "What if I wasn't a customer?"

The question startled Jennifer and she laughed. "Too late. You're already a customer."

"So you don't date ex-customers, either?"

She shook her head.

"Damn."

"I have to get back to work," she told him, smiling

as he tipped his mug at her in salute before she turned and walked away.

"What's up with Dr. Hunk?" Yolanda asked the moment Jennifer joined her behind the long counter.

"I think he worked late last night," Jennifer responded, walking past her to the big coffee urn. She checked the levels and found one nearly empty so she measured ground coffee into a fresh paper filter.

"Is that all?" Yolanda joined Jennifer and leaned forward to peer into her face, her dark eyes assessing. "It looked like he was asking you out again."

"He did," Jennifer admitted.

"I hope you said yes this time."

"Of course not. You know I won't go out with a customer," Jennifer reminded her. She'd made up the rule on the spur-of-the-moment the first week she'd worked at the diner. To her surprise, the man who'd asked her out seemed to accept it with regret but little argument. She'd used the excuse several times since with the same results and no one had ever tempted her to change her mind—until Chance.

Yolanda rolled her eyes. "That's such a crock, Jennifer. You could make an exception." She glanced over her shoulder at the booth where Chance sat and sighed loudly. "Goodness knows, I certainly would for Dr. D."

Jennifer laughed. "Don't you think your husband might object?"

"Hmm. Good point." Yolanda's dimples formed as she grinned, her eyes flashing mischievously.

"Exactly," Jennifer said with emphasis. She tossed the used filter with its damp coffee grounds into the trash bin and slipped the new one into the big coffeemaker. "You'd have to say no, too, but for different reasons. The charming Dr. Demetrios will just have to find another Cinderella to take to the ball."

"To the ball?" Yolanda repeated, intrigued. "Do you mean, literally to a ball?"

"Actually, yes. He asked me to go to the Armstrong Fertility Institute Founder's Ball with him."

"What?" Yolanda's shriek drew the attention of the diners at the long counter behind them. She glanced at them, waved a hand to tell them to return to their bacon and eggs and focused on Jennifer. "Spill, girlfriend," she hissed. "I want details."

"That's all I've got," Jennifer protested. "He asked me to be his date for the Founder's Ball and I turned him down."

"I can't believe you refused a chance to go to that shindig. It's one of Boston's biggest parties!"

A third waitress joined them to collect a full coffeepot. Yolanda caught her sleeve. "Shirley, you're not going to believe this."

The red-haired woman paused, tucking her order pad into her pocket and eyeing Yolanda with interest. "What?"

"Dr. Demetrios asked Jennifer to go to the Founder's Ball with him—and she turned him down!"

Shirley's eyes widened. "Jennifer, you can't say no! There's no way Yolanda and I will ever get an invitation so you have to go, then come back and tell us all about it."

Jenny rolled her eyes. "I can't go out with Dr. Demetrios, Shirley. If I did, no one would ever again accept my I-don't-date-customers rule," Jennifer protested.

"Not if they don't know—so swear Dr. D to secrecy and make him promise not to tell anyone," Yolanda said promptly. "He's been trying to get you to go out with him for months—he'll swear not to tell anyone you broke your rule."

"Even if I wanted to go, I couldn't," Jennifer continued, trying a different argument. "The affair is black tie. I have nothing to wear—no dress, no shoes, no jewelry. It's not as if I can go in my best jeans."

Shirley dismissed the problem with a wave of her hand. "My best friend from high school is half owner of a high-end consignment shop. She can get you whatever you might need and it won't cost you a thing. She owes me a favor. I'll ask her to let us take everything home for the weekend and I'll return them on Monday morning before the shop opens. I'm sure she'll let us."

A fourth waitress joined them in time to hear Shirley's comments and her lively face lit with curiosity. "Who's getting a designer dress and jewelry?"

"Jennifer—Dr. D asked her to go to the Founder's Ball with him."

"No way!" Linda's eyes widened with surprise and delight. "Yeah, Jennifer! You're going, of course," she said with absolute conviction.

"I can't—you know I never date customers," Jennifer replied.

"Huh," Yolanda snorted. "You don't date. Period. I don't think you've gone out with anyone but the three of us since you started working here."

"That's true," Shirley conceded and nodded with firm agreement. "You've got to expand your horizons, Jennifer. Not that we don't love having you join us for outings after work and weekends, but honey—" she laid a hand on Jennifer's forearm and leaned closer, fixing her with a solemn gaze "—you seriously need to go out with a man."

"And get to know him—in the biblical sense," Linda added.

"I'm not hooking up with a guy for sex," Jennifer protested.

"Who said it was just for sex?" Yolanda countered. "The doc is the perfect guy for a weekend fling—he's nice, you've seen him nearly every day for the past six months so you can be sure he's not an ax murderer, he's interested in you and he has a reputation for never getting involved long-term with women." She ticked off her arguments one-by-one on the fingers of her right hand. "You'll have a great time and if you end up spending the weekend having great sex, well…that's just an added benefit. You've been living like a nun and Chance is the perfect man to end that state."

"I couldn't possibly spend the weekend with anyone," Jennifer protested, though she was shocked at how tempted she was by the idea.

She hadn't dressed up in an evening gown and attended a black-tie party since before her short-lived marriage to Patrick, her daughter's father. That Harvest Ball at the country club in her small Illinois hometown had been one of many such events, distinguished only because it had been the last dinner dance she'd attended before leaving for college.

A year later, she'd been married, divorced, and was six months pregnant with her little girl.

That was over five years ago and she hadn't worn a party dress, gone out on a date, nor slept with a man since. No wonder she was tempted, she thought. With an effort, she forced herself to focus on another reason to convince her friends she couldn't go to the Founder's Ball with Chance.

"And besides," she added, "I probably couldn't find a babysitter for Annie for an evening."

"That's absolutely not a problem," Linda assured her. "My kids would love to have her spend the weekend. Just yesterday they were asking when Annie was coming over again. We'll pick her up before your date and bring her home late Sunday afternoon."

Jennifer paused, staring at the trio of faces. Could she do this? More important, *should* she do this?

"Come on," Yolanda coaxed. "You know you want to."

"I shouldn't…" Jennifer began. She glanced over her shoulder and found Chance watching her, his dark eyes unreadable. The instant shiver of awareness was nothing new—he always elicited this response in her. He made her yearn, made her want.

Seeing his unfailing gentleness with elderly Mrs. Morgenstern when she routinely stopped him in the diner to ask for medical advice had made Jennifer sharply aware of the lack of a man's strength in her own life. And the charm and dry wit with which he deftly turned aside the inevitable passes from women, all without hurting their feelings, made her wonder if his reputation as a playboy was true. He seemed to genuinely like women and go out of his way to be kind, no matter their age or degree of beauty.

All of which only increased her attraction to him— which made her more wary than ever. Her ex-husband had been charming and handsome and she'd learned to her sorrow that his goodness was a facade. Pretty words and a handsome face had concealed a shallow, faithless heart. And after her bad experience with Patrick, Jennifer questioned her own judgment when it came to men. Everything about Chance drove her to obey the urging of her body to give in and say yes. But how could she be sure Chance was one of the good guys? Should she give in just this once? Could she set aside her self-imposed strict rules—and her role as responsible single mother—and grab a few stolen hours of fun for herself?

"Go on, tell him yes," Shirley urged in a whisper behind her.

Jennifer looked back at her friends. Their faces held nearly identical expressions of encouragement and affection.

"Are you sure you don't mind having Annie sleep over for the weekend?" she asked Linda.

"I'm positive!"

With sudden, uncharacteristic impulsiveness, Jennifer nodded abruptly. "Then I'll do it."

"Yes." Yolanda pumped her fist in the air and laughed.

Linda leaned closer. "Go tell him," she prodded in a whisper. "Right now." She caught Jennifer's shoulders and turned her around, giving her a little nudge toward the booth where Chance sat, frowning down at his mug of coffee.

Jennifer took a deep breath. She could hear her coworkers whispering as she walked away from them and couldn't suppress a smile. The three women were great friends and staunch supporters. She didn't doubt they were sincere when they'd told her they expected a full report on the institute's glamorous event—and every detail about her night out with the sexy doctor.

Chance looked up just as she reached his booth.

"If the invitation is still open, I'd love to go to the Founder's Ball with you," Jennifer said without preamble.

His mouth curved in a grin and Jennifer didn't miss the male satisfaction and what she thought was a gleam of triumph in his dark eyes.

"It's definitely still open."

"Good." She took her order pad and a pen from her pocket. "It's this weekend, isn't it? What time?"

"I'll pick you up at eight on Saturday. I need your address," he added.

"Right." She nodded, scribbled her street and apartment number on the back of an order slip, tore if off the pad and handed it to him. The slow, intimate smile he gave her sent a shiver of heated apprehension spiraling up her spine and she felt her cheeks warm. "Well." She cleared her throat. "I've got to get back to work."

"Absolutely."

"Then I guess I'll see you Saturday." She turned to walk away.

"Jennifer." The seductive deep drawl stopped her and she glanced at him over her shoulder. "Thanks for saying yes."

"You're welcome." She walked back to the counter, feeling his gaze between her shoulder blades like a caress. Fortunately, a customer stopped her and during their ensuing conversation, Chance paid his check and left the diner.

She wasn't comfortable knowing she was always aware of him on some level, she thought with stark honesty. Her senses appeared to be sharply tuned to him whenever he was around her. She felt his presence and departure like a tangible force each time he entered or left the diner. Pretending to ignore him hadn't solved the problem, nor had self lectures about the sheer stupidity of giving in to the attraction.

After her divorce, she'd vowed she wouldn't subject her daughter to a series of men friends rotating through their lives. Jennifer had spent her childhood watching substitute fathers move in and out of her mother's home after her parents' divorce. When the third very nice man moved on and her mother quickly fell in love with a fourth, Jennifer had stopped viewing any of her mother's boyfriends as permanent fixtures. Her mother was currently headed for divorce court for the sixth time.

Because Jennifer's grandparents were affluent, socially prominent members of the community, she'd never wanted for the necessities of food, clothing, good schools and a lovely home. But her life felt lonely and emotionally insecure. Lunch at the country club with her grandmother and piles of exquisitely wrapped presents under the Christmas tree didn't compensate for the lack of security under her mother's roof.

She'd married young while still in college and dreamed of a life filled with home and family. With stars in her eyes, she'd quit college to take a full-time job to support her husband, Patrick, a pre-med student. Six months after the wedding, she'd been devastated when Patrick was furious the night she told him she was pregnant. He'd accused her of lying about taking birth control pills and he moved out of their apartment within a week, immediately filing for divorce. He'd told her he needed a working wife whose first commitment was to him and he had no room in his life for a child. He'd even agreed to give her full custody and let her raise their baby alone since he had no interest in visitation rights. In return, she agreed not to request child support payments from him.

When he told their mutual friends that the divorce was Jennifer's choice, they reacted by ostracizing her and Jennifer was devastated. Much as she hated the snubs and vicious whisperings behind her back, however, she refused to be drawn into a mud-slinging match.

The divorce was final when Jennifer was six months pregnant. Three months later, she gave birth to Annie, a beautiful six-and-a-half-pound, red-haired baby girl with big blue eyes.

In the five years since Annie's birth, Jennifer had kept her vow to create a better life for her daughter than the one she'd known. She went to work, attended night classes to finish her college degree, and spent her free time with her little girl. Men occasionally asked her out but she turned them down without a single regret. If celibacy and a solo adult life was the cost of giving Annie a secure, quiet life then it was a small price to pay.

Jennifer knew her friends were convinced she needed an adult social life, including a man to share her bed. But she was committed to keeping her vow to not repeat her mother's mistakes. She swore her friends to silence, and they all promised not to tell any interested men about Annie or other details of her life. Fortunately, she hadn't met anyone that stirred more than mild interest and she'd certainly never considered sleeping with anyone—until Chance walked into the diner and smiled at her.

Since then, her sleep had been haunted by vivid dreams of making love with him.

*Perhaps going out with him will get him out of my system,* she thought.

Finishing her shift at two o'clock that afternoon, Jennifer hurried home to collect her daughter from the babysitter. She chatted for a few moments with the spry seventy-eight-year-old Margaret Sullivan, before she and Annie said goodbye and headed across the hall to their own apartment. On the day they'd moved in, Margaret had knocked on their door with a plate of warm cookies and a welcoming smile. When Jennifer's babysitter moved away, Margaret volunteered to have Annie stay with her while Jennifer worked or attended classes and the three had formed a close, familylike relationship.

"How was school today, Annie?" Jennifer asked when they were home in their own small kitchen. She filled the kettle at the sink and set it on the stove, switching on the burner.

"Fine," Annie replied as she carefully took three small plates from the lower cabinet next to the sink. "Me and Melinda are working on a project."

"Really? What kind of project?" Jennifer took two mugs from the cupboard. At the small corner table, Annie was carefully arranging four peanut butter cookies on one of the plates.

"We're building a miniature house with a kennel for our dogs." Annie shifted one of the cookies a bit to the left, eyed the plate critically, then nodded with approval. She looked up at Jennifer, her blue eyes glowing with fervor. "We're practicing for when we get our real dogs."

"I see." Jennifer caught her daughter in a quick hug, pressing a kiss against the silky red-gold curls. The teakettle whistled a warning and she released

Annie to turn off the burner. Pouring hot water into the mugs, she dropped an English Breakfast tea bag into hers and stirred hot chocolate mix into Annie's, then carried them over to the table. The little girl perched on a chair, legs swinging with enthusiasm. "You know, honey," Jennifer began, "it's going to be a while before we can have a dog." She set the gently steaming mug of chocolate in front of Annie and took the chair opposite.

"I know." Annie gave her mother a serene smile and stirred her drink with single-minded concentration.

"Not that I wouldn't like to have a dog, too," Jennifer continued. "But the landlord won't let us have pets in the apartment."

"It's all right, Mommy," Annie said. She sipped the chocolate from her spoon, made a small sound of satisfaction and drank from her mug. "I'm going to ask Santa for a dog this Christmas." She narrowed her eyes consideringly. "I think we need a house with a yard, too, don't you?"

"Uh…sure." Jennifer had no idea why Annie had decided that Santa would deliver a dog and a house by Christmas. *But it's only spring,* she thought, *and with luck, I can distract her and she'll forget about it by this winter.* Given that Annie had previously demonstrated a focused determination normally found in much older children, Jennifer wasn't convinced the delay would distract her daughter. Nevertheless, it was the only plan she had. "What did you and Melinda use to build your miniature house?"

Jennifer's attempt to distract Annie worked as the little girl launched into an enthusiastic description of the two shoe boxes they'd taped together and how they'd used scissors to cut out dog photos from a magazine.

The mugs were half-empty before Annie's recital of the day's events was exhausted. Jennifer eyed her over the rim of her tea mug and smiled as her daughter broke off a chunk of peanut butter cookie and tucked it neatly into her mouth.

"I have a surprise for you, Annie," she said. "How would you like to have a sleepover at Jake and Suzie's house this weekend?"

"Oooh, yes!" Annie bounced in her chair, her eyes lit with excitement. "May I take my backpack and my Lilia-Mae doll and my Enchanted Pony so Suzie and I can play with them?"

"Yes, of course." Jennifer laughed when Annie jumped off her chair and threw herself into her mother's arms, climbing into her lap as she listed all the many things she wanted to take with her.

Jennifer felt a stab of misgiving as she cuddled the

warm, vibrant little body in her arms. This quiet apartment with Annie was her real life and she loved it—a world filled with her beautiful little girl and her busy days with work and college classes. A date with Chance Demetrios—at the ritzy Founder's Ball, no less—was a huge step outside the constraints of the life she'd built.

But her friends were right, too, she realized. Sometimes, she was lonely and longed for an emotional—and physical—connection with a partner. There was no room for a permanent man in her life just now and wouldn't be for the foreseeable future. But just for one night, perhaps it wouldn't do any harm if she seized the opportunity to play Cinderella before returning to the quiet rhythm of her busy days with Annie.

Jennifer rested her cheek against her daughter's silky red-gold curls, breathed in her little-girl smell of shampoo, soap and crayons, and contentedly listened to Annie's excited plans for spending the weekend with her friends.

Chance hadn't recognized the street address that Jennifer had scribbled on the note after she had accepted his invitation so he'd made a mental note to check it out later. He tucked the paper safely away in his pocket until later that evening, when he turned on his laptop to browse the Internet. It took his computer only a few moments to search, find a street map of Boston and pinpoint Jennifer's neighborhood.

He frowned at the screen, trying to visualize the area. He thought her apartment might be located within a mile or two of the free clinic where he volunteered. He typed in a request for directions from his own town house, in an upscale Boston neighborhood, to Jennifer's address. The resultant map details confirmed his guess that her street wasn't more than a short cab drive and probably within walking distance from the free clinic. The two addresses were in a shabby though respectable area of Boston, not far from his own home in actual miles but light-years away in real-estate prices.

Chance didn't give a damn that Jennifer's address highlighted the disparity in their incomes but it drove home the fact that he knew little about her life away from the diner.

He'd noticed her sitting in a back booth to study on her coffee breaks at the diner and when he'd commented, she'd told him that she was taking college classes. But beyond being a student and working as a waitress, she was an enigma to him. He wondered if she lived alone or shared an apartment with a fellow student.

During their brief conversations, she'd never mentioned her family and he realized that he didn't know if she had any sisters or brothers, or if her parents lived here in Boston. He couldn't help but wonder what her childhood had been like, what kind of a family she came from, and where she'd grown up. Jennifer treated Mrs. Blake, the elderly widow who counted out coins to pay for her daily coffee and donut, with the same friendly respect that she gave to the head of the Armstrong Fertility Institute. He'd never seen her react as if any of the high-powered doctors or scientists who frequented the diner intimidated her in the slightest.

Which made him think she must have grown accustomed to dealing with powerful, influential people before she arrived at the Coach House Diner.

She didn't seem to recognize the Demetrios name, however, which indicated to him that while her family may have been affluent, they didn't move in his parents' stratified circle. The Demetrios shipping empire had made his family very, very rich and by definition, made him heir to an obscenely large fortune. Chance knew his father felt he'd turned his back on the family business when he chose to become a doctor. The choice had driven a wedge between him and his parents, especially his father.

Much as he loved them, however, he couldn't ignore the deep, passionate commitment he felt to medicine.

He wondered if Jennifer's parents were happy with her career choice of waitress and part-time college student.

Which brought him full circle, he realized, to the fact that he was apparently bewitched by every facet of the mysterious Miss Labeaux.

That there was much he didn't know about the beautiful blonde only made her more intriguing. Anticipation curled through his midsection.

*I'll find out Saturday night,* he reflected.

*Chapter Two*

At seven-fifteen on Saturday night, Jennifer was well on her way to being transformed into Cinderella. Linda, Yolanda and Shirley had knocked on her door at 5:00 p.m., laden with bags. They'd dropped boxes, bags and bottles atop her bed before they raided her kitchen for wineglasses. After pouring wine and setting out a tray of crackers and cheese on her dresser, they had shooed her into the shower.

She had shampooed and scrubbed with Linda's gift of plumeria-scented gel before toweling off and smoothing the matching floral lotion over her skin.

She had heard Annie's giggles over the throb of music from the radio on her bedside table and when she had pulled on her robe and left the bathroom, she had found Annie dancing with Yolanda. The two had twirled and spun in the small carpeted space at the foot of the bed while they sang along with a 1980s disco song.

Their enthusiasm had far outweighed their vocal talents and Jennifer had laughed as the song ended with a flourish.

Jennifer replayed the fresh memories just made over the past hour. "Hi, Mommy." Annie left Yolanda and wrapped her arms around Jennifer's waist, dimples flashing in her flushed face as she grinned up at her. "We're disco dancing."

"I see that," Jennifer told her. "Very impressive."

"But now I have to dry your mom's hair," Yolanda said, handing Jennifer a glass of wine and motioning her to have a seat on a chair she'd placed at the end of the bed. "We'll dance more later, okay, Annie?"

"Okay," the little girl agreed promptly. She curled up on the bed and settled in to watch as Yolanda worked on Jennifer's damp hair.

Yolanda wielded blow dryer and curling iron with expertise and a half hour later, stood back to eye Jennifer.

"Perfect," she declared with satisfaction.

"Will you do my hair next, Yolanda?" Annie asked, gathering fistfuls of red-gold curls and bunching a handful of the silky mass on each side of her head.

"Absolutely, kiddo." Yolanda grinned at her. "Shirley's going to help your mom with her makeup in the bathroom. You can take her place over here."

Jennifer left Annie chattering away as Yolanda French-braided her long curls. In the bathroom, Shirley upended a brocade bag of makeup onto the small countertop and lined up pots of eyeshadow, brushes for the loose powder, several tubes of lipstick and a handful of lip color pencils.

Jennifer heard Annie chattering and laughing with Yolanda as she applied makeup and Shirley offered advice. At last, she slicked lush color on her lips and smoothed clear gloss over the deep red lipstick, then stood back to critically view the effect.

The mauve eyeshadow turned her eyes a deeper blue, smoky and mysterious, set within a thicket of dark lashes. Subtle rose color tinted her cheeks. She tilted her head, loving the soft brush of silky blond curls against her nape and temples.

"Perfect," Shirley pronounced, standing behind her. Their gazes met in the mirror. "Just perfect. You look fabulous, girlfriend. Time to get dressed."

"Ahem." Jennifer loudly cleared her throat and struck a pose in the doorway.

"Ooh, Mommy." Annie's awestruck voice reflected the delight shining in her widened blue eyes. "You look just like a princess."

"Thank you, sweetheart." Jennifer caught her daughter close, receiving a tight hug in return. "Now you have to scoot," she said, giving her one last hug before looking down at her. "Be good for Linda, okay? And have fun."

"I will." Annie twirled away to grab her backpack. "I'll tell you all about it when I come home on Sunday."

"I can't wait," Jennifer assured her solemnly, exchanging a glance with Linda that shared a wry understanding, one mother to another.

Fifteen minutes later, Jennifer waved goodbye from the window as her friends climbed into their cars on the street below. Annie and Linda paused to wave up at her and moments later, the brake lights of Linda's blue sedan disappeared around the corner at the end of the block.

After the laughter, chatter and teasing advice of her friends, the apartment seemed too quiet with only the radio for company. The air in the room felt hushed and expectant, as if the place itself was waiting. Jennifer swept the neat living room with a quick glance before walking into her bedroom to collect the satin wrap that matched her dress.

Turning to leave, she caught a glimpse of her reflection in the long mirror mounted on the back of her bedroom door. Jennifer paused—the woman staring back at her seemed like a stranger. The scarlet gown fit as if custom-sewn for her alone. It had a square neckline, cut low across the swell of her breasts, with tiny cap sleeves and a bodice that hugged her narrow waist. The skirt was made up of yards of floating chiffon and lace and the toes of red, strappy high heels peeked from beneath the hem.

She wore her few pieces of good jewelry—three narrow gold bangle bracelets inset with tiny diamonds and small diamond studs in the lobes of her ears. Around her neck she wore her silver locket with Annie's picture. She knew it didn't quite match, but she'd never taken it off. Yolanda had pinned her caramel-blond curls atop her head in a soft upsweep that left the line of her throat bare, but wisps curled down her neck at the back.

The designer dress truly made her feel like Cinderella, waiting for the Prince to take her to the ball. The fanciful thought made her smile as she thought ruefully of her date's playboy reputation.

A knock sounded on the outer door and Jennifer froze. Butterflies fluttered in her stomach and she pressed the flat of her hand to her abdomen, drawing a deep breath and reaching for calmness. Then she quickly left the bedroom and crossed the living room where a cautious glance through the hall door's peephole sent her heartbeat racing once again. She drew another deep breath, slowly exhaled and opened the door.

Chance stood just outside in the hallway. He wore a classic black tuxedo, a white formal shirt fastened with onyx studs, a black bow tie and polished black dress shoes. She'd thought him handsome in casual jeans and leather jacket, but she realized helplessly that he was undeniably heart-stopping in formal wear. His gaze swept over her from head to toe and back again without the slightest attempt to conceal his interest.

"Hello." His deep voice drew out the word, the raspy growl loaded with undercurrents.

"Hello." Jennifer felt the brush of his gaze and desire curled, heating her skin, making it tingle with awareness.

"Ready to go?" Chance asked. He hadn't missed her reaction to his slow appraisal and the throb of arousal beat through his veins as he watched a faint flush move up her throat to tint her cheeks. She lowered her lashes, concealing her eyes.

"I just need to collect my purse." She left him to cross the room.

He watched her walk away, his gaze intent on the gown's long skirt. It swayed with each step, outlining the feminine curve of her hips and thighs with tantalizing briefness. The nape of her neck and the pale skin of her back to just above her narrow waist was bare, framed by crimson lace and a few loose curls. She disappeared through a doorway, momentarily releasing him from the spell that held him.

His gaze skimmed the room. The apartment was as neat as the rest of the old, well-maintained building and Jennifer's living space held a warmth that was missing in his professionally decorated town house. A blue and cream-colored afghan draped over one arm of a white-painted wood rocking chair that sat at right angles to an overstuffed blue sofa. A framed poster of the New York Metropolitan Museum of Art hung on the wall above the sofa. At the far end of the room, a bookcase was stuffed with hardcovers and paperbacks, the overflow stacked in a bright pile at one end. Chance resisted the urge to walk closer and inspect the titles on the spines, curious to learn what she read. A television and DVD player took up the two shelves on a low cabinet against one wall and beyond, a kitchen area boasted a white-painted table with four chairs pushed up to it. A bright blue cloth runner ran down the center while a small stack of notebooks and what looked like a thick textbook were spread out over one end.

Just as he was about to step over the threshold, drawn inexorably by the rooms that he instinctively knew would give him a deeper insight into Jennifer, she reappeared.

"Got everything?" he asked as he watched her walk toward him. Heat stirred in his gut, just as it did each time he saw her at the diner.

"Yes." She stepped into the hall, turning briefly to lock the door before they moved toward the elevator.

Outside, the spring night was slightly chilly and Jennifer draped the long satin wrap around her shoulders and throat. She tossed one crimson end over her shoulder and let it drape down her back, covering her bare shoulder blades above the gown's skirt.

"Cold?" Chance asked as he keyed the lock and opened the door of a sleek black Jaguar sedan parked at the curb.

"Just a little," Jennifer murmured, sliding into the low seat.

"I'll turn the heater on in a second." Chance bent to tuck her skirt out of the way and closed the door.

A moment later, he slid into the driver's seat beside her.

Jennifer fastened her seat belt and stroked her fingertips over the butter-soft leather of the seat. Her gaze swept the compact, luxurious interior. "Nice car," she said, breathing in the faint scent of leather and men's cologne.

"Thanks." Chance grinned at her and winked. "I like it." His fingers moved over a series of buttons on the dash and heated air brushed Jennifer's toes. The seat warmed beneath her. "How's that?" he asked.

"Lovely." She smiled at him, feeling distinctly cosseted.

"Good—let me know if you want it warmer." He glanced in the mirrors, shifted into gear and the Jag pulled smoothly away from the curb.

"Where is the ball being held?" Jennifer inquired as they left her block and headed downtown.

"Same place as last year, apparently," Chance replied with a sideways glance and named a posh hotel that was fairly new but built in a traditional turn-of-the-century style. It had become an instant Boston landmark, its dining room and ballrooms favored by society mavens.

"I've never been there," Jennifer said, intrigued. "But I read an article in the *Boston Herald* about the grand opening. The design alone sounded fabulous."

"Rumor has it the financier was a mad count from Austria who was a distant relative of Dracula."

"What?" Jennifer's gaze flew to his. His dark eyes were lit with amusement. "You're joking."

"Nope." He raised his hand, palm out. "I swear someone actually told me that."

"And did you believe them?" Jennifer asked with a laugh.

"Not a word."

"Excellent," she responded promptly. "I'm glad to know you're a sensible man."

"Oh, I'm sensible," he replied. "Now if you'd said I was a 'nice, safe' guy, I would have had to rethink my answer."

She shot him a chastening look from beneath her lashes and found his mouth curved in a half smile that set awareness humming through her torso. "Hmm," she said. "I don't think I'll ask you why." With an abrupt change of subject, she pointed out the window. "Isn't that the hotel?"

Chance lifted a brow and his gaze met hers for a brief moment before he nodded, downshifting as he turned out of traffic and drove beneath the portico.

The lobby was a fascinating blend of old and new, with jewel-toned, blown-glass Chihuly light fixtures hanging from boxed ceilings. A broad expanse of thick black and gold carpeting covered the floors, and round seats upholstered in gold were arranged at intervals between the reception desk and the wide hallway on their left.

Jennifer loosened her wrap from her throat and let it slip down her arms to catch at her elbows. Chance took her hand and tucked it through the bend of his arm, the move securing her against his side.

She didn't shift away from the press of his body against hers although she had the feeling she was playing with fire. She was all too aware of his reputation with women; in fact, she'd overheard several diner conversations about the subject between female employees from the institute. She didn't doubt that Chance had plans for ending the evening with her in his bed. Which left only one question—did she want the same thing?

She was certainly attracted to him. She also knew that their conversations over the past six months had led to her feeling more than just physically drawn to him. Still, she wasn't sure if she wanted more from this evening than the sheer pleasure of an adult night out with a handsome man. And since she *was* undecided, she told herself to stop worrying and simply enjoy the party.

Chance led her down the wide hallway, one side lined with upscale shops. Some were filled with jewelry and designer clothing while several stores resembled Aladdin's cave, aglow with colorful glassware and gifts. Directly across from the shops was a long bank of elevators.

"Going up?" a man called, holding the door of a half-filled car.

"Yes, thanks," Chance told him, handing Jennifer ahead of him into the elevator.

They shifted to the rear of the car as three other couples entered and Jennifer found herself standing in front of Chance. When the elevator stopped on the next floor up and several other people entered, the crowd shifted backward once again, compressing the free space even farther.

Jennifer stepped nearer to Chance to avoid being bumped by the large man in front of her and Chance slipped his arm around her waist, pulling her closer and into the shelter of his body. By necessity, however, the move brought her bare back flush against his chest, his arm a warm bar across her midriff.

She felt surrounded by him. Each breath she took drew in the faint scent of his cologne and shifted the texture of his black jacket against her mostly bare arms, pressed the round black shirt studs against her waist.

She closed her eyes, flooded by sensations as her awareness of him intensified. She wanted to sink against his powerful body, wanted to pull his arms closer and wrap them around her, but instead, she forced her eyes open. And caught her breath when she gazed directly into the mirrored elevator wall and the reflection of Chance's heavy-lidded eyes. Heat flooded her, matching the burn in his dark stare.

She stood still and his hand tightened at her waist, muscles flexing in the hard body that held her close. The moment was taut with silent tension. She nearly groaned with frustration when the connection was abruptly broken by the ping of the elevator when it came to a smooth stop. The doors opened with an audible whoosh, the sound further shattering the moment.

"Our floor," Chance murmured in her ear, his voice deeper, rougher.

Jennifer didn't reply, unsure if her voice would actually function. She and Chance moved with the crowd, conversation unnecessary amid the laughter and chatter. Chance's hand rested at the small of her back, a warm weight that tied her to him as surely as if it were an invisible chain.

Never had she been so conscious of the differences between male and female, nor so compelled to explore the undeniable pull on her senses that drew her inexorably toward him.

They reached a wide archway and the guests around them slowed, forming a straggling line as they waited to enter the dining room.

"Dinner should be great," Chance murmured. "I happen to know one of the chefs." He took a square, gold-embossed, cream-colored card from his inner jacket pocket as the line moved forward.

"Good evening, Dr. Demetrios." The tuxedo-clad man standing just outside the door smiled with warmth, nodding at Jennifer. "Ma'am."

"Hello, Frank," Chance replied. "Tell your boss I'm glad he's doing the catering tonight. I was seriously considering skipping the dinner until I heard he was the chef."

"I'll tell him." The man's smile broadened. He took the invitation from Chance and consulted a seating chart. "You and your lady are with the senator and his wife at a front table." He snapped his fingers and a waiter instantly appeared. "Joseph, show the doctor and his guest to table number four."

"Yes, sir. This way, please." The young man

sketched a quick, respectful nod and led the way across the room.

Jennifer tried not to stare as they crossed the beautifully appointed art-deco dining room. White linen tablecloths covered round tables, each set for eight guests with polished silverware, gold-trimmed china, sparkling crystal glasses and fresh floral centerpieces. Crystal chandeliers were spaced at intervals down the ceiling and glittered and gleamed, adding their brilliance to the recessed lighting in the boxed ceiling.

"Chance!" A tall man with a mane of white hair and sun lines fanning from the edges of shrewd blue eyes stood as they reached a table just to the left of the speaker's podium. "I told Emily Armstrong to make sure we sat at your table. I'm glad it worked out."

"Hello, Archie." Chance shook the man's outstretched hand before draping an arm over Jennifer's shoulder. "Jennifer, this is Senator Claxton and his wife, Evelyn. Their son, Ben, was my best friend from kindergarten through college. Archie and Evelyn, this is Jennifer Labeaux."

"Good evening," Jennifer held out her hand and received a firm, warm handshake.

"Glad to meet you, Jennifer," the senator said, his eyes kind, his smile welcoming.

Seated on his left, his wife nodded and smiled. "It's nice to meet you, dear." The silver-haired woman leaned forward. "We must make a pact to keep Archie and Chance from talking politics or funding for medical research all during dinner. When they get started, they argue for hours."

"Then we definitely need to divert them," Jennifer told her as she slipped into the chair Chance held. "You lead, I'll follow."

"Excellent." Evelyn nodded with approval.

"Now, Evie," her husband protested as he and Chance settled into their seats. "I don't know how you can object to a little friendly discussion, especially since tonight is a fundraiser for the institute and it's one of your pet projects."

"Oh, I certainly want to raise money for research," Evelyn said serenely. "I just don't want you and Chance to spend all evening discussing nothing but political funding. Especially when there's bound to be so many other interesting subjects to talk about tonight. Like for instance," she continued as she tilted her head, her voice lowering, "the not-quite-divorced starlet who just walked in on the arm of a certain land-development billionaire. Don't stare!" She caught the sleeve of her husband's tuxedo jacket to keep him from turning to look.

"Shoot, Evie," the senator grumbled. "How do you expect me not to react when you hit me with one of your bombshells?"

"I'm continually amazed at the depth of your knowledge about society's movers and shakers and the gossip they stir up," Chance teased. He lounged in his seat, one arm resting across the gold-trimmed back of Jennifer's chair. His fingers moved lazily, brushing her arm just below the edge of her capped sleeve. Goose bumps lifted in the wake of his touch.

"A senator's wife has to have something to occupy her while her husband is off doing governmental things," the older woman told him. "I just happen to have access to a very well-informed network of gossips." She winked at Jennifer.

Jennifer laughed, charmed by the couple. Before she could respond, however, two other couples arrived to take their seats at the table and there was an ensuing flurry of introductions and conversation.

She felt as if she'd been dropped back in time to the country club in her hometown. The Claxtons reminded her of a couple who had been longtime friends of her grandparents and their comfortable, loving repartee had her laughing out loud along with Chance. They clearly adored Chance, too, which

Jennifer took as an endorsement of her growing conviction that he was definitely one of the good guys.

One of the other couples at the table had a four-year-old daughter and Jennifer had to make a conscious effort to keep from sharing stories about Annie at that age. The husband was a TV producer and his wife was a local Boston news anchor. Jennifer often watched her on the late-night broadcast and was delighted to learn that she was every bit as nice in person as she seemed on television.

When dinner—which was truly delicious—was finished, the doors were opened into the adjoining ballroom. Lush music filled the high-ceilinged room from the orchestra seated on a dais, edged with potted palms, at the far end of the polished floor.

Shoulder propped against the wall, his hands thrust into his pockets, Chance waited at the edge of the ballroom while Jennifer disappeared into the ladies' room.

"Hey, Chance."

The tap on his shoulder had him straightening from the wall. Behind him were Paul Armstrong and his siblings Derek and Lisa.

"Evening, everybody," Chance smiled at the twin brothers and winked at the petite, dark-haired Lisa. The two men wore traditional black tuxedos with pristine white shirts and bow ties, while Lisa's dress was clearly a designer gown, the oyster-and-bronze-colored dress held up by a collar of jewels. It left her back and shoulders bare and Chance reflected idly that both she, and her brothers, looked every bit the society powerhouses they were. "This is quite a party."

"Yes, it is, isn't it?" Lisa said with a smile of satisfaction, her gaze sweeping over the crowded ballroom. "Everyone seems to be having a good time."

"I'd say so," Chance agreed. He flagged down a passing waiter and took champagne flutes from the tray, handing one to each of the Armstrongs. "Congratulations, you three. I'm guessing the institute's coffers will grow after tonight."

Chance lifted his glass in salute and they all sipped.

"Is the whole family here?" He glanced past the trio to briefly scan the crowd for their sister and her husband. "I don't think I've seen Olivia and Jamison."

"Oh, yes, they're here," Lisa assured him. "We were just talking with them."

"Yeah," Paul said with a shake of his head. "They were telling us about their adoption plans."

"Adoption plans?" Chance echoed, surprised. "I didn't know they were thinking of adopting a child."

"Children—plural," Derek told him. "Two brothers. The younger one is autistic."

"Really?" Chance wasn't sure what to say. Adopting an autistic child was a noble action but a very big challenge for the parents—especially when one parent was a busy junior senator with one eye on the White House. "That's quite an undertaking."

"I agree," Lisa said, worry underlying her tone. "I can't help but wonder if they're truly prepared for the impact of a special-needs child in their lives."

"I think Olivia is determined," Paul said with a shrug. "Only time will tell but my money's on her and Jamison."

"Excuse me, sir." A woman, carrying a clipboard and wearing a unobtrusive "Staff" button on her green evening gown, interrupted them with an apologetic look. "Senator Claxton would like to introduce all of the Armstrong family members to a friend of his." She lowered her voice to murmur, "The senator asked me to tell you the friend is a potential donor to the research program at the institute."

Derek slipped his arm through Lisa's and clapped Paul on the shoulder. "Then we'd better go meet-and-greet."

"Duty calls. See you later, Chance." Paul let his brother urge him into motion.

"Have fun," Lisa called over her shoulder as the three followed the clipboard-carrying woman into the throng.

Chance lifted his half-empty flute in farewell.

"Who are they?" Jennifer asked, having returned in time to see the Armstrongs leave.

Her voice stroked over his senses, lush, sensual, and when he turned, the sight of her did the same.

"My bosses—and coworkers," he answered, dismissing them with a wave of the champagne class before deftly depositing the flute on a passing waiter's tray. "They were called away to meet potential donors. For them tonight is both business and pleasure. I'd like you to meet them—hopefully we'll see them later and I'll introduce you." He held out his hand. "Dance with me?"

She smiled shyly. "I'd love to."

Chance swept Jennifer onto the floor. They circled the room amid the crowd of dancers, moving gracefully to the strains of a waltz.

"I feel like Cinderella," Jennifer murmured.

Chance tucked her closer, his leg brushing between hers as he executed a turn. "Does that make me the prince?" he asked.

She tilted her head back to look up at him. "I'm not sure," she said. "I think the jury's still out."

"Damn." His smile was wry. "And I've been on my best behavior tonight."

His eyes twinkled, inviting her to laugh.

"After listening to you and the senator tell stories about the pranks you and his son pulled on your friends in school, I'm not sure you grasp the concept of 'good behavior,'" she teased.

"Isn't there a statute of limitations on being a dumb kid? Dave and I did most of that stuff in high school and college," he protested.

"Nothing recently?" she pressed with a smile, unconvinced.

"No," he assured her. "We had a lot of fun in school but my days of setting up practical jokes are over. I wish I had time to see more of the senator's family," he added. "But for the past few years, Ted and I have been too busy with our research."

Her gaze softened. "You work too hard. Lately when you come into the diner, you seem exhausted."

"There have been a few weeks when sleep was a rare commodity," he admitted.

"What exactly do you do at the institute?" she asked, insatiably curious about every aspect of his life.

"I treat women with fertility issues," he told her. "Part of my day is spent with patients in one-on-one appointments and procedures. The rest of the day is spent in the lab with my partner. We're searching for a way to increase the success rate of implanted embryos, among our other projects."

"That's marvelous." Jennifer couldn't help but think about how difficult it must be for couples who wanted children but couldn't conceive. Annie was the most important thing in her life—what if she couldn't have gotten pregnant? "I can't imagine doing anything more important."

"That's how I feel. How I've always felt." His voice deepened, eyelashes half-lowering over dark eyes. "You understand and you've only known me a few months. I started bandaging the neighborhood dogs when I was eight years old but my parents still can't understand why I want to be a doctor."

"Why not?" Baffled, she searched his features. "Most parents would love to have a doctor in the family."

"They wanted me to go into the family business. My father especially. He's the CEO and he wanted me to take his place." He shrugged. "If they'd had more children, it might have been easier for them to accept my decision but unfortunately I'm an only child."

"It must have been difficult for you to disappoint them," she murmured in response to the hint of regret underlying his words.

"Yeah," he admitted. "It was—still is, sometimes."

"But you love your work so it's worth it to you," she guessed.

"Yes." He smiled at her, his dark eyes warm. "How about you? Do you like working at the diner?"

"I do," Jennifer replied. "I like the customers, the other waitresses, even my boss. I plan to keep working there until I get my degree."

"What are you studying?"

"Education—I want to be a teacher."

"Good for you." His smile held approval and respect. "What kind of classes are you taking?"

"An English lit class, which I love," she told him. "And a psychology class, which I don't like very much. Still," she added, "at least it's not an art class."

"You don't like art?"

"Oh, I love art," she assured him. "I love going to museums and looking at sculpture, oil paintings, watercolors…I especially love Impressionist paintings. But I have very little artistic talent, unfortunately, and I need a passing grade in several art classes to finish my degree."

"How many hours are you at the diner every week?" he asked with a frown. "Aren't you working full-time? How do you have time to study?"

She smiled impishly. "I don't date. It's amazing

how much free time a woman has when she cuts men out of her life."

His arms tightened, pulling her closer. "That's got to change," he growled.

She laughed, her breasts pressed to the muscled strength of his chest, his powerful thighs hard against hers. Excitement and heat shivered through her and she tilted her head back to look up at him. "But I have to earn my degree if I want to become a teacher—and I really, really want to be a teacher."

His gaze studied her before he nodded. "I can see you being a teacher—little kids, right? Or are you thinking of teenagers?"

She shook her head. "I'm more interested in grade school."

"Yet another thing we have in common," he commented. "Both of us want careers where we can help people."

She stared into his eyes, struck by the truth of his comment. They did seem to have a lot in common—and with each new revelation, her feelings for him deepened.

Conversation lapsed as they danced, the brush of their bodies casting a spell that held them, growing stronger, hotter with each movement of body against body as they swayed to the music.

When the orchestra took a break, Chase tipped his head back to look down at her.

"Thirsty?"

Jennifer nodded and Chance released her, his hand stroking in a warm caress down her arm before he threaded her fingers through his and led her from the crowded dance floor.

Guests strolled the periphery of the ballroom, sat with wineglasses at small tables, or gathered in groups to chat and observe the colorful swirl of other guests in the center of the room.

The champagne fountain sat on a white linen-covered table. Chance handed a filled crystal flute to Jennifer and lifted a second one.

"Hello, Chance. Frank told me you were here."

Jennifer looked over her shoulder, her eyes widening at the lanky, blond man in a white chef's coat. His features were movie-star handsome and a counterpoint to Chance's dark masculinity.

"Jordan," Chance greeted him with a wide grin. The two men shook hands and then Chance slipped his free hand around Jennifer's waist to draw her closer. "Jennifer, this is Jordan Massey, the best chef in Boston."

"Pleased to meet you, Jennifer." The swift glance Jordan raked over her was pure male interest.

Jennifer felt a subtle tension in Chance. The possibility that he might be jealous of the good-looking chef was intriguing but she dismissed the notion. Instead, she smiled and held out her hand. "It's lovely to meet you, Jordan. I'm so glad I have an opportunity to tell you how wonderful our dinner was—I can't remember when I've enjoyed a meal more."

"Thank you." He took her hand, holding it a second too long and giving her fingers a light squeeze before releasing her. He lifted an eyebrow at Chance. "She's beautiful and she loves my cooking. Where have you been hiding her, Chance?"

"Never mind." Chance's voice held a definite possessive warning. "Back off."

Jordan laughed and winked at Jennifer. "Duty and my kitchen calls but we'll have to talk later, Jennifer, and you can tell me how you've managed to make my friend so possessive."

"I'm just protecting her from the wolves," Chance drawled.

"Of course," Jordan said blandly. "Enjoy the evening, my friend."

Jennifer didn't miss the enigmatic look he gave Chance before he disappeared into the crowd.

"Where did you meet him?" she asked Chance, curious about the chef.

"His sister was a patient of mine," he told her. "He threw a party when the baby was born and after everyone else went home, we killed a fifth of Scotch toasting his new niece. We've been friends ever since."

She sipped her champagne, her gaze drifting over the glittering gathering before stopping on a couple. The man wore a tux and the woman's gown was a formfitting sapphire blue, her hair a long, wavy mane that gleamed like silk beneath the chandelier's light. The two had eyes only for each other—until the man glanced up, grinned and waved.

"There's Ted," Chance commented, lifting his champagne glass in salute.

"Who's the woman with him?" Jennifer asked.

"His wife," Chance replied. "And I'm damned grateful Sara Beth said yes when he proposed. I work with him and he's been a pain in the…well, let's just say he was in a bad mood until he worked things out with her."

"They look very much in love," Jennifer said softly, her gaze on the two as the man brushed the woman's long wavy hair over her shoulder and smiled down at her.

"They are." Chance emptied his champagne flute and caught her hand. "Let's dance." He deposited their glasses. "I'm glad to know I was right," he said as they circled the room.

"About what?" she asked, a tiny frown drawing her brows into a vee.

"The food," he replied easily as he guided her out through open French doors and onto the wide balcony where other guests danced beneath the night sky. "Unless you were lying to Jordan. You did enjoy dinner?"

Her brow smoothed and a smile curved her mouth, lighting her eyes. "Oh, yes. The lobster was wonderful and the chocolate mousse was perfect."

"I told you the food would be worth the cost of the ticket," he said with satisfaction, executing a series of smooth, sweeping turns to move them down the length of the wide stone balcony. "Jordan doesn't serve tiny slivers of artsy-looking food. His food is elegant without being precious—you know, no tiny portions that leave a guy so hungry that he has to stop for a burger on his way home."

Jennifer looked up at him, a smile curving her lips. "It sounds suspiciously as if you've been forced to sit through dinners filled with…maybe, cucumber sandwiches and tea?"

He laughed. "Not since my grandmother made me eat them when I was a kid. Since then, though,

I've had to attend dinners where we were served rubbery chicken or tiny plates with three or four artfully arranged celery and radish slices." He shuddered. "Makes me hungry just to think of it."

"I'm guessing it takes more than celery and radishes to fuel a guy your size," she joked.

"You guess right," he said with a nod. "Lots more. I have a big appetite." He winked at her.

She studied him, contemplating an answer to what was clearly an invitation.

His lips brushed her ear. "Aren't you wondering what other appetites I have?" he teased, lazy amusement underlaid with darker, more volatile emotions.

She tilted her head and his mouth brushed over her cheek, with scant inches separating his lips from hers. "I was considering asking," she said quietly. "But decided I should give the subject more thought before asking questions that might provoke dangerous answers."

"I'd be happy to answer any questions, Jennifer," he told her. "Dangerous or not." Heat flared in his dark, heavy-lidded gaze.

"I've never been a woman who courts danger," she murmured. "I've always preferred safe and sane."

"You're safe with me, Jennifer," he muttered,

pressing his lips to her temple. "I'd never hurt a woman, especially you." His arms tightened as he swept her into a series of fast, graceful turns.

"I believe you," she replied softly once she was back in his embrace. "At least, not physically. But you're a very attractive man, Chance, and a woman could lose her heart to you."

"Could she?" he rasped, his voice deeper.

"Yes." She nodded, her hair brushing the underside of his chin and his throat. "I don't want a broken heart, Chance."

"I won't break your heart. Come home with me, Jennifer." His fingers trailed over her cheek, tucked a tendril of soft hair behind her ear, and returned to brush over her lower lip. "I've wanted you since the first time I saw you."

"I don't sleep around," she told him honestly. They'd stopped dancing but still stood within the circle of each other's arms. Beyond the balustrade, the lights of the city glowed while on the street below, the faint sounds of traffic drifted upward. Down the length of the stone veranda they'd traversed, a series of French doors were thrown open to the ballroom. Gold light poured out, illuminating the guests at the other end of the veranda as some strolled or leaned on the wide, chest-high stone bulwark and some danced, swaying in time to the orchestra's lush notes. Chance and Jennifer were alone at their end of the long veranda, shadowed except for the spill of soft light that fell through the glass panes of the French doors beside them, drawn closed against the crowded ballroom inside. The yellow light highlighted his face and she searched his features. "In fact…I haven't been with a man since my divorce, and that was more than five years ago."

His eyes darkened, his mouth a sensual curve. "Honey, that's a damned shame. A woman as beautiful as you should be loved often and well." He bent and brushed his mouth over hers, then lingered to slowly trace her lower lip with the tip of his tongue. "Come home with me. Please."

He urged her closer until she rested against his chest, her thighs aligned with his. Jennifer shuddered at the press of her breasts against hard muscles.

"I don't want to complicate my life," she managed to get out. She struggled to remember why she needed to resist him, closing her eyes against the heat that bloomed beneath his lips as he traced the arch of her throat. "Or yours," she added.

"This doesn't have to be complicated," he murmured, his lips on her throat, just below her ear. "It can be whatever we want it to be."

An enticing shiver ran down her spine, and Jenny knew she couldn't resist him. "Just tonight," she whispered. She forced her eyes open and leaned back, cupping his jaw in her palm to tilt his head up. Beard stubble rasped faintly against the sensitive pads of her fingertips, his eyes ablaze with need. "No complications—and after tonight, we go back to waitress and customer. Can we do that?"

She read the objection that flared in his eyes and saw the swift refusal on his face as his jaw flexed and muscles tightened beneath her hand.

"Please," she said softly, desperate to hold on to some shred of control. "I can't make promises beyond tonight."

His fingers tightened on her waist and then he nodded. "All right. If tonight's all you can give me—" he brushed a kiss against her cheek "—I'll take what I can get."

His mouth covered hers with searing heat. Her senses were fogged and she was reeling with want when he lifted his head. He tucked her along his side and led her to an exit. After waiting—for what felt like an eternity—for the valet to bring his car, they were off. Threading her fingers through his to keep her close, he laid her hand palm down on his thigh and covered it with his own as they sped through

Boston traffic, his touch anchoring her to him. Desire seethed, swirling and heating the air between them in the close confines of the car.

Jennifer was only peripherally aware of the neighborhoods they drove through, her senses focused on the man beside her. When he tapped a control on the dash and then turned off the street and beneath a still-rising garage door, she caught a brief glimpse of the exterior of a brick town house before they pulled in.

Chance switched off the engine, the sudden silence enfolding them. His gaze met hers, heat blazing. "If I touch you before we're inside, we won't make it out of the garage."

She swallowed, throat dry. "Okay."

He smiled, the sudden amusement easing the tension. "Unless you have a fantasy about making love in the backseat of a Jag."

She blinked, distracted by the curve of his mouth. "Um, no."

"Too bad," he said, his voice suddenly lower, huskier. "The idea has possibilities. But I don't want our first time to happen in this car, either, so let's go."

## Chapter Three

Chance took Jennifer's hand and led her up the stairs, then down the hall to his bedroom.

The clatter of nails on the polished oak floors below was followed by a loud bark.

"That's Butch," Chance reassured her.

Jennifer's eyes widened at the size of the dog racing down the hallway toward them. The black and tan rottweiler skidded to a stop and sat, panting up at Chance with what looked like an ear-to-ear grin.

"I think he's glad you're home," she said, unconsciously inching behind Chance.

"I think you're right." He tugged her forward and into the bedroom. "I'm going to put him in the kitchen with food and water. I'll be right back." He bent, his mouth taking hers with heated possession. Then he disappeared into the hall, the big dog by his side, tail wagging.

Her legs unsteady, Jennifer sat on the edge of the bed, drawing a deep breath into oxygen-starved lungs. She'd barely gotten her bearings when Chance returned. He strode across the room and caught her hands, drawing her to her feet and into his arms. Her wrap slid to the floor in a pool of red silk at her feet, her small evening bag joining it.

Chance cupped her face in his hands, his gaze intent.

"I can't tell you how many times I've thought about you being here—in my room. And in my bed."

He brushed kisses over her jawline, cheeks, temples. Jennifer's eyes drifted closed and his lips moved softly over her lashes and against her sensitive skin. Just that quickly, she fell back into the haze of need and desire so abruptly interrupted moments before.

She threaded her fingers into the thick, silky dark hair at the nape of his neck and urged him closer until his lips met hers.

Heat built, quickly becoming a firestorm as the kiss turned urgent. Without taking his mouth from hers, Chance lowered the zipper at the skirt of her dress. The backless gown had a sewn-in bra and his fingers stroked over the bare skin of her back.

Jennifer reluctantly lowered her arms from around his neck, a quick shrug sending the loosened gown free to pool at her feet. She knew a moment of self-consciousness when Chance stepped back, his dark eyes searing as he swept her from head to toe with one swift glance. She wore only a tiny pair of red lace bikini panties, thigh-high sheer hose and the red stiletto heels.

"Damn, you're beautiful," he murmured, bending to brush a quick, hard kiss against her mouth before taking a step back again.

His gaze focused on hers, he stripped his tie loose and dropped it on the floor, shrugged out of his tux jacket and tossed it behind him.

He caught her waist in his hands and drew her nearer.

"Unbutton my shirt," he instructed, his voice husky with arousal. His thumbs moved in slow circles, as if he was unable to stop caressing her.

Reassured, Jennifer took only seconds to slip the black studs free. When she finished, Chance took them from her cupped hand and dropped them on the nightstand before holding up his hand. Jennifer unfastened the cuff links, one by one, and dropped them on the pile of studs. Chance immediately shrugged out of the shirt, pulling her flush against him, his hands threading into her hair to tilt her face up to his. When his mouth settled over hers, Jennifer sank into the sensation of his soft lips, gentle and demanding all at once.

The hard muscles of his bare chest teased her sensitive breasts, the fabric of his tux slacks faintly rough against her thighs. And his lips on hers sent desire throbbing through her veins.

She murmured incoherently and Chance laid her back on the bed before he stood, toeing off his shoes, pulling off his socks, unzipping and shoving his pants and boxer shorts down his legs. He bent and pulled open the drawer in the bedside table, ripped open a packet and a second later, rolled on protection. Then he leaned over her, slipping his thumbs under the narrow bands of red lace on her hips to tug her panties down her legs. He dropped the bit of lace and silk on the floor behind him before bending to press a kiss against the faint outward curve of her belly.

Jennifer gasped at the heated brush of his mouth against her sensitive skin. He stroked his tongue over the indentation of her belly button and she moaned. Frantic to have him closer, she tugged at his arms, fingers clutching the hard muscles of his biceps to urge him nearer.

He surged on top of her, his mouth taking hers with urgency, one knee nudging hers apart to make space for him. Then he was inside her. Jennifer cried out, drowning in pleasure and need.

It had been too long for her and, all too soon, Chance drove her over the edge.

Sated and drowsy, she opened her eyes and found him gazing at her, a slow smile curved the sensual line of his mouth.

"I'm guessing it was good." His words weren't a question but she nodded, too satisfied and boneless to speak, nonetheless.

"Let's try it again," he murmured against her mouth.

And a moment later, despite being certain she couldn't move a muscle, Jennifer was again burning with heat, twisting urgently beneath his mouth, hands and the steady thrust of his powerful body.

Just after midnight, hunger lured them out of bed and downstairs to raid the refrigerator. Dressed only in Chance's white tux shirt, the long tails hitting her at mid-thigh and sleeves rolled to her elbows, Jennifer perched on a tall stool and propped her elbow on the island countertop, leaning her chin on her hand. The kitchen was beautifully appointed and everywhere she looked, something drew her eye. But after a quick glance around the room, her gaze returned with fascination to Chance. Grey boxer shorts hung low on his hips as he bent to peer into the refrigerator. His powerful shoulders and chest were bare as were his thighs and long legs. Despite the long hours they'd just spent in the bedroom upstairs and although she'd felt sated and content only moments earlier, heat stirred in her belly once again. She shivered as she contemplated running her palms over his back while his weight pinned her to the bed.

"How do you feel about spaghetti and cheesecake?"

Her eyes widened and she straightened. "Yum. What kind of cheesecake?"

He turned to look at her over his shoulder. "Regular, I guess, except it has chocolate on the top."

"Even better," she said promptly.

He grinned at her, eyes warming. "You like chocolate?"

"Of course, who doesn't?" she responded.

"I definitely do. The local café has chocolate crepes so good they can make a grown man cry. We'll get you some for brunch tomorrow." He turned back to the refrigerator and moments later, nudged the door closed with his hip because his hands were full of food containers.

"Here, let me help." She jumped down from the counter and hurried to take a plate of cheesecake from him. He'd balanced it on top of a deep blue casserole dish, where it tilted and wobbled precariously.

"Thanks." Chance slid the casserole onto the tiled counter and removed the glass lid. He stirred the red sauce and spaghetti noodles and popped the dish into the microwave, set the timer and closed the door.

"I think we should seriously consider cutting a bite of cheesecake while we wait for the spaghetti," Jennifer told him, eyeing the swirls of dark chocolate on top of the cake.

"Sure, why not." He took a knife and a fork out of a drawer and joined her, bracketing her against the counter with his arms and body. "You cut." He laid the utensils on the countertop on each side of the cheesecake and bent to nuzzle his face against her nape. His hands settled on her hipbones.

Jennifer closed her eyes, her body going boneless as she melted back against him. His hands slipped beneath the hem of the white shirt and stroked upward, over her belly and midriff to cup her breasts.

"Ohhhh, that's not fair," she moaned as her nipples pebbled against his fingers and her hips settled into the cove of his. She tilted her head back against his shoulder, the thick silk of his hair brushing her throat as he bent over her to press his mouth against the upper curve of her breast.

She twisted in his hold, slipping her arms around his neck, her body pressed flush against his as she tugged his mouth down to hers. His hands cupped her bottom, lifting her higher, and the kiss turned hotter, more carnal.

Behind them, the microwave alarm buzzed loudly as the timer went off.

Chance eased back from the kiss and lifted his head.

"Want to skip the spaghetti and cheesecake and make love on the countertop?" he asked, his voice rasping with need.

Jennifer was torn but before she could decide, her stomach growled. They both laughed.

"That's it. Food wins," he declared, pressing one last hard kiss against her mouth and stepping back. "First we'll feed you, then we'll get naked again. Let's go back to bed."

He reached behind her and picked up the cheese-cake plate, handing it to her with the knife and fork. "You carry this, I'll get the spaghetti."

"What about plates? And don't we need another fork?" she asked, still disoriented and flushed.

"Nope." He used hot pads to remove the casserole of spaghetti and closed the door with his elbow.

"We'll share. But we might need napkins. Grab a couple out of the drawer by your hip, will you?"

Jennifer found snowy-white linen napkins and preceded him down the hall and up the stairs to his bedroom.

Chance tossed the sheet to the bottom of the bed and disappeared into the bathroom, reappearing with a thick blue towel. He spread it on the center of the bed and set the casserole on it.

"We're having a picnic," she said with delight. "I love picnics and I've never had one in bed before."

"The mattress is more comfortable than the floor." Chance crooked his finger at her. "And when we're done eating, the bed's more comfortable for making love."

She laughed, balancing the cheesecake in one hand and utensils in the other as she climbed onto the bed, shuffling on her knees to the far side of the folded towel. "Plus," she told him, setting down the cheesecake, "there are no ants. Always a good thing."

Chance grabbed her free hand and tugged, tumbling her toward him. He threaded his fingers into her hair and kissed her, his mouth hot. "I love the way you find the good in everything. You're easy to please."

"You offered me cheesecake with chocolate." She raised an eyebrow. "Why wouldn't I be pleased?"

"Lots of women would be offended if they weren't offered champagne and caviar."

"Hmm." She eyed him. "I think you've been dating the wrong women."

His eyes laughed at her. "I think you're right."

He stabbed the fork into the spaghetti, twirled it, and lifted the pasta to her mouth. "Tell me if it's hot enough."

Obediently, she parted her lips and took the bite.

"How is it?" he asked.

"Excellent," she told him. "Try it."

They took turns, Chance insisting on feeding her.

When the bowl was empty, Jennifer rolled off the bed and carried the casserole dish to the long oak entertainment center across from the foot of the bed. A flat-screen TV was mounted on a wall bracket and on the polished oak surface below was a stack of books.

"You have a copy of the new Tom Clancy book," she exclaimed. "I didn't even know it was out."

"It's not. I have a friend at the publishing house and he sent me a copy before the release date."

Jennifer tilted the stack of books, reading the titles. "You have mystery, suspense and a couple of nonfiction titles." She picked up one of the books and read the back cover copy. "What other genres do you like? Do you read romantic suspense?"

He frowned. "I don't know. I don't think I've ever read one. Unfortunately, I have to read a lot of medical journals so often my fiction reading has to take second place behind articles."

"I know what you mean. Textbooks have to come first with me, too."

"Come here." Chance patted the bed beside him. "We still have cheesecake to eat." Jennifer put down the stack of books and walked back to the bed, tucking the shirttails neatly beneath her as she sat.

"I bet you were a cute little girl," he told her as he cut the cheesecake with the fork.

"What makes you think so?" she teased, opening her mouth to let him feed her.

"Because you sat down as if your mother trained you to tuck in your skirt and sit properly," he told her with a grin.

"It was my grandmother," she said without thinking, after she'd swallowed.

"I bet you were your grandmother's favorite granddaughter," he told her.

She fed him the bite, fascinated by the movement of strong throat muscles as he swallowed. "I was her only granddaughter," she murmured absently, trailing her fingertips down his throat to his shoulder.

"You're an only child, too?" he asked, surprised.

"Yes." She forced a small smile, deciding to confirm what he probably already knew—that her background was light-years away from what had clearly been his privileged home life. "The only child of divorced parents. My mother declared she didn't want any more children. She was far too busy meeting new men and having fun. I heard that my father remarried several times and had more children but I've never met any of my half-siblings." She kept her gaze on the cheesecake, precisely cutting another bite. "I doubt my childhood was anything like yours."

"Hey," he murmured. His hand cupped her chin, tilting her face gently up until her gaze met his. His dark eyes searched hers. "Except for wishing you were happy, it doesn't matter to me what your parents were like or where you spent your childhood, Jennifer. All I care about is that you're here with me now."

Emotion flooded her. She knew there couldn't be a future for them. All her time over the next few years was already committed to work, school and Annie. But for this night, she could forget about tomorrow and responsibilities. And if she felt things with Chance she'd never felt with anyone before, she'd worry about that tomorrow, too.

"All we have is right now," she whispered, lowering the fork to the plate so she could slip her arms around him. "Let's not waste a moment."

His dark eyes turned hot. Without releasing her, he shoved the towel, cheesecake and utensils onto the floor and bore her backward, his mouth taking hers as his weight settled over her.

Jennifer welcomed the instant rise of desire that swept over her, erasing all thought of tomorrow. There was only this moment and the heavy, powerfully muscled body on hers as Chance's fierce passion carried her over the edge once again.

Jennifer was half-awake the following morning when Chance left the bed. He bent over, kissed her, chuckled and with a pat on her bottom covered by the sheet, left her to disappear into the bathroom. She smiled, half opening her eyes and noting the bright sunshine pouring through the open drapes. Then she yawned and rolled over.

It seemed like only a moment before Chance came back into the bedroom, several pieces of clothing tossed over his arm.

"Hey, sleepy woman, wake up! I promised you crepes for breakfast." He tossed the clothes on the end of the bed. "My mother left some things in the guest room the last time she was here," he told her, dropping onto the bed to stretch out beside her. "The slacks might be a little short but they're bound to fit better than a pair of my jeans."

The bed dipped under his weight, rolling Jennifer toward him. He grinned and caught her, tugging the sheet lower until she was bare from her tousled hair to her belly button.

Chance's head bent and he trailed his lips over the upper curve of her breasts. "Mmm," he muttered. "You taste as good as you look."

Jennifer buried her fingers in the silky thickness of his hair, cradling his head to hold him close as her eyelids drifted closed.

"If we're going out, I have to shower and get dressed," she protested drowsily, smiling as he growled in protest. She closed her fingers into fists and tugged his hair, the strands sliding like rough black silk against her fingertips and palms.

Reluctantly, he obeyed her silent demand and lifted his head to look down at her. "We could skip going out and order in—eat Chinese food in bed," he suggested.

"No." She laughed softly. "I'm starving and those chocolate crepes sound wonderful." And she wanted to see a bit more of the pieces of his day-to-day life. The need to know him better, to learn more about the man behind the handsome face and powerful male body, grew stronger with each moment she spent in his company.

"All right," he grumbled good-naturedly, his hands trailing over her midriff as he rolled onto his side, releasing her so she could slide out of bed. "We'll take Butch for a walk and get brunch at the café. Then we'll come back and pick up where we're leaving off. Deal?"

"Deal." She flashed him a sassy grin, caught up the pile of clothing from the foot of the bed and slipped into the bathroom. For a moment, she leaned back against the door, eyes closed, a smile on her lips while she reveled in the sheer happiness bubbling through her veins.

A half hour later, Jennifer had showered, pulled her hair up into a high ponytail, smoothed on the lipstick and mascara she'd tucked into her evening bag the night before, and was dressed. She paused to run a quick, assessing glance over her reflection in the long mirrors bracketing the door.

The pale pink silk slacks fit well except for being a trifle short in the leg, the hem hitting her at her anklebone. *Which is actually a good thing,* she thought, since if the designer label slacks had been longer, she would have surely tripped over them while wearing the strappy red heels. The white silk tank top was snug and since she didn't have a bra to wear, she'd pulled on a clean white shirt from Chance's closet. It was much too big, of course, but after rolling the sleeves to her elbow, she decided it worked well enough to conceal her braless state.

In fact, she thought, turning to look over her shoulder at her back view, the outfit was rather chic. The slim-cut slacks hugged her thighs below the hem of the loose white shirt, and the red heels added a touch of Vogue-model fashion to the outfit.

Thanks to Chance's mother leaving clothes in his guestroom, Jennifer reflected, she was reasonably covered. She'd had a few qualms about the clothing, suspecting it might have really belonged to one of Chance's girlfriends. But the silk slacks and tank top had a small label with "A. Demetrios" beautifully embroidered in blue and gold thread. Chance had mentioned his parents, John and Anastasia, and Jennifer was confident the "A. Demetrios" was surely his mother.

She left the bathroom, a spring to her step, and went searching for Chance. She found him in the kitchen, reading a newspaper spread out over the island countertop.

"Hey." He looked up when she entered, his eyes lighting up as he swept her from head to toe and back again.

"Hi." Suddenly self-conscious under his intent

stare, she glanced down. "I'm glad your mother left her slacks and top here. Are you sure she won't mind my borrowing them?"

"I'm positive," he told her, abandoning the paper on the counter. He reached her in two long strides and wrapped her close, pressing a quick, hard kiss against her mouth. When he lifted his lips from hers, his eyes were molten. "And if we don't leave the house right now, I'm going to carry you back upstairs. Come on. Let's feed you. You're going to need energy when we get home."

He released her, threaded her fingers through his, and tugged her after him toward the front door.

"Come on, Butch."

The big dog obeyed Chance's command with enthusiasm, pushing past them to race down the hall and wait just inside the front door.

Chance took a leash from a peg on the antique coatrack and clipped it onto Butch's collar, then pulled open the heavy oak door.

Jennifer stepped outside, relishing the balmy air and the quick warmth of sunlight on her bare forearms.

Chance locked the door behind them, pocketing the keys before catching Jennifer's hand in his, and with Butch leading the way at the end of the leash, they set off down the street.

"I love your neighborhood," Jennifer told him, taking in the neat facades of town houses and bright flowers filling window boxes. She tilted her face up and spring sunshine warmed her cheeks, filtered through tree leaves.

"Good morning."

The friendly greeting drew Jennifer's attention and she smiled hello at the young couple passing by, pushing a stroller with a little boy that babbled excitedly, hands outstretched to Butch.

"Good morning." Chance nodded at the couple, letting the little boy pat Butch on the nose, then pulling the big dog away before he could lick the toddler's face.

"Who was that?" Jennifer asked, curious.

"The Carmichaels." Chance expertly steered Butch around a trio of giggling schoolgirls in jeans and sandals walking toward them, three abreast on the sidewalk. "They moved into the house two doors down from me just before their little boy was born. I met them when I was out walking Butch."

"Butch seems to be a great ice breaker," Jennifer commented. "You must meet a lot of people when they stop to pet him."

"Yeah, I do." He grinned at her and tugged her nearer, releasing her hand to sling an arm over her shoulder and tuck her close. Their hips bumped companionably as they walked. "Nobody can resist a big, friendly dog."

Jennifer privately thought it was probably the combination of Butch's friendliness and Chance's charm.

"Here we are." Chance drew Jennifer to a halt outside a small restaurant. "Do you mind sitting outside? I can't take Butch inside."

He nodded at the area to their right. Several round wrought-iron tables with colorful red and white umbrellas shading their chairs were clustered along the front of the café, the uneven line two tables deep. Just then a patron exited, the café's open door releasing a waft of aroma that was mouthwatering.

"Yes, let's." Jennifer drew in a deep breath. "It smells fabulous. I can't believe anyone has the willpower to walk by and not stop to eat."

Chance bent to brush his lips against her ear. "The food's great but it doesn't taste as good as you."

Jennifer shivered with awareness and felt her skin warm.

His arm tightened in a brief hug before he released her and pulled out a chair at an empty table at one end of the row.

He knotted Butch's leash around the arm of a chair. "Stay," he told him as he dropped into the seat.

Butch obligingly lay down between Chance and Jennifer, technically outside the dining area. Ears perked, eyes alight with interest, he watched the diners at the neighboring tables.

The cute young waitress who took their order clearly adored Chance.

"You have another admirer," Jennifer teased as the teenager disappeared into the restaurant.

"Carrie?" he asked. When Jennifer nodded, he grinned at her. "Nah, I'm helping her brother study for his SATs, that's all. He's a bright kid but the family doesn't have the money to send him to a top-notch med school. If he scores high on the SAT, he'll have a better shot at scholarships."

"What a lovely thing for you to do," she told him. "You're a surprise, Dr. Demetrios."

"Why?" he asked, resting his forearms on the tabletop and leaning forward, his gaze searching hers.

"Because you have a reputation as a playboy, which infers you're shallow. But the more I get to know you, the more complicated you seem."

He smiled, a slow upward curve of his lips. "I'm not complicated," he murmured, his voice husky with need. "At the moment, I've got only a single interest."

"And what would that be?" she asked, mesmerized by the heat in his eyes and the sensual curve of his mouth.

"You." He closed the few inches between them and covered her mouth with his.

The kiss was sweet, slow and filled with heat. Jennifer felt her toes curl as desire moved like languid fire through he veins.

"Um, excuse me." The hesitant female voice had Chance lifting his head.

"Ah, coffee." He sat back to give the waitress room to empty her tray, setting steaming coffee cups in front of them and a carafe in the center of the table. "Thanks."

The fresh-faced teenager smiled shyly in response and whisked away.

Jennifer was disoriented and slightly dizzy from the kiss, while Chance appeared to have gone from arousal to casual friendliness in a matter of seconds.

Determined to match his seemingly unflappable coolness, she sipped her coffee, eyeing him over the rim while she scrambled for casual conversation.

"Did you grow up here in Boston?" she asked, settling for a standard, getting-to-know-you topic.

"No." He shook his head. "I spent my childhood in upstate New York. I moved here when I took the job at the Armstrong Institute. What about you—did you grow up in Boston?"

"No, I lived in a small town in Illinois until I moved here last year."

"What made you choose Boston?"

"I had a friend from high school who moved here. She encouraged me to join her. She loved the city, especially all the American historical sites. We used to visit a national historical treasure nearly every weekend."

"Used to? Why did you stop?"

Jennifer shrugged. "Renee met the man of her dreams and it was love at first sight. They married after dating for three weeks and have been traveling the world ever since. He's an archeologist and they're currently living in Central America while he helps excavate a Mayan temple."

"No kidding?" Chance looked intrigued. "Now there's a job that sounds interesting."

Jennifer laughed. "Every guy who hears about Renee's husband's job says that. There must be a frustrated adventurer hidden in every male on the planet."

"Maybe." He grinned.

The waitress arrived with their food, interrupting their conversation. Jennifer indulged in crepes drizzled with chocolate sauce while Chance tucked into a Spanish omelet. By the time they'd finished eating and had poured a second round of coffee, they were deep in a discussion of movies they'd seen.

"You like chick flicks," Chance told her. "Most of the movies on your best-of list are romantic comedies."

"I liked the movie *Hunt For Red October* and that's not a chick flick," Jennifer protested.

"No kidding—you like that movie?" He lifted his brows in surprise. "I've seen it about a dozen times."

"Me, too." Jennifer sipped her coffee. "Of course," she added, "the film's stars are Sean Connery and a young Alec Baldwin. To be honest, I'd be tempted to watch it over again just to see them."

"So the big attraction isn't the incredible under-water sub maneuvers or the great suspense plot, it's the handsome actors?"

She considered the question, eyes narrowed, before nodding firmly. "Pretty much."

Chance's face lit with amusement, his deep, rich laughter drawing the attention of nearby diners.

Jennifer suspected her smile was besotted but she couldn't help it. The sunlight gleamed in his black hair, laugh lines fanning at the corners of his eyes.

His gaze met his and his laughter died.

"Let's go home," he said roughly, the curve of his mouth sensual.

"Yes," she breathed, caught up in the heat that flared between them. "Let's."

Jennifer woke slowly, stretching and smiling contentedly at the warmth against her back. A weight lay over her waist, anchoring her to the hard male body she lay tucked against and she realized Chance was curled around her, his arm holding her close.

There was a great deal to like about waking up with a man, she thought with a smile.

She opened her eyes. Just beyond the edge of the white sheet-covered mattress was the oak nightstand with a brass clock, its numbers glowing in the dim bedroom.

Her eyes widened. It was almost four o'clock. And Linda had promised to return Annie to the apartment by 6:00 p.m.

Her weekend was over.

She wasn't ready to let it go. She'd lost track of the number of times they'd made love and yet she wanted more. But reality intruded and she bit her lip, knowing she had no choice.

Carefully, she lifted Chance's arm and slipped out from beneath his hold. He muttered, protesting, and she froze beside the bed, holding her breath and hoping he wouldn't waken. Then he shifted, sprawling on his stomach over the place where she'd lain moments before. His eyes remained closed and the tension eased out of his big body as he relaxed, clearly asleep again.

Jennifer lingered a moment, her gaze tracing the beard-shadowed line of his jaw, the black lashes fanning against his olive skin and the sensual curve of his mouth. The white sheet was bunched at his waist, leaving the powerful muscles of his upper body and arms bare.

Reluctant to leave him, she forced herself to turn her back and pad silently into the bathroom where she'd left her borrowed clothes earlier. Dressing quickly, she slipped through the connecting door to the hall and let herself out the front door of Chance's town house.

As she hurried down the street on her way to the bus stop on the next block, she was assailed by a barrage of memories of the hours spent with Chance.

He was a man she could easily fall in love with, she realized. She hoped fervently that she hadn't already done so—because she knew there wasn't, could never be, a future for them together. She reached the end of the block and a bus wheezed to a stop, the doors opening. She climbed the steps, determined to put Chance Demetrios out of her mind.

Whether she could put him out of her heart remained to be seen.

Chance knew the moment he woke that Jennifer was gone. He swept his hand over the sheet but felt no warmth left by her body. He sat up, scrubbing his hands over his face, then tilted his head, listening. The complete silence was broken only by the soft ticking of the bedside clock.

"Damn it," he said into the stillness. He'd wanted to take her home. He hadn't counted on being so relaxed and wrung out from making love this morning and last night that he'd sleep through Jennifer's leaving.

Nails clattered on the oak flooring and Butch nosed the hall door open wider before bounding across the room, tail wagging. He laid his head on the bed, big brown eyes pleading with Chance.

"What?" Chance groaned. "I suppose you want to go out?"

The big rottweiler barked, one sharp, approving sound that made Chance wince.

"Not so loud, buddy," he muttered. "I'm getting up."

He tossed back the sheet and sat on the edge of the bed.

Butch barked again and nosed the sheet a few inches

from Chance's hip, burrowing beneath the sheet until his head was out of sight beneath white cotton.

"Hey, cut that out." Chance tossed the sheet aside. Silver glittered and he pulled the sheet aside to find a necklace peeking out from under the pillow. He grabbed the chain and locket just before Butch could reach it. A low whine rumbled from the dog's throat and his brown eyes were reproachful. "Oh, come on." Chance ran his hand over Butch's head and scratched him behind his ear. "You know this is Jennifer's. And you know you're not supposed to have it."

Butch plopped down on his haunches and eyed the locket, dangling by its chain from Chance's fingers.

The oval-shaped locket had a delicate latch. Chance felt as if his fingers were giant-size as he carefully maneuvered the tiny mechanism. The locket opened and he held it on his palm. One side held a photograph of a little girl, her impish face smiling up at him. The other half held a tiny curl of auburn hair, gleaming brightly against the silver metal.

*Cute kid. I wonder who she is?* He ran the pad of his index finger over the small, bright curl. *And I wonder if this is her hair?*

He had no answers, but he was going to ask Jennifer as soon as he saw her again. There were lots of things he wanted to know about her. Their one date—

and the best sex he'd ever shared—had only led him to be more intrigued about her.

Butch whined and nudged his damp nose against Chance's knee.

"Okay, big guy," Chance told him. "I'll let you out."

He grabbed his jeans from the closet and pulled them on. Then he jogged barefoot down the stairs and through the kitchen to open the back door. Butch barreled happily past him and out into the small backyard.

"I've got to teach him better manners," Chance muttered to himself. He turned back into the kitchen to make coffee—and wondered if Jennifer was thinking of him, as he was thinking of her.

Jennifer stepped out of the silk slacks and folded them atop the hamper. She knew by the label that the slacks had probably cost more than her monthly salary, the nubby raw silk pure tactile pleasure to touch.

*I'll drop them at the cleaners after work tomorrow,* she thought. *Along with the top. Then I'll mail them back to Chance.*

She pulled the tank off over her head, folding it neatly atop the slacks, before she turned on the sink taps. Cupping her hands, she splashed cool water on her face, reaching blindly for a hand towel. She blotted moisture from her skin before tugging the band from her ponytail. As it pulled free and let her hair tumble about her shoulders, she ran her fingertip over the base of her throat. The gesture was pure habit. She'd worn the locket with Annie's picture and lock of hair since her daughter was born.

But this time…the chain wasn't there.

Dismayed, Jennifer stared with consternation at her reflection in the mirror. She knew she'd been wearing it earlier in the day when she'd dressed to go out to brunch. Frowning, she mentally reviewed the afternoon and realized that the last time she'd noticed the locket was after they'd returned to the town house. Chance had rushed her upstairs and stripped off their clothes before tossing her on the bed. He'd joined her immediately and she remembered the slide of cool metal over her skin when Chance's lips brushed the locket aside, replacing it with his mouth.

*Maybe I lost it in his bed,* she thought. She hoped the locket had ended up tangled in Chance's sheets rather than broken and lost on the street or the bus.

She would have to call Chance and ask if he'd found her missing locket. Misgiving warred with delight at the thought. She wasn't sure she had the fortitude to walk away from him a second time.

The night with Chance was a fairy tale—a few days stolen for herself, Jennifer thought later that evening.

With Annie tucked into bed after telling Jennifer about the fun things she did with Linda's children, Jennifer walked back into the living room and dropped onto the sofa.

She switched on the television, browsing through channels with the remote control and finally settling on a news station. Dressed in pajama bottoms and a white cotton camisole, she tucked her legs under her and stared blindly at the TV screen. She couldn't make herself care about the political news or the latest scandal caused by a local state representative.

She couldn't stop thinking about Chance.

It wasn't just the sex—which had been amazing. It was his sense of humor, the discovery that they both loved or disliked some of the same movies. They'd argued hotly in defense of book titles the other had merely shrugged over but, each time, the contention had ended with laughter and kisses.

She'd never met anyone like Chance before.

And now that her night with him was over, she had to admit that spending time with him meant more to her than a brief, spicy interlude to her nonexistent dating life.

She had feelings for him. She wasn't sure exactly what those feelings were, or how deeply they ran, but the ache in her heart wasn't simple. That nothing could ever grow between them only made her chest hurt more.

There was no possible future between a waitress at the Coach House Diner and a doctor at the Armstrong Fertility Institute. Their lives were too different; the disparity in their background and income too great. She wouldn't see him anymore, outside the diner.

Jennifer knew it was for the best but somehow the thought of going back to pouring Chance his morning coffee while knowing she'd never be more than a one-time date made her pain grow.

*It's no good yearning for the moon,* she told herself stoutly, wiping dampness from her cheeks. *I knew when I agreed to go out with him that it was a one-shot deal. No future dates, no building dreams of a relationship.*

She switched off the television and the living-room lights, entering her bedroom where the bedside lamp threw a pool of soft white over her solitary bed.

*It's time for Cinderella to go back to her real life,* she told herself as she climbed into bed and switched off the lamp. The room was plunged into darkness except for the faint glimmers from the streetlights outside marking the edges of the window blinds.

Resolutely, she closed her eyes but when at last she slept, she dreamed of Chance.

Chance had barely shrugged into his lab coat on Monday when the phone on his desk rang. The caller was Paul Armstrong's secretary, who relayed a message that he was needed in Paul's office immediately.

Wondering what could possibly have happened to impact his research funding this time, he left his office and headed down the hall.

He tapped on the half-open door to Paul's office and stepped inside. "Morning, Paul…Ramona."

"Good morning, Chance." Paul leaned against the front of his desk, hands tucked into his slacks pockets. Ramona Tate, the institute's blonde, blue-eyed public relations expert—and Paul's fiancée—smiled warmly.

Chance didn't miss the worry on both their faces, however, and he mentally braced himself. "Is everything all right?"

"I'm afraid not," Paul said grimly. "There's no easy way to tell you this so I'll just say it—a former patient has filed a paternity suit and named you as the father of her baby."

Chance was stunned. Of all the possible subjects for bad news, this one had never occurred to him.

"That's crazy," he said when he could speak. "Totally insane. Who filed the suit?"

"Georgina Appleby."

Chance bit off a curse.

"I know." Paul grimaced, shifting to cross his arms across his chest. "The institute is behind you one hundred percent in this, Chance. Whatever we can do to help, we will. Just let us know."

"I'm so sorry," Ramona said with sympathy. "The timing of this lawsuit is just terrible. You've barely had time to relax after proving how false those outrageous allegations were about funding for your research with Ted."

"I have no doubt you'll win the day in this, too," Paul told him resolutely.

"Thanks." Chance frowned and raked one hand through his hair, thinking out loud. "I should call my attorney. Has the institute been officially served with copies of the documents?"

"Yes. I had my secretary run a copy for you." Paul picked up a sheaf of papers and handed them to Chance. He turned back to his desk and picked up a copy of the *Boston Herald,* passing that over, as well. "The newspapers already have the details."

Chance took the paper, folded open to the society page. Heavy black marker circled two paragraphs of the gossip column with quotes from Georgina Appleby. "She stops just short of slander," he said grimly.

"No one who knows you will believe it," Ramona stated firmly.

"Maybe," Chance commented, rereading the last paragraph, coldly furious. "I'd like to take this to my attorney, as well."

"Keep it," Paul told him. "I read it on the way to work this morning."

"I'd also like to take a short leave of absence to deal with this," Chance suggested. "The smear against my reputation is probably unavoidable, at least temporarily, but I don't want to damage the institute's image with bad personal publicity."

"Take as much time as you need," Paul said.

"Thanks. My hope is that my attorney can expedite arrangements for an HLA paternity test. Once the results are back, I can prove the case has no merit and I can come back to work. Without being followed by reporters and bad press," he added, shaking his head.

"Sounds good," Paul replied.

"I didn't get to see much of you at the Founder's Ball," Chance noted in a purposely abrupt change of subject.

"We saw you with a stunningly lovely blonde

woman," Ramona commented, following his lead. "But you left before we had a chance to learn who she was."

"I'm keeping her identity a secret," Chance told her with a faint grin.

"Oh, yeah?" Paul lifted an eyebrow, the look he gave Chance speculative.

"Yeah." Chance didn't respond further, guessing that Paul had picked up on the possessive note in his voice. "How's your mother, Ramona?"

Ramona brightened, exchanging a quick glance with Paul. "My half sister, Victoria, has agreed to donate bone marrow so I'm very hopeful that her prognosis will improve."

"I'm glad to hear that," Chance told her. "Very glad."

"Dr. Armstrong?" Paul's secretary tapped on the door panel, then peered into the room. "I'm so sorry to intrude, but Senator Johnson is on the line. He wants to talk to you about a potential donation from a constituent."

"I'm sorry, Chance. I have to take this call." Paul pushed away from the desk.

"Of course. I'll let you know about any developments." Chance headed for the door.

"Take care," Ramona called after him. "Remember, we're here if there's anything we can do to help."

"I appreciate that." Chance lifted a hand in reply

and left the office, striding down the hallway and back to his own office.

He shrugged out of his lab coat and pulled on his leather jacket. Within seconds, he left the office with the sheaf of lawsuit papers in his hand. His partner, Ted, was at his desk and apparently deeply immersed in a report when Chance paused in the doorway.

"Hey, Ted." He waited until Ted looked up. "I'll be out of the office for a few days but if anything comes up, you can reach me on my cell phone."

Ted blinked in surprise, frowning. "What's up? You okay?"

"I'm fine." Chance lifted the lawsuit documents. Ted's gaze flicked to the papers and he frowned as he looked back at Chance. Before he could ask, Chance interrupted him. "Long story. I'll explain later."

"All right."

Chance nodded and turned to leave, stopping when Ted called after him. "Hey, if you need me, call."

Chance glanced over his shoulder and grinned. "I will. A guy never knows when he might need help disposing of a body. I'll keep you on speed dial."

Ted snorted and Chance strode off down the hall.

It was good to know he had friends who would stand by him if he needed help.

Not that he'd need help with this, he thought with

a dismissive frown. Georgina Appleby was a young woman with emotional problems. Even if he'd wanted to compromise his professional principles to sleep with her, her emotional vulnerability would have stopped him.

He'd been concerned about her stability when she'd originally come to him for help with fertility issues. His doubts had deepened when her actions became erratic. He'd referred her to a fellow physician who specialized in patients with her particular combination of conception problems and emotional issues.

Though he'd known she was emotionally unstable, it hadn't occurred to him to consider whether she was mentally unbalanced.

*Which is what she must be to file a paternity suit when a blood test will easily prove I'm not the father of her child,* he thought grimly. He could only imagine the kind of lawyer who would agree to take such a frivolous case.

He dialed his attorney's office while walking to his car and having confirmed a meeting within a half hour, drove away from the institute. The route to his attorney's office took him down the street, past the Coach House Diner.

*Damn it,* he thought with frustration. He didn't want to spend the day fighting another unfounded allegation against his good name. He'd been scheduled to run a test analysis in the research lab today. Then he'd planned to order a dozen roses and knock on Jennifer's door to deliver them in person. The night she'd spent in his bed had rocked his world and he was uncharacteristically unsure of her. He felt driven to cement their connection as soon as possible.

He smacked the heel of his hand against the leather-covered steering wheel in frustration. He had to get rid of the paternity suit and return to his normal life—and Jennifer.

The meeting with his attorney went well. He advised Chance to go home and search through his patient files to identify all contact with Georgina Appleby. The attorney wanted details of each time she'd had an appointment with Chance.

He had also been adamant that Chance maintain a low profile—and specifically told him not to date anyone, warning him that he was likely to be followed by reporters in search of fuel for the gossip columns.

Their conversation convinced Chance that he needed to protect Jennifer from unwanted publicity—which meant that just as he would stay away from the Armstrong Fertility Institute offices, he also had to stay away from the diner.

Fortunately, an appointment for the HLA blood

test was set within the week and once the results were back, Chance knew he'd be cleared—and free to see Jennifer again.

Still, putting his plans on hold, though necessary to protect her, didn't sit well.

He dialed her home number from his cell phone but reached her answering machine. Finally, unwilling to explain the situation without speaking to her in person, he left a brief explanation telling her that something important had come up and he would be in touch in about a week.

Edgy and restless, frustrated that he hadn't been able to talk to Jennifer in person, he drove home. His neighborhood was bursting with spring color—pale green leaves unfurling on trees and window boxes blooming with brilliant purple, blue, yellow and pink flowers. Although he'd chosen to buy his town house in part because of the charming neighborhood, today Chance barely noticed his surroundings. He was preoccupied with how much he'd wanted to talk to Jennifer in person. If he couldn't see her, he needed to hear her voice.

He tossed his car keys on the kitchen's tiled island countertop and switched on the coffeemaker. Within moments, the aroma of brewing coffee filled the air. Just as the timer beeped to announce the coffee was ready to pour, the door knocker sounded, its rapping echoing through the entryway and into the kitchen.

Chance strode down the hallway and pulled open the door. A distinguished, silver-haired man in a gray suit stood on the porch, a chauffeur-driven, long black town car parked at the curb behind him.

"Hi, Dad." Chance stepped back, holding the door wide. "This is a surprise—I didn't know you were in town."

"I have a dinner meeting with a group of investors tonight." Jonathon Demetrios walked past his son and into the oak-floored entryway. "Since I have a free hour, I thought I'd drop by to say hello."

*Not bloody likely,* Chance thought, wondering what had really brought his father to Boston. Whatever it was, he knew from past experience that it was easier to let John Demetrios have his say, then usher him out the door as quickly as possible.

"Come into the kitchen," he said aloud. "I just made a fresh pot of coffee."

When his father was seated on one of the chrome and black suede stools, a mug of coffee on the counter in front of him, Chance picked up his own steaming mug.

"Why don't you tell me why you're really here,

Dad," he said, leaning his hips against the cabinet counter behind him.

"All right." John took a newspaper clipping from his inner jacket pocket and slid it across the counter toward Chance. "Your mother and I are concerned about this woman you're dating."

Chance picked up the clipping, his gaze narrowing over the black and white picture. The photographer for the Boston newspaper's society page had captured him dancing with Jennifer. There was no use denying the expression on his face or hers—the photo highlighted the smoldering attraction between them.

"Nice snapshot," he commented.

"That's not the point," John said impatiently, frowning.

"What *is* the point, Dad?"

"The point," John urged with emphasis, "is that this young woman is a waitress at a local diner. Certainly not the kind of person my heir should be escorting to an important social event."

Chance bit off a curse. He didn't bother asking his father how he knew Jennifer was a waitress and where she worked. John Demetrios had a staff of attorneys at his beck and call. He'd probably had an investigator's detailed report about Jennifer on his desk within twenty-four hours of seeing the photo. He scrubbed his hand down his face and eyed his father wearily. "Don't tell me that you're here to deliver the proper-behavior-for-the-Demetrios-heir lecture again, Dad. I thought you realized I won't listen after the last time we did this."

"The last time you dated inappropriate women was your senior year in college," John snapped. "In the intervening years, your mother and I assumed you'd matured and now had better sense. You have obligations, Chance, whether you want to acknowledge them or not."

Chance held up his hand, palm out. "Don't, Dad. Just…don't." He drew a deep breath to keep from raising his voice. "Who I date is my business. And I will never choose a woman based on a set of antiquated rules created by you and Mom. Certainly not based on whether the woman is suitable for a Demetrios heir. And when I marry—*if* I ever marry," he added when his father flushed with anger, his mouth opening to speak, "I'll choose the woman. And it's not likely she'll be someone from the handful of families approved by you and Mom."

"You have an obligation to the family name," John spoke tightly. "For years, your mother and I have been tolerant of your rebelliousness, hoping you'd eventually take your proper place…."

"Father." Chance held on to his temper with an effort. "My proper place is helping my patients. I'm a doctor. I'm never going to live the life of a trust fund baby. I told you and Mother when I entered med school—my first obligation will always be to my patients."

"I suppose this waitress you're dating thinks she's struck gold," John condemned scathingly. "Not only is she dating a doctor, but you're a Demetrios."

Chance considered the older man while he fought to hold on to his temper. "You know," he said slowly, "I doubt she even knows who the Demetrios family is. Or that she would give a damn."

"Humph." John stood, straightening his jacket with annoyed tugs. "That's highly unlikely. Young women in her class always want to move up. She knows who you are, all right."

"I'm going to forget you said that," Chance said evenly. "But in the future, don't make disparaging remarks about Jennifer."

His father's eyes widened, his expression taken aback. "Are you saying you're actually serious about this woman?"

"I'm saying I don't want her harmed because my father is a snob," Chance explained bluntly.

"You may think I'm a snob, but I've had more experience in these matters than you," John told him flatly. "Getting involved with women outside our class invariably leads to disaster. I've seen it happen over and over again with friends and family."

"We'll have to agree to disagree," Chance countered, as unconvinced now as he had been by his parents' arguments on the subject since he was fourteen. "Is Mother looking forward to the cruise you booked for her birthday?"

Fortunately for Chance's temper, his father allowed the change of subject and didn't return to his warnings about dating Jennifer. A half hour later, Chance closed the door on John's departing back.

"I love them but my family makes me crazy," he muttered to himself as he headed down the hall to his home office. And he considered himself damn lucky they didn't seem to know about the paternity suit yet.

But unfortunately for Chance, the picture of him and Jennifer at the ball and the gossip column paragraphs weren't the only items that included the Demetrios name. The following afternoon, he opened the *Boston Herald* and found a quarter-page article with the details of the paternity suit featured prominently in the local news section. The story was accompanied by a grainy photo of Georgina Appleby side-by-side with a photo of him.

He swore out loud and headed for the shower. Dressing in record time, he drove to the diner. Much to his frustration, Jennifer had already completed her shift and gone home.

"Will you tell her I came by?" he asked Linda, the blonde waitress he'd seen often talking with Jennifer.

"Sure." She poured coffee in his mug. "But why don't you just give her a call? Or drop by her apartment?"

Chance didn't want to confess he'd left several messages on Jennifer's answering machine but she hadn't returned his calls. He was beginning to suspect she was having second thoughts about spending the night with him. And if she'd read about the lawsuit, he wouldn't blame her.

"I can't go by her apartment. I'm being followed by a photographer for the *Boston Herald*'s gossip columnist. I recognized him when I parked in front of the clinic," he informed her. "And I don't want the guy following me to Jennifer's house. I'd just as soon keep her off his radar."

Linda's eyes widened. "Is this because you took Jennifer to the Founder's Ball?"

"No." He shook his head. "Something else."

"Is he following you now? Where is he?" she whispered, glancing furtively behind her.

"Sitting in the booth nearest the door."

She twisted, craning her neck to see around an older couple on their way to the exit. "The little guy with the hat? Is that him?" She looked back at Chance and sniffed. "He doesn't look like he's big enough to cause you any trouble."

"Maybe not, but that camera of his makes a powerful weapon," Chance said dejectedly.

The waitress leaned closer. "Would you like us to keep him here while you leave out the back?"

"I appreciate the offer, but he's been parked outside my house so he knows where I live. He'd just go back there and wait for me."

"What on earth did you do that has a reporter following you?" Her eyes were curious.

"Not a damn thing," Chance growled. "But it's going to take a week or so to clear up what he *thinks* I did and in the meantime, I'm stuck with having reporters tailing me."

"Well, keep him away from Jennifer," Linda advised. "I don't think she'd appreciate having a reporter camped on her doorstep. She's a very private person."

That was just what he was afraid of, Chance thought, though he didn't voice his concern about dragging Jennifer into the gossip storm currently harassing his personal life. "I respect that," he said instead. "And I don't want the gossip columnists to know I'm seeing her."

Linda smiled at him with quick warmth. "It's nice to see a guy concerned about her protection."

Something about the way she phrased the statement set off warning bells for Chance. "That sounds as if somebody hasn't protected her in the past…"

Linda grimaced and waved a hand dismissively. "The last guy she was involved with was her husband. I've never met him but he sounds like a jerk," she said bluntly. "If any of Jennifer's friends thought you were anything like him, we'd form a posse and come after you," she warned.

Chance nodded solemnly, acknowledging the not-so-subtle threat. "If I treated her badly, I'd deserve it," he conceded.

"Good to know." She lifted her head, glancing over her shoulder to nod at the cook. "I have to go." She looked back at him. "Are you sure I can't get you something besides coffee?"

"No, thanks."

She leaned closer, her expression serious. "Take care of our girl, Doc. We think a lot of her."

"So do I."

His response seemed to satisfy her and she nodded abruptly before hurrying off.

Chance drained his mug and rose, shoved a hand in his jeans pocket for cash and counted out bills before tossing several on the table. Then he headed for the exit, pausing to allow an elderly woman to hobble past before he left the diner, the doorbell jingling musically.

At the moment Chance walked out of the Coach House Diner in Boston, in New York City, Jonathon Demetrios finished reading the article detailing the paternity action involving his son.

His mouth tight with anger, he closed the door to his office to keep his wife from hearing and dialed a number while walking back to the desk.

"Maxwell Detective Agency."

"I want to speak with Andrew Maxwell."

"One moment, please."

While he waited, Jonathon reread the article, his anger growing.

He knew very well his son would be furious if he ever learned his father had interfered. Nonetheless, the scandal threatened the entire family with damage to their good name.

*And while I'm having this Georgina Appleby investigated, I might as well have Andrew look deeper into the background of this waitress, too,* Jonathon decided.

"Maxwell here." The deep voice was abrupt, businesslike.

"Andrew—this is Jonathon Demetrios. I want you to investigate two women. I need the information as soon as possible."

## *Chapter Four*

When Jennifer arrived at the diner for her normal shift the following morning, Linda and Yolanda immediately dragged her into a corner.

"The gorgeous doctor was here yesterday, looking for you," Yolanda told her.

"And someone is following him, so he can't come to your house," Linda added. "He said a photographer was trailing him."

"We saw him," Yolanda interjected, her eyes bright.

"Chance? Or the gossip columnist?"

"No, Jennifer—we saw the photographer. And

then, we saw the article." Linda ducked down to take a folded newspaper from beneath the counter. The five seats at the end of the counter where the trio stood were empty and Linda spread open the paper on the countertop.

With a sense of dread, Jennifer slipped onto one of the stools and read the article. The grainy photos weren't very good likenesses but the man was unquestionably Chance—and the information in the article was undeniably damaging. The reporter quoted the woman as saying she was "heartbroken by the betrayal of the man she loved—and whom she believed loved her." She'd gone on to say Chance had "treated her unkindly and abandoned her."

"I don't believe any of this," Jennifer stated with conviction. She tapped her fingertip on the paper. "The man we've observed every morning for months is not the man she's describing." She folded the paper and handed it back to Linda. "I simply don't believe it."

"But, honey," Yolanda pointed out kindly, "nice men accidentally get women pregnant, too—it happens all the time. Okay, so this woman made some harsh accusations about Chance. But if you set those aside, it's still possible that he's the father of her child. He has quite a reputation with the ladies."

Yolanda was right—Jennifer knew she was right and, much to her dismay, the possibility that Chance had been careless and created an unwanted child with another woman sent a shaft of pain through her chest.

*He's not mine,* she told herself. *And there never was any possibility of a relationship between us, certainly nothing serious.*

So why did it feel as if her heart was breaking?

With painful honesty, Jennifer realized that on some level, she'd been secretly dreaming that Chance would want a future with her. Had fantasized that the two of them would find a way to be together.

Which was ridiculous, of course. The knowledge made her want to cry.

*It's a good thing I haven't returned his calls,* she decided, making a vow she wouldn't return any in the future either, no matter how many messages he left.

A clean break was surely best.

A week passed before Chance appeared at the diner. Jennifer had her back turned, handing an order slip to the cook, when she heard the strap of bells on the door jingle. She glanced over her shoulder and her heart leaped.

Chance's dark gaze met hers, his eyes warm. An exiting customer walked between them, blocking him and he shifted, smiling at her before he moved down the aisle to reach a booth in her section.

Jennifer passed Yolanda as she walked behind the counter. "Will you tell the boss I'm taking my break now?"

"Sure." Yolanda looked up. "What are you…?" She glanced past Jennifer and saw Chance sliding into the seat of a booth. "Oh."

Chance stood as Jennifer reached the booth, waiting until she took the bench opposite him.

"Hello," she said gravely.

"Hello," he responded, voice husky. "I've left messages on your machine. You didn't call back."

"I didn't think I should," she explained truthfully. "We agreed that our…date…was a one-night thing. And that after it was over, we'd return to our normal lives as if it had never happened."

"That's right, we did." A faint frown veed his brows, his gaze intent on her face. "Is that what you want?"

"I thought it's what you wanted," she commented. "When you didn't come into the diner all week, I was certain of it."

"I couldn't come near you," he told her grimly. "Not without involving you in a scandal."

"You mean the paternity suit?" she asked quietly.

"Yes." He thrust his hand through his hair, raking

it back from his forehead. "I suppose you read about it in the papers?"

"It was hard to miss," she told him.

"Yeah, it was." He frowned, a cynical twist to his mouth. "And of course, the columnist who broke the story didn't bother to comment on the conclusion."

"The conclusion?"

"I called in a few favors and had my blood tests expedited. The results came back today. They prove I'm excluded as a possible father of the child."

Relief flooded through Jennifer and she realized that in some hidden part of her heart, she'd been unsure of his innocence. His words soothed some bruised, wary place inside her. She leaned forward, impulsively covering his hands with hers atop the table. "I'm so glad this was resolved so quickly for you, Chance. Linda and Yolanda told me you were being followed by a photographer. That must have been awful."

"The photographer is the reason I haven't tried to see you." Chance turned his palms upward, capturing her hands in his. "If he'd seen us together, our photo would be splashed all over the papers the next day. That kind of attention isn't comfortable—I wanted to protect you from it."

Touched, Jennifer squeezed his hands. "That was

very sweet of you. And very considerate," she added, thinking about how awful it would have been if Annie had been photographed and their lives laid bare to public gossip.

"No," Chance said, his thumbs moving in slow, rhythmic strokes over the back of her hands. "It should never have happened." He leaned forward, his gaze intent on hers. "The woman who accused me of fathering her child was an ex-patient. I can't discuss details but I want you to know that I never touched her, other than in a purely professional way. I was her doctor for a short time and then referred her to a physician friend who I felt was more qualified to deal with her situation. There was never the slightest moment of inappropriate contact between us. Our relationship was strictly doctor and patient."

"I believe you," Jennifer assured him. His features eased, lines disappearing from around his mouth and eyes, and she realized that he'd been unsure of her reaction. "Chance, I've watched you interact with other customers here in the diner over the past six months. You've been unfailingly kind and considerate to people, whether young or old. And I've never once seen you respond with anything but friendly politeness when women have obviously been coming on to you. Not that I'm unaware of your reputation as a lady-killer," she added with a wry smile. "Goodness knows, the female half of the institute's employees who have lunch here seem to spend fifty percent of their time speculating about your love life."

"I can't help what people say about me," he told her, his eyes serious. "And I admit I like women and that I've dated quite a few over the years. But I would never get a woman pregnant and then abandon her. Kids are too important. I'd never walk away from a child of mine."

Jennifer's heart clenched. Her ex-husband hadn't wanted a baby and by filing for divorce while she was pregnant, he'd effectively abandoned her. That Chance obviously felt strongly about the father standing by the mother of his child sent elation bubbling through her veins.

Perhaps there truly were men in the world with a sense of responsibility, she thought. And who would have expected a well-known playboy to be one of those men?

"It's wonderful to know you wouldn't ignore your responsibility to your child, even if conception was unplanned," she reiterated. Emotion trembled in her voice and she didn't miss his quick frown of concern. Before he could ask her any questions, however, she rushed into speech. "Will the lawsuit be dismissed, now that the test results have excluded you?"

He nodded. "My attorney is working on that now. I suspect my former patient filed the case as leverage to negotiate a settlement. There are no grounds for a payoff now, of course."

"She damaged your reputation and caused all this trouble because she wanted money?" Jennifer's eyes widened, shock giving way to outrage on his behalf.

"I'm sure that was the motive." He shrugged, his mouth curving into a wry smile that didn't reach his eyes.

"Has this happened before?" Jennifer asked, struck by his calmness.

"Not with a paternity suit." His dark gaze was unreadable. "I have a good income from my medical career, Jennifer, but my parents are…fairly well-off, too. Over the years, several people have tried various schemes to extract money from us." He shook his head. "We've never given in."

Appalled, Jennifer couldn't speak for a moment. "Have you ever been hurt?" she asked, horrified images of television reports of kidnappings and robberies flashing in her brain.

"No." He shook his head again. "Never—the

attempts have involved what police might refer to as white-collar crime, always civil law actions."

"That's terrible." She had no experience to compare with this. Jennifer couldn't imagine dealing with criminal or civil greed targeting her.

"Mostly it's just annoying," he told her. "The family has excellent attorneys and I've learned to let them handle these situations." He squeezed her hands. "It does no good to worry over it—and in the meantime," he continued, "life goes on." He leaned back and shoved one hand into his jeans pocket.

"I've wanted to return this to you all week," he told her, holding out his hand. A delicate silver chain dangled from his hand, a silver locket suspended over his palm.

"My locket!" Jennifer exclaimed with pleasure. "Where did you find it?" She took the pretty necklace from his outstretched hand and fastened it around her neck.

"Butch found it." He dropped his voice to a deep murmur. "In my bed."

Her gaze flew to his and she felt her cheeks heat. She couldn't look away, memories swirling as his deep chocolate eyes turned hot.

"I, um…" She faltered, drawing a deep breath.

"I want to see you again, Jennifer."

"You are seeing me," she noted.

"I mean outside the diner. I know we had an agreement," he said. "But one night wasn't enough. If anything, all it did was convince me that we should see each other again."

Jennifer badly wanted to say yes but she was torn. She'd vowed before Annie was born that she wouldn't expose her daughter to a succession of men friends. At least, not until she knew the relationship was serious. And she had no clue whether Chance contemplated a future. Given his history with women, she doubted it.

Not to mention that she had so little free time between her job at the diner, caring for Annie and her college classes.

Still, she'd discovered during the night she'd spent with Chance that he was more complicated, more complex, more loving and certainly more fun than she'd expected.

She wanted to know him better. But how to do that without breaking her commitments to Annie, work and school?

"I have a class tonight that I can't skip," she said slowly. "But I can meet you for coffee afterward, if you'd like?"

"I'd like," he agreed promptly.

They arranged to meet outside the campus library after her class and Chance said goodbye.

"Did he tell you about the paternity suit?" Linda asked when Jennifer relieved her behind the counter.

"Yes, there were blood tests and they proved he's not the father." Jennifer walked the length of the counter, pouring coffee into customers' cups and exchanging hellos with her regulars before returning to the center section where Linda waited. "We're meeting for coffee after my class tonight."

"Yes!" Linda crowed, her smile wide. "That's terrific, Jennifer."

"I'm not sure if it is or isn't, but I know I want to see him again."

"Trust me," Linda said firmly. "You and the doc are great together. Dating him is going to be soooo good for you."

"Who's dating?" Shirley asked as she and Yolanda joined them.

"I'm meeting Chance tonight after my class," Jennifer whispered, aware of the interested customers within hearing range.

"Cool." Shirley's eyes were bright with approval.

"Now you're doing the smart thing," Yolanda told her. "That man is fine." She rolled her eyes and the other three laughed out loud.

"Hey, are you four working or talking?" the boss yelled from the pass-through window into the kitchen.

They exchanged guilty glances and dispersed, Yolanda winking at Jennifer as they left the counter to wait on customers in the booths.

When Jennifer called her neighbor and babysitter, Margaret Sullivan, to tell her that she was meeting someone for coffee after class, Margaret was delighted. She assured Jennifer she was happy to stay later than usual with Annie and told her to enjoy herself.

Since Annie was accustomed to having Margaret stay with her while Jennifer was at class, Jennifer didn't feel too guilty about staying out later than usual. In any event, Annie was always asleep when Jennifer returned and would never know if her mom was out later than usual.

Try as she might, Jennifer had difficulty concentrating on the classroom lecture. Although she took as many pages of notes as usual, her attention wasn't fully concentrated on the speaker. When at last the instructor released the group, she took a moment to slick a fresh coat of color on her lips before leaving the lecture hall.

Chance leaned against a waist-high wall outside the library entryway. His hands tucked into the pockets of faded jeans, he scanned the passing groups of chattering students, looking for Jennifer.

He saw her hair first. Long caramel-blond silk caught up in a ponytail, she walked a few steps behind a quartet of younger students. Lust stirred as he watched her walk toward him, her long legs encased in jeans, a plain white scoop-necked T-shirt tucked in the belted waistband, simple black flats on her narrow feet and a pale blue sweater over her shoulders.

He wanted to take her to bed. Now. But strangely enough, he was willing—hell, he was even happy—to know he'd get to spend innocent time talking with her at a coffee shop.

His stomach growled.

He needed more than coffee, he realized, counting the hours since he'd grabbed a sandwich at lunch.

"Hi, there." She reached him just as he pushed away from the wall.

"Hello, beautiful." He couldn't resist bending to brush a kiss against her cheek, just at the corner of her soft mouth.

Even in the light from streetlamps and the library windows behind them, he could see the color flush her cheeks.

"Are you hungry?" he asked, hooking an arm around her shoulders to anchor her against his side. He took the books from her hands and tucked them under his free arm before urging her into motion. "Because I just realized I missed dinner and I'm starving."

"I had a cup of soup before class but I guess I could have a bite of something." She looked up at him, her ponytail brushing silkily against his cheek as she moved. "Did you have somewhere in mind?"

He nodded. "There's a great Italian restaurant just down the block. How do you feel about pasta?"

"I love pasta," she told him.

"Great."

A half hour later, they were seated across from each other at a table covered with a red-checked cloth. The table was lit with a white candle in a squat wine bottle, its green glass half-covered with drippings of melted wax. Plates of lasagna, green salad and stemmed glasses filled with ruby red wine sat in front of them.

Jennifer took another bite of lasagna and sighed, half closing her eyes as she swallowed. "This lasagna is fabulous," she said.

Chance nearly groaned at the sensual expression on her face as she savored the food. He forced himself to focus on her comment, instead of the overwhelming urge to lean over the table and cover her mouth with his. "Uh, yes, it is, isn't it. I used to eat here at least twice a week."

"You must really love Italian food—this isn't exactly in your neighborhood," Jennifer commented.

"I taught a few classes here," he told her. "Before I took on a few other medical duties and had to cut back on teaching."

"Did you like doing it? Teaching, I mean?"

"Yeah, I did." He smiled at her, lifting his glass to salute her. "Another thing we have in common—we both like to teach."

Jennifer tipped her glass at him in response and sipped. "I don't know if I'd ever want to teach at the college level," she admitted to him. "I'm more interested in teaching young children."

"An honorable goal," he agreed. "And little kids are a lot of fun. What subject do you see yourself teaching?"

Time slipped by as they ate, drank wine and talked.

The restaurant's crowd was growing thin when Jennifer glanced at her watch and gasped. "Oh, my goodness—look at the time!" She looked at Chance, her expression apologetic. "I really have to go. I'm working the early shift and have to be at the diner by 5:00 a.m. I'll be staggering if I don't get some sleep."

"Much as I hate for the night to end, I don't want to be responsible for you being exhausted tomorrow,"

Chance assured her. He stopped a waiter to request the bill and moments later, they left the restaurant.

Despite needing sleep, Jennifer wished the drive back to her apartment wasn't quite so short.

"Wait," Chance muttered as she twisted her key in the lock of her apartment door.

Jennifer paused, looking up at him, and he bent his head, his mouth covering hers in a kiss.

Sweet, sensual and so arousing that Jennifer's insides melted like warm chocolate, the kiss lured, enticed and made desire and need beat through her veins.

When at last he lifted his mouth from hers, she realized that she was pinned between his hard body and the wall next to her door. The cove of her hips cradled his, the hard proof of his arousal snugged against her abdomen, and the tips of her breasts ached under the pressure of his chest.

"Honey," he rasped against her throat, "it's damned hard to leave you."

She smiled, eyes half-closed at the caress of his lips against her skin when he spoke. "I know," she murmured. "It's hard to let you go." She planted her palms against his shirt and gently pushed.

He retreated a bare half inch, and his head lifted so he could look down into her face.

"But if you don't leave, I won't sleep and that's why you brought me home, remember? So I could sleep." She wasn't sure if she was reminding him— or herself.

"Damn." He sighed, a short gust of air that stirred the tendrils of loose hair curling at her temple. "You're right."

He pressed a final hard kiss against her lips and stepped away from her. The loss of his weight and warmth made her want to grab him and pull him back.

A smile lit his dark eyes and his lips curved in a half smile.

"I know how you feel, honey. If you didn't have to work early tomorrow, I'd kidnap you and take you home to bed." He reached past her and pushed the door partially open. "I'll see you tomorrow at the diner for breakfast."

"Okay," she whispered breathlessly. "Good night."

The door clicked shut behind her and she twisted the lock, sending the dead bolt home.

"Did you have a good time?"

Margaret's voice behind her snapped Jennifer out of her daze.

"Yes." She turned, carrying her books into the kitchen area to drop them on the end of the table. "I had an absolutely lovely time."

Margaret's eyes sparkled behind the lenses of her glasses. "I'm glad—and I'd like to meet the man that put that glow on your face," she teased.

Jennifer laughed. "He's pretty terrific, Margaret."

"Good. It's about time you met someone terrific." The older woman turned to collect her knitting, tucking the length of cable-knit red and cream-colored afghan into her bag. "I'm heading home so you can get to bed. Now what did I do with my book?" She searched and found a paperback mystery stuck between the cushions. She slipped the book into her knitting bag and took out a key chain. "Walk me to the door?"

"Of course." Jennifer freed the dead bolt and opened her apartment, waiting in the doorway while Margaret crossed the hall to unlock and go inside her own home.

"Good night." Margaret lifted her hand and closed the door.

Jennifer waited until she heard the click of the locks sliding home across the hall before closing and securing her own front door.

The apartment was quiet without Margaret's cheery presence. Jennifer turned off the living-room lights and went to her bedroom, switching on the bedside lamp before tiptoeing into Annie's bedroom.

The little girl was sprawled on her back, red-gold curls a tangle on the pillowcase and the blanket half on, half off the bed.

Jennifer straightened the blanket and tucked it in at Annie's waist before leaning over to kiss her daughter's cheek. Annie mumbled and stirred, rolling over to snuggle her face against the soft fur of the stuffed brown bear in her arms.

A surge of love and affection swept over Jennifer. Once again, she was caught off guard and staggered at the depth of her love for her daughter. Annie was a treasure and in so many ways, a constant source of surprise for Jennifer. The little girl enriched her life in ways she'd never envisioned before she became a mother.

And Jennifer loved every one of them.

She moved quietly back into her own room, stripped out of her clothes to take a quick shower, then pulled on her pajamas and climbed into bed and switched off the light.

After a long time, her world now seemed to be full and the future stretched ahead of her, filled with possibilities.

*What could possibly go wrong?* she thought with a drowsy smile just before she fell asleep.

\* \* \*

Jennifer's sense of well-being and happiness lasted less than twelve hours.

Due to working a split shift at the diner, she was alone in her apartment just before noon the next day. Annie was at school and Jennifer was almost dressed and ready to return for her second four-hour shift, padding about barefoot as she quickly dusted and neatened the rooms after assembling a casserole and tucking it into the refrigerator for Annie's and Margaret's dinner.

A knock on her door interrupted her and, thinking it might be Margaret, she hurried out of the kitchen. A quick glance out the apartment door peephole startled her speechless and she froze, staring at the man who stood outside in the hallway.

"What on earth is *he* doing here?" she murmured to herself, nonplussed.

The man knocked again, an impatient rap of his knuckles against the door panels.

Annoyed, Jennifer threw the dead bolt and yanked open the door. "Hello, Patrick."

"Hello, Jennifer." Her ex-husband smiled, exuding boyish charm.

His endearing smile had no effect on Jennifer.

Fortunately, she thought dispassionately, she'd been well and truly inoculated.

"What are you doing here?" she asked.

"I'd like to talk to you." He peered over her shoulder and gestured at the room behind her. "But I'd rather not have this conversation in the hallway. Won't you ask me in?"

Jennifer narrowed her eyes, studying him. She knew very well that Patrick wanted something but she couldn't imagine what it could be. He'd blithely walked away from their short marriage before Annie was born and hadn't contacted her since.

Nevertheless, whatever he wanted to talk to her about, it was probably best done in the privacy of her apartment.

"Very well, come in." Reluctantly, she stepped back and waved him inside.

"Nice," he commented, his gaze running over the small rooms. "You always did have a natural ability for decorating, Jennifer."

Jennifer ignored the comment, knowing full well his compliments were always charmingly insincere. "I have to leave for work, Patrick, so maybe you can cut to the chase and just tell me why you're here."

His gaze sharpened with swift annoyance and then

he shrugged, his expression bland once more. "You always were appallingly direct, Jennifer."

"I prefer to call it being honest," she told him. "So…?"

"Very well." He reached into the inner pocket of his suit jacket and took out a newspaper clipping, handing it to Jennifer.

She unfolded the newsprint, frowning when she saw it was the photo of her and Chance, dancing at the Founder's Ball, and the accompanying gossip column notation listing their names.

"I'm afraid I don't understand." She looked at him, confused.

"It appears you're dating Dr. Chance Demetrios."

"And if I am?" Jennifer couldn't imagine where this conversation was going. Granted, she hadn't dated anyone since the divorce but surely Patrick wouldn't care if she went out with someone.

"I don't know if you're aware, but I've finished med school and completed my internship."

"Congratulations." She eyed him, waiting, wishing he'd get to the point.

"I'm applying for various positions—including an opening in the research department at the Armstrong Fertility Institute."

Jennifer stared at him, beginning to guess where

the conversation was going. "And you're telling me this…why?"

"Dr. Demetrios and his partner are doing cutting-edge research in his field. I want to be a part of that research team."

Slow anger began to churn in Jennifer's midsection. "What does this have to do with me?"

Patrick smiled, shaking his head at her. "Jennifer, Jennifer," he chided. "I'm sure you can see my point. I want you to use your influence with your boyfriend to move my name to the top of the hiring list."

"No." Jennifer shoved the newspaper clipping into his hand. "If that's all you wanted to talk to me about, I really have to get to work." She walked to the door.

"How's Annie?"

Jennifer froze, hand on the doorknob, then slowly turned to stare at him. "I'm surprised you know her name."

"Of course I know her name," he said, faintly reproachful. "After all, she's my daughter."

Unease shivered up Jennifer's spine. "I thought we resolved your connection to Annie when you agreed to give me full custody in return for my not asking for child support. You've never shown any interest in her before."

"That's true," he agreed blandly. "But I've been re-thinking my position as her father. I'm wondering if I shouldn't ask the court to set up a visitation schedule so I can get to know my daughter."

"You don't want to get to know Annie," Jennifer told him, coldly furious. "You're using her to threaten me so I'll ask Chance to hire you."

"You always were quick to grasp the basics," he conceded. "I don't want to take you back to court and force you to let me have Annie for alternate weekends. If I were involved in demanding re-search, perhaps I would be too busy to have her with me, anyway."

"This is blackmail," she said, fighting to keep her words even. Anger warred with worry, threatening to make her voice tremble.

"Blackmail is such a harsh word, Jennifer," he informed her. "I prefer calling this a…negotiation for mutual benefits."

"You've always been good at hiding your selfish interests behind pretty words," she retorted bitterly. "I won't do it, Patrick. I can't do it. Chance and I don't have that kind of relationship but even if we did, I wouldn't ask him to hire someone like you." She pulled open the door and stood back. "Now get out of my house."

"I suggest you think it over." He moved toward her, stepped into the hallway. "I'll call you soon."

"Please don't," she insisted. "My mind isn't going to change."

He merely smiled and walked down the hall.

Jennifer closed the door with quiet force and threw the dead bolt before she turned, the solid door panel supporting her when she slumped.

Eventually she'd learned Patrick hid a snake's personality behind the charming, handsome facade. Their divorce had certainly shown her a side of him that was unattractive and selfish, but threatening her with Annie's welfare if she didn't help him use Chance to further his career…well, it was beyond belief, even for Patrick.

Glancing at the clock again, she realized more time had slipped away than she'd realized.

"And now I'm going to be late for work," she grumbled, hurrying to the bedroom to grab her shoes.

She wasn't sure how she was going to stop Patrick without endangering Annie, but she was determined to do so.

Jennifer was certain that the day that began with the unexpected visit from her ex-husband could not get any more complicated.

Never had she been so wrong.

\* \* \*

Midafternoon found Chance pushing open the door to the diner and striding inside, pausing to swiftly scan the long room. He didn't see Jennifer and a wave of disappointment washed over him.

*Damn.* He scanned the room again, slower this time, but still didn't see Jennifer's blond hair.

Enthusiasm dampened, he took a step toward his usual booth but paused abruptly, his gaze sharpening. A little girl sat in the back booth where he'd often seen Jennifer studying on her breaks. The child's head was bent over a book lying open atop the table, long red-gold curls falling forward over her shoulder as she focused intently on the crayon she moved over the page.

She looked up, her gaze unerringly finding his as if she'd felt his stare. Chance went still—he knew those deep blue eyes. They were duplicates of Jennifer's—same color, same shape beneath the arch of delicate brows. He had an instant mental image of a small curl of red hair tucked into the silver locket he'd found in his sheets after the unforgettable night Jennifer had spent in his bed. This child's hair had the same sheen of glossy, burnished red-gold. And the pixie face framed by that mane of curls was the same as in the locket's tiny photo.

Intrigued, he immediately changed direction.

"Hi, there," he said when he reached the back booth.

The little girl studied him gravely, her blue eyes inspecting him with curiosity. "Hi." Her childish voice was a clear treble. "Who are you?"

"I'm Chance. Who are you?"

"Annie."

"Nice to meet you, Annie. You have blue eyes just like my friend Jennifer. Do you know Jennifer?"

"That's my mom!" A smile lit her face and she beamed up at him. "I'm waiting for her till she gets off work."

"I see." Despite his suspicions, Chance was stunned when the little girl cheerfully confirmed his guess. Jennifer had a child and she'd never told him. In fact, she'd never even mentioned being a mother. Why not? Was she keeping the child a secret? He glanced at the papers and books spread out over the tabletop. "What are you doing?"

"Coloring."

He tilted his head to better view the page under her hand. "Nice," he commented. The ballgown on the drawing of a gold-crowned princess matched the magenta crayon in her hand. "Who is she?"

"She's a princess and her name is Cinderella,"

Annie told him with a reproving stare. "Don't you know a princess when you see one?"

"Uh, well…" Amused and charmed, he shrugged, a smile tugging at the corners of his mouth. "I thought I did, but maybe not."

She pointed a small, imperious finger at the seat opposite her. "I know all about princesses. If you sit down, I'll tell you. Princesses are important."

Intrigued and entertained, Chance slid onto the bench seat and propped his elbows on the table.

"I'm guessing you're a princess, right?" he asked.

"Sometimes." She nodded.

"And what about your mom—is she a princess, too?"

"No," she said promptly. "She's a queen."

"Yes," Chance agreed. He had a quick mental image of blond hair, long legs, graceful carriage and wise eyes. "She certainly is," he added softly.

## *Chapter Five*

Jennifer left the restroom and returned to the diner's main room just in time to see Chance standing next to the booth where she'd left Annie. Stunned, she froze for a moment, staring with disbelief as Chance leaned slightly forward to look at Annie's coloring book, the two exchanging words. Then Annie pointed at the seat opposite and Chance slid onto the bench to join her.

*Oh, no,* Jennifer nearly groaned aloud. Once again, Chance was sweeping aside an iron-clad rule she'd established for her life. He was like a force of nature and, apparently, virtually unstoppable.

Jennifer started toward the two, determined to send him on his way, out of her daughter's booth and firmly outside Annie's small sphere of male influences. Unfortunately, her progress was stopped by customers. Filling four different requests for coffee delayed her and it was ten minutes later before she reached Annie's booth.

"Hi, Mommy." A smile lit Annie's pixie face and she beamed up at Jennifer. Dressed in a navy-blue school jumper with a white blouse and pink sweater, the little girl's legs and small feet in black Mary Jane shoes were tucked beneath her as she knelt on the red vinyl seat. The crayons lay scattered now, clearly forgotten as she'd chatted with the big man seated opposite her. "Chance likes dogs, too."

"Call him Dr. Demetrios, Annie." Jennifer's gaze met Chance's, momentarily distracted by Annie's unexpected comment.

His dark eyes sparked with amusement. "I suggested a rottweiler like Butch or a Great Pyrenees but Annie seems to be leaning toward something bigger."

"Bigger?" Jennifer felt her eyes widen. "What could possibly be bigger?"

"A Newfie," Annie told her with conviction. "I really like Newfoundlands, Mommy. They have the sweetest faces and kind eyes. I saw a picture of one in a book." She switched her gaze to Chance. "I go to school and my teacher takes us to the library," she said confidingly.

"Pretty cool teacher," he agreed with a grin. "Especially if the library has dog books with pictures."

"Oh, yes," she assured him. "It has lots of dog books—I counted four." She looked back at Jennifer. "I think we should get a black Newfoundland and name her Sadie."

"Sadie's a very nice name," Jennifer conceded. "And Newfoundlands are known for being even-tempered and sweet-natured dogs but, honey—" she paused, mentally picturing a very, very large dog "—I think they weigh over a hundred pounds. I'm not sure she would fit, even if we had a house with a yard. Maybe you should consider a smaller breed, like a miniature dachshund or a Chihuahua."

"I don't think so, Mommy," Annie replied, her expression serious as she leaned forward to peer up at her mother. "I think we need a big watchdog. 'Cause we don't have a daddy that lives with us to keep us safe from burglars and things."

Startled speechless, Jennifer could only stare as she tried to think of a reasoned reply. But she drew a blank. "I didn't know you worried about burglars, Annie."

"I don't so much," Annie said blithely. "But until we find us a daddy, we should have a dog."

Jennifer felt her eyes go round. She glanced at Chance and found him watching her. His mouth wasn't curved upward but laughter danced in his dark eyes. She frowned at him and he grinned, lifting his hands as if to disclaim any responsibility for Annie's comments.

"When did you decide this?" she asked Annie, turning away from Chance so she couldn't see his amusement at what must have been obvious astonishment on her face. She wasn't going to admit that Annie had taken her completely by surprise. Not that it would have done her any good to deny it since she was sure her expression must have been clear enough.

"Today at school. Melinda said she'd share her daddy but I think we should get one of our own." A small, worried frown creased her brow. "Do you think it will be hard to find one that likes Newfoundland dogs?" She turned to Chance, leaning on her elbows to get closer. "What do you think, Chance?"

"I think any man worth his salt would like to have a Newfoundland dog named Sadie." He bent forward to lean his forearms on the tabletop and the move narrowed the distance between them across the table to barely a foot. "And if the package included a little red-haired girl named Annie, it would be a deal too good to turn down."

Annie beamed at him with approval before turning to Jennifer. "See, Mommy? We're a good deal."

"You and Sadie certainly would be," Jennifer agreed. She glanced at her wristwatch. "My shift is finished and it's time for us to head home. Why don't you put your things away in your backpack while I go get my purse and jacket."

"Okay."

Jennifer switched her attention to Chance and opened her mouth to say goodbye but he spoke first.

"I've got my car outside. I'll give you a lift home."

"That's a lovely offer, Chance, but Annie can't ride in a car without a child's safety seat and I'm sure you don't…"

"You can borrow the one out of my car," Linda interrupted eagerly, slowing on her way past them with a tray of dishes. She paused, balancing the tray on one hip while she fished a key ring from her pocket. "Here you are, Chance. It's the blue sedan parked directly across the street."

"But…" Jennifer protested. Linda merely winked at her.

"Thanks, Linda." Chance took the key and stood.

"I'll be right back, you two." He leveled his index finger at Jennifer. "Wait for me."

"Well, I…"

Annie tugged at her arm. "Please, Mommy," she whispered loudly. "I don't want to ride the bus today. I want to go with Chance."

"Dr. Demetrios," Jennifer corrected absentmindedly, giving in to the plea in Annie's blue eyes. "All right." She glanced at Chance. "We'll be here."

Chance didn't wait for Jennifer to say anything more. He left the diner and jogged across the street to Linda's sedan. It only took a few moments to remove the safety seat from the rear of Linda's vehicle but it took a bit longer to install it in the back of his Jaguar. As he adjusted the seat belt, he thought about the little girl. Damned if he didn't like the kid, he thought with a rueful grin. She'd chattered non-stop, her conversation about her love of all things Disney Princess–connected and her desire for a large dog interspersed with questions. He'd been down-right charmed by her and had given her answers to blunt questions that he would have adroitly avoided had she been twenty years older.

Annie seemed to have the same effect on him as her mother, he reflected as he jogged back across the street. None of the usual rules applied to them.

He found the little red-haired girl enchanting. And she seemed equally pleased with him.

*And how crazy is that?* he thought as he pushed open the door and reentered the diner. He didn't dislike kids, exactly, but he'd never had a particular interest in them, either. Until Annie.

"Do you ladies have plans for dinner?" he asked as they drove away from the diner. "I've been craving pizza all day—not just any pizza, but my favorite pizza at Giovanni's."

"I love pizza!" Annie exclaimed from the backseat.

"That makes two of us who vote for pizza. How about you, Jennifer?" Chance inquired when she remained silent. "Do you love pizza?"

She glanced sideways at him, her expression closed, her eyes wary. "I like pizza," she confirmed. "But I have a casserole in the fridge for dinner tonight, and I have to be at class at six-thirty so I'm afraid we can't—"

"Please, Mommy," Annie pleaded. "I really, really want to have pizza. We can have the casserole tomorrow night."

"I'm not sure we have time to go out for dinner, Annie. I have to take you home, then go to class..."

"I'll drive you," Chance put in. "It would be my pleasure."

She gave him an uncertain look.

"But if you truly can't make it tonight, then I'll take you home and wait while you settle Annie before driving you to the campus," he told her. "We can go out for pizza another time."

"Well, I…" Her fingers worried the strap of her purse in her lap.

Chance felt like a heel. She clearly was torn and though he didn't know why, her concern was obviously focused on his invitation to dinner. "I didn't mean to pressure you, Jennifer," he murmured. He covered her hands with his for one brief squeeze of reassurance. "Don't worry about it. Just tell me what you want to do."

He braked for a red light and looked at her to find her gaze on him, intent. Stiffly held shoulders slowly relaxed and she nodded with decision.

"Pizza sounds good—and Annie's right, the casserole will keep until tomorrow night."

"Great." He grinned at her and Annie's whoop of delight in the backseat had Jennifer smiling back. "Giovanni's restaurant is only a couple of blocks from here."

The light turned green and he switched his attention to the street, weaving expertly through traffic before he slotted the sleek Jaguar into a parking spot.

The moment they exited the car a short half block

from the restaurant, the wonderful smell of yeasty bread and Italian sauce reached them. And when Chance held the door wide and ushered Jennifer and Annie into the restaurant, the aroma surrounded them.

"It smells yummy in here," Annie whispered loudly as they took seats.

"I think that's one of the reasons I like coming here," Chance told her.

"I love it," Annie proclaimed with a definitive nod.

"Well, I guess that's the seal of approval," Chance indicated to Jennifer.

She rolled her eyes at him. "Annie's nothing if not decisive. I suspect she'll grow up to be the first female president of the United States. Or maybe CEO of Häagen-Dazs since she loves the ice cream and she'd get free samples."

Chance laughed out loud, drawing indulgent smiles from surrounding tables.

The spontaneous late-afternoon meal went by too quickly. After dropping Annie off at home in the care of Margaret, Chance drove Jennifer to the campus and all too soon, it was time to say goodbye.

"Thanks for coming to dinner with me," he told her. "Your daughter is terrific. I enjoyed getting to know her."

A tiny frown drew the feathery arches of Jennifer's brows into a vee. "About Annie, Chance…" She paused, seeming to search for words.

"What about Annie?" he prompted. Without thinking, he smoothed his thumb over the little worry lines between her brows, his fingers trailing down the line of her cheek and jaw in a lingering caress. Her skin was silky soft beneath his hand and a rush of fierce emotion shook him. He could deal with lust— he expected it. But this feeling of protective affection, this was something else.

"I haven't dated, mostly, because I didn't want Annie getting attached to men who were just casual friends," she explained. "I didn't want her to get hurt."

"So I'm the first guy she's seen with you since the divorce."

"You're the first man she's seen with me, period. Her father and I were divorced before she was born and he's never met her."

Chance bit off a curse. "You mean to tell me that little girl's daddy isn't part of her life?" He was incredulous.

"Patrick was furious when I told him I was pregnant. He'd never wanted children. He moved out that night and filed for divorce within a week."

He tried to assimilate the blunt words. "What an ass," he said finally.

"Yes, he was." Her mouth quirked and she smiled at him, eyes sparkling.

"Jennifer…" He cupped her chin in his palm, his gaze holding hers. "Some men are just brainless. But I'm not—and I'd never harm Annie or you. I'm not sure what this is between us but I'd cut off my arm before I'd see either one of you hurt."

Her blue eyes misted. "You're a good man, Chance Demetrios," she said softly.

"Hell, no, I'm not." He kissed her, savoring the sweetness of her mouth as her lips softened beneath his and she kissed him back.

When at last he lifted his head, her hands clutched his shirt and they were both breathing hard.

"Can I wait and give you a ride home?" he asked.

"No, thanks," she murmured. "This is the night our class lets out early and one of my study group members gives me a ride home. She says she doesn't mind dropping me, even though it's out of her way, because it gives us a little longer to study."

Reluctantly, Chance let her go. She turned at the doorway to wave, then disappeared inside the lecture hall.

She hadn't been completely convinced that both she and Annie's hearts were safe with him, he thought as he drove away.

*I could have told her I think I'm falling in love with her,* he thought somberly. *That might have re-assured her.*

But he wasn't sure he was ready to admit he'd finally met the one woman who could turn him inside out and stand his world on end. Even to himself.


"Put your pajamas on, sweetie," Jennifer called as she blotted water from the bathroom floor the following evening. She made a mental note to toss a couple of towels on the tile tomorrow night before Annie took her bath. The child splashed water as if she were a dolphin in a pool.

She wondered if Chance was still in his office at the institute. He'd called earlier in the day to say he had to work late that night but wanted to invite her and Annie on a picnic the following Saturday. She'd been surprised by the depth of disappointment she'd felt that she wouldn't be seeing him sooner but decided it was probably a perfectly normal reaction. She hadn't dated anyone in so long she could hardly remember what constituted "normal."

She dropped the damp towels in the hamper and folded Annie's crumpled jeans and T-shirt, laying them on the counter next to the sink.

"Annie," she yelled in an attempt to hurry her

daughter. "As soon as you're dressed, we'll pop over to Margaret's apartment to see how she's feeling."

"Okay." Annie appeared in the doorway, her voice muffled as she pulled the top to a pair of pink princess pajamas over her head. Her mop of soft curls was damp, curling wildly around her face. "Margaret coughed a lot this afternoon, Mommy."

"Did she?" Jennifer hung the wet towel over a bar, cast a quick glance around the neat bathroom, and joined Annie. "That's why we're going to go check on her."

Annie dashed ahead of her, waiting for Jennifer to slide the dead bolt free before they crossed the hall. When Margaret didn't immediately answer the door-bell, Annie knocked on the door panel. When at last Margaret opened the door, Jennifer understood the delay. Her neighbor's face was pale, the only color a faint flush over her cheekbones, and her mouth was taut with distress.

"Margaret, my goodness." She took the older woman's arm and steadied her, concern heightening when she felt the usually spry body tremble and lean heavily. "Annie, come in and close the door," she commanded, waiting until the little girl had done so before she guided Margaret to a seat on the sofa. "How long have you…" She was interrupted when the older woman began to cough, a hacking, painful sound in the quiet apartment.

Jennifer laid her palm on Margaret's forehead. "You feel warm. Have you taken your temperature—do you have a fever?"

"Just a slight one," Margaret responded, her voice weak and faintly raspy.

"That's it," Jennifer said with decision. "You need to see a doctor."

"No, no," Margaret protested but with a distinct lack of her usual energy and forcefulness. "I'm sure it's just a cold and I'll be fine in a day or two."

"Maybe." Jennifer was unconvinced. "I certainly hope you're right. But in the meantime, let's have a doctor at the free clinic check you out, just to be sure." Her gaze met Margaret's. "I don't like the sound of that cough, nor the fact that you're running a temp. If you need an antibiotic, the sooner it's started, the better."

Margaret sighed. "Very well."

Her easy capitulation worried Jennifer even more. Margaret was too compliant and very unlike her usual self. As she helped the older woman dress, even tying her shoes, Jennifer became even more concerned.

"We need to make a quick stop in our apartment so Annie and I can grab a light sweater—and I need my purse," Jennifer said as she collected Margaret's apartment keys and purse, locking up behind them.

"Mommy, do I get to wear my pajamas outside?" Annie asked as Jennifer unlocked the door to her own apartment and helped Margaret inside.

"Why don't you pull on jeans over your jammies," Jennifer suggested. "Or just change clothes—but hurry, we don't want to keep the cab waiting."

"Take the money for the cab out of my wallet," Margaret told her, eyes closing as she laid her head back against the sofa.

Jennifer would have insisted on paying herself but she knew Margaret would argue and the older woman seemed too weary.

"Of course, Margaret, I'll do that," she agreed, catching up a sweater from where it hung on the back of a kitchen chair. It took only a moment to collect her purse from the bedroom and she hurried back into the living room. "Annie," she called. "Are you ready?"

"Yes, Mommy." The little girl appeared, dressed in laced-up sneakers, jeans, a T-shirt and pink sweater. She carried her backpack, bulging at the seams.

Jennifer glanced at her watch. "Great, let's head downstairs. The cab should be here soon."

Luck was with them, for they'd barely reached the

exit to the street when a cab pulled up to the curb, lights bright.

"Thank goodness," Jennifer murmured. She handed Margaret into the cab, Annie scrambled inside and Jennifer gave the driver the address for the free clinic.

Dusk was falling and streetlights glowed outside the medical offices. Jennifer helped Margaret climb the three shallow steps to the entry as the cab drove away. Annie walked beside them, uncharacteristically quiet. Backpack slung over her shoulder, she grabbed the handle with both hands and with an effort, pushed the heavy door inward, holding it while the two women made their way into the reception area.

The room was nearly empty. Only two other people sat there—a young woman with a crying baby in her arms and an elderly gentleman sucking on an unlit pipe.

Jennifer helped Margaret to a seat on a vinyl-covered sofa against the wall and Annie sat next to her, eyeing the woman and small baby with concerned interest.

"Good evening." The receptionist smiled when Jennifer walked to the counter. "What can we do for you?"

"My neighbor has a bad cough and a temperature. She needs to see a doctor." Jennifer looked over her shoulder when Margaret began to cough, the sound grating.

"I think we can get her in quickly," the receptionist assured her. "The doctor is in with a patient now, and the other folks here are waiting for test results to come back so it should only be a few moments. I'll need you to fill out a form with her personal stats and insurance information."

The paperwork took only a few moments and once finished, Jennifer joined Margaret on the sofa, Annie tucked between them.

"It shouldn't be too long, Margaret," she began. "The receptionist said the doctor was…"

The door to the inner rooms opened and a young man exited, his hand wrapped in thick white bandages. A tall, dark-haired man in a white lab coat followed him.

"Next time, try to be more careful when you're slicing vegetables," the doctor said.

"Thanks, Doc, I will."

Jennifer stared at the doctor, blinking in disbelief. The voice she knew so well, the face she saw in her dreams and the doctor who worked in the halls of the Armstrong Fertility Institute was here.

What was Chance Demetrios doing in the free clinic? It was the last place she'd expected to see him.

"Look, Mommy, it's Chance." Annie hopped off the sofa and dashed across the tile floor.

"Hey, Annie." Chance grinned at her. "What are you doing here?" The smile disappeared and he looked up, scanning the room. His features cleared when his gaze met Jennifer's and he walked toward her. "Hello, Jennifer."

"Hi." She stood. "I didn't expect to see you here."

"I work here," he said simply. "Why are you here—are you and Annie okay?"

"Oh, we're fine," she assured him quickly. "It's Margaret, our neighbor."

On the sofa, the older woman stirred, opening her eyes and sitting up straighter.

"I see," Chance said. "You must be Margaret," he told her, his voice gentle, his eyes assessing. "Why don't we get you into an exam room?"

He helped her to stand, his big hand cupping her elbow.

He glanced over his shoulder. "You can come with us, Jennifer. You, too, Annie."

They followed down a short hallway, slowly as Chance let Margaret set the pace. When she was settled on an exam table, he gestured for Jennifer to take a seat on the single, straight-backed wooden chair in the small room.

Annie perched on her mother's lap, her eyes bright, round as she watched Chance.

"So, what's going on, Margaret?" he queried, wrapping a blood pressure cuff around her thin upper arm.

"I have a cold," she told him. "Well, it started as a cold," she amended. "But late this afternoon, I noticed I was feeling hot and my thermometer confirmed I had a temperature."

"I see." Chance noted the blood pressure stats and removed the cuff from her arm. "There's a lot of flu going around," he informed her. "Let's check your temperature. Hmm," he said a moment later. "It is a little elevated."

Margaret nodded, clearly weary. "I thought so."

Jennifer managed to contain her worry until Chance had finished his examination.

"Does she have the flu?" she asked when he began making notes on a chart.

"I'm afraid so," he told her. "I'd like to have her spend the night in the hospital. We'll give her fluids and watch her to be sure the she doesn't get worse."

"I don't want to go to the hospital," Margaret argued, a hint of her normal asperity in her weary voice.

"I know you don't," Jennifer assured her gently. "But a single night being cared for is better than having you go home, get worse, and then perhaps face several days in the hospital."

"True." Margaret's response was grudgingly agreeing.

"You're doing the wise thing," Chance stated, patting her thin shoulder. "I'll make arrangements for transporting you to City General. I'll be right back."

"I'd much rather go home. I don't like hospitals," Margaret grumbled, lying back on the exam table as the door closed on Chance's back.

"I know," Jennifer soothed. "And I don't blame you but I think Dr. Demetrios is right—you've made the wise choice."

"Perhaps," she said wearily.

Chance returned shortly, his presence seeming to fill the room. "Your ride is here, Mrs. Sullivan."

"Goodness, that was fast." Margaret peered owlishly up at him. "Are you a magician?"

"No, ma'am." He smile flashed, his teeth white in his suntanned face. "An ambulance was in the neighborhood when my receptionist put in a call for transport. I think we just got lucky here."

"Good," Margaret murmured. "It's about time. I could use some luck."

"I suspect we'd all like a little more luck," Chance told her.

Voices sounded in the hall outside and Chance pulled open the exam-room door. "The patient is in here," he called. "The EMTs are going to need room so let's step outside, Jennifer, Annie."

"We'll see you tomorrow morning, Margaret," Jennifer promised, bending to brush a quick kiss against the older woman's pale cheek.

"Me, too, Margaret." Annie carefully followed her mother's example with a brief kiss. "We love you, Margaret."

A smile lifted the corners of Margaret's mouth. "I love you, too, sweetie."

Her eyes drifted closed as Annie stepped back. Jennifer took her hand, following Chance into the hallway to make room for the two ambulance attendants and their gurney. The pair quickly and efficiently transferred Margaret to the stretcher, tucking a blanket around her small frame and strapping her securely.

"See you tomorrow, Margaret," Annie repeated as the two men wheeled her down the hallway to the exit and their waiting ambulance. Her fingers clutched Jennifer's and when the back door closed, she turned her worried face up to her mother's. "She's going to be okay, isn't she, Mommy?"

"Chance says she will be and he's a very good doctor, honey," Jennifer reassured her, smoothing

her palm over the silky mop of curls in uncon-
scious comfort.

Annie's blue gaze switched to Chance, questioning.

He dropped to his heels in front of her. "Your
friend is going to be just fine, Annie. The nurses at
the hospital will keep watch over her tonight and
she'll get medicine so that she can come home in the
morning. Okay?"

"Okay." Annie's cupid mouth tilted in a brief
smile and Chance's big hand cupped her small chin
for a moment.

Then he stood, his gaze soothing as he met
Jennifer's.

"I'll pick you up around ten tomorrow morning
and you two can come to the hospital with me. I have
to do rounds to check on several patients and you can
visit with Margaret until I'm finished. Then I'll give
you all a ride home."

"Thank you," she said simply. She might have
declined, given her determination to be independent,
but it would be much better for Margaret if Chance
chauffeured them home in his comfortable car.

"I'd take you and Annie home tonight but my shift
doesn't end for several hours. I had my receptionist
call a cab—it's waiting outside," he told her. His gaze
flicked assessingly over Annie's face. "I know you

could take the bus but humor me. It's late and Annie looks like she's about to fall asleep on her feet."

Jennifer knew Annie was tired. The weight of her small body leaned against her side and the hour was way past her usual bedtime.

"All right."

Relief spread over his features and he smiled at her with such warmth that her knees went weak.

"Thanks," he murmured as he walked them down the hallway, through the reception area and out to the waiting cab. "I'll feel better knowing the cab will take you straight home."

"Good night, Chance." Annie's farewell was interrupted by a jaw-cracking yawn as she slid onto the worn leather seat.

"Good night, and thank you, Chance," Jennifer said.

"I'll see you in the morning," he promised.

For a moment, she thought he was going to kiss her, but then he closed the door. He leaned in the open window of the cab's passenger front seat.

"Take good care of my girls," he indicated, handing the driver folded bills.

"You bet," the driver replied, taking the currency.

Chance stepped back and the cab pulled away from the curb.

*His girls?* Jennifer wasn't sure how she felt about

the possessive note in Chance's voice. But affection for the big man and his obvious concern for her, Annie and Margaret curled warmly through her body. It had been a long time since anyone made her feel so cared for and she liked it, maybe too much, she thought soberly.

Was she coming to depend too much on Chance's place in her life? And if she was, how painful would it be when he moved on, as surely he would?

She pushed the thoughts aside, determined not to spoil the happiness she felt with Chance today by worrying about the future.

The following morning, as promised, Chance collected Jennifer and Annie and took them to the hospital with him. They dashed through the rain from the car to the double-doored entrance, their jackets quickly growing damp from the spring storm. He left them on Margaret's floor, promising to collect them in an hour or so.

Fortunately, Margaret was feeling much better and by the time they returned to their apartment building to settle the elderly woman into her own bed, it was well past noon.

"Are you sure Margaret is okay by herself?" Annie asked, her little face worried. "Maybe she should come stay with us till she's all better."

"She wants to rest in her own bed, honey," Jennifer told her. "But we're just across the hall so we can run in and out often to make sure she's all right and has everything she needs."

"Like lunch?" Annie climbed onto a kitchen chair and leaned on her elbows. "I'm hungry. I bet Margaret is, too."

"She had an early lunch at the hospital, remember?" Jennifer recalled. "But we didn't so I'm not surprised you're hungry. What would you like for lunch?"

"How about Chinese?" Chance put in. "I noticed there's a take-out place on the corner."

"Yeah! I love Chinese food," Annie instantly crowed with approval.

Chance leaned against the counter, arms crossed over his chest, and cocked an eyebrow at Jennifer. "How about you? Do you love Chinese food?"

"Yes, but you'll soon learn that Annie claims she loves all kinds of ethnic food, whether she's actually tasted it or not," Jennifer said dryly.

"Good, that simplifies matters," he told her. "Do you have a take-out menu for the restaurant?"

Jennifer pointed past his shoulder. "There's one on the fridge."

A half hour later, they sat around the table, a dozen boxes of food opened and plates in front of them.

"I like this stuff," Annie proclaimed. "What is it?"

Chance leaned over to inspect the bite of food on her fork. "That's almond chicken," he informed her.

"It's yummy."

He grinned at Jennifer. "She likes it."

"I guess we can add it to the short list of ethnic food she's actually tried," Jennifer decided.

"I want to use chopsticks, too," Annie said.

"A fork is lots easier to eat with," her mother insisted.

"Chance uses chopsticks."

"True." He glanced at Jennifer for permission, waiting until she nodded before he tore the wrapping off a pair of plastic chopsticks from the restaurant and handed them to Annie. She held them awkwardly, stabbing a piece of chicken but dropping it before it reached her mouth. "Not that way," Chance instructed. "Here, I'll show you."

He stood, rounding the table to lean over her, moving her little fingers to properly grip the two sticks, then helping her pick up a bite.

Jennifer clapped when the small piece of chicken disappeared into Annie's mouth and her eyes lit with success.

"Look, Mommy," she said, her mouth full of chicken. "I can use chopsticks."

"Yes, you certainly can." Jennifer exchanged a mutually amused look with Chance.

Outside, the rain came down, pattering against the windowpanes and watering the spring flowers and budding trees. Inside, the three of them finished lunch, neatened the kitchen and then settled around the coffee table for a game of Clue. Jennifer switched on the CD player and the raspy voice of Louis Armstrong sang the lyrics of a 1940s blues tune. She lowered the volume until the music was a pleasant background, adding to the apartment's cozy, comfortable air.

Chance rolled the dice and moved his playing piece on the board.

"Oh, no," Annie groaned dramatically. "You're in the library and with Miss Scarlet!"

Chance laughed. "I haven't played this game since I was a kid but I seem to remember that when a fellow player doesn't want me landing in a room, it probably means she knows something about who killed who."

Annie gave him an impish look. "Maybe, maybe not." She tossed her head, her ponytail of red-gold hair gleaming in the lamplight. "I'll never tell."

Jennifer leaned sideways to whisper loudly. "I should warn you—Annie almost always wins this game."

"Aha. Now you've challenged me," he told them. "This is serious. I have to win to prove guys can play this game well, too." He gave the two females a fierce frown and they laughed, identical blue eyes sparkling with merriment.

*Damn,* he realized with sudden insight. *I'm having fun, playing a board game with a kid and her mom.* Nothing could be further from the polished, sexually willing debutantes and black-tie events that had often been the focus of his past social life. Was it possible his conviction that he wasn't wired for family life was only because he'd never met the right woman? The thought was startling—and he shoved it to the back of his mind, to be considered later. Maybe much later. At the moment, he was enjoying himself too much to ponder weightier subjects.

Later that evening, when Chance had left the apartment and Annie was asleep, snuggled beneath the pink princess coverlet on her bed, Jennifer curled up in her own.

The lamplight cast a circle of gold light over the book on her lap and the notebook with her pen. She'd planned to study but kept thinking about the afternoon just past.

There was such a disparity between Chance's playboy image and the man who'd sat cross-legged on her floor, arguing spiritedly with her daughter over who was the culprit in their game of Junior Clue.

A smile curved her mouth, her eyes going unfocused as she replayed the scene in her mind's eye. In some ways, the afternoon had been bittersweet because it had created an image for her of what life would have been like had Annie's father been a man she could have loved and respected. And if he had been an honorable man who had remained in their lives, she thought.

The phone rang, startling her out of her reverie. She leaned sideways to pick up the portable from the bedside table.

"Hello?"

"Hi, Jennifer."

She almost groaned as she recognized Patrick's voice. "Hello, Patrick."

"I'm calling to check back with you. Have you thought about my request?"

"I told you, Patrick, I'm not going to ask Chance to give you a job."

"I'm sorry to hear that," he said smoothly. "Perhaps we can discuss it further over coffee tomorrow."

"No, I don't think so. Frankly, Patrick, we have nothing to discuss."

"Oh, but we do." His voice turned harder. "We can

certainly leave it to our attorneys but I thought you might want to discuss arranging a visitation schedule in private, just between the two of us. Before my attorney asks for a court date to resolve the issue."

"You have absolutely no interest in seeing Annie," she argued, anger sharpening her tone.

"But I have the right to visit," he told her, "if I choose to exercise that right."

"Fine," she conceded. "I can meet you before I start work."

She gave him the address of a nearby Starbucks and rang off, her fingers trembling as she returned the phone to its base.

## Chapter Six

Jennifer was still angry when she walked into the Starbucks the following morning.

Her ex-husband sat at a small round table near the back. He stood, waving at her when she entered. She threaded her way through the tables, the crowd of prework customers thinned at midmorning.

Patrick held her chair before taking his own seat, fastidiously straightening the crease in his suit slacks when he sat. "I ordered a low-fat vanilla latte for you," he told her with a friendly smile. "I remember you used to like them."

"Thank you." She'd vowed to remain polite and to use this meeting to elicit information and gauge Patrick's determination to follow through with his threat. She still had no intention of complying with his request to ask Chance to help his job search. Nevertheless, she didn't want him to start legal proceedings and threaten the stability of Annie's life. She sipped the coffee, eyeing him over the rim of her paper cup. "I confess, Patrick, I'm curious as to how you located me. The newspaper photo and brief comments about my being Chance's guest at the institute's ball didn't list anything about me except my name."

"You're correct. I didn't find you through the newspaper photo," Patrick confirmed. "It was the private investigator who gave me the details, including your current address."

"Private investigator?" Jennifer hoped she concealed her surprise.

"Yes. He didn't specifically tell me, but I gathered he was hired by the Demetrios family to check out the background of the woman their son and heir is dating." Patrick's eyes narrowed. "You do realize who Dr. Chance Demetrios is, don't you?"

Jennifer lifted her brow in cool inquiry, refusing to comment.

"You don't know. Jennifer—" he clucked and

shook his head, amused "—you just might be the only woman in Boston who doesn't know that Chance Demetrios is the only son of Jonathon Demetrios and heir to the Demetrios shipping empire."

Stunned, Jennifer's mind moved at whirlwind speed, trying to remember bits and pieces that might have told her Chance was more than a little rich. But his custom-tailored tuxedo, beautifully appointed town house and the luxurious Jaguar car didn't seem to point to a man who had access to ultrarich funds. Surely a doctor in his position would have those things?

"Of course, when the investigator asked me several extremely personal questions about you, I realized the family was taking the situation seriously—your dating Dr. Demetrios, that is." He spread his hands, his expression smug. "Which, of course, was serendipitous."

"Why is that?" she asked evenly, trying to keep a lid on her anger when she wanted to dump her hot latte over his head.

"Because here am I, having recently graduated from med school and filed an application with the Armstrong Fertility Institute. And here are you." He gestured at her. "My ex-wife, dating a man who's very influential at the institute. And between us, a daughter we both want the best for, I'm sure."

"I've told you, I won't introduce you to Chance or try to influence him in any way to help you obtain a position at the institute. You'll have to rely on your own qualifications. Annie and I have nothing to do with your being hired there."

"Perhaps not," he said smoothly. "But you, Annie and me are connected in a very basic way. Perhaps we should discuss our parental duties and whether it's in our daughter's best interests for you to deny me a father's right to visitation."

"You have absolutely no interest in seeing Annie," she said accusingly, her voice scathing. "You never did, so don't pretend you do now."

"Perhaps," he conceded. "But if you choose not to cooperate with me, I'll have my attorney take you back to court and sue for visitation rights—maybe even for custody."

Jennifer felt her body go cold. "You wouldn't dare," she ground out.

"Of course I would," he assured her amiably, his eyes cold. "I intend to have a prestigious position on the Armstrong research team—any way I can get it." He leaned closer, his voice lowering threateningly. "Don't stand in my way, Jennifer."

"You're despicable," she told him, her voice trembling with fury.

He leaned back with an easy shrug. "Call me what you like—as long as you do what I ask. If you don't," he warned her, "make no mistake, I will exercise my parental rights."

Jennifer stood, unable to bear another moment in his company. "I'll have to think about this. I don't know how I could possibly influence Chance since I have no connection to his work. In fact, I'm not even sure what he does at the institute since he doesn't talk about it."

"You don't have to know what he does," Patrick told her, rising. "Just make sure you convince him to arrange to give me the position. I'm willing to give you a couple weeks, maybe a bit more, but then I'll have to pay a visit to my attorney."

Jennifer didn't answer. In truth, she wasn't sure she could have spoken without outright refusing him. So she bit her tongue and walked away, seething.

She couldn't bring herself to ask Chance to hire Patrick. The man was a snake and, besides, she couldn't use Chance, not even to save Annie.

But how could she keep Patrick from gaining access to her daughter?

After the rainy afternoon playing Clue, Chance found himself spending as much time as possible in Jennifer and Annie's company.

Although lust was a constant, slow-burning flame in his gut whenever he was with Jennifer, he found himself unwilling to pressure her to spend the night with him. Instinct told him that he needed to court her, to give her time to come to terms with his presence in her—and Annie's—life.

He knew she'd looked on their date for the Founder's Ball and the night they'd spent together as a one-time thing.

But he was determined to have her in his bed again.

He suspected Jennifer was still struggling to shift her goals for her life and decide how letting him into her world would also allow her to meet her commitment to protect Annie.

With each day that passed, Chance was more convinced that he wasn't going to be a temporary man in Jennifer's life. He was slowly coming to believe that maybe, just maybe, his life would only be complete if Jennifer and Annie were a permanent part of his world.

Just before lunch on Saturday morning, Chance arrived at Jennifer's apartment with Butch.

She pulled open the door, a smile lighting her face when she saw him. Butch bounded over the threshold, wriggling with pleasure.

"Come in," she told Chance, as she bent to give the big dog a hug. He woofed, one deep sound of greeting, and tried to lick her face.

"Mommy? What was that noise?" Annie entered the living room and stopped abruptly, her eyes widening with surprise. "It's a dog!"

"This is Butch," Chance told her. "Butch, say hello to Annie."

Butch planted his rear on the floor and uttered one more deep woof of hello, ears up, big brown eyes trained on Annie with interest.

"Hello, Butch." Annie looked at Chance. "Can I pet him?"

"Sure." He beckoned her closer. "Hold out your hand and let him sniff it."

If the adults had any concerns about the big dog accepting Annie, they were quickly laid to rest. Within moments, dog and child were seated on the floor, Annie's arm around Butch's neck while she murmured in his ear. He watched her with unflagging interest, his eyes bright.

"I'm just making lunch," Jennifer told him. "Would you like to join us?" She led the way into the small kitchen and he followed, making himself at home as he opened a cupboard door to take down a mug, then poured himself coffee.

"Let's pack those sandwiches and take Annie on a picnic at the park near my house," Chance suggested.

Jennifer looked up. He leaned against the island's countertop, coffee mug in hand, his brown eyes warm.

"We can take Butch, too," he continued. "And the Frisbee, of course. I'll teach Annie how to toss it for Butch to catch. He's pretty good," he added with a grin.

"Annie would love it," Jennifer said. "Are you sure you're up for dealing with one very active little girl in a park, with lots of room to run?"

"Are you suggesting I can't keep up with her?" he asked. His appalled, disbelieving expression was undermined by the amusement in his dark eyes.

"I'm saying I doubt I can keep up with her," she corrected him. "But if you're game, I'm willing to give it a try."

"Great." He set down his coffee cup and strode across the kitchen. He wrapped his arms around her and swung her off her feet, planting a hard kiss on her mouth. "I'll go tell Annie and collect Butch." He set her down and glanced at the counter behind her. "Want some help packing the sandwiches?"

"No, I'm good." She shooed him out of the kitchen, shaking her head with affection as she took plastic containers from the pantry.

A half hour later, Chance parked the car outside his house and they unloaded, then set off for the park.

"How far is it to the park, Chance?" Annie asked, dancing backward in front of him.

"Six blocks," he told her.

"Okay." She spun around to skip forward once more, next to Butch.

The big rottweiler paced happily at the end of the leash, sniffing the warm spring air. He responded to Annie's frequent pats with a quick lick of his tongue and a woof of shared excitement.

"They're quite a pair, aren't they?" Jennifer murmured to Chance. "I'm not sure who's the most excited about this outing—Butch or Annie."

"I think it's a draw," Chance told her.

Jennifer glanced sideways at him. He held Butch's leash in one hand, easily controlling the eager big dog. A bright red blanket was tossed over one shoulder and he carried the wicker picnic basket in the other hand. His long legs were encased in faded jeans that clung faithfully to powerful thigh muscles, his feet covered with polished black boots. At his wrist, a Rolex watch glinted in the sunshine, his arms bare below the short sleeves of a navy polo shirt.

Just looking at him made her happy, she realized.

He glanced sideways at her, met her gaze, and lifted a brow in inquiry. "What?" he asked.

"Nothing." She smiled. "I'm just happy."

His dark eyes warmed, heating with slow promise. "Good to know." His voice was deeper, gravelly.

Jennifer shivered in reaction, anticipation curling slow tendrils of heat low in her belly.

"Look, Mommy, it's the park!" Annie's voice rose with delight.

Jennifer wrestled her thought under control and looked ahead. A half block away, the entry to a large expanse of green grass and trees.

"It must be two full blocks, at least," she commented, looking at Chance for confirmation.

He nodded and glanced at Butch. "The park is one of the reasons I bought a home in the neighborhood. If you want a dog, it's good to have a park nearby. Not to mention—" he grinned at her "—a large supply of plastic bags."

"Plastic bags?" she queried, confused.

"For picking up dog poop. It's a city ordinance, punishable by a fine, if owners don't clean up after their dogs."

"Eeww." Annie grimaced, her gaze meeting Chance's. "That's disgusting."

"Nah," he told her. "You just use a plastic bag and

then tie the ends and toss it in the park trash container. No big deal."

Annie looked unconvinced.

"That's part of being a dog owner," Jennifer told her gently. "If you have a pet, you have to take care of it properly."

"Well." The little girl eyes Butch consideringly. "I guess it's worth it." Her small chin tilted with purpose.

"She's so much like you," Chance murmured to Jennifer, low enough to keep Annie from overhearing.

"And that's a good thing, right?"

"Of course," he said promptly. "Conviction, determination, commitment—what's not good about that?"

They turned off the sidewalk, entering the park and following a winding concrete pathway beneath trees rustling with pale green leaves. On both sides of the walk, freshly mowed green lawns were dotted with beds of bright red, yellow, purple and blue flowers.

The park wasn't crowded but quite a few couples and family groups were taking advantage of the warm spring sunshine. They'd gathered on blankets spread on the grass, brightening the green sward with spots of color. Children ran and laughed, many with blue, red or green balloons tied to their wrists.

"Where are we going to have our picnic, Chance?" Annie asked.

"There's a great spot just a little farther," he told her. "It's just off the sidewalk and near the creek."

"Oooh, there's a creek, too? Fun!" She skipped ahead of the adults, keeping pace with Butch who paced happily at the end of his leash.

Her long red curls bounced as she moved, bright tendrils against the white sweater she wore over a pale blue sundress.

"Where does she get all that energy?" Chance said with wry disbelief, watching Annie's nonstop movement.

"I don't know, but I'd give anything to have just a tiny bit of it," Jennifer told him with a grin.

"Kids are pretty amazing, aren't they?"

"I don't know about all of them," she answered. "But I think Annie is. Of course, she's my daughter and I'm probably prejudiced."

"Yeah, you probably are," he told her. "But speaking as an objective bystander, I think you're right."

Impulsively, Jennifer went up on tiptoe and brushed a kiss against his cheek.

"What was that for?" he asked, his eyes heating.

"Just because."

The moment was broken when Butch and Annie came racing back to drop onto the blanket.

"We're hungry, Mommy," Annie declared. "Can Butch have a sandwich, too?"

Jennifer looked at Chance. "Is Butch allowed to eat a peanut butter and jelly sandwich?"

"It will probably stick to the roof of his mouth but he'll love it," Chance replied with a grin.

Jennifer put a sandwich, chips and a fat dill pickle on each plate and passed them out. She hesitated before sitting a paper plate in front of Butch. "What about pickles?" she said dubiously. "Does he like dill pickles?"

"Butch has a cast-iron stomach," Chance said drily. "And anything that's edible, he loves."

"Do you feed him like this all the time?" she asked as they began to eat and Butch wolfed down his food.

"No, he usually gets dry dog food and the occasional piece of meat, or a big bone to chew." He reached over and tucked a stray tendril of blond hair behind her ear, his fingers brushing in a slow caress over her cheek. "The vet told me he can occasionally have people food. It won't hurt him."

"Oh, good." She would have said more but an elderly man walked by, followed by a trio of golden retriever puppies and their mother on leashes.

Butch woofed and started to rise.

"Butch." Chance's voice was quiet. "Down."

The rottweiler dropped back to the blanket but he quivered with excitement. The puppies heard him and tugged free of the older gentleman to gambol near, touching noses to Butch's, crawling and tumbling over the big dog. Their mother was more cautious but friendly.

Annie caught up one of the puppies and hugged the wriggly, warm body close. "Mommy, I want a puppy like this one."

"Honey, you want a puppy like every one you see," Jennifer chided her with a smile.

Chance and Jennifer helped the elderly man disentangle the darling puppies from Butch and finally he hobbled off down the path toward the bridge across the pond.

"Can we throw the Frisbee for Butch now?" Annie asked when only crumbs were left on the blanket where they sat.

Stretched out beside the little girl, the big dog lifted his head inquiringly when he heard her say his name.

"Sure," Chance answered. He looked at Jennifer. "If your mom says it's okay."

"Fine with me." Jennifer smiled fondly as the three left the blanket, Annie darting ahead, Butch trotting after her, with Chance ambling behind. He'd auto-matically deferred to her for permission to release Annie to play, she thought, and how nice was that?

"Morning."

Chance looked up from his desk. His partner, Ted Bonner, stood in the doorway, a steaming cup of coffee in his hand. His hair was mussed as if he'd been running his hands through it. The two had gone to Stanford med school together—Chance recog-nized the signs of frustration.

"Morning. Come in, close the door and tell me what's wrong," he told him.

"What makes you think something's wrong?" Ted closed the door and strolled into the room, dropping into one of the chairs facing Chance's desk.

"Your hair and that face." Chance leaned back in his chair and propped his feet, ankles crossed, on the end of his desk.

Ted gave him a baffled look. "What face?"

"The one under your messed-up hair," Chance told him, pointing the hand holding his coffee cup. "It looks like you've been shoving your hands through it and trying to pull it out."

"Hell." Ted grunted and ran his palm over the crown of his head. "Better?"

Chance shrugged. "Now tell me what's wrong."

"I've heard some bad news," Ted said gloomily.

"The lab test results on our latest research weren't what we hoped they'd be?" His mind was already thinking of options if this was the problem. They could try a new theory he'd been working on…. He was beginning to wonder whether the lower percentage of viable pregnancies from the current in vitro procedure might be solved with adding more specific vitamins and minerals to optimize the mother's health six months prior to conception. The lab tests so far seemed to indicate their current limited specific regimen was working.

"No, they're fine. Pretty much right on target."

Chance stared at him. "All…right," he said slowly, giving Ted time to spill his knowledge without prodding.

"Sara Beth told me a secret audit was conducted at the institute. The results show significant financial problems."

"Damn." Chance looked stunned. "Is she sure about this?"

Ted nodded. "Lisa told her about it."

"Pretty reliable source," Chance said. Lisa Armstrong wasn't only a member of the institute's founding family, she also was the head administrator for the medical facility. If Lisa had told Ted's wife, then the story was probably true. "Did Lisa say anything else?"

"Evidently the problems are severe enough that the institute's financial survival is at stake."

Chance swore again with feeling. "How could this have happened? I heard the Founder's Ball was a success at raising funds and donations have increased. What the hell's going on?"

"It doesn't seem to add up, does it?" Ted agreed, eyes narrowing in thought.

"No, it doesn't," Chance agreed. He thrust his fingers through his hair, raking it back off his forehead. "This comes at a critical point in our research," he said grimly. "I don't want to think about what would happen if we had to start all over at another lab."

"I know," Ted agreed morosely. "It could set us back months, if not years."

"I can't believe how many scandals the institute has been hit with over the past months," Chance commented. "It's amazing it hasn't sunk beneath the weight of bad news."

Ted nodded as he took a swig of coffee, his mouth grim. "I have to believe it will survive—after all, look how many storms it's weathered over the years."

"I hope you're right." Chance dropped his feet to

the floor and stood. "In the meantime, I suggest we go down to the lab and take a look at those test results."

For the rest of the day, Chance immersed himself in the work that both challenged and frustrated both he and Ted. The meticulous lab work from a large group of volunteer patients was time consuming and sometimes tedious but necessary if they were to prove their theory. The opportunity to increase a couple's chance to conceive and have a healthy baby was worth it to both men.

Later that evening, he headed for Jennifer's apartment, stopping on the way to pick up a family movie on DVD and a pizza. It didn't escape his notice that lately, when confronted with problems at work, he instinctively turned to Jennifer.

She opened the door with a smile and he bent to catch her in a quick, hard hug. She slipped her arms around his waist and held him tight for a moment before he released her.

"Is everything okay?" she asked, her warm blue gaze scanning his face.

"Just some problems at work," he told her. "And now that I'm here, I feel better already."

"Good." She caught his hand and drew him into the apartment. "Annie," she called as she closed the door behind him. "Chance is here."

"Goodie." The little girl bounced into the room, eyes lighting when she saw the box he carried. "Pizza!"

Chance grinned, handing her the DVD case to carry. She danced around him, waving the movie over her head, as he carried the pizza to the kitchen table. Jennifer took down plates, glasses and silverware.

"Can we eat in the living room while we watch the movie, Mommy? Please?" Annie pleaded, showing her mother the movie case.

"All right, just this once."

They transferred pizza slices to plates, filled glasses with ice water and settled on the sofa as the movie credits began to roll. When the plates and glasses were empty, Annie stretched out on the floor, chin on her hand, to watch the movie.

Chance helped Jennifer carry the dinner things into the kitchen and load them into the dishwasher. Just as they finished, the telephone rang.

"Go back and watch the movie," Jennifer told him. "I'll join you as soon as I take this call."

He brushed a kiss against her mouth and walked into the living room, dropping onto the sofa just as Jennifer picked up the phone.

Glancing sideways, he saw her slim body stiffen and her mouth tighten just before she turned her back, murmuring into the phone.

Curiosity piqued, he only half listened to the movie dialogue and still Jennifer's conversation in the kitchen was inaudible. But her body language was loud and clear.

"Everything okay?" he asked when she joined him on the sofa.

"Fine." She gave him a brief smile before she tucked her feet beneath her on the cushion.

Chance slipped his arm around her shoulder and eased her back until her shoulders were against his chest, her hair brushing his throat.

He'd wait until Annie was asleep, he decided. But regardless of what Jennifer had said, he knew by her pale face and the worry in her eyes that everything in her world was not "fine."

Two hours later, Annie was tucked into bed. Chance hit the mute button on the TV control and turned on the sofa to face Jennifer.

"Tell me about the call you got earlier," he suggested.

Her gaze flew to meet his, her eyes widening.

"You could tell me it was no one, and nothing," he went on. "But I saw your face after you hung up and I know the call upset you. So, tell me," he urged. He nudged her backward and lifted her feet into his lap, big hands kneading her stocking-covered feet.

"Umm, that's positively decadent," she murmured, half closing her eyes on a deep sigh.

"Yeah, yeah," he told her. "No changing the subject. Tell me what it was about that phone call the bothered you."

She opened her eyes and looked at him, her face somber. "It was my ex-husband."

Chance's hands stilled, then returned to kneading her instep. "I didn't know you two were still in touch."

"We aren't—at least, we haven't been since the divorce," she stated. "But this is the third time I've heard from him in the past month."

"What does he want?" Chance asked, frowning.

"You won't believe it," she warned him. "It's just too ridiculous."

"Tell me," he commanded gently.

"Patrick saw the photo of us dancing at the Founder's Ball. He's recently finished med school and applied for a position at the institute, and he wants me to ask you to hire him."

Her words were blunt, straightforward, but without inflection.

"I have the distinct impression that you're not telling me the whole truth," Chance said gently, circling his thumb over her arch, just below her toes.

"You're amazingly good at that," she sighed, stretching with a moan.

His thumbs stilled, poised motionless over her foot. "You're avoiding the subject again."

"All right, all right, I'll tell you. Please don't stop rubbing my foot."

"Fine." He stroked her arch and she nearly purred. "Tell me the rest of it."

"He threatened me with Annie."

"What?" Chance stopped rubbing her foot and leaned over her to grab her shoulders.

"Hey." Jennifer's eyes rounded.

"Sorry," he muttered, easing back a foot and patting her shoulder awkwardly before gently cupping her chin in one hand. "Tell me what he said about Annie."

"He threatened to take me back to court and sue to get visitation."

"I thought he voluntarily gave up any rights as her father when you two were divorced?"

"He agreed to leave us alone if I agreed to never ask him for child support," Jennifer corrected. "I was pregnant when he filed for divorce and he listed our marriage as 'without children.'"

"What a jerk," Chance ground out. "Why did you marry the guy? What could have attracted a smart, savvy woman like you to him?"

"You think I'm smart and savvy?" Her smile was brilliant, her eyes meltingly warm.

"Of course I do. And don't change the subject," he told her for the third time.

"I was very young and he was very charming. Not a good excuse, obviously, but the truth is that I was naive and fell for the wonderful exterior. My only defense is that I left when I discovered that Patrick's interior wasn't so great." She paused. "But the marriage wasn't a total loss—because it gave me Annie."

"It sounds to me like that's your ex's one redeeming feature," he told her. "I thought he'd signed away his parental rights but evidently he never did?"

"No, he didn't." Jennifer's eyes darkened. "Frankly, it never occurred to me that he'd want to exercise his rights as her father. He's never even seen her—never wanted to. And he doesn't really want anything to do with her now. He's just using Annie as a means to force me to cooperate." Her gaze turned fierce. "Let's make something clear, Chance. I am *not* asking you to help Patrick get a job at the institute. I don't know what I'll do about him threatening Annie but I'm hoping he'll drop the whole thing when he realizes it won't get him anywhere."

"Honey, it never occurred to me that you'd cooperate with him," Chance declared. "And neither will I." He pulled her into his arms, her slim body lying trustingly against his. "I don't want you to worry about Annie. We'll figure out a way to stop him. If we need to, I'll call my family's legal representatives. They've never lost a case for the family yet."

Jennifer pressed closer. Chance slid his fingers into the silk of her hair and tugged gently, tipping her face up to his.

"No one's going to threaten you and Annie." His tone was fierce but the kisses he brushed against the corner of her mouth were gentle, soothing. He felt her sigh and stir against him, her lips seeking his.

A half hour later, they were both aroused, breathing unevenly and too fast, when Chance sighed and pulled Jennifer up from the sofa.

"Unless you're going to take me to bed, I'd better go home. I only have so much control and I've about used up my quota for the night."

"Chance, I'm not sure…" she began.

He stopped her by laying his finger against her lips, damp from the press of his.

"I know. You're not ready." He tucked her against his side and walked to the door. The kiss he gave her before pulling open the door sizzled with heat and frustrated longing. "Lock the door after me," he told her as he stepped outside.

"Good night," she murmured.

"I'll see you tomorrow," he told her. He waited until he heard the locks click shut then moved down the hallway.

Before he reached his car, he'd placed a call on his cell phone to the investigative agency his father used. Assured they would locate Jennifer's ex-husband by tomorrow morning, Chance drove home, his mind churning with how to remove the man from her life for good.

By the time he reached his town house, he knew exactly how he wanted to proceed.

"Dr. Demetrios, your three-o'clock appointment is here."

"Send him in." Chance flicked off the intercom and leaned back in his chair. Except for a thin file and a pen directly in front of him, the polished expanse of mahogany desktop was bare, creating a wide barrier between him and the group of four leather armchairs facing the desk.

The door opened and a man entered.

Chance stood slowly, assessing Jennifer's ex-husband. He was medium height with a compact body and he wore an expensive gray suit with a conservative blue silk tie. His features were boyish and he had an affable smile that Chance shrewdly suspected would charm women.

Chance disliked him on sight.

"Patrick Evans?"

"Yes." Patrick reached the desk and the two men exchanged a quick handshake. "It's a pleasure to meet you, Dr. Demetrios. I've followed your work here with great interest over the past several months."

"Thanks. Sit down." Chance waved him to a chair and resumed his seat behind the desk. He tapped the file in front of him with his forefinger. "Your application states you've recently completed your residency at Chicago General. What made you decide to apply to the Armstrong Fertility Institute for your first position?"

"Your research," Patrick said promptly. "I'm very interested in emerging methods of in vitro procedures and the efficacy of the process. The Armstrong Institute is on the cutting edge of research in the field. I want to be part of the team."

He punctuated his comments with a sincere smile.

"I see," Chance said evenly. "I understand you were once married to Jennifer Lebeaux."

"Yes, I was." Patrick's expression turned wryly regretful. "We were too young and the marriage didn't last, unfortunately."

"Hmm," Chance said noncommittally. He wasn't surprised that Patrick had a ready, glib response since he could have anticipated Jennifer would tell Chance about their marriage. Still, his fingers half curled into fists before he purposely straightened them. "And you have a daughter?"

"Yes, her name is Annie." Patrick shifted in his chair and his features reflected a faint sadness. "Circumstances have kept me from seeing her as much as I'd like, but now that my residency is finished, I hope to change that."

Chance had heard enough and seen enough phony emotion from Patrick. His original analysis of Jennifer's ex-husband hadn't changed with a face-to-face meeting. The man was an ass who didn't give a damn about Annie.

"I suggest you rethink your relationship to Annie." Chance's neutral tone shifted, an undercurrent of menace running through his words.

Patrick blinked. "I beg your pardon?" he said warily.

"I've had my attorney draw up two documents. You will sign them, relinquish all parental rights to Annie and agree to her adoption by a man who is capable of being a real father to her."

Patrick shoved back his chair and stood, anger painting flags of red across his cheekbones. "What makes you think you can order me to sign anything?"

Chance stood, leaning forward to plant his fists on the glossy desktop. He made no attempt to conceal the contempt he felt. "I have the power to keep you from being hired in damn near every research facility on the eastern seaboard, maybe even in the entire U.S."

"You can't do that," Patrick protested. But his color faded and his eyes shifted to the file, then back to Chance.

"Try me." Chance's voice deepened, turned more lethal. "And if you ever threaten Jennifer or Annie again, I won't waste time calling your boss or my attorney. I'll come looking for you myself."

"Just because you're a Demetrios doesn't mean you can get away with forcing me to sign away my rights to my child," he blustered. Color ebbed and flowed in the younger man's face, mottling and changing the boyish good looks with sulky dislike.

"I don't need my family's money or good name to take care of you. But I'll use whatever I have to," Chance said grimly. He opened the file and took out two legal documents, sliding them across the desktop, the pen on top. "We both know you couldn't care less about Annie or Jennifer. Sign the consent papers."

Patrick glared at him for a moment in one last gesture of obstinacy and stubbornness before he snatched up the pen. The writing was fast, slight shaky, and then he shoved the documents back across the desk to Chance.

Chance flipped the pages, making sure they were signed properly, then slid them into the file.

"I have your word you won't blacklist me with your friends at other research facilities?" Patrick demanded with belligerence.

"You do."

The other man turned on his heel and strode to the door, yanking it open.

"If any of this conversation leaks, I'll know who spread the rumors. And if I find out you've talked," Chance said with lethal intent, "all bets are off. I'd take a great deal of pleasure in making sure you never practice medicine."

Patrick's face whitened. Without a word, he left the room, closing the door quietly behind him.

Muscles tight with the effort it had taken to keep from throwing Patrick physically out of his office, Chance forcibly unclenched his fists and rolled his shoulders. Adrenaline still surged through his veins and he strode to the window to look down on the parking lot below. He waited until Patrick exited the building, climbed into a sedan and drove with a rush of speed out of the lot.

"So much for Patrick Evans," Chance muttered aloud. He knew a deep sense of satisfaction that the man no longer had any claim on Jennifer or Annie. The documents he'd signed only legally established what Chance was convinced had always been true—Evans had never really loved Jennifer or their daughter.

*What a fool the man is,* he thought. If he'd ever been lucky enough to have a wife and child like Jennifer and Annie, he never would have let them go.

*And I won't now,* he thought with sudden clarity and fierce determination. He wanted Jennifer and her little girl in his life permanently, here in his home, sharing his life. He wanted the legal right to protect them both—and that meant marriage and Annie's adoption.

He didn't know how long he'd been thinking of Jennifer as his but he knew he wasn't going to wait to make her his.

He just hoped she felt the same.

He caught up the file and headed for the door, intent on driving directly to Jennifer's apartment to talk to her. He just stepped over the threshold when his secretary hurried toward him.

"Chance, there's an emergency with Mrs. Mac-

Quillen. Her husband called 911 and the ambulance is taking her directly to the hospital."

"I'm on my way." Chance strode off down the hallway, punching in numbers on his cell phone as he went. Much as he wanted to see Jennifer, his patient came first. Ralph MacQuillen answered on the third ring, his voice distracted. "Ralph, this is Dr. Demetrios."

Chance calmed the anxious husband and told him they'd meet at the hospital. Moments later, he drove out of the parking lot, knowing it may be hours before he could talk to Jennifer, his mind switching to Mrs. MacQuillen's pregnancy.

Earlier that same day, Jennifer tried to reach Chance at his office but was told he was out. Dashing out the door to catch the bus to work, she wondered where he was and hoped he'd come by the apartment later that evening. She didn't have a class and over the past three weeks, she'd come to count on seeing Chance on her free nights.

*I wonder if that means this is a relationship,* she wondered.

Later that evening, the hour grew late and Chance didn't appear. Disappointed, Jennifer bathed Annie before reading two chapters from an Eloise book and turning off the light.

Alone in the darkened living room, she clicked through channels on the TV, finding nothing that caught her interest.

She missed Chance, she realized. Resolutely, she located a mystery series and tried to concentrate on the story.

Just after 10:00 p.m., someone rapped on her door. After checking her visitor through the door's peephole, Jennifer pulled open the door.

"Hi." She held the door wide and Chance entered.

He pushed the door shut and dragged her close, wrapping her tightly against his body while his mouth covered hers.

"Hi," he rasped when he finally lifted his head. "Did you miss me?"

She laughed. "It hasn't even been twenty-four hours but yes, I missed you. I thought you would be here earlier."

"I've been busy," he told her. "Making sure your ex-husband can never threaten you or Annie again."

Her eyes widened. "Chance, what have you done?" Worry veed her brows as she frowned. "You didn't buy him off, did you? I didn't want you to give in to his blackmail. If you helped him get a job at the institute, you'd never be able to trust him."

"I didn't do what he wanted," Chance assured her.

He reached into the inner pocket of his leather jacket, removed a folded sheaf of papers and handed them to her. "These are for you."

Confused, Jennifer took the papers, unfolding them as Chance shrugged out of his jacket and tossed it over the seat of the rocking chair.

She read the legal documents twice, hardly daring to believe what she thought the wording meant. The documents were signed by Patrick and stated that he abandoned his legal parental rights to Annie and specifically agreed to an adoption.

"I don't know what to say," she said, stunned. "How did you convince Patrick to do this?"

"It was simple," he told her. "I threatened to tell certain influential people at the best research facilities in his field that he wasn't a good candidate." Chance shrugged. "I'm not without influence in the arena and he knows it. So he agreed to give up Annie." His face tightened, a muscle flexing along his jawline. "In return, I said I'd refrain from discussing his lack of character with potential employers. And I didn't think he and the institute were a good fit."

"Oh, Chance..." Jennifer's mouth trembled and tears welled, threatening to spill down her cheeks.

"Don't cry, honey." He pulled her into his arms

and she burrowed closer, pressing her tear-damp face against his throat. He cupped the back of her head in one big hand. "I'm not sure you're ready to hear this, but I need to say it. I want to marry you and adopt Annie."

She tipped her head back, her gaze searching his. His dark brown eyes were fierce with conviction.

"Say yes, Jennifer. I'm in love for the first—and last—time in my life. Living without you isn't an option." His arms tightened, pressing her closer.

"I didn't know—you didn't tell me you loved me," she whispered.

A wry half smile curved his mouth. "I didn't think you were ready to hear it. Plus, I've never felt this way about a woman before, not the way I have you. I guess I thought it was obvious I was head over heels in love with you."

"Not to me," she murmured. "But maybe that's because I'm head over heels in love with you, too."

His fingers flexed in reaction, stroking her sensitized skin.

"I'm glad you said that," he muttered with a sigh of relief. "Because if you didn't, I had no plan for what to do next."

"What was your plan if I said yes?" she asked, smiling as she turned her head and kissed the warm, strong column of his throat, breathing in the faint trace of cologne and a scent that was his alone. Her heart raced, thudding in her chest.

"I was hoping you'd take me to bed." He tilted his head back to look down at her, arousal painting a slash of color over the arch of his cheekbones. "I haven't pressed you because I know you vowed Annie would never wake and find you in bed with someone—and I respect that decision. But we're going to be married, as soon as possible, I hope. And I don't want to leave you tonight."

"And after tonight?" she asked, holding on to the moment.

"I want us to elope—you and Annie and me. And I want you to move in with me. I have plenty of room at my house." He smoothed the pad of his thumb over her cheekbone. "Say yes, Jennifer. I don't want to spend any more nights without you."

"Yes." She smiled through misty tears. "Yes, I'll marry you."

He grinned, dark eyes lighting. "I feel like I've just won the lottery." He pressed a hard kiss against her mouth. "Annie's going to love living with Butch and he'll be crazy about having her there," he said when he lifted his head.

"We'll have trouble separating them at night," she agreed.

"I vote for not fighting that battle. Let's just move Butch's bed into her room," Chance said dryly.

"You know Annie so well." She laughed.

With decision, she stepped back, taking his hand in hers. "Come to bed with me, Chance," she murmured, relishing the words. "And stay until the morning. When Annie gets up, we can all have breakfast together and tell her the news."

His eyes darkened to black, fierce emotion filling them.

She led him into the bedroom, to her turned-down sheets and comfortable bed—the bed that she'd slept in alone since before Annie was born.

But no longer. Chance's broad shoulders and big body would crowd her bed just as his love filled her heart.

As he tugged her T-shirt over her head and bent to take her mouth with his, Jennifer was swamped with a rush of emotion. Chance made her feel all the things she never thought she'd be—happy, safe, cherished, challenged and loved.

Just before he stripped off their clothes and lowered her onto the bed, she vowed she would love and cherish him, as well. The future glowed with promise, bright and beckoning.

It seemed she'd finally found her Prince Charming.

* * * * *

# THE TEXAN'S
# HAPPILY-EVER-
# AFTER

BY
KAREN ROSE SMITH

First published in Great Britain 2011
by Mills & Boon, an imprint of Harlequin (UK) Limited,
Eton House, 18-24 Paradise Road, Richmond, Surrey TW9 1SR

© Karen Rose Smith 2010

ISBN: 978 0 263 88876 8

23-0411

Harlequin (UK) policy is to use papers that are natural, renewable and recyclable products and made from wood grown in sustainable forests. The logging and manufacturing processes conform to the legal environmental regulations of the country of origin.

Printed and bound in Spain
by Blackprint CPI, Barcelona

Dear Reader,

I'll always remember the first time my husband and I really talked. In sharing, we connected on a deep level, inspiring trust that has lasted throughout the years. To form that bond, we had to become vulnerable to each other.

My hero, Shep McGraw, is a strong, silent Texan. A marriage of convenience teaches him he must lower his guard to trust his new wife. By risking vulnerability. He discovers the love and understanding that can lead to happily ever after.

I hope you enjoy Shep's transformation from guarded single dad to my heroine Raina's white knight. Shep and Raina's romance is Book 5 in my THE BABY EXPERTS series.

Readers can learn more about THE BABY EXPERTS at www.karenrosesmith.com.

All my best,

*Karen Rose Smith*

To Sis and Bern, our son's godparents.
Thanks for the difference you made in his life.
Happy birthday, Sis. Bern, we miss you.

Author's Note

Adoption procedures may vary according to state,
individual circumstances and agencies.

Award-winning and bestselling author **Karen Rose Smith** has seen more than sixty-five novels published since 1992. She grew up in Pennsylvania's Susquehanna Valley and still lives a stone's throw away with her husband—who was her college sweetheart—and their two cats. She especially enjoys researching and visiting the West and Southwest where her latest series of books is set. Readers can receive updates on Karen's releases and write to her through her website at www.karenrosesmith.com or at P.O. Box 1545, Hanover, PA 17331, USA.

# Chapter One

Shep McGraw hurried to the emergency-room door. In his arms, two-year-old Manuel let out a cry that echoed in the hospital's parking lot.

Tension and worry tightened Shep's chest. He'd been through this before with Manuel's earaches. Thank goodness Dr. Raina Gibson, the boy's ear, nose and throat specialist, had been on call for her practice tonight. He thought about his two other sons, who were with their nanny. They hadn't liked him leaving this late at night.

As Shep rushed through the automatic glass doors, he remembered another fateful E.R. visit many, many years ago. He shoved that out of his mind and hugged Manuel closer.

The woman in charge at the registration desk looked him over—from his tan Stetson to his fine leather boots—and he had to rein in his frustration with red tape. "My name's Shep McGraw. I'm meeting Dr. Gibson here to treat my…son."

"Mr. McGraw, if you'll have a seat—"

Manuel's crying had tapered off slightly, but now he screwed up his cute little round face and howled loud enough to scare his black wavy hair into disarray.

Shep shifted Manuel to his shoulder. "My boy needs someone to look at him *now*." He was about to add that the Lubbock hospital had all of his information on file, when Dr. Gibson came through a side door and crossed to the desk.

Although Manuel's crying still rent the waiting area, the beautiful doctor's appearance impacted Shep as it always did. Her Native American heritage was attractively obvious in the angles of her cheekbones and chin. Tonight she'd pulled her long black hair back into a low ponytail and clasped it with a beaded barrette. The white coat she wore molded to her long legs as she hurried toward him.

She greeted the woman at the desk as she reached for Manuel. "I'll take him back, Flo."

After patting Manuel's back and making soothing noises that quieted him, she said to Shep, "Give Flo your insurance card so she can put through the paperwork." Then she headed for the door leading to the examination cubicles, motioning him to follow.

Shep took out his insurance card, slapped it onto the desk and followed Raina. He couldn't help but admire her graceful stride, the straightness of her shoulders, even as she held Manuel and headed for the exam room. He had to smile at the sneakers she wore that made her look more like a runner than a doctor.

All was quiet for the moment in this part of the E.R. wing. Manuel's cries had faded to tiny hiccups. Shep felt so sad sometimes for this little boy, who'd been neglected, taken away from his mother and put in a foster home. Shep knew all about foster homes firsthand, though there was no indication the couple who'd cared for Manuel was anything like the foster parents Shep had lived with.

At the door to the exam room, Dr. Gibson paused and waited for Shep to precede her inside. Although Shep considered himself more cowboy than gentleman, he motioned her to go ahead of him. With a small smile and a quick nod, she did. But when she passed him, he caught the scent of lemon and his stomach twisted into a knot, as it did whenever he got too close to her. He didn't get too close to her if he could help it—for lots of very good reasons.

Raina glanced at Shep as she settled Manuel on the gurney. "On the phone you told me this started about an hour ago?"

"Yes. Before I put him in his crib. At first I thought he was just overtired or didn't want to go to bed. But then he started pulling on his ear, so I took his temperature and saw he had a fever."

"I'll take it again," she assured him with quiet efficiency. Her gaze met his. The earth seemed to shake a little and they both quickly looked away.

With coiled energy wound tight inside him, Shep moved to the gurney to hold Manuel. He hadn't intended it, but somehow his hands got tangled up with hers before she pulled them away from the little boy. Their gazes connected again…and this time held. Shep's blood rushed fast, and in that instant, he thought he saw returned interest in the pretty doctor's very dark brown eyes.

A moment later, he guessed he was mistaken. In a small town like Sagebrush, Texas, where they both lived—about fifteen minutes from Lubbock, where this hospital was located—certain people had a higher gossip profile than others. Dr. Gibson was one of them.

He'd asked his nanny, Eva, if she knew any particulars about the doctor, and he still remembered what Eva had said. "Her husband was a firefighter in New York City. He died saving others on September eleventh. Somehow, she picked up her life and finished her schooling, then returned here to be with her family. I can only imagine what she's gone through, and it's not something I ever want to even *think* about going through."

As Shep studied Raina Gibson now, he saw no signs of a tragic past—unless it had carved those tiny lines under her eyes and fostered the ever-present quiet and calm he sensed about her.

She went to the counter, where she took an ear thermometer from its holder. When she returned to the table, she focused solely on Manuel. "This little guy has been through so much. I feel so sorry for him. Another ear infection is the last thing he needs." She cut Shep a sideways glance. "Or *you* need. How are Joey and Roy?" She had treated eight-year-old Joey last year for a sinus infection that wouldn't quit.

"They're good. They get upset when Manuel's sick, though. Roy's afraid he'll lose more of his hearing."

Raina studied Manuel's temperature and frowned. "It's one hundred one." Seconds later she was examining the toddler with the otoscope and then her stethoscope. Finally, she gave Shep her verdict. "I don't like the looks of this, Mr. McGraw."

"Shep," he corrected her, not for the first time. After all, Manuel had seen her at least three times over the past six months.

Now she didn't avoid his gaze, but looked him directly in the eyes. That was his first clue he wasn't going to like what she had to say.

"Okay, Shep."

That was the second clue. He had the feeling she'd used his first name to soften the blow.

"I'll give you a prescription again for Manuel, to get this cleared up. But I have to recommend that you let me do a procedure to put tubes in his ears. I'm afraid if we don't, he'll lose his hearing altogether."

Before he caught himself, Shep swore. "Sorry," he mumbled. "I just don't want to put him through anything else." He picked up his son from the table, easily lifted him to his shoulder where Manuel snuggled against his collarbone.

Raina's gaze was sympathetic, her voice gentle. "I know what he's dealt with already. But he's in your care now, and I can see that you love him. You have to think beyond the procedure to when he's three or four. You have to do what's best for him long-term."

Shep patted Manuel's back. Finally, he said, "Tell me what's involved."

Taking a few steps closer, Raina stopped within arm's reach. "The surgery's called a myringotomy. I make a tiny incision in the eardrum and any fluid will be removed. Then I'll insert a tympanostomy tube into the drum to keep the middle ear aerated. We'll leave the tubes in from six months to several years."

She was close enough that Shep was aware of her body heat as well as his. "Will he have to have surgery to remove them again?"

Tilting her head, she ran her hand over Manuel's hair then brought her gaze back to Shep. "No. Eventually they'll extrude from the eardrum and fall into the ear canal. I'll be able to remove them during a routine office visit, or they'll just fall out of his ears."

Shep could hardly imagine his small son in this big hospital, with medical personnel caring for him. "And you believe we have to do this?"

"Shep, Manuel has already lost some hearing. You know that from the assessment I did. I'm afraid if we don't do this, he'll have speech problems, too."

"And the downside?"

"I'll give you a sheet of information and you can read about the pros and cons. As often as you're bringing Manuel to me, I don't think you have a choice."

"I hate hearing statements like that," Shep muttered.

Manuel began crying again and Shep rocked him back and forth. "How long will this operation take?" he asked over the baby's heartbreaking distress.

Raina leaned closer to him, as if in empathy…as if she might want to take Manuel into her arms again…as if she hated seeing a child cry.

"Ten to fifteen minutes. It's done on an outpatient basis. Manuel will be given anesthesia. Once he's recovered from that, he can go home. Chances are good he'll feel better right away, because that pressure in his ears will be released. He's been suffering with this for too

# Get 2 books Free!
## Plus, receive a FREE mystery gift

If you have enjoyed reading this Cherish romance story, then why not take advantage of this **FREE** book offer and we'll send you two more titles from this series absolutely **FREE**!

Accepting your **FREE** books and **FREE** mystery gift places you under no obligation to buy anything.

As a member of the Mills & Boon Book Club™ you'll receive your favourite Series books up to 2 months ahead of the shops, plus all these exclusive benefits:

- 🌹 FREE home delivery
- 🌹 Exclusive offers and our monthly newsletter
- 🌹 Membership to our special rewards programme

We hope that after receiving your free books you'll want to remain a member. But the choice is yours. So why not give us a go. You'll be glad you did!

**Visit www.millsandboon.co.uk for the latest news and offers.**

Mrs/Miss/Ms/Mr ............................................ Initials ............................

BLOCK CAPITALS PLEASE

Surname ......................................................................................

Address ......................................................................................

..............................................................................................

..............................................................................................

.................................................... Postcode ....................................

Email ........................................................................................

S1DIA

MILLS & BOON®

NO STAMP
NEEDED!

MILLS & BOON®
Book Club

FREE BOOK OFFER
FREEPOST NAT 10298
RICHMOND
TW9 1BR

If offer card is missing write to: The Mills & Boon® Book Club™, PO Box 676, Richmond, TW9 1WU

NO STAMP
NECESSARY
IF POSTED IN
THE U.K. OR N.I.

long. And so have you," she added with an understanding Shep found almost unsettling.

Again, their gazes locked and neither of them seemed to be able to look away. Shep didn't know what was happening to him, but he didn't like it. Every time he stared into those impossibly dark eyes of hers he felt unnerved, and if he was forced to admit it, aroused. That wasn't what he should feel, standing in this cubicle with her while he held Manuel. He should feel grateful...nothing else.

He must have been scowling from here into the next county, and she misinterpreted his expression. "I know you're worried. Every parent worries when anything is wrong with his child. But try to anticipate a positive outcome. Think about Manuel *not* having any more painful earaches."

"The anesthesia bothers me," he admitted.

"You must trust the doctors here. Give us a chance to help him."

Shep was used to being in control. His history had taught him not to let anyone else run his life...let alone his son's. "How soon do you want to do this?"

"How about next week?"

"That soon?"

"You have a housekeeper, right?"

Did she remember this kind of information about all of her patients? "Yes, Eva. She'll be able to take care of Joey and Roy if I'm not home."

Obviously thinking that distracting him for a minute might be a good thing, Raina said, "Roy's and Joey's adoptions are final now, aren't they?"

"Yes, they are."

"And Manuel's?"

"I'll be his dad in a few months, if all goes well."

"I admire what you're doing, Mr. McGraw."

"Shep," he reminded her again, suspecting she used his surname to distance herself. Why would she need to distance herself? Could she be as interested in him as he was in her? It had been a long time since he'd wanted to pursue a woman….

"Shep," she repeated, her cheeks coloring a little. "Giving these boys a home is so important. And you obviously care about them a great deal."

"I wouldn't have decided to adopt them if I didn't. The foster-care system—" He shook his head. "It's not like it once was, but it's hard for children to feel loved when they don't know where they'll be sleeping the next night."

After being abandoned by his mother, a series of foster homes, as well as a chief of police, had convinced Shep he wasn't worthy of anyone's love…until a kind rancher named Matt Forester had proven differently. Matt had been Shep's role model and he was determined to give Roy, Joey and Manuel the same leg up in life that Matt had given him and his friend Cruz.

Raina was looking at him thoughtfully, as if there were more to him than she'd ever realized. Her intense gaze made his interest in her reach a new level, and he had to tamp down a sudden urge to touch her face.

He felt warm and uncomfortable, and now just wanted to get the prescription for Manuel and leave.

The doctor cut through the awkwardness between them by suddenly pulling a pamphlet from a stack on the counter and a pad from her pocket. She wrote out the prescription, then handed the papers to him. "Go home and think about the procedure. Look at the pamphlet I've given you. I'll be in my office tomorrow. Call me if you have any questions."

Someone knocked on the door.

Raina went to it and opened it, then returned with a few papers. "You need to sign these before you leave."

As he signed the forms, he tried to make conversation—anything to distract himself from her quiet beauty. "Did you come in just for Manuel, or have you been here all day?"

She gave a shrug. "This has been an exceptionally long day. I had office hours this morning, surgeries this afternoon and a complication that kept me here." At his look, she was quick to assure him, "Not for anyone who had tubes inserted in their ears."

Shep smiled the first smile that had come naturally since he'd entered the emergency room. "You knew I was going to ask."

"You're the type who would."

"Type?"

"You *care,* Mr. McGraw. You ask questions and you want answers. That's a good type to be when you're a parent." There was admiration in her voice.

"You're going to have to practice using my given name."

Another blush stained her cheeks. "Maybe I will. I'll walk you out."

As they strode side-by-side to the reception area once more, Manuel stilled on Shep's shoulder. He could tell the little boy was almost falling asleep. His crying had exhausted him.

Raina must have seen that, because as they stopped

at the entrance to the hallway leading to the pharmacy, she peered around Shep's shoulder at Manuel's face, and then gently patted him on the back. "I imagine he'll get more sleep tonight than you will."

"You probably imagine right."

Standing there like that, staring down into her eyes, Shep felt totally unsettled. His gut tightened, his collar felt tight and he was overcome by a desire to kiss her.

He was absolutely *crazy.*

A woman like Raina Greystone Gibson wouldn't give a man like him a second look. Her husband had been a hero.

And Shep?

He was no hero…and because of his past, he never would be.

The following Wednesday, Raina hurried to the day-surgery waiting room. Manuel had been her last surgery of the day, and she was eager to bring his father good news. However, when she reached the doorway to the waiting room she stopped cold as her gaze went immediately to an obviously nervous Shep McGraw.

To her dismay, she felt flustered, knowing she was going to have to talk to him again. That was ridiculous! She didn't fluster easily. But something about this tall, lean cowboy got to her, and she couldn't figure out why. Since Clark had died, no man had made her feel much of anything. But then, the way Clark had died probably had something to do with that.

Closing her mind to memories she didn't revisit often, she watched Shep McGraw for a few seconds. He sat alone, away from the others in the waiting room, staring at the cable-channel news on the TV. But she could tell he wasn't really absorbing what he was watching. He'd checked his watch twice since she'd stood in the doorway.

Why did he get to her? Because he was such a concerned dad? Shep had had such a difficult time stepping away from Manuel to let the baby be taken to surgery. Still, she'd seen concerned fathers before. Maybe he got to her because he was a single dad doing the best he could with the boys he was adopting?

That had to be it. After all, she knew Manuel's story because Shep had given her the baby's history the first time she'd treated him. Manuel had gone into foster care malnourished and sickly when he was almost seventeen months old. A month after that, Shep had received a call from a contact working in the system who'd told him about the boy, asked if he was interested in adopting a third child. Shep had gone to see Manuel and made the decision on the spot. Thank goodness the toddler's mother had finally cared enough to sign away her parental rights. Manuel's father was nowhere to be found.

Raina suspected some particular motivation drove Shep to save children from the system. She was becoming more and more curious as to what that motivation could be. Not for the first time, Raina reminded herself her interest couldn't have anything to do with Shep's six-foot height, dark brown hair, the very blue eyes that reminded her of a Texas sky on a clear summer day. He could probably crook his finger at a multitude of women and they'd come running. But he wasn't crooking his finger, and she wondered why.

She'd heard he was well off. He'd bought a huge

ranch on the outskirts of Sagebrush, invested in a barnful of horses, remodeled the house and refurbished the barn. He'd also purchased a business—a lumberyard. He might look like a cowboy on the outside, but inside she got the feeling he was a shrewd businessman. He'd supposedly made a bundle selling commercial real estate in California before moving to Sagebrush. Yet he didn't flaunt his wealth. In fact, the locals said he spent a good bit of time at the lumberyard as well as working his ranch.

He glanced at the doorway. Spotting her, he was on his feet in an instant.

She stepped a few paces to the side of the doorway for a little privacy, faced him and smiled. "Manuel came through the procedure with flying colors. He's in recovery. If you'd like to come sit by his bed while he wakes up, that's fine. After he's aware that you're there, we'll wait another half hour or so until the anesthesia wears off. Then you can take him home."

"Just a half hour? Are you sure he'll be okay? And you said something about instruction sheets and eardrops."

Impulsively, she reached out and clasped his arm. "Shep, he'll be fine. We won't let you leave without the instruction sheets."

As her fingers made contact with his tanned skin, sensations registered from her fingertips to her brain—his heat, the strength of the muscle in his forearm, the tingling in her belly that seemed to come from nowhere. His eyes met hers, and for a moment they were both aware of the contact. She quickly released his arm.

He was wearing a Stetson, and he took it off now and

ran his hand through his hair, ruffling it. "Will you take me to him?"

"Sure."

They walked side by side down the hall. Shep was six inches taller than she was—a couple of inches taller than Clark. But where Clark had been husky, Shep was lean. Clark had worked out with weights to keep his body in prime condition for his job. But she had the feeling Shep McGraw's muscles came from his work on the ranch and at his lumberyard.

She shook her head to clear it from such insane thoughts. "Will your housekeeper be available this evening?"

Shep arched a brow at Raina.

"I just wondered if she'll be helping to care for Manuel tonight."

"More than likely she'll keep Roy and Joey busy so that I can take care of Manuel. Eva often jokes that I moved from laid-back California to Wild West Texas never expecting life to be as unpredictable as it has been. But I don't regret one day of it and I don't think she does, either. I'll show her anything you show me, in case she needs to know."

"Is she...older?" Raina asked, telling herself she needed the information for purely professional reasons.

"Don't let *her* hear you say she's older," he joked, with a wry smile. It was a crooked smile that made Raina's pulse beat just a little faster. "She's in her fifties," he went on, "but won't say exactly *where* in her fifties."

Raina chuckled. "She sounds like a woman after my own heart. We should never have to divulge our age."

"Let me guess," Shep said. "You're thirty-seven."

"How did you—?"

"Gotcha," he teased. "I have a friend who's a doc in Santa Fe. I know how long med school took him. And you started practicing here after your residency, right?"

"A year and a half ago," she confirmed with a nod.

"That's about when Joey and Roy came to live with me."

"And Manuel joined you six months ago."

"That's right. It's been a roller-coaster ride."

She laughed. "You're a brave man, Shep McGraw, taking in three boys and having the confidence to raise them."

"Confidence or insanity," he muttered.

She laughed again.

They reached a door with big black letters—Authorized Admittance Only. Raina opened the door and let Shep inside. He spotted Manuel right away and made a beeline for him, Raina hurrying to catch up. She glanced at the monitors, then asked the nurse at Manuel's side, "How's he doing?"

"He's doing great."

Shep caught a stray stool with the toe of his boot and dragged it to Manuel's bedside. He sank down on it and took the little boy's hand. "How are you doing, kiddo? There's nothing to worry about now. I'm here and we're going home soon."

"Home?" Manuel repeated, his eyes still a little unfocused.

"Yep, home. Joey and Roy and Eva are waiting for us."

Raina went to a side counter, picking up a sheaf of papers. She brought them over to Shep, then went over the instructions for giving Manuel the eardrops, as well as changing the cotton in his ears. "Everything's explained here. If he runs a fever or if anything seems out of the ordinary, call me immediately. My service can page me."

Shep's attention shifted from her to his son in the bed. His gaze ran over Manuel—from the little gown he was wearing to the cotton in his ears.

Shep was quiet for a moment, then he swiveled around on the stool to face her. "Are you done here for the day?"

"Yes, I'm off to run some errands. But as I said, my service can always contact me."

"How would you like to do something a little more exciting than running errands?"

"And what would that be?" She was really curious.

"How would you like to come to the Red Creek Ranch and get a taste of just how wild the West can be?"

## Chapter Two

Raina was stunned by Shep's invitation.

"Why do you want me to come to the ranch?"

For a moment, he looked as if he was going to clam up, pull down the brim of his Stetson and walk away. But then he gave a small shrug, stood, lodged his hands in his back pockets and studied her. "You're a no-nonsense kind of woman, aren't you?"

"Does that require an answer?"

"No," he drawled, with a lazy Texas slowness that made her stomach jump. Then he became more serious. "After what you've been through, I imagine you don't have time for crap. Life's short, and you know it."

No one had ever approached the subject of her widowhood quite like this before. She was even more intrigued by this man who had been getting under her skin a little every time he had an office visit with one of his kids. "That's one way of putting it," she admitted wryly.

Sliding his hands out of his pockets, he dropped them to his sides. "The truth is…" He hesitated and then said, "I like you and I trust you. Manuel had an operation and anesthesia. The hospital is sending him home just an hour afterward. That doesn't sit comfortably with me. On top of that, I need to do some things, like the drops and all, and I don't want to make a mistake. I'll be glad to pay for your time. I'm not asking you to do this for free."

He *liked* her. She decided not to focus on that. "So you'd consider this a house call?" If she looked at this in professional terms—

"Yeah, sort of. Maybe a little longer than a house call. After all, it's going to be suppertime soon. You could stay and eat with us."

There was nothing obvious in the way Shep was looking at her, and yet…she was very aware he was a well-built man. From those silver sparks in his blue eyes, she had the feeling he appreciated who she was, white lab coat and all. This was the oddest situation she'd ever found herself in. Over the past nine years, she hadn't taken a second look at a man, and had always put up a shield or run quickly if one looked interested. Why wasn't she running now?

Because this was mainly about Manuel, she told herself.

"I don't usually make house calls."

"Is it on your list of things you never wanted to do, or on your list of things you just never have done?"

In spite of herself, she had to laugh. Shep's sense of humor was one of his charms. Raina thought about the

Victorian where she lived. It would be empty tonight. She'd missed Gina Rigoletti the day she'd moved out to live with her fiancé at his estate. Gina's sister, Angie, had moved in with her last week. But as a pediatric nurse, she was working the night shift. And her friend Lily was away in Oklahoma with her recently deceased husband's family. Her husband had been killed in Afghanistan while serving his country.

Raina suddenly realized that at one time she'd craved solitude, but that wasn't the case now. After Clark died, her grief had gotten held up by everything surrounding September eleventh—the immensity of everyone's loss, the days of horrible nightmares, the government settlement. She'd watched way too much TV, unable to tear herself away from it, hoping to learn more…to see Clark's face *somewhere*. Grief had finally overtaken her the day she'd gone to Ground Zero, seen all the pictures posted and been overwhelmed with the realization that the man she loved was never coming home. Now, nine years later, she felt as if she'd finally found herself again. Returning to Sagebrush, being near her family, had helped her do that.

So here she was, with this rugged single dad asking her to his ranch. "Basically, you want my help with Manuel?" she asked Shep directly.

"Yes. I'll pay you outright. Insurance won't be involved."

"You could hire a nurse, though I really don't think you need one."

"First of all, I don't want a nurse. I want *you*." The way he said it seemed to disconcert him a little. The muscle in his jaw jumped. But he went on anyway. "And secondly, I have two other boys to think about. They're going to be worried about Manuel. I want to make sure they don't have anything to be afraid of by the time they go to bed tonight."

Making a sudden decision—from sheer instinct—Raina said, "No need to pay me. Let me tell my house-mate where I'll be. She's working upstairs. Then I'll come home with you for a little while, just to see how things are going."

After an automatic last check of Manuel's monitors, a look into his adorable dark brown eyes, Raina left the recovery room, wondering what in the heck she was doing.

As Raina's hybrid followed Shep's shiny new blue crew-cab truck down the gravel lane, she thought about how absolutely different she was from the rancher. The types of vehicles they drove were only the tip of the iceberg. So why was she following him to his ranch as if…

As if she were attracted to the man?

She was here for Manuel's sake. That was the beginning and the end of it. Though she *was* curious how a single rancher managed to handle two rambunctious boys and a baby. Wasn't it part of her duty as a doctor to find out?

The beautifully maintained split-rail fencing lined the lane. Pecan trees and live oaks kept the road in shade. To the left she spotted horses, at least ten or twelve, and a new-looking lean-to that could shelter them from the weather. When she drove a little farther, she caught sight of a huge red barn with Red Creek Ranch painted in shiny black letters above the hayloft doors. On the right stood a spacious two-and-a-half-story ranch house that looked as if it had been recently refurbished with tan siding and dark brown shutters. The wide, white wraparound porch appeared to be an addition to the original structure. A swing hung from its ceiling. She caught sight of curtains fluttering at the windows and was surprised to find herself thinking the house looked like a home.

To the left of the house, set back, a three-bay garage stood waiting. Shep headed for the parking area in front and she followed, her tires crunching on the stones as she parked beside him. Then she went to the back of his truck to help him with Manuel. The little boy was awake, but not altogether himself.

"He's usually yelling and screaming to be let out of his car seat by now."

"Give him some time to get back to normal."

As Shep reached for Manuel, the two-year-old began to cry. "What did I do?" Shep asked worriedly.

"Are you grumpy after you have a tooth drilled?"

"Sometimes," Shep answered warily.

"Well, think about how Manuel must feel."

To Shep's surprise, when he held Manuel in the crook of his arm and closed the back door of the truck, the little boy reached toward Raina.

"Do you think she can do a better job of making you feel better?" Shep asked, half serious, half joking.

Manuel stared at his dad for a few seconds, then reached for Raina again.

Shep shrugged. "Go ahead."

"This has nothing to do with your ability to take care of him," Raina assured him as she cuddled Manuel close and let the baby lay his head against her hair.

"There's a basic difference between men and women," Shep decided. "That's what this is all about."

"And that difference is?" Raina asked, not sure she wanted to know.

"Women are softer. Men are harder. It's a matter of comfort."

Raina couldn't help but hide a smile as she followed Shep up the porch steps to the front door and into the house.

A ceiling fan hummed in the large living room and tempered the noise coming from beyond. Raina caught a glimpse of a colorful sofa, its covering stamped with rodeo cowboys and horses. Black wrought-iron lamps and comfortable-looking side chairs complemented the casual decor. Sand art on the wall appeared to be hand-crafted, as did the mandala over the sofa and the blue pottery painted with gray wolves high on the bookcase. The big flat-screen TV was a focal point in the room.

Manuel tucked his face into her neck and she snuggled him closer. She liked the feel of a baby in her arms. Once she'd hoped a child would be a possibility. But so many possibilities had died on September eleventh, along with her husband.

At first, she'd thought about him twenty-four hours a day, seven days a week. Memories still popped up now and then without her summoning them. But time was taking its toll, and life went on, whether she grieved and remembered or not. Life had swept her along with it, and she'd stopped resisting its force, though a deep ache was always there.

As they neared the kitchen, loud boys' chatter turned into more of a shouting match. Six-year-old Roy and

eight-year-old Joey were coloring at a large rectangu-
lar pedestal table. But Joey was now drawing on Roy's
picture, and in retaliation Roy was drawing on Joey's.

They were pointing fingers and making accusations
while a woman in her fifties, with white-blond spiked
hair and long dangling earrings stirred a pot on the stove
and firmly called their names. "Roy. Joey. Stop squab-
bling. You don't want your dad to come in and hear you."

"Dad's too busy to hear us," Joey said defiantly, his
dark brown eyes snapping in his mocha-skinned face.

Roy nudged his brother's shoulder. "Dad don't want
us to fight."

"We're not fighting," Joey declared, making another
mark on Roy's paper. "We're just drawing."

"Drawing very loudly," Shep admonished them as he
stepped through the doorway into the kitchen. "Eva,
shouldn't they be helping you get supper ready?"

"We did help her," they both chimed in unison,
running to him for a hug.

"Oh, I just bet you did."

Suddenly Joey looked around Shep and saw Raina.
"What are *you* doing here? Did she come to do something to Manuel or to me or Roy?"

Raina couldn't imagine what they thought she'd do.
She'd examined Joey when he had a sinus infection, but
that had been about the extent of it.

"Why is she carrying Manuel?" Joey wanted to know.

Raina suddenly wondered if any parent could answer
all of the questions a child might ask in one day.

"Dr. Gibson came home with me to make sure
Manuel feels okay," Shep responded, and quickly intro-
duced her to his housekeeper, who had kind, hazel eyes.

"The doctor came home with you so you can spend time with *us*," Roy decided, looking happy at *that* idea.

From their exchange Raina guessed Manuel's earaches had shifted most of Shep's attention to him, and the older boys didn't like it.

"Supper in fifteen minutes," Eva called. "Boys, you'd better wash up."

Their heads swung to Shep almost in unison, and he nodded. "Do what Eva said."

But before they ran off to the bathroom, Roy studied Raina again. "Are you staying for supper? We're having chili. Eva doesn't make it so hot, 'cause I don't like it that way."

Raina laughed. "I don't know if I'm staying."

"We'd like you to," Shep said quietly.

Eva added, her eyes twinkling, "I made plenty."

She really hadn't intended to stay and share a meal. Sharing a meal formed a...bond. But with little Manuel clinging to her, Roy looking at her hopefully, Joey studying her a little suspiciously and Shep standing only a few feet from her, giving off signals that he wanted her to stay, she agreed. "All right. Thanks for the invitation. My mom makes chili, too, and I don't like it too hot, either."

At that, Roy grinned and ran off with his brother to wash up.

Manuel cuddled against her, looking up at her with big brown eyes. "How do you feel, little one?" she asked gently.

He reached for her chin, and when his fingers made contact he said, "Rocky, rocky."

Raina looked to Shep for an explanation. He was

watching Manuel's fingers on her skin. He was looking at her lips. She felt hot and cold, and much too interested in what Shep was thinking right now.

Eva explained, "When Manuel first came here, all he wanted Shep to do was to rock him in the big rocking chair in the living room."

Raina bought her attention back to Manuel's words. "I suppose he's associated rocking with comfort. I can do that."

"I can hold dinner longer, but the boys are going to get their hands dirty again," Eva warned.

"There's a solution," Shep assured her. "I'll bring the rocker to the table."

"She still won't be able to eat if she's rocking Manuel."

Since Raina would rather talk with than be talked about, she assured them, "I can rock and eat at the same time. It might get a little messy, but maybe I can get Manuel to drink."

Eva nudged Shep's shoulder. "I can see why you brought her along. She's on top of things."

"I'll say she is," Shep said, looking at her almost as if he didn't *want* to be looking at her. The same way she knew she shouldn't be looking at him?

Dinner was a rowdy meal, as the boys dipped corn bread into their chili and talked with their mouths full. Roy told Raina about his bus ride that morning and afternoon. Joey talked, mostly about Roy—but not about himself.

After supper, the boys helped Eva clean off the table and Raina was impressed. "I could never get my brother to do that unless I bribed him."

"Your brother's the police officer, right?" Shep asked.

"Don't tell him I told you about the bribing. I'll never live it down."

"Rumor has it he's a good detective."

She knew small towns listened to the rumor mill more than cable news channels.

Thoughts of Sagebrush's gossip line faded as Manuel stirred. She brought her head down to his and whispered close to his ear, "You're such a good little boy."

He looked up at her as if he'd heard every word, and gave her a smile.

Shep was sitting next to her in a high-backed wooden chair that looked like an antique. He leaned closer to her. "Whispering words of wisdom in his ear?"

With Shep's face so close to hers, she became breathless when she gazed at his lips. "Just some positive reinforcement. You can do that for him anytime."

"I'll remember that," Shep returned in a low, husky voice, then leaned away.

To distract herself from the magnetic pull Shep exuded, she complimented Eva on her chili, as well as on the corn bread, the coleslaw and the ginger cookies she'd baked for dessert.

Suddenly Shep stood. "Okay, boys. How about if you go get ready for bed? Morning comes a lot quicker when you have to go to school."

Roy's "Aw, do we have to?" and Joey's quick look at Raina had Shep arching a brow. "I'm going to get Manuel changed into pj's, too. I want you two finished by the time I'm done."

Both boys mumbled, "Yes, sir," slid last peeks at Raina, then scrambled off.

After they were gone, Eva said to Raina, "They find

toys to play with and forget to put their pajamas on. I'll go up and make sure they don't get too sidetracked."

"Thanks," Shep called to her, and Raina could see he meant it.

"I guess it's time to put those eardrops in," Shep said with a frown. "Is there a right way and a wrong way?" he asked Raina.

"If we coax him to lay on his side, that will make it easier."

Shep motioned through the doorway to the living room. "Let's go to the playroom. I set up a changing table in there."

Raina wasn't used to being around a man who put kids first. Gina's fiancé, Logan, did. He'd had to. But Raina didn't know Logan all that well yet.

Shep took Manuel from her, his large hands grazing her midriff as he securely took hold of the little boy. She was surprised by her body's startled awareness of the man's touch. Her cheeks flushed and she felt oddly off-balance.

Shep looked down at her, their gazes locking for a few intense moments. Neither of them said anything as Shep carried Manuel, and Raina followed him to the playroom.

They passed what looked like a guest bedroom, then entered a bright, sunny room with yellow walls. There were two long, floor-to-ceiling windows that looked out over the backyard and smaller ones in a row on the other side.

"Was this once a porch?" she asked.

"Yes, it was. I closed it in, put a smaller porch on this entrance and fenced in the yard."

"Did you do it yourself?" If he did, she was curious

why. He could have hired an entire crew! Now she really *was* curious about him.

"A contractor did most of the work on the ranch for me. I wanted it restored rather than razed and rebuilt. But I did this. I learned to work with my hands early on. I like building things. I guess that's why I bought the lumberyard, so I could help other people do it."

He took Manuel over to a dark wood chest with a changing table on top. The room had been furnished with kids in mind—a couple of royal blue beanbag chairs, a game table with stools, cupboards and shelves that held toys—everything from remote-controlled vehicles to drawing sets. This room created a pang of longing in Raina, a pang she hadn't experienced in a very long time. Clark had wanted children badly. So had she.

"What are you thinking about?" Shep asked her.

With that question, Raina knew he could be a perceptive man. But she didn't share her private thoughts very easily. "I was just thinking about parents and kids. When did you know you wanted to adopt?"

As he undressed Manuel, Shep seemed to consider her question very carefully. "I knew about foster care firsthand. I grew up in the system. It wasn't pretty. Once I got a start in life and learned how to make money, I had a goal—to find a place I could turn into a real home for kids, kids who needed a family as much as they needed a roof over their heads."

Shep set Manuel's shirt aside, but it began to slip from the table. Raina caught it. Closer to Shep now, she could almost feel the powerful vibrations emanating from his tall, hard body. She sensed he was all muscle, all cowboy, silent much of the time, only revealing himself when he chose or had to.

"Why Sagebrush?" she asked.

"Why *not* Sagebrush?" he responded with a quick grin that she realized he used to disarm anyone who maybe got too close. That grin had the power to make butterflies jump in her stomach. She hadn't felt that sensation for so long she almost didn't recognize it. But when she felt a burning heat crawling up her neck again, she knew exactly what it was. Attraction. She'd been fighting it ever since she'd met Shep McGraw.

Concentrating on their conversation, she took a quick breath. "This isn't an area of Texas most people think about when they want to move somewhere. I just wondered how you landed here."

Shep helped Manuel into a pajama shirt covered with horseshoes. The toddler yawned widely as Shep concentrated on the tiny buttons, his fingers fumbling with them.

"My father came from Sagebrush. He died when I was four. Then my mother and I moved to California. So you might say I just returned to my roots."

Raina knew she should back away from Shep and his story, which was bound to deepen her awareness and sympathy. She didn't want to get involved with *anyone.* She'd lost her husband in the most awful of ways, and the aftermath had been heart-wrenching. Moving on had been an almost insurmountable task. But she *had* gone on. She was past tragedy. And she wanted to keep it that way.

Still, she was *so* intrigued by a cowboy who could run a ranch and a lumberyard, yet change a diaper, too. Trying to be as tactful as she could, she asked, "And you lost your mom, too?"

"Yeah, I did."

When Shep didn't say more, Raina moved a step closer to him. "I'm sorry."

Stilling, he peered down at her. He was so much taller than she was. The blue of his eyes darkened until she felt a tremble up her spine.

"Don't be sorry," he said, his voice husky and low. "Everything that happened to me back then made me who I am now."

Who *was* Shep McGraw, beyond a rancher and a dad? Did she even want to find out? Wasn't that why she had accepted his invitation tonight?

The moment was broken when Manuel began kicking his legs and reached his arms out to Shep. "Up, Daddy, up."

Shep broke eye contact and concentrated on the little boy. "Not yet. Let's get you changed so we can put your eardrops in."

"Dwops?" Manuel repeated.

"I left them on the kitchen counter," Shep told Raina. "Would you mind getting them?"

No, she didn't mind. She felt as if she needed a breather from him and the obvious love he felt for his sons.

A few minutes later Raina distracted Manuel as Shep squeezed in the drops. Both of them seemed to be going out of their way not to get too close, not to let their fingers touch, not to let their eyes meet.

Footsteps suddenly thundered down the stairs. "Dad! Dad!" Roy and Joey called as they ran through the living room towards the playroom.

"I'm right here," he said with a laugh, "not out in the barn."

His gentle rebuke didn't seem to faze the boys. "We want to say good night to Dr. Gibson. Eva said we could."

Raina drank in the sight of the two little boys, her heart lurching again. What was wrong with her tonight? Joey was dressed in pj's decorated with racecars. Roy's were stamped with balls and bats. "I'm glad you came down."

"We're not going to bed yet," Joey explained. "We can read in our room before we go to sleep. Dad says that quiets us down."

Raina couldn't help but smile. "Sometimes I read to quiet *me* down before I go to sleep."

"We wanted to ask you somethin'," Roy volunteered.

Raina glanced at Shep but he just shrugged. "What did you want to ask me?"

"Can you come back and see the horses sometime?"

She didn't know how to respond. What did Shep want? What did *she* want? Did that even matter, when these two precious children were staring up at her with their big, dark eyes? "I suppose I can."

"Promise?" Roy asked, possibly sensing her hesitation.

Joey added, "If you promise, you have to do it. Dad says no one will be your friend if you can't keep a promise."

Again her gaze sought Shep's. His expression was friendly but neutral. Apparently, this was her decision. She liked the idea of him teaching his sons about promises being kept.

"I promise," she said solemnly.

"If you come Saturday, we can go for a ride after we do chores," Joey informed her, as if warming to that idea.

"You can *help* with chores!" Roy added enthusiastically.

At that, Raina laughed out loud. "Well, maybe if I'd help you with chores, I'd develop some muscles. My brother's always telling me I should work out."

"You have a brother?" Roy asked, wide-eyed.

"Sure do." She thought about her schedule Saturday. "I'll tell you what. I have to go to the hospital Saturday morning, but then I'll stop by here afterward." She looked at Shep. "Is that all right?"

"That's fine," he replied, still giving nothing away.

Eva came into the room then, and asked Shep, "Is Manuel ready?"

The two-year-old had cuddled against Shep's shoulder. Now Eva took him and said, "Come on, boys. Let's head on up." As they followed their nanny, they turned around and stared at their dad.

He assured them, "I'll be up in a few minutes. Go on. Pick out a book you want me to read to you." He said to Eva, "I'll bring along some of that oat cereal for Manuel."

After Roy waved at Raina, both boys took off after Eva.

Feeling awkward, Raina checked her watch. "I'd better be going."

"I'll walk you out."

Raina gathered her purse from the counter, feeling Shep's gaze on her as she went to the door and he followed. She wondered what he was thinking. She knew what *she* was thinking.

The end-of-August evening was warm. As they stepped outside, the breeze tossed the ends of her hair. They walked to her car in silence.

The motion-detector light on the side of the house glowed as they neared her car. She knew she was going to have to ask Shep the question in her mind. Distracting herself for the moment, she pressed the remote and her doors unlocked.

Shep opened the driver's-side door for her.

Rather than climbing in, she faced him, close enough to him to see the beard shadow on his face. "Do you want me to come out on Saturday?"

"You have to. You promised."

"I know. I wasn't sure what to say. When Roy looked at me with those big eyes, I didn't know how to refuse."

Shep chuckled. "I know exactly what you mean."

"You didn't answer my question." She needed to know if he wanted her here or not.

"I like you, Dr. Gibson. It won't be a hardship to take you on a trail ride."

"Raina," she said softly. "If we're going on a trail ride, first names seem more…comfortable."

"Comfortable," he agreed, looking down at her with interest she hadn't noticed in a man's eyes for years. He shoved his hands into his pockets, though he didn't step away. "Thanks for coming over tonight."

"I really enjoyed myself."

Awkwardness settled between them, the kind of awkwardness that happened after a first date, she thought. Only, they hadn't been on a date. Still, she felt pulled toward Shep. Yet something else urged her to move away—probably memories, heartache and regrets over a love lost.

After she slid into the driver's seat, Shep closed the door. Then he laid his hand on the open window and bent down, his face close to hers. "Remember, a promise given is a promise that should be kept."

She had the feeling his boys had had promises made to them that weren't kept. He was protective of that and protective of them. "I'll remember," she murmured, unable to take her gaze from his face.

Shep straightened and stepped away from the car.

With a trembling hand, she pressed her smart key to start the engine. As she backed out of the parking space and drove away, his words echoed in her mind.

*A promise given is a promise that should be kept.*

Did Shep McGraw keep *his* promises?

## Chapter Three

"You are wrong!" Roy yelled. "Wrong, wrong, wrong."

"I am not," Joey yelled back.

"Boys," came a stern voice.

Raina had parked beside Shep's ranchhouse and, hearing voices at the barn, headed to it. She walked toward the corral, guessing the boys were outside the stall doors. At the fence, she stopped.

Shep had crouched down in front of Roy. His voice wasn't stern now, as he said, "It's still early. Not even lunchtime."

"But she said she'd be here this morning."

Raina had gotten tied up at the hospital and intended to phone on her way to the ranch, but her cell phone had lost its charge.

"Hey, everybody," she called, cheerily now, letting them know she was there. "Am I too late for chores?"

"Dr. Gibson!" Roy cheered, brushing away his tears. "You came." He turned to his brother. "I told you so. I told you she'd keep her promise."

Shep slowly rose from his crouched position. Without any accusation, he said, "The boys were a little worried you'd forgotten."

Opening the corral gate, she stepped inside the working area for the horses. "I'm sorry I'm late. I got tied up at the hospital." She lifted her duffel bag. "I brought old clothes and riding boots."

"You can change at the house or in the tack room," Shep informed her.

"The tack room is fine."

"She's a girl," Joey said with disgust. "She thinks about clothes and getting them dirty."

Raina could see Shep was trying hard to suppress a laugh. He knocked his Stetson higher on his head with his forefinger. "Listen, Joey, part of a woman's job is to think about clothes. You ought to do it once in a while."

As Joey crinkled his nose, Raina laughed and headed for the tack room. A few minutes later, she returned in her old jeans and short-sleeved blouse, her dad's navy paisley kerchief tied around her neck. "Just tell me what you want me to do."

"We saved mucking out the stalls," Roy told her.

"I'm thrilled about that," she responded with a straight face.

He took a good look at her and smiled. "You're teasin'."

She ruffled his hair. "Yes, I am. I guess no one really likes mucking out stalls, but it has to be done."

"You're really going to do it?" Joey asked.

"I did it before, when I was about your age. My uncle had a ranch and a couple of horses."

"In Sagebrush?" Shep asked.

"Yep. On the east side of town. When hard times set in and he had to sell it, a developer bought it. There's a whole bunch of houses there now, where his ranch used to be."

Her gaze met Shep's and one of those trembles danced through her body again. It was like a preliminary tremor to an earthquake. She told herself she was being foolish. She was just off balance, being out of her comfort zone, being with Shep and his boys again.

"We'll get the shovels," Joey told Raina as he and Roy headed into the barn.

After they were out of earshot, Shep asked her, "Did you have second thoughts?" His blue eyes demanded a straight answer, not a polite excuse.

"I did. But I'd made a promise."

"Should I ask why you had second thoughts, or leave it alone?"

"You're direct, aren't you?"

He shrugged. "I try to be. Life is complicated enough, without beating around the proverbial bush."

When she hesitated before answering, he settled his hand on her arm. "It's okay. You don't have to explain."

She'd worn a short-sleeve blouse because of the early September heat. Shep's long, calloused fingers were warm and sensual on her skin. When she looked up at him, she felt tongue-tied. It was an odd experience, because she usually wasn't at a loss for words.

Finally, she admitted, "There are a lot of reasons why I had second thoughts." The awareness between her and Shep wasn't one-sided. She knew that now. She could feel his interest, and she wanted to run from it.

He released her arm and held up one finger. "The first reason is me." He held up a second finger. "The second reason is me." He held up a third finger. "And the third reason is probably me."

"No ego there," she muttered.

He laughed. "It has nothing to do with ego. I just figure— Hell, Raina. I know about your husband. I also know for the past six months you did everything you could not to make eye contact with me."

"Manuel was my patient."

"Yeah, I know that."

"Well, *you* didn't show any interest, either."

"No, I didn't. I pretended there wasn't any, just like you did."

"I wasn't pretending," she protested. "I wasn't interested. I'm *not* interested. I loved my husband, and when I lost him—" She stopped. "I can't ever explain what it was like—waiting and not knowing, waiting and hoping, waiting and waiting and waiting. And finally accepting, and having to deal with grief deeper than I've ever known." She shook her head, struggling to maintain her composure. "I never want to feel anything remotely like it ever again."

"I can understand that."

She saw empathy in Shep's eyes. Real empathy. He'd lost his parents, and she didn't know who else he might have lost along the way. Maybe he knew, too, that nothing was forever…nothing lasted.

"I came because I made a promise," she repeated.

A smile crept across Shep's lips. "Then Roy was right to trust you."

The way Shep said it, she had the feeling *he* didn't trust many people. Because of the way he'd grown up?

"Roy and Joey don't fight often. For a couple of years, all they had was each other."

"For a couple of years?"

"When their parents were killed in an accident, they were put into the system. But being biracial, and being brothers, the system had trouble placing them. So they stayed in foster care."

"Maybe the fact that they're fighting means they don't have to depend on each other quite so much, since they have you."

"I'd like to believe that's true, but they still hold back with me. Especially Joey. He likes to keep things to himself, and sometimes that causes him trouble."

"Do *you* keep things to yourself?"

"Oh, terrific. My boys had to ask a *smart* lady to come to the ranch for a trail ride."

This time *she* laughed. The scent of horses and the sun's heat beating on old wood rode the corral air. Although Shep didn't always say a lot, he was easy to talk to. He made her feel…safe. She'd returned to Sagebrush to feel safe, to be close to her mother and brother, to establish roots that had somehow slipped away on that terrible day in 2001. She'd felt safe in the Victorian with Gina, and now Angie. But not safe in this way. Not protected like this. She suspected Shep was a protector, and that gave her an odd feeling. Clark had been a protector, and because of that he'd died.

"You're thinking sad thoughts."

How could Shep do that? How could he know? "Not for long. As soon as your boys hand me a shovel, I'll only be thinking about getting finished and going on that trail ride."

Shep motioned her inside the barn. "Then let's get started."

The barn was old. Raina could tell that there were signs of it being refurbished—fresh mortar between stones on the walls was lighter gray and without cracks. Some of the wooden stall doors looked new, their catches and hinges shiny and untouched by time.

"How old is the barn?" she asked, realizing the boys were nowhere in sight.

"The buildings on the property date back to the 1850s."

"You bought a piece of history."

"That's the way I look at it. That's why I didn't raze everything to the ground and start over. I liked building on what was here, making the old stand up to the test of time. Do you know what I mean?"

"I do. It's nice to know something will last with a little help." As she took in the stalls and the feed barrels, she asked, "Where are the boys and their shovels?"

Shep shook his head. "I know where they are. Come on." He led her past the tack room, and when they rounded the corner, she saw Joey and Roy leaning over a pile of hay bales. The hay was stacked wide and high. But the boys were sort of in the middle of it, two bales up, peeking over the edge of one bale.

"Kittens?" she guessed.

Shep nodded, smiling. "You *have* been around barns. They wanted to bring them up to the house, but I told them the babies are still too little. They haven't even learned how to climb out of their nest yet. Give them a few more weeks and they'll probably be sleeping with the boys."

"You sound resigned."

He chuckled. "I know kids can get attached to animals. Pets can give them security, so I'm all for it."

Without thinking twice, Raina climbed up the bale and sat next to Joey. She peered over the edge and saw a mama cat nursing four little ones whose eyes were barely open.

"They know where to go to eat," Roy told her, as if that was important information.

Joey added, "Dad says we shouldn't touch them until they climb out. Their mama wouldn't like it."

"Your dad's probably right. The mama cat might move them and then you wouldn't be able to find them."

"Until they're old enough to run around," Joey said, as if he were challenging her.

"Yep, that's true. But in here they're protected from the weather and anything else that might bother them. So it's a good place."

Joey seemed to think about that. "Yeah. I like the barn. It's even neater when the horses are in here making noises."

"I'll bet," Raina responded, holding back a grin.

"Come on, boys. If we don't get those stalls cleaned out before lunch, you don't go on a trail ride," Shep reminded them.

Without grumbling, they crawled down the bales, rushed into the tack room and emerged with three shovels. Roy handed one of them to Raina. "Dad uses a pitchfork, but he won't let us touch that."

"It's locked in the tool closet," Shep explained. "I'll go get it and meet you at stall one."

Chores went quickly, and Raina noticed Shep did most of the work. He wanted the boys involved, to have a good work ethic, but he wouldn't give them more than they could handle.

By the time they reached the third stall, Roy was slowing down.

Raina said, "Why don't I give you a hand?" She put her shovel aside and stood behind Roy, helping him scoop and carry to the outside bucket.

He grinned up at her. "That was easier."

Joey didn't say a word, but there was no indication he resented his little brother having help when he didn't.

When they'd finished with the third stall, however, Shep suggested, "Let's take a break. Go on up to the house and tell Eva we're ready for lunch. Wash up. We'll be along."

A few minutes later, Raina stood beside Shep, watching the boys race out of the barn through the corral gate and across the lane. "They're hard workers."

"Yeah. And sometimes I think they'll do anything for my approval. That's not always a good thing."

"I don't know what you mean."

"I want them to be themselves. I want them to be who they are with each other when they're in their room alone. When I'm around, they're more guarded."

"They've been with you what—a year and a half?"

"Yep. And you'd think they'd be more comfortable with me by now."

It was easy to see that Shep was the strong, silent type. She wondered how much sharing he did with his boys. How much he told them what he was feeling. But she didn't know him well enough to say that, so instead she said, "There's distance between me and my mom, even now. But my brother and I are really close."

"You don't tell your mother what you're thinking?"

"No."

Shep didn't ask why, and his look told her he wouldn't pry if she didn't want him to. So, instead of keeping her childhood hidden, as she usually did, she brought it out to examine once again. "My father was Cheyenne, and proud of it. He told me and my brother about the old ways of living, of thinking, of believing. My mother didn't like that. She wanted us to fit in. Sometimes being proud of our heritage didn't help us fit in. Ryder and I were often made fun of, but we had each other and I didn't tell her about it. That sort of set the standard for our relationship. I tried to be what she wanted me to be—the perfect daughter. Daddy and I could always talk, but my mom and I couldn't. He died when I was ten, and nothing was ever the same after that."

Shep nodded as if he knew all too well exactly what she meant. "Did your mother work before your dad died?"

"At the library. But afterward, that wasn't nearly enough, so she started driving a school bus, too."

"Gutsy lady."

"I think in her heart she always wanted to be a teacher, but never had the money to go to college. She practically runs the library now. She gave up bus driving a few years ago to take the head position."

"She sounds as interesting as you are."

Raina wasn't sure what to say to that, so she fell back on what had affected her life most deeply. "My mom never got over losing my dad. It was like that part of her, the romantic side of her, just stopped existing."

"Has that happened to you?"

Raina really had not seen the connection before, and

now she did. "I think that's happened to me because of the way Clark died."

"I suppose that's so. Your husband was a hero. His memory is bigger than life, so there's no room to have a romantic dream again."

"How do you understand that so well?"

"I've been around."

Sometimes Shep's attitude was too enigmatic, and she found herself wanting to dig down to deeper levels. So she asked a question that had been niggling at her for a long while. "If you wanted a family so badly, why didn't you get married?"

"Because having a family didn't depend on me marrying."

"That's not an answer," she protested softly, wanting to step closer to him, and yet afraid of feelings that were starting to tickle her heart. So afraid, she wanted to run.

He seemed to have an inside battle with himself, then finally said, "I don't trust women easily. I have good reasons to believe they leave when the going gets tough. Or they stay for the wrong reasons."

"The wrong reasons?"

"Yeah. Things like money. Fancy cars. A house in the best neighborhood in town."

So he'd gotten burned by a woman who had wanted what he could provide for her? Or had the trust issues started much earlier than that?

"Everyone's got baggage, Shep. It's what we do with it that matters."

When he angled toward her, she wasn't sure what was going to happen next. She was a bit surprised when he took hold of a lock of her hair and let it flutter through his fingers. "You're a captivating woman, Raina. Do you know that?"

"No," she said seriously. "Each day that passes I figure out more about myself."

"What did you figure out today?" He let his hand drop and she was sorry when he did.

"I figured out that mucking out a stall is as good an exercise as I can get in a gym. And that little boys always have a next question, even when you think you've answered them all."

He chuckled. "Isn't that the truth?"

He looked as if he wanted to kiss her. To her amazement, she wanted him to do it. But why—so she could feel like a desirable woman once more? So she could really start living again? So she could wipe out some terrible memories and replace them with sparkling new ones?

Whatever the reason, it didn't matter, because Shep took a step back. "We'd better get up to lunch before there isn't any. Those boys have big appetites after doing chores."

Shep had let her down easy. They'd gone back to friendly. His trust issues and her past could be hurdles that might prevent even a meaningful friendship from beginning.

*What* had gotten into him?

Shep gave his horse a nudge up a small hill, watching his sons in front of him as they did the same. Raina rode between Joey and Roy, talking to them as they bounced along.

Shep rarely discussed his background or his breakup with Belinda. Only with Cruz now and then. Granted, he hadn't given Raina much, but he'd said more than enough. He wanted to forget Belinda's gold-digging motivation for getting engaged to him…the indifference to children she'd kept well-hidden. He needed to forget that kid who'd gone through life without an adult to really care about him. He longed to forget landing in jail at the age of fourteen. He'd never tell Raina Greystone Gibson *that* story.

He'd been so rebellious back then. He'd hated his foster parents and their neglect. Not only of him, but of Cruz, too. Cruz had been younger, more vulnerable, not as experienced as Shep about the ins and outs of the system. Shep had felt he had to look out for him. But in protecting Cruz, he'd broken the law.

No matter their foster parents had left them alone for the weekend. No matter Cruz had taken ill and had a raging fever. No matter Shep hadn't known what to do except hotwire that old truck and take Cruz to the closest E.R.

The chief of police had thrown him into that dirty jail cell and not cared a whit. If it hadn't been for Matt Forester rescuing them, Shep wasn't sure where he or Cruz would be today. Maybe in prison. Maybe on the streets.

Nope. He'd never tell Raina about that chunk of his life. She'd never understand the desperation that had driven him to rebel against authority figures for his sake as well as Cruz's.

He'd sensed that same defiant spirit in Joey and suspected it had developed while he was in foster care.

The brothers had had loving, caring parents until they'd been killed. With no relatives to take care of them, they'd been thrust into the system. Then five,

Joey had acted out, and his aggressive behavior had made placement even harder. They'd been through two foster couples before Shep had decided to take them.

He believed there were three secrets to turning kids around. Matt Forester had taught them to Shep and Cruz. You gave children safety. You gave them love. And you gave them a reason to trust you. If Shep could accomplish that, Joey, Roy and Manuel would be on their way to being confident and finding a future that fit them.

Breaking Shep's consideration of his past and present, Joey turned around and called, "Can we show Dr. Gibson Red Creek?"

"Do you remember how to get there?"

"Yep. We go right at the bottom of this hill."

"Lead the way."

Joey grinned and pushed his fist up into the air, as if he'd just been given a gift. The gift of confidence, Shep hoped, as he urged his horse to catch up to Raina's.

"They're good riders for their age," she remarked as the two boys trotted ahead.

"You're pretty good yourself."

"I must have inherited good riding genes from my ancestors who roamed the plains."

He couldn't tell if she was being serious or tongue-in-cheek. "You said your heritage meant a lot to your dad. Did it mean a lot to you?"

"That's not an easy question."

"Tell me," he said, surprising himself. Usually when conversations with women got into sticky waters, he swam in the opposite direction. But he wanted to know more about Raina, wanted to uncover everything she kept hidden deep in her soul.

"Is it a long way to the creek?" she asked with a wry smile.

"Long enough that if you haven't ridden for a while you're going to be sore tomorrow."

"I guess I'd better soak in a hot tub tonight."

"It wouldn't hurt." He suddenly had visions of her sinking into a tub full of bubbles. But before she slid into those bubbles—

He had to quit imagining her in something less than a blouse and jeans.

When she canvassed his face, he wondered what she saw. He could hide quite a bit with his Stetson. Every cowboy knew how. But they were riding in the sun, and the shadows from his brim didn't hide everything. Could she see his interest in her was physically motivated? Since Belinda's rejection of a future he held dear, all he'd looked for from a woman was physical satisfaction.

He and Raina were so blasted different. The ways were too numerous to count. So why was he here? And why was *she* here?

Curiosity, pure and simple.

She was still studying him when he said, "You changed the subject."

"You helped it along."

"I did. And if you really don't want to talk about it, that's okay."

She was silent as they rode through pockets of wild sage, scrub brush and tall grass. As her horse rocked her, she turned the kerchief around her neck, the frayed edges brushing her skin. "This was my dad's. He wore it whenever he went riding. He liked to tease that it would come in handy if a dust storm came up. His stories about his father serving in World War II, as well as his own experiences in Vietnam, were written down in a diary he kept. My mother gave it to me on my twelfth birthday."

"Why your twelfth?"

"I was having trouble fitting in at school. I didn't know how to handle being Cheyenne, and at times growing up, it made me feel like an outsider. Ryder faced the same problem, but a guy can be a loner and that can be attractive by itself. He knew who he was when he hit his teens. He also knew he wanted to be a cop. I just felt…different from everyone else."

"When did you stop feeling different?"

"I never did. But I learned to *like* being different. Remembering the myths and fables my father told me helped me see how life fit together, how the past becomes the present, how being Cheyenne is something to be proud of. But it wasn't always so, and I feel guilty about that."

"You were a kid."

"Yeah. A kid who should have listened more. Who should have known better. If I had listened to the stories my father told, instead of trying to deny my heritage, my life might have made sense sooner."

"I think you've done one heck of a job with your life."

Raina shook her hand. "Shep, you don't know me."

He reached over, clasped her arm and they both stopped their horses. "Med school isn't a walk in the park. I know you're a fine doctor who cares about her patients. I can see you love kids and should have a bunch of your own."

"Oh, Shep."

He wasn't sure, but he thought her eyes were a little shiny. His hand slid from her arm down to her hand. "What's wrong?"

Then he swore. "That was really a stupid thing to say. And a stupid thing to ask. You're wishing you did have a bunch of kids with your husband. You want the life back that was so brutally taken away from you."

She took a deep breath. "It's been nine years. The first five, that was probably true. The next couple, I tried not to keep looking back, because that only brought anger and sadness and regret. Returning to Sagebrush made a difference for me, and I probably should have done it sooner."

"Getting away from New York?"

"Yes. Stepping away from the memories and starting over."

Shep watched Raina's dark hair blowing in the wind, saw the determination in her eyes to forge a new future. But determination wasn't always enough to push regrets aside.

After a long look at each other, they headed toward the sound of the boys' laughter.

Fifteen minutes later, at the bank of the creek, Shep dismounted and so did Raina, without any help from him. She was definitely an independent woman, one who charted her own course.

He went to help Roy dismount and saw Raina go to Joey. She hadn't asked if she should help. She just saw the need and handled it. But he noticed she waited to see what Joey could do for himself, obviously not wanting to step on the little boy's pride.

She'd make a wonderful mother.

*Now, where in the heck had that thought come from?*

He and his little band were just fine on their own, although he had to admit, their caseworker seemed to doubt his ability to handle a toddler. But he'd shown her so far that he could, and he had Eva to help with practical matters. He didn't need anyone else.

But as he moved to stand beside Raina, watched the boys walk a little farther down to listen to the bubbling creek, he had to admit he was damn attracted to her. A night in his bed—

He cut off the thought. She wasn't that kind of woman. After the obviously loving marriage she'd had, she'd only look for another committed relationship. If she looked at all.

And to be honest, he couldn't commit to a woman because he didn't trust them.

Cruz had tried to analyze him. More than once his friend had suggested that his trust issues stemmed from his mother abandoning him at a mall when he was six…from his foster mothers not really caring…from Belinda wanting what Shep could give her materially rather than emotionally. Shep didn't know about all that. He just knew it was hard for him to open up to anyone—to trust anyone.

Yet, standing beside Raina, inhaling the lemony fragrance of her that carried to him on the breeze, appreciating the lines of her profile and the soft fullness of her lips, his groin tightened and all he thought about was kissing her.

Her gaze met his and he knew she'd caught him. She didn't play coy games, but said simply, "You were staring. Do I have hay in my hair? A smudge of dirt on my nose?" Her question was light, but he sensed the underlying tension.

"You look like you belong out here, with the horses and the wind, breaking trails and maybe riding shotgun."

She laughed. And he smiled. And then they were leaning a little closer to each other.

"Hey, Dad. Come see the rock I found," Roy called to him.

*Saved by the voice of a child,* Shep thought as he leaned away from Raina, tapped his Stetson more securely on his head and went to see the treasure his son would be carrying home.

His life was his boys. And he couldn't—wouldn't—forget that.

*Chapter Four*

"It seems longer than a few weeks since we really talked to her," Raina said on Sunday evening. She stood at Lily Wescott's front door with Gina Rigoletti and her sister, Angie.

They were all worried about Lily. A few months ago, she'd been so happy in her marriage, fulfilled in her work helping women conceive. Then a little over a month ago, she'd become a widow. Shortly after her husband, Troy, had been deployed to Afghanistan, he was killed in action. A shock to them, and Lily had been devastated. She and Troy were only married for a year.

"I know," Gina agreed, pushing her black curls behind her ear. "Phone calls just aren't the same. But she needed to be with Troy's family in Oklahoma."

Angie pushed a lock of dark wavy hair out of her

eyes. "I wasn't sure I should come. After all, I don't know her as well as you two do."

"Lily can use all the friends she can get right now," Raina assured her new housemate. "We'll just have to take our cues from her. But she needs us right now. I've been through this. I know that when the casseroles and the cards and the phone calls stop, sometimes you lose your compass. You don't even know if breakfast comes before lunch."

Gina put her hand on Raina's shoulder. "You've never really talked about how it was for you."

"Did your family stay with you in New York?" Angie asked.

"Mom did. Ryder had to get back here to work, and I understood that. Actually, it was a relief when Mom left and friends stopped coming by at all hours of the day. Don't get me wrong, I appreciated all of it. I don't know what I would have done without the support. But I also needed time alone, just to sit and realize that Clark was never coming back. I imagine that's what Lily's doing now," Raina said, sighing. "Our situations aren't so very different."

"Maybe she can talk to you about it," Angie ventured.

"Maybe. We'll see."

When Gina rang the bell, they all seemed to hold their breath.

A few seconds later Lily opened the door. Her blond hair was pulled back into a tight ponytail and she had purple smudges under her eyes. She gave each of them a hard and long hug, then wiped a few tears from her eyes. "I thought all the tears were gone. I don't know how any can be left."

The front of Lily's apartment was a huge, open space. The kitchen flowed into the dining room, which flowed into the living room, with no barriers except some furniture in between.

Lily went to the kitchen, the rest of them following, then stood there as if she'd lost her purpose. "I'm a mess," she admitted. "After I arrived in Oklahoma, Troy's family didn't leave me alone for a minute, and I appreciated their support. But then last night, when I got in, after I called you, I just…I just couldn't figure out what to do next." Her gaze went to Raina's. "When will I feel like I'm back in my body again? That the world's real and I'll understand Troy isn't going to walk through that door?"

Her eyes filled up and Raina went to her and put her arm around her. "Everyone's different. But little by little you'll find a new normal."

"I can't even *imagine* normal! I go into the garage where Troy had his workshop and see the furniture he'll never finish. I put my hand on my tummy and it seems impossible that he's gone and I'm going to have our baby. A month ago—" She stopped abruptly. "I'm sorry. I'm a put-one-foot-in-front-of-another sort of person. Now I look in the mirror and I don't even know who I am."

Raina took Lily by the arm and pulled her into the living room. They all sat on the long sectional sofa.

Angie said, "I've never gone through anything like this, Lily, but when I have a crisis, work helps. When are you going back?"

"I don't know. I called Mitch last night, too. He understands since he served in Iraq. He said to come in whenever I'm ready. How will I know when I'm ready?" She sighed, then took a deep breath. "I have to start thinking about the baby. I have to figure out my options."

Soon after Troy had been deployed, Lily had happily e-mailed him that she was pregnant. *Maybe now her baby could help her through her loss,* Raina thought.

"Options for what?" Gina asked.

"I don't think I can stay in this apartment. It's so painful being here. We were going to buy a house as soon as Troy came home."

Raina and Angie's gazes connected at the same time. Angie gave a small nod.

"You shouldn't make impulsive decisions right now," Raina advised her. "You should weigh the pros and cons of each one. But if you decide you do want to move, you're welcome to move into the Victorian with me and Angie."

"You're serious?" Lily asked, surprised.

Both women said at the same time, "Yes, we are."

"There's only one problem. If I move in with you, then I'll have to move again when I have the baby in late March."

"Why?" Raina asked. "Won't you need babysitters?"

Lily looked from Angie to Raina, then over at Gina. "Are they kidding?"

"I don't think they are," Gina assured her with a smile.

"I'm a pediatric nurse," Angie reminded her. "I like babies. Just think of all the expert advice I can give you."

Lily actually gave her a small smile.

"We would love to have you, Lily," Raina reiterated. "And I'm a sucker for babies, too. Yesterday, Shep McGraw's baby stole my heart. When Manuel put his little arms around my neck—"

She stopped. No one had heard about her visit to Shep's. She'd kept it to herself.

Lily murmured, "Troy knew Shep. He bought supplies from him."

Raina had forgotten that, as a general contractor, Troy might have dealt with Shep.

"You were at Shep McGraw's?" Gina asked. "How did *that* happen?"

Lily piggybacked on that. "What did you do while you were there?"

Angie asked, "Didn't you do a procedure on his son Manuel recently?"

Raina held up her hand. "Whoa, now, everybody. I shouldn't have brought it up."

"But you did," Gina reminded her, "which probably means you want to talk about it."

"No, I don't. I just mentioned it because—"

"Because Manuel stole your heart," Angie filled in.

"I never should have brought it up," Raina murmured again.

Lily shook her head. "Don't be silly. I'm all for anything that helps me think about something else for a while."

Raina could see that, even though Lily was talking a good game, she wasn't going to be able to think of anything else but Troy for a very long time. Still, if this conversation would help distract her a little… "I think Shep was nervous about Manuel's procedure and his care afterward. When he found out I was finished for the day, he invited me to go along and see his ranch. I did, and somehow his two boys, Joey and Roy, asked me to come back on the weekend. We went on a trail ride. It was really a nice afternoon."

"Nice?" Gina asked with a raised brow. "Does that mean you like Shep McGraw?"

"Shep's an old-fashioned cowboy." She felt herself blushing. "We're very different."

"Are you going to see him again?" Lily asked.

"I don't know. I don't know if I'm ready. And he has his hands very full with those three boys. I don't think a lasting involvement is on his mind right now."

"He's the love 'em and leave 'em type?" Angie asked.

"I've heard rumors. But for the past year, all I've seen is that he's trying to be a good dad."

"Taking in three boys from foster care is noble," Gina agreed.

Raina noticed that Lily was staring out the picture window, no longer hearing the conversation that swirled around her.

Raina touched her friend's hand. "Would you rather we left you alone? Or should we try to come up with a meal we can all make and enjoy together tonight?" She knew Lily might have a tendency to forget to eat and that wouldn't be good for her, especially because of the baby.

Lily saw through that ploy right away. "You're trying to take care of me."

"No," Gina protested, "we're trying to help you take care of yourself."

Lily looked from one of them to the other and then her gaze fell on a picture of Troy in his uniform that was sitting on a side table. "All right," she decided, pushing herself up from the couch. "Let's comb my cupboards for something exotic we can make."

Raina knew exotic wouldn't help Lily stop missing her

husband—it wouldn't help her forget she was a widow. But cooking a meal with her friends could be a start.

As Shep sat in an examination room at the Family Tree Health Center the following Wednesday, one thought kept racing through his mind—he should have kissed Raina when he had the chance.

He felt awkward now, sitting here while she examined Manuel. And he hadn't felt awkward at any time on Saturday. Not even after he'd almost kissed her.

Shep waited until she stopped examining Manuel's right ear. "We had a good time on Saturday." When she met his gaze without hesitation, he added, "*I* had a good time on Saturday."

"I did, too," she admitted.

Shep's blood ran faster. The exam room suddenly got hotter.

Breaking eye contact, Raina crouched down to Manuel. "You were such a good boy for me today. How about a sticker for your shirt?" She reached over to the counter, grabbed a strip of stickers and held it out to Manuel. "Can you point to the one you'd like?"

Manuel glanced up at her and then back at the stickers. He pointed to one of a cowboy and a horse, with a rope that sparkled with glitter.

"Good choice," she assured him with a smile, peeled it off its backing and put it on the right side of his shirt.

He kicked his legs and said "Horsey," then ran his finger over the silver rope.

"So he's healing like he should?" Shep asked.

"He's doing great. If there aren't any problems, I won't need to see him for three months."

Three months might be okay for Manuel, but it wasn't for Shep. He cleared his throat. "So you enjoyed the trail ride?"

Her arm around Manuel, she met Shep's gaze again. "Yes."

"How about you and I go on a trail ride together *without* pint-size chaperones?"

She looked surprised. Before she could say no, he added, "Maybe we could pack a picnic and explore Red Creek a little more. What about your day off?" He was keeping it light, easy and as casual as he could.

Raina hesitated. "I have two surgeries tomorrow morning, but then I don't have office hours for the rest of the day."

"Tomorrow?" It took him a moment to wrap his head around that. He thought he'd have time to get prepared, to ready himself for the idea. But then again, he didn't want her to change her mind.

He'd been leaning against the wall, arms crossed over his chest. Now he unfolded them and approached the table where Manuel was seated. Raina was wearing a smock printed with cartoon characters today. Underneath, a pale pink silky blouse was tucked into cream slacks.

This close to her, the rush of heat targeted very strategic parts of his body. "Can I ask you something personal?"

"You can ask."

"Have you dated since your husband passed on?"

"No, I haven't. Some of my friends in New York thought I should, but I couldn't. I guess I just wasn't ready."

"And now?"

"Are we going on a date?" she asked with a half smile that revved up his libido even more.

He chuckled. "That's a fair question. I'd like to think of it as one, if that doesn't rattle you too much."

"If I just think of it as a picnic and trail ride, I won't get rattled."

"Are you sure?" He gazed deeply into her eyes and could feel the undeniable attraction pulling between them.

She ducked her head.

But he wouldn't let her get away with that. He gently put his thumb under her chin, and she raised her gaze to his once more. "I think we should call a spade a spade," he said.

"Or a date a date?" she teased.

"Yeah."

After a hesitant moment, she asked, "What time do you want me there?"

"Whenever you're done here." He dropped his hand to his side, wanting to smooth his fingers over her cheek…brush her hair behind her ear…taste her lips.

She was looking at him as if she might want to do the same. "I'll make sure my cell phone is charged this time." Then she confided, "Shep, the boys made it easy last Saturday. When it's just you and me… I haven't dated for a *very* long time."

"I hear it comes back easily. It's just like riding a horse. You never forget how." Then he did touch her again. He just couldn't help it. He brushed the back of his hand over her cheek. "We're just going to spend a little time together, Raina. We can talk, ride, hike—whatever we want. No pressure. No expectations."

"That sounds good."

"Wide horsey?" Manuel asked, interrupting them.

Shep lifted his son from the table, held him up in the air and made him squeal. "You're a little young for a horsey. At least a real one. Maybe at Christmas, Santa will bring you a make-believe one."

Gathering Manuel into his arms, Shep carried him to the door. He was already looking forward to tomorrow.

No pressure. No expectations. For either of them.

Raina had been jittery on the drive to Shep's. But now, as they stood in the corral, the jitters were gone because she was worried he'd change his mind. He'd seemed distracted ever since she arrived. She wasn't going to stay if he didn't want to go on this trail ride.

He held the reins to her horse for her so she could mount. But she didn't. Instead, she said, "I know you probably have a hundred other things you need to be doing."

He looked surprised at her comment. "Why do you say that?"

"Because you seem far away. I don't want to keep you from—"

"You're not keeping me from anything." He rubbed his hand over his face and gazed at her with consternation. "You're too—"

"Perceptive?" she filled in sweetly.

He laughed then, a genuine laugh. "That's one of the words for it."

She waited, already knowing Shep used an easy grin and warm humor to deflect a discussion he didn't want to have.

"I'm concerned about Joey," he admitted. "But being

concerned about him isn't going to change anything right now, so let's just head into the sun and enjoy being alive." As soon as the words came out of his mouth he grimaced. "I always step into it with you, don't I?"

"Shep, you don't have to watch what you say. I'd like nothing better right now than to ride with the sun on my face."

He stepped toward her slowly, as if he wanted to touch her. In fact, she thought he might play with the tips of her hair as he had once before. Excitement—and apprehension—tingled through her down to her fingertips, and she knew that was because she'd like to touch him, too.

But instead of reaching toward her, he took a step back. "Do you need a leg up?"

"No. As long as you hold Lazybones, I'll be fine." Though she didn't know if she really would be. Her hands were shaking now. She couldn't recall the last time a man had made her feel exactly like this.

She reached for the saddle horn, put her foot in the stirrup and took a hop up all at the same time. She was in the saddle now, but Shep was standing beside her, just in case she'd have a problem climbing up. She considered herself a supremely independent woman. Yet Shep's protective manner made her feel feminine and looked after.

Their horses walked side by side as they rode out of the corral. A whispery breeze lifted her hair, brushed her face and seemed to cleanse her. The week of surgeries, appointments, her concern about Lily—it all seemed to shed from her shoulders until she felt renewed.

Shep kept pace with her as they soaked in the brush and the crooked fence line, the end-of-summer colors. One field was still dotted with yellow flowers. In the distance she caught sight of the fields of white cotton, and farther away, wind turbines that seemed to stand like protective sentinels. All of it was Texas now, the old and the new, the wild and the tame.

As she turned toward Shep at the same time he glanced at her, she realized he was still part of the wild side of Texas, even though on the outside he sometimes seemed tame. Was that why he excited her? Was that why she could forget the past when she looked into his blue eyes and got lost in a sensual haze? Tall, with a physique that showed he wasn't afraid of hard work, he rode a horse as if he were one with it.

They rode along the same trail they'd taken with the boys, but when they reached the creek they turned east instead of west.

"I know a spot," Shep said, "where the horses will be happy. There's a clearing for a picnic and more wild-flowers than brush. I stuffed one of those NASA space blankets into the saddlebag, too, so we won't have to worry about ants crawling on our plates."

She laughed. "You thought of everything. Do you do this often?"

"I bring the boys out here a lot. They think walking along the creek is pure fun. But it's a chance for me to teach them about marking a trail, learning what plants to stay away from—things like that."

Shep seemed to know that the best ways to parent were the most subtle. But she often got the impression he wasn't sure at all about how he was handling his sons. Was it because he hadn't had a good role model?

That was none of her business, especially since he'd shied away from talking about his childhood.

Shep led them through tall grass, sage and tiny yellow flowers, where butterflies darted here and there. Riding beside Shep, Raina couldn't imagine a more beautiful day.

Eventually he slowed and pointed ahead. "We can climb down here and tether the horses under those trees."

Shep quickly dismounted and stood by Raina's side, making sure she hopped to the ground safely. Standing close by, he waited until she was safely on the ground, then tethered the horses. The clearing under pecans and cottonwoods seemed to be a peaceful bit of paradise, as the creek water rushing over rocks into a natural dam sent crystal spray into the breeze.

"Would you like to hike first, or eat first and then work it off?"

"Maybe we could just sit and talk for a while and then decide."

Shep gave her a long look. "Anything in particular you want to talk about?" He sounded a bit wary.

"Not really. I thought maybe you could tell me what the problem was with Joey."

"You really want to hear that?"

"They're good kids, Shep. If there's anything I can do to help, I'd like to."

After he gave her another studying look, he nodded. "Let me get that blanket so the grass doesn't poke us."

She had to smile. Shep was definitely a practical man, and she appreciated that.

Once he'd spread the silver blanket on the ground, they settled under a canopy of leaves. Raina kicked off her boots and tucked her legs beneath her. "So tell me what's wrong. You really seemed worried this morning."

Shep stared into the creek, then brought his gaze to hers. "Last week the nurse from the school called me. She said Joey didn't feel well. He had a stomachache. So I picked him up and brought him home. He was mopey for a couple of hours but then seemed to be fine. I thought maybe he'd eaten something he shouldn't have."

"No fever or other symptoms?"

Shep shook his head. "No. I took his temperature. I watched him that day and the next. But he ate okay. He played with his brothers and didn't act sick."

"Did something else happen?" she asked.

"Yeah. Monday he didn't want to go to school. He said his stomach hurt again. He cried and threw a fit, so I let him stay home. But something about it just didn't feel right, so I took him in to see Tessa Rossi."

"Tessa's got a good eye, and she's thorough."

"Yeah, she is. She examined him and asked him a list of questions. She didn't find anything. She said we could run a bunch of tests, but I hate to put him through that without good cause. Especially when she thinks something else could be going on."

"Like something at school?" Raina guessed.

"Possibly. I don't know. I can't get him to talk to me. And Roy is just as close-mouthed. If he knows anything, he's not saying."

"Did you speak with Joey's teacher?"

"That's next on the list. I have a phone conference with her tonight."

Raina couldn't help moving a little closer to Shep, reaching out and touching his arm to offer comfort. But as soon as she did, everything changed between them. Instead of just engaging in friendly conversation, she felt connected to him in an elemental way. Her heart beat so fast she could hardly breathe, and the air around them seemed electrified.

Somehow, she managed to find a few words. "You'll figure it out."

The blue of his eyes had suddenly deepened. She knew he, too, felt the change in the air between them.

His voice was husky when he said, "This could be up to Joey. If he can't trust me, it's going to be hard going for us both."

Shep shifted, leaned forward and sandwiched her hand between his and his arm—his very strong forearm. "I didn't bring you out here today to talk about the boys."

After only a moment's hesitation, she asked, "Why *did* you ask me out here today?"

"Because I like you," he said simply. "And because when I'm with you, all I can think about is kissing you."

Her stomach did a flip. Her heart fluttered. The sun seemed even brighter and the sky even bluer.

"Say something," he muttered. "If you want me to get back on my horse and forget this conversation ever happened—"

"I don't want you to get back on your horse," she almost whispered.

He took off his hat and set it on the blanket, out of the way. When he leaned in closer to her, she closed her eyes.

But his mouth didn't cover hers. Instead, she felt his lips touch, whisper soft, slightly above her ear. "A kiss shouldn't be too quick." His voice was husky with desire.

"No?" she asked, her pulse pounding in her temples, her cheeks getting warm.

When he brushed his jaw against her cheek, she noticed only the slightest bit of stubble. The sensation was so erotic she felt her nipples harden.

His hand, still covering hers, now moved up her arm and under her hair. "If a man goes for a woman's lips right away, the kiss is over too fast. So I like to ease into it."

His lips brushed the corner of her mouth and her breaths came fast.

"Or would you rather just get it over with?" he asked against her mouth.

She shook her head, and when she did, her lips rubbed back and forth across his. Like flint on tinder, heat sparked. Suddenly they were kissing, with no chance to go back to slow and easy. He held her head with both hands as his tongue slid into her mouth.

Her response was instinctive and inflammatory. It had been too long since she'd felt like this. So long. Shep made her feel beautiful and desirable, protected and wanted. She let those feelings rule her as she wound her arms around his neck.

She couldn't seem to get enough of him. The kiss that had started easy, that had grown sensual, had now turned into raw hunger. The excitement of the moment and the heat they were generating drove them on.

Shep stretched out his long legs against hers. Side by side they held on to each other. She was driven by something she didn't understand, something she didn't want to think about right now. She just wanted to feel—feel like a woman, feel Shep, feel him touching her. He *would* touch her if she touched him.

She slid one hand under his shirt placket and unfastened the snap. Her fingertips met hair and bare skin.

Shep groaned and lifted her T-shirt to unfasten her bra.

Raina had never been impulsive, never been impru-
dent, not in her whole life. But now she felt reckless and
invigorated and awake to her sensuality in a way she
hadn't been for almost a decade. She wanted Shep's
hands on her body. She wanted to know she was capable
of responding. She needed this tough, enigmatic
cowboy to make her come alive.

He seemed to need her, too. He invited her taunting
caresses by murmuring, "That's it, Raina. That's
exactly right."

When he'd given her breasts enough attention to make
her grip his shoulders tightly, she cried, "I want more."

"More of this or more of something else?"

"More of *you*," she said almost mindlessly.

He unzipped her jeans and pulled them down far
enough that he could insert his hand into her panties. Then
he stroked her until she didn't have a coherent thought.

In a frenzy of desire now, they feverishly undressed
each other. When they were both naked, Shep covered
her body with his, kissed her once more and asked, "Are
you ready?"

Her desire for Shep seemed to consume her. "Yes,"
she told him, breathlessly.

At first, Shep slowly guided himself inside her. She
moaned, tasting passion, so hungry for it she could only
arch up to him and clutch his shoulders, pleading for
more. He plunged into her, and the speed at which they
took each other robbed them both of all their breath.
Raina's body wound tight, tensed and released with
shattering tremors that made every nerve ending quiver.
She felt Shep's climax end in a groaning shudder.

Raina held on to him tight, needing to feel his body against hers to prove what they'd just experienced had been real.

She was fine, really okay, until Shep rolled off her and onto his side. Then she closed her eyes and took a deep breath. Suddenly she had to blink fast to force away tears. But blinking didn't help.

So many emotions assaulted her—regret, confusion, guilt, pent-up feelings of loss. Yet joy and tingling pleasure were still alive in her body from Shep's touches, caresses and kisses.

What had she done?

Giving in to feelings she couldn't push back, she finally had to let her tears run down her cheeks, because they had nowhere else to go.

## Chapter Five

"What's wrong?" Shep asked, looking horrified that he'd caused this reaction in her.

Raina couldn't stop her tears long enough to tell him none of this was his fault. She couldn't even catch her breath.

Really worried when she didn't answer, he rolled to his side. "Did I hurt you?"

"No!" The word was a burst of emotion into the stillness of the peaceful day.

"Then what's wrong?"

She shook her head and just held up her hand to signal she needed a few moments to figure it all out.

Quickly, he pulled on his briefs and jeans and buckled his belt. Then he waited without touching her.

She figured she'd spooked him as much as she'd spooked herself.

He handed her her panties and jeans and didn't look away as she dressed, obviously determined to find out what was going on. Eventually, after she'd adjusted her bra and rebuttoned her blouse, her tears slowed.

Thoughts zipped through her mind and she said the first one that found its way to her mouth. "This was a mistake. I shouldn't be here with you."

The lines along Shep's mouth became more pronounced, and she could tell he was restraining his response. "Why?" he asked, calmly.

She was grateful for his calm. If he had turned angry or frustrated or impatient, she probably would have kept all her thoughts to herself. But Shep's concerned blue eyes and his gentle waiting urged it to all pour out.

"Do you know what the date is?" Without waiting for him to answer, she continued, "It's September ninth, and Saturday is September eleventh."

"Raina."

The caring in his voice undid her even more. "You don't understand," she said, before he could say he did. "I know it's been nine years, and I didn't think another anniversary would be so raw. But it's not just Clark and what happened to him and all the others. It's the memories of everything about it—going to the Family Assistance Center, applying for the death certificate, forever hearing the fire bell clang at the Ground Zero memorial service. And most of all, the finality of that sound." She shook her head, as if that could stop the memory. "Every year I remember the private memorial service we had, too. Clark's friends and relatives told stories and I made a collage of pictures. His brother pieced together videos of him."

She took a deep breath and pushed her hair back from her face with both hands.

"Tell me about it," he requested, as if he sensed more was bubbling up inside her and could form a thick wall between them if she didn't let it out.

After a long silence, sorting out the words that could express all of it, she said in a low voice, "I didn't go to class. I hardly ate. My mom stayed with me for a while, but I sent her home. Everyone kept saying they were sorry, and I didn't know what to say back. I just couldn't make sense of it."

She turned to face Shep. "When I finally returned to class, I was like a robot. But then the pace and complexity of med school gave me a routine to hold on to. Weeks and months passed, and I had a goal—to become the doctor Clark wanted me to be. That was all I thought about and all I lived for. It was my way of holding on to his memory. As the years passed, I found a rhythm. I concentrated on children and I helped them. By helping them I helped myself."

The burble of the creek and a call of a bird were the only sounds until Shep asked, "Why did you come back to Sagebrush?"

"Because I knew that to move on, I couldn't stay in New York. So I came back home to be near my family, to share a practice and make a difference here." She had told a bit of this to her friends, but had never let it pour out to this extent. Why had the dam fully burst open with Shep?

His hand clasped her shoulder for a few moments, and then, as if the contact was still too incendiary, he took his hand away. "I never meant for things to get so out of hand today."

She could hear the sincerity in his voice, still feel the warmth of his hand where it had lain. "I know you didn't. I never expected—" She dropped her face into her hands for a moment, then glanced at him again. "This isn't *me,* Shep. As I told you, I haven't dated since Clark died. I've just ignored that side of me. Yet, when I came out here today, I felt so alive, and the place is so beautiful, and you— I hadn't felt a connection like that in a very long time. I wasn't thinking of the anniversary date. I guess, subconsciously, I just wanted to feel alive." She let out a long sigh. "And that's why it happened."

"And afterward, why the tears?" he probed. "Because I wasn't your husband?"

Closing her eyes, she thought about her reaction. "It's not that simple. I just got bombarded by all the emotions a woman feels when she joins with a man. Sex was never just a physical release for me, and I guess I'm too old for it to be now. I know it is for guys, but I'm just not wired like that. It seems odd that pleasure and joy should let everything else crash in, but that's what happened."

"I knew you weren't the kind of woman to have recreational sex," he admitted. "That's why I've kept my distance. I've got three boys who need me. I'm not looking to partner up and make my life more complicated than it is."

Partner up. Was she relieved he didn't want to? Or hurt he didn't want to? What she was, was confused. "That's honest," she murmured, glad he could be.

"You were honest with me. I thought I should return the favor."

He'd already told her he didn't trust women. She'd sensed from the beginning that he was a loner and intended to run his life without having to answer to anyone else. They'd made a huge mistake today, and they both knew it.

"Do you want to go back?" he asked her.

She knew if she said "Let's have a picnic" they would have it, no matter how awkward it would be. But why put them through it? Why put them through having to make small talk and pretend they hadn't been as intimate as two people could be?

"That would probably be best," she responded, and saw the relief in his eyes. Whatever had been brewing between them had ended today—because neither of them were ready for it.

On Saturday, Shep leaned against the kitchen counter, trying to look more relaxed than he felt as Manuel's caseworker inspected his cupboards and refrigerator.

He hated these visits, but he knew they were necessary. Still, he felt one wrong move, one wrong word and she could swoop Manuel out of their lives.

"Did you find what you're looking for?" he asked, with some attempt at levity.

Uncharacteristically quiet, Roy and Joey sat at the kitchen table eating lunch. Manuel poked at the noodles on his tray, smearing cheese on the vinyl and then across his mouth.

Carla Sumpter, a tall brunette in her forties, gave a weary sigh. "Mr. McGraw, you know this is just routine. Could I have a word with you on the porch while the boys finish their lunch?"

Manuel suddenly decided he'd had enough of lunch. "Daddy, Daddy. Up! Up!"

Ignoring Carla for the moment, Shep went to Manuel, lifted him from his high chair and took him to the sink, where he proceeded to wash his hands and face. Manuel shook his head from side to side, avoiding the damp paper towel, but Shep made a game of it and soon the little boy was giggling.

"Mr. McGraw." The caseworker reminded him she was there.

He faced her and said, "The boys come first, even before your report. Just give me a few seconds and I'll come out on the porch with you." Crossing to the table, he said to Roy and Joey, "Each of you can have two cookies from the bakery box. I know how many are in there, so don't try to fool me." He winked at them. "I'll be right outside."

Roy crooked his finger at Shep.

Shep leaned down toward him.

Roy asked, "She's not going to take Manuel with her, is she?"

Roy asked this every time the caseworker visited. "No, she's not. Now eat a cookie and drink your milk. I'll be back."

Two minutes later, he was standing on the porch with Mrs. Sumpter. He took his key ring out of his pocket and handed it to Manuel to keep him occupied.

Shep had to admit he was distracted today. He had been for the past two days. In spite of his attempt, he hadn't been able to stop thinking about Raina. Especially today—September eleventh. He'd thought about calling her. But his gut told him to leave her alone—for now. In a few weeks, he'd have to check on her. They hadn't used protection, and he would have to find out if she was or wasn't pregnant.

Although images of Raina and their day together had kept him awake the past two nights, he shifted his focus to Manuel.

Carla wiped a little smear of cheese from Manuel's cheek with her forefinger, and he grinned at her. She smiled back. "I'm glad his operation went well. He does seem to be hearing better. You said your housekeeper is shopping today?"

"Yes. Some sale she wanted to go to in Lubbock. She'll be driving to Amarillo later in the month to see her sister. She needs a few things for that."

"How long will she be away?"

"Three or four days."

"And you think you can handle all three yourself?"

"I spend as much time with them as Eva does." He tried to keep his voice from showing his impatience. "When she leaves after supper, it's me and them. On her days off, it's me and them. Believe me, Mrs. Sumpter, we'll be just fine when she's away."

She peered inside the kitchen where Roy and Joey were comparing the size of their cookies. Then her gaze returned to Manuel again. With her purse under her arm, she descended the steps. "I hope so, Mr. McGraw. I do hope so."

As he watched her make her way to her car, he looked forward to the day when her visits would end. He looked forward to the day when he was officially Manuel's dad.

Smoothing his hand over his little boy's hair, he thought of Raina again and how good she was with his boys. Did they need a mother?

Not as much as they needed one stable person in their lives who would never leave them. Shep knew he was that person.

For the past few days, Raina had told herself not to panic. Yes, her period was late. But it could just be...stress.

The problem was—she was never late. Never, ever. Not even through the most horrible time of her life.

So she'd done what any woman in this position would do. She'd gone out and bought two pregnancy tests last night on her way home. Angie had just switched to the day shift and left for work. Raina was alone in the house.

Despite reminding herself once again not to panic, she still was. A few minutes later, she waited in the bathroom, staring at the thermometerlike stick lying on the vanity. She read the code on the display window.

Her head swirled as she realized what the message meant. She was pregnant. Hurriedly, she unwrapped the second package, hoping the first was a mistake and would say something different.

But deep down she already knew the reading was true. She was carrying Shep's baby.

It would take a few minutes until her world righted itself and she could figure out what she was going to do next.

"You're pregnant?" Ryder Greystone's voice was filled with astonishment.

"That's what I said." Raina sat quietly beside her brother on his patio Sunday evening, looking up at the sky, trying to decide what to do.

"Who's the father?" Her brother's voice was gruff,

and she knew this was hard for him. He'd always been the kind of big brother who wanted to take care of his little sister.

"Shep McGraw." Raina explained how she'd met Shep and the boys.

"I heard he was adopting three boys. What's his story? Why did he do it?" As a cop, as a detective, Ryder was always looking for motives.

"He was born in this area. Then he and his mom moved to California after his dad died. He ended up in the foster-care system there. He insists his goal is to give kids more than a temporary home, a home like he never had."

"So this guy blows into town, buys a ranch, a lumberyard, and adopts a few kids. I think I'll do a background check."

"Ryder."

Ryder's suspicions stemmed from the fact that he'd seen his share of domestic violence, as well as women harmed by con men. But Shep didn't fit into either category.

"Just let me check around, Raina. I don't want you getting involved with someone you shouldn't get involved with. And don't lecture me on how you have to live your life on your own terms. Go ahead, do that. Just let me be in the background making sure those terms are good ones. You deserve the best. And if this guy isn't the best, you need to know."

"He's a wonderful dad. I think that tells a lot about a man."

"How long have you been dating him?"

That one was hard to answer. She didn't want her brother to know their first date had ended in making love under a cottonwood. "Ryder, Shep and I connected. It happened fast."

"You're not impulsive."

"I was this time. Isn't that obvious? We didn't use protection. We didn't even think about protection."

"Too much information," Ryder said with a shake of his head.

"You were grilling me. I get confused between an interrogation and what a brother should know."

He chuckled. "Raina, sometimes I don't know what to do with you."

"Just don't tell Mom yet. Once I know what I'm going to do—" The cell phone in her purse beside her chair beeped. She plucked it out, thinking it might be Lily. However, the number on the screen was Shep's. Her heart started beating even faster than it had when she'd told Ryder her news as she answered the call.

"Hi, Shep." That was lame, but she didn't know what else to say, not yet anyway.

"Raina, hi. How are you?"

"I'm fine." Had he called for that reason? Had he called to see if she was pregnant?

"I don't know if I believe you. You weathered September eleventh okay?"

Had he been thinking about her that Saturday? It sounded as if he had been. "I weathered it." She didn't want to go into it now, with her brother listening.

"I thought about calling you. But it seemed better just to let everything…settle."

She knew exactly what he meant. "Is that why you called tonight?"

"I called for more than one reason. But I don't want

to talk about them on the phone. For starters, do you by any chance have the name of a nurse I could call who would come to stay with the boys overnight?"

That question hadn't even been on her clipboard. "A nurse? Why do you need a nurse?"

"I don't need a nurse per se, but I've got a sick horse, and Eva's away in Amarillo. I might be able to take Roy and Joey to the barn with me and let them sleep in bedrolls, but I can't do that with Manuel. All I would need is the caseworker showing up and finding out about it. So I've got to do this right."

"You have to stay with the horse all night?"

"Possibly. He has colic. I don't want to lose him."

An idea rolled around in her head, and she knew she should dismiss it. But she did need to talk to Shep, and at least she'd have a reason for being at the ranch. Before she changed her mind, she said, "I'm not on call this weekend. Why don't I come out and stay overnight with the boys and get them ready for school in the morning. Do you think that would be okay with them?"

"I'm sure that would be fine with them, but are you sure you want to do it?"

She knew what he meant. When she'd left his ranch, she'd had no intention of seeing him again. Or he her. But now everything had changed. "We do need to talk. Besides, I've missed the boys."

"They asked me about you, when you'd be coming to the ranch again."

"What did you tell them?"

"The truth. That I didn't know."

She could just blurt out the fact that she was pregnant. But that wasn't the way to handle this. She didn't know exactly what was—she just knew that wasn't the way. "I'm at Ryder's now. I'll have to go back home to pick up a couple of things. But then I'll be there. It will probably take about a half hour."

"You're a godsend, Raina. Thanks for offering to do this. If you have second thoughts on your way, though, and you can think of the name of someone else to call, let me know."

"I'll be there, Shep."

"A promise?"

"A promise." She could almost see his crooked smile as she closed the phone.

"You're driving out there tonight?" Ryder asked with a bit of disapproval in his tone.

"Shep has a sick horse and needs help with the boys. He can't leave them alone."

"I thought he had a nanny."

"She's away."

"How much older is she than he is?"

"Ryder!"

"How much?" he grumbled.

"About fifteen years. There's nothing going on between them except respect and affection."

"I'm still going to do a background check."

"I don't want you to. You're not going to find anything. He's a good man."

"Men who have been away for years and then return have a past. In that past, sometimes there are secrets."

Did Shep have secrets? Didn't everybody?

Standing, she went over to her brother and hugged him. "Please, Ryder. Just let me live my life. Okay?"

He didn't answer her.

Straightening, she picked up her purse and shoved the strap over her shoulder. "Remember, don't tell Mom anything."

"You *are* going to tell her you're pregnant."

She sighed. "In good time. I have to figure out what I'm going to do first."

"Keep in mind one thing, will you?" he asked soberly.

"What's that?" She thought he might insist she didn't have to be involved with Shep McGraw simply because she was carrying his child.

He told her something else. "I want you to think of yourself this time, Raina."

She wasn't sure what he meant. "Do you want to explain that?"

"When you married Clark, you supported his lifestyle as a fireman. You fit yours around it. After Clark died, you thought about his family, about his friends, about grants you could give to fire companies in his name, instead of using that money to make your life easier and secure."

"I used some to finish med school. That was all I needed."

"I know what you used. You needed a lot more than you gave away. The fact is, I don't think you really thought about yourself until you moved back here. Don't stop now. You consider what's best for you and your baby."

"I will," she promised him, already focused on the life growing inside of her. She would always do what was best for her baby.

Parking next to the veterinarian's van, Raina closed her car door. As she began walking toward the house, Shep strode across the lane from the barn, holding Manuel.

Roy and Joey were tight on his heels. Roy asked in excitement, "Are you going to put us to bed tonight?"

"I think I am."

Her gaze met Shep's and the world shook a little, a leftover seismic tremor from what had happened between them that day under the cottonwoods.

"Thanks for coming."

She felt herself blushing, something she couldn't remember happening before she'd met him. "Have you been trying to take care of the kids, the ranch and a sick horse all by yourself?"

"I'm definitely not super-rancher," he said with a crooked grin. "The man who tends to the horses most days stayed late. He just left when the vet arrived. I do know my limits."

In a way, she guessed that Shep thought he didn't have many limits. She wasn't sure what had given her that idea. He seemed to be able to tackle anything, and do a good job of it, whether it was adopting the boys or seeing to the ranch and handling the lumberyard business. She considered what Ryder had said about doing a background check and she liked the idea even less now than she had earlier. She'd have to tell him again to let it go.

As they started toward the house, Roy tucked his little hand in hers and a warm feeling enveloped her. She hadn't thought much about being a mother over the past few years—not since losing Clark. Now, with Roy's hand in hers, and the knowledge that she had a little life growing inside of her, she realized a forgotten dream could come true.

Once they were on the porch, she held out her hands to Manuel. He pursed his lips, made a sound like an engine and then lunged toward her. She caught him with a laugh, holding him close.

When Shep touched her elbow, she felt a shaft of heat rush through her. "I might have to spend most of the night in the barn. In the morning, we can talk."

Raina nodded, her throat suddenly tight. All she wanted to do was blurt out the words and see Shep's reaction. Yet, on the other hand, she wanted to keep the secret to herself, just in case telling Shep would change her life in a way she didn't want. She wasn't sure what to expect from him. Just how well *did* she know him?

Ryder's point exactly.

"We can talk when the crisis is over."

"Sometimes there seems to be one after another."

Releasing her arm, he ran his hand over Manuel's hair. She wondered what kind of dad Shep would be with a daughter. Protective, that was for sure. Probably doting, too. But he already had three children. Would he want another? And if he did, then what? How would she handle having him in her child's life? In *her* life? Attraction was one thing. Parenting was another.

"The boys had showers before supper. You can skip Manuel's bath tonight, if you'd like."

"I don't mind. We'll make a playtime of it."

"I've been putting cotton in his ears in case he splashes. I have those little earplugs, too. They're on top of the chest in his room."

"I won't forget," she said, amused that he'd think she would.

"No, I guess not," he responded with some chagrin. "I'm just trying to think of anything that could crop up."

She raised her eyebrows. "I'm thirty-seven, Shep, and my coping skills are pretty good. Even if your boys throw me a curve, I'll try not to strike out."

He laughed at her sports imagery. "Okay, I get the picture." His gaze lingered on hers for a few more seconds, and that made her tummy shimmy—and not from evening sickness.

"I can show you to the guest bedroom upstairs—"

"We'll show her," Roy piped up. "It's next to ours," he explained to Raina.

Shep gave Roy a pat on the back. "Thanks. I know you and Joey will make Dr. Gibson feel right at home."

Showing Raina just how prepared he was, Shep pulled a card from his pocket. "That has my cell phone number on it. I'll have it with me. If you need anything, just call."

Again she nodded.

After a last, long look at her and Manuel, he said, "I'll see you in the morning, boys," turned and jogged down the steps, not stopping his fast pace until he reached the barn. There he tossed another look over his shoulder at her and disappeared inside.

During the rest of the evening, Raina played mom. She had to admit, giving Manuel a bath while Joey and Roy brushed their teeth and put on their pj's felt natural. After settling Manuel in his crib, she sat on the boys' twin bed, Joey and Roy on either side of her, and read them their favorite story. The words rolled off her tongue as if she'd read it before, but she hadn't. They laughed and asked her to read their favorite pages over.

As Joey leaned forward to point to a picture, a medal

on a chain swung from around his neck. Raina asked, "That's St. Christopher, isn't it?"

Joey's fingers closed around the medal. "Yeah, it is. My dad who died gave it to me. He said it would always keep me safe."

"I have one, too," Roy remarked, as if he didn't want to be left out. "Mine's in a box in my drawer. I was afraid I'd lose it. So my dad…" He hesitated. "My dad in the barn said that's best for now."

"I think your medals are wonderful remembrances," she said softly.

Obviously wanting to change the subject, Joey asked, "Can we get a drink of water?"

The brothers tried to stall their bedtimes, but finally they settled in, tired from a weekend full of activities with Shep. Joey had seemed quieter than Roy, but then he always was. She wondered about the stomachaches, if he was still having them, but didn't bring them up.

Before she'd given Manuel his bath, she'd deposited her backpack in the guest bedroom and hung her outfit for office hours the next day in the empty guest-room closet. Apparently Shep didn't have overnight visitors often.

After taking her own shower, slipping into feminine pink plaid boxers and a T-shirt, she lay on top of the covers with a magazine she'd brought along, thinking she'd read for a little while, just in case the boys didn't go right to sleep. However, she must have been as tired as they were, because she drifted off.

The next thing she knew, she felt a hand on her shoulder—a large, warm hand. Thinking she was dreaming, she leaned her cheek against the fingers, remembering Shep's sensual touches by the stream.

"Raina?"

His voice was husky, deep, louder than a dream.

Instantly, she came awake and found Shep leaning over her.

## Chapter Six

The light from the hall cut a swath into the guest bedroom, putting Shep in silhouette as he gazed down at Raina.

The same look had been in his eyes before they'd made love. No, not made love. They didn't know each other well enough for that. Still, she couldn't have had sex with him if she hadn't felt a deep connection. Did he feel that connection, too? Or had it only been pleasure he'd been after—a relief from his life with his boys.

He dragged a wooden chair from alongside the bed and sat facing her. "It's around midnight. I wanted to make sure everything was okay up here."

"How's the horse?"

"Buttermilk is coming along. Ed came back to help out. He's walking him while I make us some coffee."

Shep was looking at her pink T-shirt, appraising her plaid boxer shorts. She'd left the window open and hadn't bothered to cover with the sheet. Now she felt a little uncomfortable, especially without a bra. "The boys are fine. I read them a story while Manuel fell asleep."

"How many glasses of water did they ask for?"

"Three, but they only got two."

He chuckled. "If I don't set a boundary, they'll test me until I draw one."

"Manuel's the sweetest baby, and since I was here last, he's picked up more words and syllables. The surgery worked—I don't think he'll be far behind at all."

Okay, they'd covered the subject of the boys, and now they both knew what was coming. The pulse in her ears was pounding hard.

She hiked herself up to a sitting position and laid the magazine to the side of the bed.

"How did you really cope with September eleventh?" Shep asked, real concern in his voice.

She shrugged. "I spent most of the day with my friend Lily. She lost her husband recently and she's pregnant. We definitely understand each other right now."

"Lily Wescott? I knew her husband. Troy was a great guy."

Raina thought about how life was one big circle... just like life in Sagebrush. "I called Clark's family. Angie and Gina came over, too, late that evening. We went through photo albums. I do that every year and allow myself to relive the pain and cry. I found if I don't, if I try to ignore the day, if I think everything's going to be okay, then it isn't. Grief has a way of bleeding upward from your heart through your whole body, so it's better just to take it on."

"You're a brave woman, Raina."

She shifted on the sheet, uncomfortable with his assessment. "No, I'm not brave. I've just learned what works for me. Lily will have to find her own way. In the meantime, we can support each other. That's what friends are for. She's thinking of moving into the Victorian, and that would be terrific. We'll all help her raise her baby." Raina suddenly felt the color drain from her face.

Apparently Shep noticed. "What is it?" He took her hand, and the gesture made her confession so much harder.

She slipped her hand from his, needing her wits about her. "I'm pregnant, Shep. Two pregnancy tests were positive."

He looked stunned for a moment, took off his Stetson, twirled it in his hands, then set it back on the top of his head. "I know this pregnancy is my responsibility as much as yours, but I need a little time to take this in."

That really wasn't the reaction she'd expected, but Shep often did the unexpected. "Okay. I'll go back to sleep up here, and you can think about it while you're walking Buttermilk."

He took her hand again and this time held on. "I don't want you to feel alone in this, but right now I can't stay. I have to get back to the barn."

"I understand." And she did. But they couldn't resolve anything if they didn't talk. Obviously, Shep wasn't a big talker until he knew what he wanted to say.

Pushing back the chair, he stood, leaned down and kissed her forehead. It was a tender, light kiss, almost like a whisper. She might have imagined it.

After he put the chair back where it belonged, he went to the doorway. "Light off or on?" he asked.

"Off is fine. I need to go to sleep so I have energy for the boys in the morning."

"Remember, call me if you need me."

She had her phone on the bedside table and his number beside it. But she wasn't going to call him—because she didn't think he *wanted* her to need him.

Raina took the tray of cinnamon toast from the oven and carried it over to the table, where the boys were already starting on their scrambled eggs.

"What's that?" Joey asked.

"Cinnamon toast. My mom used to make it for me and my brother when we were your age. It's hot. I'll put a piece on your plates. You have to let it cool a little."

They had kept her stepping this morning—getting Manuel up, dressing him and readying the other two boys for breakfast, too. It was a challenge she'd enjoyed. The same thing with cooking breakfast. She hardly ever did that for herself, just grabbed a container of yogurt and a piece of fruit and ran.

She knew Shep was occupied with the veterinarian. As she cut pieces of cinnamon toast for Manuel, she wondered how the horse was faring. She wondered even more what Shep was thinking about her pregnancy.

A sudden knock at the door interrupted the boys' chatter. "Wait a couple more minutes before you try that toast," she warned them, and went to answer it. As soon as she opened it, the woman on the other side stepped back, surprised.

"Hello! I'm Carla Sumpter, Shep's caseworker. And you're…"

"I'm Raina Gibson." She could see in the caseworker's eyes that she instantly made a connection with information in Shep's file.

She wasn't sure whether to let the woman in or not. Maybe she should call Shep. But she didn't have to. Over Mrs. Sumpter's shoulder, she spotted him jogging toward the porch.

"Mrs. Sumpter! This is a surprise this early on a Monday morning. How can I help you?"

"I just thought I'd stop by for that follow-up visit and see how everyone is."

"Excuse me," Raina said. "I don't want to leave Manuel for too long."

The caseworker wouldn't need to talk to her, so she hurried back to the kitchen, where she put bite-size pieces of toast on Manuel's tray. He already had some scrambled eggs in his hair, and she tried to brush them away.

Roy looked up at Raina. "*Her* again?"

Raina tried to suppress a smile. "You don't like when she visits?"

Roy shook his head vigorously. "She puts ants in my pants."

Joey explained, "That means she makes us all nervous, especially Dad."

Raina had never seen Shep nervous, but then the boys probably sensed more than they saw.

As if on cue, the caseworker and Shep came into the

kitchen. "What are we having this morning?" Mrs. Sumpter addressed the boys.

"Something new," Roy told her. "Cinnamon toast."

"I see. Does Dr. Gibson cook for you often?"

Raina's mouth opened but she wasn't exactly sure what to say. She didn't have to worry because Roy filled in for her. "This is the first time. She stayed last night."

Shep's gaze met Raina's. "I explained about the horse being sick and you sleeping in the guest room."

"She gave Manuel a bath," Joey said helpfully.

"Wasn't that nice," Mrs. Sumpter said, even though Raina wasn't sure she meant it.

"Take another bite of toast, then get your things together," Shep ordered Joey and Roy. "You don't want to be late for the bus."

The brothers hurriedly took two more bites of toast, drank some milk and ran to the playroom to get their backpacks. The silence in the kitchen was awkward until they returned.

"I'll take them down the lane to the bus stop," Shep told the women. "If it's on time, I should be back here in about ten minutes. Will you be all right?" he asked Raina, in spite of Mrs. Sumpter being there.

She squared her shoulders and encouraged Manuel to eat another bite of toast. "I'll be fine."

Shep nodded to both women and led the boys to the door. After they called noisy goodbyes, they followed their dad to the bus stop.

In spite of the caseworker's attention focused on her, Raina pulled up a chair beside Manuel and offered him a sippy cup with milk.

"So. Mr. McGraw says you're Manuel's doctor," the caseworker said, prompting her.

"Yes. I've also treated Joey."

"And the two of you struck up a friendship?"

"You could say that."

"Now you're here, so I assume the two of you have some connection."

Oh, they had a connection all right, but she wasn't about to tell this woman about it.

"Are you planning to stay here while Eva is away?"

This woman was fishing. True, it was her job, but Raina still didn't like it. "No, I'm not. Shep called me and asked if I knew of a nurse who could stay overnight, and on such short notice, I volunteered myself. I've become fond of the boys."

"And Shep?"

"We respect and admire each other."

"How quaint."

Now Raina's hackles were up. "Excuse me?"

"Well, *admire* and *respect* are old-fashioned terms in a world that doesn't understand them very well."

Holding her temper, Raina returned, "That doesn't mean they can't exist."

"How old are you, Dr. Gibson?"

Taking a breath, warning herself to be tactful, she answered, "Thirty-seven."

"I assume you're single?"

"Yes. I'm widowed."

"You're young to be a widow. I assume your husband was the same age?"

"He was a few years older."

Apparently Mrs. Sumpter wasn't going to stop poking until she got the information she wanted. So Raina might as well put her life on the table. "Clark was a fireman. He died on September eleventh. I really don't want to discuss that with Manuel in the room."

"But he doesn't understand—" Mrs. Sumpter began.

Enduring enough, Raina interrupted her. "My former housemate is a baby-development expert. She believes children pick up mood and tone, as well as a sense that surrounds words when they're spoken. I remember that when kids are around. Maybe in your profession, it would be good if you did, too."

"I've been managing my job for fifteen years just fine."

"I'm glad about that. That should make Shep feel so much easier about adopting Manuel. I hope there won't be any surprises."

"That depends. If Shep is involved with you, the adoption could be delayed."

Footsteps on the porch were definitely Shep's this time. After entering the kitchen, he picked Manuel up out of his high chair. "How was breakfast, buddy?"

Manuel nodded and touched Shep's face with sugar-sticky fingers.

"Oh, so I'm going to wear cinnamon as aftershave this morning," he teased. He found a Busy Box for Manuel to play with on the table as the child sat on his lap.

Shep asked Mrs. Sumpter, "Why did you really come by this morning?"

"I'd like to finish up my questions first."

He glanced at Raina. "Does Raina need to stay?"

"Dr. Gibson is part of these questions. I want to know what the two of you are to each other."

Raina's heart felt like a high-speed train on a newly polished track.

Shep hadn't taken off his hat, and the shadow hid part of his face. "What if I told you we're trying to figure that out."

"I won't ask the obvious question, since you said you were in the barn all night and she was in the guest bedroom. But if you get married, that could add months onto the course of the adoption until we make a portfolio on Dr. Gibson. The relationship has to be examined to make sure it's healthy for Manuel."

Shep unbuttoned the top button of his shirt and looked angry. "You don't think Raina would be good for the boys?"

"I didn't say that."

"That's what you indicated. Don't you think they might need a woman's influence, kindness and warmth?"

"Every child deserves that, Mr. McGraw. But I have to see with my own eyes to know it's true. You have bonds with these boys. I know that. If Dr. Gibson is going to be in their lives, I have to see how they relate to her, too." She looked from Shep to Raina, and although they were sitting at least a foot apart, Raina wondered if the caseworker could feel the sexual tension between them. She herself certainly could. Whenever Shep was in the same room, everything seemed to buzz.

Mrs. Sumpter cast a final glance at Manuel. "All right. I think that's all I can do here today. You don't need to see me out. I can find the door. It was nice to meet you, Dr. Gibson. Maybe we'll see each other again sometime soon."

After the caseworker was gone, Raina heaved a sigh of relief. "That sounded like a threat."

"No, she just keeps her word. I'm sorry you had to go through that."

"Is she like that every time she comes?"

"She has a reason for each of her visits. This—" He pointed to her and then himself. "This just cropped up today, so she pounced on it. You handled her well."

"I told her what she wanted to know." Raina was a bit disgusted with herself about that.

"I imagine you just gave her the essentials. That was good."

"And what are the essentials, Shep? That we're friends? Is that what we are?"

The tension between them had coiled inside of her so tight that her chest hurt. She needed to know what Shep was thinking, whether or not he was going to be involved in her life and her—their—baby's.

An expression passed over his face that was something akin to determination. She didn't understand it until he rose with Manuel and settled him into his play saucer. Once the toddler was occupied, Shep stood right in front of her, staring down at her, big and looming and male. An excited thrill shot through her and, in a flash, she remembered being naked with him, joining with him, feeling guilty and confused because the pleasure had been so wonderful and taken her totally off guard.

"Marry me," he demanded, the two words jumping into the air as if he'd been waiting all night to say them.

Since they rammed into her, stealing her breath, she simply repeated them. "*Marry* you?"

His hands settled gently on her shoulders as if to

prevent her from running away. "You're carrying my baby. I want to be a dad to this child just as much as to Manuel, Joey and Roy. I want to be there when this baby's born. I want to see his or her first smile, first step, first everything. Manuel has changed and grown before my eyes, and I don't want to miss a minute of this new baby's life."

Raina swallowed hard. "I know you like being a father, Shep, but what about *us?*" Her mind was spinning with all the ramifications of what he was suggesting.

Shep's jaw tightened, as if what he was going to say was hard for him. "I've never been married. So I can only imagine what your husband meant to you, and I'm not aiming to pretend that what you and I have is anything like that. But I do know there's something between us. When we're together, we want each other. That's what led us to where we are now. We can build on that."

*Did* they have something to build on? As she'd told the caseworker, she respected and admired him. If she was truly honest with herself, she also had to admit she was falling for him. But *marriage?* "I don't know, Shep. I'm a doctor. I never imagined I'd settle down on a ranch."

Still clasping her shoulders, working his thumbs up and down her neck, he asked gently, "Are you panicked by the idea of having a baby?"

"A little."

"You don't have to be. You don't have to give up your career. Eva will help us. Our baby will have three brothers."

"But getting married might affect your adoption."

"Actually, I think it will help. You'll have to have interviews with Mrs. Sumpter and eventually appear with me before the judge. But I don't see why there would be a problem. Two parents are better than one, if they both love kids."

"You know I love kids, Shep. Yet I never imagined I'd be the mom of four—practically overnight."

"It *is* a lot to think about," Shep agreed. "I've been mulling it over in my head all night. But if you want a family and kids as much as I do, I think it's the best thing to do for all of us. But whatever you decide, I want to be a father to our baby…whether we're married or not."

Parental rights. Custody issues. A child being shuttled back and forth between two parents. How confusing would that be?

Raina considered her past nine years—her loneliness, her loss, her own childhood growing up without her father. Then she considered a life with Shep and his boys here on the ranch. In vivid recall, her tryst with him under the cottonwoods played like a movie in her mind. She could see in Shep's eyes that he was remembering, too, and he leaned forward to kiss her. His lips had almost settled on hers when Manuel began banging on his play saucer, tired of the toys there, tired of not being the center of attention.

Shep straightened, touched her cheek tenderly, then scooped Manuel from his saucer. "Marriage *is* a lot to think about. Our life together could be a challenge in a lot of ways. There's something else you might want to think about. We should have a prenup to protect us both."

Watching Shep with Manuel, studying the play of his muscles under his shirt as he hefted the toddler higher in his arms, she suddenly realized what the most challenging aspect of their marriage could be. Shep had said several times he didn't trust easily. What kind of marriage could they have without trust?

"I need time to think about all this."

Manuel leaned toward her, reaching his arms out. She lifted him and felt the joy of holding a baby, realized that in June she'd be holding *her* baby.

When her gaze met Shep's, she saw desire there…and hope. Could they have a life together?

Was she crazy for even considering his marriage proposal?

On the patio at the back kitchen entrance to the Victorian the following evening, Raina stood with Lily, looking over the yard at the purple-and-gold sunset. "I'm glad your bedroom furniture fit."

With a loud bang, Angie backed out of the screen door from the kitchen, carrying a small side table. "I think this will look great out here."

Lily gave them both a forced smile. "I should probably sell everything I put in storage, but I can't just yet."

Raina tugged Lily down to the glider rocker that had already been positioned on the patio. "You have to give yourself time. Don't do anything that doesn't feel right."

"Moving in here feels right."

"Good," Angie said. "Feel free to add whatever personal things you want. The house reflects all of us, though it might just be the two of us, once Raina makes her decision about Shep's proposal."

Last evening Raina had told Angie and Lily about Shep's proposal. Now it was time to tell them her decision. She'd been mulling over everything since yesterday.

"Do you two think I'm crazy if I say yes?"

"Depends on your reasons," Lily insisted, her full attention on Raina.

"First and foremost, I've always wanted a big family, and at thirty-seven I might not get another chance. And second, Shep is a wonderful father—those boys love him. Doesn't my baby deserve that? Doesn't *our* baby deserve two parents and a family atmosphere?"

She raised a third finger. "And the last reason is that Shep is a good man. I've been alone for so long, and he's the kind of man who makes me feel protected. I think we could have a good marriage." She blushed a little, remembering the passionate intimacy she'd experienced with Shep.

"You're really attracted to him, aren't you?" Angie asked.

"I am. I can't figure it out. My heart races and my stomach gets butterflies whenever he's close."

Lily spoke. "You've given us good reasons why marriage might work, but what do you feel about him? Because in the end, that's what's important."

"To be honest, I'm confused. All these years, I felt as if I was still married to Clark. It's hard to turn off that life to start a new one. I don't want to ever forget what we had, who he was, how brave he was—though I know I can't hold on forever. With this baby coming, I have to look forward."

"We'll be pregnant together," Lily said with a real smile.

Raina laughed. "Yes, we will." Then she became serious again. "But I feel if I do this, I'm deserting you when you've just arrived."

"That's nonsense," Lily assured her. "Angie will be here, and you and I can still see each other. It's not as if you're going to fall off the face of the earth."

"No, but handling three kids, plus having a new husband and being pregnant, is going to make for long days and maybe even long nights."

The women laughed.

"Don't forget about the horses," Raina added, getting a quiver in her stomach just thinking about all of it.

"Do you really want to marry Shep?" Angie asked her.

Raina hesitated, not knowing if she was making the right decision. But she answered, "Yes, I do."

"Do you think you'll move your things to his place?" Lily asked.

"I'm not sure. He already has a house full of furniture. I could move my bedroom suite to my mom's garage."

"That's silly," Angie decided. "Just leave whatever you don't move here, then if…well…if things don't work out, you'll have a place to come home to."

The three women had been totally involved in their conversation, so involved that all three of them were startled when a deep male voice beside the patio said, "Howdy, ladies."

Raina swung around. "Shep!"

"I rang the front bell but no one came. Then I heard voices from back here. I didn't mean to interrupt."

As Lily went over to Shep to introduce herself, Raina wondered how much of the conversation he might have overheard. What must he be thinking?

Lily said, "I'm Lily Wescott. I work at Family Tree with Raina. I just moved in today."

Shep gave Lily's hand a firm shake. "It's nice to meet you. I knew your husband and I'm so sorry for your loss."

Lily seemed to swallow hard, but managed to say, "Thank you."

Angie crossed to Shep now and he shook her hand, too. She smiled. "I'm Angie Rigoletti, a pediatric nurse at the hospital. I work with Raina now and then, and I moved in here in August."

"I see." He studied each of the women as if he was wondering about their bonds and what made them want to live together.

Lily and Angie exchanged a look and Raina wasn't surprised when Lily asked, "Angie, do you want to help me empty some boxes?"

"Sure thing," Angie agreed. Then she added, "We have a lot to do upstairs, so don't worry about us interrupting you."

Lily and Angie were through the kitchen door before Raina could blink.

"I didn't mean to chase them away." Shep stepped up onto the patio. "If this is a bad time—"

"No, it's not a bad time. I was going to call you."

"The boys have been asking me about you."

"Is that why you stopped over?"

"No," he replied. "I came to get your answer. I need to know what direction we're headed and what steps to take next."

What steps to take next—as far as custody went? Custody worried her as much as everything else. If he was really determined to be a father, he'd want equal rights to his child. She couldn't bear the thought of a son or daughter of theirs shuttling back and forth between two households. Her decision really was the best one to make for their baby.

"I've made my decision. But are you sure you want to consider marrying a stranger?"

He closed the distance between them, smiled his crooked smile and assured her, "You're *not* a stranger. You're my baby's mother."

"Our baby," she remarked, quietly. "And if your proposal still holds, yes, I'll marry you."

She wasn't sure what she thought would happen when she said the words, but nothing did, and that surprised her a little. Attraction was still rippling between them. She felt goose bumps on her arms whenever he looked deeply into her eyes, as he did now. But he was examining her expression and she wondered what that meant. She soon found out.

"I overheard part of your conversation when I was walking along the side of the house."

"Shep—"

He held up his hand to stop her. "Look, I know this is an unusual situation. But if I commit to this marriage, I want you to know I intend to make it work. So I guess my question to you is, do you intend to do the same? Leaving your furniture here is one thing. Leaving part of your resolve here is another."

She should have realized strength of commitment would be important to Shep. They really didn't know each other, yet he seemed willing to take this step without completely trusting her. What would that mean for their marriage? Could they learn to trust as well as learn to love? After all, she knew now she was falling in love with Shep. Otherwise, she couldn't do this.

"When I marry you, Shep, I'll do everything I can do make it work. Lily and Angie are good friends and they just want to be here for me, no matter what decision I make."

The silence that fell between them was a bit awkward. "When should we tell the boys?" Raina asked. She wished Shep would touch her. She wished he'd reassure her that this ready-made family would fulfill both their dreams.

"How about tomorrow night. Why don't you come over for dinner? Then we'll tell them." He ran a hand through his hair. "I've got to be getting back so Eva can leave. By the way, she's willing to stay on and help with the baby. I didn't know what you might want to do about your practice after the baby's born."

"I don't know yet, but I have some time to think about it."

"Yes, you do. And we have a lot to talk about."

Did Shep mean practical things like prenuptial agreements, nannies and four children to raise? Or did he mean they had a lot to discover about each other?

She saw the heat in Shep's eyes before he reached for her. Then his arms were around her and his lips were on hers, firm and demanding, and a little more possessive than they'd been before.

All too soon, he pulled away and cleared his throat. Then he touched his lips to her forehead and murmured, "Good night, Raina."

The sensation of his lips on her skin was so sensual, she savored it for a moment. When she opened her eyes, she caught a glimpse of Shep's back as he headed around the side of the house.

What had she done?

## Chapter Seven

"We're getting married," Shep told his sons the following evening, as Raina held her breath in anticipation of their reaction. She thought the boys liked her, but with children, you never knew what they were thinking.

Roy immediately clapped his hands, jumped up and down and ran to her. "Are you going to be our mom?"

"No," Joey answered before she could. "She's just marrying our dad. She'll be our *step*mom."

Raina didn't think now was the time to split hairs. She didn't know what would happen with Manuel's adoption, whether it would go forward with just Shep, or if she would be included. They'd be sitting down with the caseworker soon to discuss that.

So she simply said, "I'd like you to think of me as your mom."

"That's all right, isn't it?" Roy asked his older brother. But Joey didn't look so sure. "I guess so."

Raina saw that Shep had been right in his decision not to tell them about the baby yet. This change was enough for now. She hugged Roy, crossed to Joey and knelt down before him. "It's a big decision, whether you want somebody for your mom or not. So you could just call me Raina until you decide."

"Instead of Dr. Gibson?" Joey looked to Shep for confirmation.

"If that's what Raina wants, then that's what you can do," Shep said, looking approving at how she was handling this. His approval meant a lot to her, and that surprised her.

"So you're going to live here with us?" Joey wanted to make sure he had it right.

"After we get married, I will. We're not sure when that will be yet, but we'll let you know. Tonight, I just came over to cook dinner with you. Your dad says you like tacos."

"I love tacos," Joey replied, still with a bit of wariness.

"I make my own salsa. Do you want to help?"

Again Joey looked at Shep, and Shep gave a nod. With a roll of his shoulders, he agreed. "Okay."

Apparently, Joey still firmly had his guard in place. She hoped this new situation wouldn't make his walls even sturdier. Only time would tell what was in store for all of them.

Manuel had toddled over to her and now wrapped his arms around her legs.

She stooped and picked him up. "Do you want to help, too?"

Roy made the decision for his little brother. "He can taste it."

They all laughed, and Raina hoped this was going to be the start of their new family life. It might be different from her first marriage, but just as fulfilling in its own way.

The preparations for supper were noisy and fun, with Shep exchanging glances with her often. Those glances held questions and doubts and anticipation and excitement.

After dessert, she and Shep played board games with the boys, and spin-the-top with Manuel. They put the toddler to bed first, then read stories to Roy and Joey. Finally, everyone was tucked in for the night.

They were almost out the door when Joey called Shep back in.

Raina gave them some privacy and went downstairs. She straightened up a bit, surprisingly feeling as much at home here as she did at the Victorian. Afterward, she stood at the coffee table and looked around the room, letting its warm, comfortable ambiance seep into her.

When Shep came downstairs, he found her like that and asked, "Looking for something?"

"Nope."

His face sobered. "I guess I should have asked what you want to change."

She crossed to him, feeling their attraction wrap around her as she gazed into his blue eyes. "I was looking at it through a mom's eyes, or trying to. I wouldn't change a thing."

His brows arched, and he seemed surprised at her answer. "Most women would want to come in here and redecorate."

"I'm not most women, Shep, and I don't think you'd be marrying me if I was. You've done a fine job with the place. Everything's comfortable and sturdy and made for boys. The decorations speak of your Texas heritage."

Taking her hand, he brought it to his lips and kissed each of her fingertips. She felt shivery all over. But they weren't married yet, and they still had a lot to talk about until they were.

"What did Joey want, or is that a private matter?"

"Nothing too private. He just asked me if you were going to sleep here overnight again."

"What did you tell him?"

"I told him, after we were married, you'd be moving in here and we'd be sleeping in the same bedroom. I thought I might as well be honest about it."

"Did he ask any more questions?"

"No, he just turned over and went to sleep."

After Shep led Raina to the sofa, he sat beside her. "We should go to the courthouse and fill out the applications for a license next week. How do you feel about that?"

"That would be fine."

"If you want a church wedding, we could wait."

"I don't need a church wedding, Shep." She saw a flicker of something pass over his face. Disappointment, maybe? "Do *you* want to get married in a church?"

He gave a shrug. "It doesn't matter."

"Do you want the boys to be there?"

"I think they should be. Also, I called Carla Sumpter and she said she can meet with us around six on Friday, if that's okay with you."

"That's fine. I have surgery in the morning and appointments until four. I should be free by then. Will our getting married prolong the adoption?"

"Let's not jump ahead of ourselves. We'll see what she has to say."

"I don't want to jeopardize your adoption of Manuel. We can always wait, or—"

"Getting cold feet already?" he asked with a penetrating assessment.

"No, but—"

"No *buts,* Raina. Manuel's going to be *our* son. And our baby is going to know both parents, however we have to do this."

*However we have to do this.* He was marrying her for their baby's sake, and she'd better remember that.

"You said you wanted a prenuptial agreement?"

"I think we both need one, don't you? There was a lot of information in the news about the Victims' Compensation Fund and the settlement. You need to protect what you have."

"I don't have much to protect. I used some for med school—what my scholarships didn't cover. But the rest, and any donations that came in, I gave away."

"You gave them away?" he repeated, looking shocked.

"I set up a grant program for fire companies that are affected by disasters."

"You are full of surprises," Shep said with admiration.

"I did what was right for me. And with the prenuptial agreement…" She'd considered it since he'd mentioned it, and made a decision. "Why don't we have our lawyers just draw up papers saying we take out of the marriage whatever we brought into it? That way it won't be complicated."

"I'm a wealthy man, Raina. I will definitely provide for our child and his or her future. Some should be yours if things don't work out. We're both going into this with the best of intentions, but you never know."

Suddenly she needed to get his doubts on the table. "You think I'm going to leave, don't you?"

He was silent.

"Shep, tell me why you can't believe I'll be as committed to this marriage as *you?*"

"Let's just say, history has been a forceful teacher."

"Were you involved in a serious relationship and got hurt?"

"You don't really want to hear about my past love life," he said, teasing, trying to make light of what she wanted to find out.

She met his gaze. "Yes, I do."

For a few ticking moments he was silent, staring straight ahead. When he spoke, his voice was tight. "There was a woman in California. It turned out we didn't want the same kind of life."

It was obvious he'd felt betrayed, and she wanted to know more. But she sensed Shep's protective walls wouldn't let him say more.

He was still holding her hand, and now he turned it palm up and rubbed his thumb over the center. "You're not like any woman I've ever met, and that's a good thing. I want to believe that you'll stay. But as I said, neither of us knows what will happen next." Then he smiled. "Except that you're going to have a baby—and he or she will belong to both of us."

"There's something else we need to do. Maybe

tomorrow evening we could meet with my mother and brother and tell them we're getting married."

"Are you sure you don't want to tell them without me first?"

"I've already told Ryder I'm pregnant, so he knows we're involved. Mom doesn't know anything yet."

"What did your brother say?"

"He's always on my side, no matter what happens, but he's protective. He's an older brother, so I'm not sure how he'll react to the idea of me marrying you this quickly. But that's the whole point, Shep. We *are* getting married, and I'd like to tell them together."

"If that's what you want, then that's what we'll do."

When she gazed into Shep's eyes, she saw determination and humor and desire. But if she looked deeper, she could see he'd been through a lot in his life. Telling her family they were getting married wouldn't be difficult for him. Would he eventually confide in her about his life up until the present?

In a flash of insight, she suddenly realized why facing her family wouldn't faze him. "You're willing to go through all this to be a father," she said softly.

"Yes."

Shep was a man of few words. Would he become more open with her as their relationship deepened? That was her hope.

"You're taking on a lot more than I am." He turned toward her, his thigh lodging against hers, his voice going a little husky. "Joey and Roy can be a passel of trouble, and at two, Manuel's growing into his independent stage. He says 'no' to me now," Shep added with a half smile. Showing he was thinking about their future, he continued, "I think we should build a guest cottage where Eva can stay. If you want to go back to work, maybe we can find some additional help."

Was he trying to convince her that her decision to marry him had been the right one? "Shep, moms handle three or four kids all the time."

"Not suddenly, like this. I don't want you to feel you've taken on more than you can handle."

"I'm a do-it-yourself kind of person, just as you are. Someone else helping is fine, but I think we'll want to raise our own kids. I've wanted children for a long time. The idea of taking on all of them *is* daunting, but I feel I'm ready for it. I want to be a mom just as much as you want to be a dad."

The warmth in Shep's eyes slowly turned to desire. He slipped one hand under her hair as if he relished the silky feel of it. Then he tilted her head up until her lips were very close to his. A warm breeze blew through the living room window, bringing with it the scents of overgrown fields and night dampness that was primal and filled with earthy secrets. Then there was the masculine scent of Shep, the cotton of his shirt, a trace of cologne, male pheromones. Her response to him was quick and without thought, as it always was. She twined her arms around his neck and gave herself up to the wishes that were awakening in her heart.

She'd been lost in his kiss for a few seconds…for a few minutes, when she realized Shep was pulling away. *He* had kissed *her*—but then his enthusiasm had seemed to wane. Or was it simply his restraint taking over? She felt foolish, giving in to hormones. The children were upstairs.

She was rushing headlong into this marriage because she wanted to be a mom. She wanted to protect her rights to her child, wanted a connection to a life partner that she'd missed since Clark had died. She'd fallen for Shep's strong and determined approach to life, his humor, his desire.

But had this kiss been an indication of what was going to happen in their marriage? That he'd always keep himself guarded and restrained with her? Did he want her as much as he wanted their baby?

The sobering thought had her sliding her fingers from his hair and drawing her arms to her sides.

He caught the change. "We can't expect too much," he said, leaning back against the sofa, still keeping his gaze on hers. "We have to take this slow and just see what comes."

"Are you afraid?" she asked.

"No. Just concerned that everything will work out the way we want it to."

"You mean that we'll have a good marriage?"

He nodded.

"You've never been married. I have. It does take work."

"I've never been afraid of work," he replied with a shrug and a smile. That smile made her heart flutter again, and her stomach twitter. He was one sexy cowboy.

And she was going to have to do one heck of a job selling this marriage to her family.

"This Victorian is at least a hundred years old," Shep told Raina as he walked the rooms the next morning, examining it with a builder's eye. "The way it's built, it will be here at least a hundred more."

Raina had told him they would meet her family at the Victorian, rather than at her brother's place or her mother's. She felt neutral territory was best. But Shep wasn't so sure. He'd suggested the ranch, where they could introduce the family to the boys. But Raina had wanted to go slower than that.

Shep wandered back into the kitchen where Raina was preparing iced tea.

"Be right back," she said, slipping outside onto the patio.

Trying to settle his nerves, he lifted the dessert dishes from the counter to the table and set out the napkins and silverware.

Raina returned with a smile and a handful of fresh-scented leaves. "Fresh mint." She took a sprig and held it up to his nose.

He sniffed. "That's mint, all right."

She laughed at his expression. "You're wondering why I bother. I just love the smell of mint when I'm sitting out on the patio. And it's just perfect dropped into a glass of iced tea. Will I be able to have an herb garden at the ranch?"

His large hand went around her smaller one before she could take the leaf away. "An herb garden would be nice." He took a bite of the mint leaf. "Definitely fresh."

After she took a bite, he lifted her chin. "Now let's see if we taste like mint."

He knew her mother and brother would be there any minute, but that didn't matter. The desire he felt was reflected in her gaze. Remembering their last kiss, he knew how damn hard it would be to restrain himself. This time he let a little more passion give way as his tongue searched for hers, easily tasting her and inviting her to taste him.

But she pulled away all too soon. "I don't have much time to get ready," she said breathlessly.

"It looks to me as if you *are* ready."

There was one small dish of pastries, another of cookies, a hand-painted plate with wedges of cheese and fruit. "I just have to take the corn bread from the oven. Sometimes Ryder isn't into sweets. Can you make a pot of coffee? He won't be crazy about mint tea."

Shep wasn't sure how *he'd* feel about mint tea, but he wasn't about to say so. This was Raina's evening, and he was letting her take it as far as she wanted to.

He told himself he was prepared for anything. "Is your brother going to want to throw my butt in jail for getting you pregnant?" He wasn't nervous about it, but he just didn't want to start out with her brother angry at him. Since she was close to him, Shep didn't want to interfere with that.

"Ryder's a reasonable man."

"You're saying the words, but I don't see it in your eyes."

Suddenly they heard the front door open, and Angie came hurrying in. After greeting them, she assured them, "I won't interrupt. I'll slide out the back if your mom comes in the front. I just need my laptop."

"Work?" Raina asked.

"No, Gina's wedding. All my notes are on my computer. We're going over the checklist. With the big day only a little over two weeks away, she and Logan are finally going to decide what they're doing about a honeymoon."

Raina explained, "Angie's sister Gina used to live here, too. She's marrying Logan Barnes."

"He has a son, Daniel, doesn't he?" Shep remarked.

"Do you know Logan?" Angie asked.

"He ordered supplies from us for the day-care center he built at his factory. I supervised the delivery of a lot of it and he and I got to talking. Daniel and Manuel are close together in age, so we thought they might like to play together sometime."

"That would be wonderful," Angie said enthusiastically. "We'll have to have a barbecue and invite them over. Maybe Tessa and Vince and their kids, too. Do you know Tessa Rossi, the pediatrician?"

"Yes, my boys go to her."

"Tessa used to live here, too," Raina remarked. "And one of her housemates, Emily Madison, is a midwife who works with my obstetrician. He's her husband. I'd like Emily to deliver my…our baby."

"Midwife?" Shep's chest suddenly got tight. "You're not thinking of having the baby at home?"

"What better place to have a baby? Now don't worry, Shep. You and Emily can have a nice long talk and she'll explain how safe it is, how much better for me and the baby."

Angie leaned close to Raina and whispered, "Don't spook him before the wedding."

Raina grinned at her friend. "He needs to know what he's getting into."

Raina's gaze found Shep's, and he knew she was as uncertain as he was about this marriage. Yet, he was determined to take responsibility for his child. He was also determined to look after her—and knew having her under his roof was the easiest way to do it.

*Just look after her?* the voice in his heart asked, the voice that kept him honest.

All right. He wanted her in his bed every night. He wanted to wake up to her face each morning. He wanted to watch her play with the kids.

Maybe he wanted too much.

When the doorbell rang a few minutes later, Angie hurried out the back, while Shep considered the best way to deal with a mom who would be concerned about her daughter's welfare and a cop who might look on him as the enemy.

A few minutes later, in the quaint but comfortable atmosphere of the Victorian's living room, Shep found himself offering his hand to first Raina's mother, Sonya Greystone, and then her brother. "I'm Shep McGraw," he said to the gray-haired woman who wore her hair in a sleek, chin-length cut. She had finer features than Raina, but he couldn't miss the resemblance.

Her brown gaze studied him quizzically, as if she wasn't quite sure why she was here. "It's nice to meet you, Mr. McGraw."

"It's Shep," he said with as friendly a smile as he could muster. He wasn't sure what Raina had told her family, but he could see they were unprepared for the news they were about to receive.

On his part, Ryder gripped Shep's hand hard, and the two men sized each other up quickly. Shep innately understood that Ryder Greystone would protect his sister at all costs.

After introductions and an uncomfortable moment, Ryder tossed out a conversational gambit. "I heard you turned the lumberyard around in a short amount of time and took on a few more men."

"When business is good, I can keep a stronger workforce."

"How can business be so good, with home construction down in this area?"

Shep could see Raina's eyes were already shooting daggers at her brother. But he could hold his own. More than his own.

"True, but home repairs are up," he replied to Ryder. "I have a couple of contractors who specialize in additions, and they like my products. Plus we're even trucking to outlying Lubbock areas. My suppliers are faster than some others. I can go on with other ways we've revved up business, but I'd probably bore you."

Raina motioned toward the kitchen. "Let's sit down. I have coffee, iced tea and snacks."

Shep's hand naturally settled at the small of Raina's back as they moved into the kitchen. He was aware that both Raina's mother and brother seemed to take note of the gesture. He waited for Raina to be seated first, and then he took the chair across from her brother.

"Raina tells me you have three boys, Mr. McGraw," Raina's mother said.

"Please call me Shep," he reminded her with a smile. "And yes, I do. Roy is six, Joey is eight and Manuel is two."

"Yes, she mentioned you have a toddler. He must keep you stepping."

"They all do."

"Do you have family in the area to help you with the children?" Mrs. Greystone asked.

"I have a housekeeper. She's good with them, as Raina can tell you." Raina was being awfully quiet, and that concerned him a little.

"I see," Sonya murmured. "You said you wanted me to meet Shep," she said to her daughter. "Are the two of you dating?"

Raina sat up straighter and met her mother's gaze. "We're not just dating, Mom. We're going to get married. That's why I invited you here. We wanted to tell you together."

Sonya pushed back her chair and stood, as if the words propelled her up. "Married? You aren't serious?"

Ryder looked from one of them to the other. "I think they're very serious, Mom."

"But how can this be? You didn't even tell me you'd met someone."

"I'm telling you now," Raina said calmly. "I also have something else to tell you. I'm pregnant."

At that, her mother seemed absolutely thunderstruck. The silence in the room was suffocating.

Shep took Raina's hand, not only to give her comfort, but to show her family they were a solid unit. "Mrs. Greystone, I know this news is surprising to you. But I want you to know I'll take good care of Raina and our baby."

"Have you ever been married?" Ryder asked.

"No, I haven't."

"Are you getting married because of the pregnancy?"

"Ryder, I don't think that's your concern," Raina answered.

"He's trying to make sure you're going to be happy." Shep could feel the tension in her hand, and he wished he could make this easier for her.

He addressed her brother. "I care about your sister and what happens to our child."

"Will you sit down, Mom?" asked Raina. "Let's talk."

The older woman sank down into her chair. "All right. But I don't think talking will change anything. You two have obviously made up your minds." She looked directly at her daughter. "I thought you might not marry again...after the way Clark died. I couldn't marry again after your father died."

"I know you couldn't. And I know you still love him. Just as a part of me will always love Clark."

"Just because you're pregnant doesn't mean you have to get married," Ryder advised his sister.

Anger flared in Raina's eyes. "Don't question my decisions, Ryder. I don't question yours."

"Maybe that's because mine are a little more well thought out."

Shep squeezed Raina's shoulder. "I think your family needs to let our news sink in."

Sonya still looked a little stunned. "Have you started planning a wedding?"

"We're going to get married in the gazebo at the courthouse," Raina replied quickly. "Probably in about a week. I want you to be there. You will come, won't you?"

"To the courthouse? Not a church?" Her mother seemed appalled by the idea.

Raina slipped away from Shep and went to her mother, crouching down beside her. "Mom, I'm pregnant and Shep's involved in an adoption. Our marriage will probably delay his adoption of Manuel. I need to go through interviews, and we'll have more home visits. We'd like to keep that process moving. Getting married quickly is the best way to do this."

"If you and your mom and brother would like to talk," Shep offered, "I can step outside." He didn't want to come between Raina and her family, yet he had *his* family to protect, too.

Raina shook her head. "No, you don't have to leave."

Raina's brother looked stern as he stood. "I think we should go. As you said, we need to absorb your news. Mom, what do you think?"

Sonya Greystone's gaze swung from Raina to Ryder. "Maybe that would be best. Raina, it's not that I don't wish you happiness. I do. But this is so sudden."

"I know, Mom."

Shep didn't like Raina's family leaving this way, but he couldn't see what he could do to make things any better right now. Hopefully, in time, both her mother and brother would realize he was going to be good to her, and to the baby she was carrying.

"Could that have been any more uncomfortable?" Raina asked with exasperation as she and Shep stood in the foyer, hearing Ryder's SUV pull away.

He rested his hand on her shoulder, wondering if her family had stirred up a hornet's nest of doubts. "You can still change your mind."

She was quiet for what seemed to be an exceptionally long moment. Finally, she replied, "I don't want to change my mind. Do you?"

After a look into her vibrant, dark eyes, he shook his head. "No, I don't. But if you need more time so your family's with you on this, I'll understand."

"I can't base my decisions on my family."

"Your circumstances are a little different than most. I can understand your mother's concerns."

"Oh, Shep. I've been alone for nine years! I want

a family. My mother can't expect me to live my life like hers."

"And your brother?"

"My brother will just have to get over himself. Where he's concerned, no one will ever be good enough for me after Clark."

With a gentle nudge, Shep tipped up her chin. "And what about the wedding? Are you sure you don't want to have it in your church? Your mother seems to think that's important."

Raina shook her head. "A judge will be fine."

He couldn't wait to bring Raina into his life. Yet something about her impatience to get married bothered him. Did she not want to get married in a church because she and Clark had been married in a church?

He remembered what her friend Angie had advised. *Just leave whatever you don't move here, then if things don't work out, you'll have a place to come home to.*

He knew he had to trust Raina if he wanted this marriage to work. He knew he had to forget Belinda and the fact that she hadn't wanted to share his life…just his bank account.

Bending to Raina, he kissed her. Chemistry took over, quickly arousing him. Raina's response was satisfyingly fervent. A low fire always burned between them, ready to burst into flames.

They had that. But would it be enough?

## Chapter Eight

The day of their wedding, Shep straightened his bolo tie and couldn't keep a grin from his face. Alone in his bedroom—he heard Eva corralling the boys downstairs—he thought about tonight. Raina would be his wife, under his roof, and if he was lucky…in his bed. This morning he felt like the luckiest man in the world.

He had to call Cruz. He had to tell his best friend on the planet he was getting married today. Picking up his phone, he hit a speed-dial number.

"What's going on?" Cruz asked. He and Cruz didn't talk often. That wasn't their nature. But when one called the other, something important was happening.

"I'm getting married today."

He heard Cruz's sharp intake of breath. "Who?"

"Raina Gibson."

"Manuel's doctor?"

They had spoken the night before Manuel's surgery when Shep's nerves had been jangling. "So you were listening and caught her name?" Shep joked.

He knew they always listened to each other. When they'd been kids under the Willets' "care," they'd only had each other. The Willets had invited them in when Cruz was eleven and Shep was thirteen. Shep had already had enough of foster homes and folks who didn't want to adopt an "older" child. He'd admit he'd become rebellious at the Willets', uncommunicative and defiant of authority, just waiting for the day he could be on his own.

He'd stood up to Bob Willet more than once when the man was drunk and angry in order to protect himself and Cruz. They'd made a pact to bide their time until Shep was eighteen and could try to spring Cruz from the system. They'd been naive. But they'd been like brothers then and still were now.

"I more than listen," Cruz assured him. "I heard something in your voice whenever you mentioned her name. What's the story?"

"She's pregnant."

This time Cruz remained silent.

"I know. It was stupid on both our parts. But that day— Hell, neither of us were thinking."

"Obviously," Cruz remarked drily. Then he asked, "Do you *want* to get married?"

"I do." He realized those were the words he'd be using later this morning. "She's great with the boys. And…she's different, Cruz. This isn't about money or what I can give her. It's about family and making one of our own."

"Why didn't you call sooner so I could fly out?"

"We made the arrangements quickly. And I know this is a bad time for you to get away from the ranch." After the night Shep had spent in jail, he'd been angrier than he'd ever been at authority in the form of the chief of police of Sandy Cove. So in the morning when a big man with a deep voice had shown up and invited Shep to come to his ranch—he'd be taking Cruz there, too—Shep had agreed. Anything was better than the Willets' or jail. That day had changed both his and Cruz's lives.

Matt Forester lived a couple of hours north of Sandy Cove. Shep had never known exactly how Matt had heard about his situation and Cruz's. But it hadn't mattered. After months of testing Matt, seeing if he was like all the others, Shep and Cruz had realized he was a kind man who wanted the best for them both. Matt had saved their young lives and given them a real home.

"I could get away if you wanted me to," Cruz offered.

"Maybe later this year when things are more settled."

Cruz wised up to that excuse right away. "You haven't told your wife-to-be about the foster homes and jail and Matt taking us in, have you?"

"No. Her husband was a hero, Cruz, a fireman who died on September eleventh. How would she feel if she knew I almost had a record?"

"She'd understand if she cares about you."

"I'm not so sure about that. Women want their knights to be spotless. I'm not."

"You don't trust her, do you? You still don't trust that a woman will stay. Every woman isn't your mom. Every woman isn't Belinda."

"I know."

"You *don't* know. But if you're making the leap into marriage, something must have changed."

"Raina *is* different," he repeated, maybe to reassure himself. "We just haven't known each other for long."

"But you're getting married anyway. For the boys."

"And for our baby. He or she will have two parents, brothers and a good home."

"I hope you know what you're doing."

"I do."

"Then congratulations."

After Shep closed his phone, he thought about everything Cruz had said. He thought about his troubled teenage years and the people who'd turned their backs on him.

He'd *always* be there for his kids. Today Raina would promise to be there, too.

His gut told him she really did know how to keep a promise. He hoped to heaven his gut was right.

Raina stepped into the white gazebo on the front lawn of the Lubbock courthouse, her hands clammy in spite of the warm, early October day. Handsome in his dark suit, Shep held out his hand to her, looking sober, but the boyish gleam in his eyes chased away some of her nerves. She took his hand, holding on to her bouquet with the other, and together they stepped forward and stood before the judge.

The enormity of what they were doing solemnly overtook her. Yet, as she felt the presence of her mother and brother, of Lily, Gina and Logan Barnes and Angie, of Shep's boys and Eva holding little Manuel behind them, she decided once more she was doing the right thing.

Roy suddenly called out, "Hey, Dad, are you gonna say 'I do'?"

Raina laughed as she looked over her shoulder at the brothers.

Joey jabbed Roy in the ribs, giving him a scowl, but Shep answered, "You bet I am."

A second later, Shep's gaze collided with hers, and there was something in his blue eyes that made her insides twitter with an excitement that had *nothing* to do with the pregnancy. She didn't know exactly what she was getting into, but this was going to be an adventure of a lifetime.

The judge cleared his throat, ready to begin. Then he welcomed friends and family and began a ceremony that seemed to be over in the blink of an eye.

Afterward Raina remembered keeping her gaze on Shep's and saying vows. He'd done the same. She twisted the gold band on her finger and knew she'd put one on his finger, too. Yet the ceremony was somehow a foggy blur. Because she remembered much too well her wedding to Clark? Because his voice sometimes still whispered in her ears? Because so long ago sometimes seemed like yesterday?

Yet, when Shep held her in his arms, bent his head and kissed her, she was nowhere but here—in this gazebo, in front of the courthouse, kissing him. Shep's kiss was all about the two of them, and not the past. Maybe she *was* as important to him as their child. She became totally involved, totally responsive, awesomely excited, even here, even now…with a world of people watching.

Applause rang out as the kiss ended. Everyone was clapping—except for her mother and brother. What was she going to do about that? How could she convince them to support her decision?

Her mother might be easier to win over than her brother, especially if she spent any time around Shep's children. She'd have that chance in a little while. Gina had offered to host their reception on the Barnes estate. At first, Shep had refused, saying they could throw the party at the ranch. But Gina had come to both of them, convinced Shep that she and Raina were good friends and she and Logan wanted to do this for them. He'd reluctantly given in. Raina understood he didn't want to be beholden to anyone, something else she'd learned about her new husband.

Before Shep let her go, he murmured close to her ear, "You look beautiful today."

She'd chosen a Western-cut, cream lace dress with a fringed neckline and hem, and cream leather platform sandals. Along with that, she wore a Western-style hat with off-white tulle tied around it.

"Thank you," she whispered to Shep. "You look pretty good yourself." In spite of the early-afternoon heat, he wore a Western-cut suit, white shirt and bolo tie, and looked exceptionally handsome, exceptionally like a dressed-up cowboy.

"Did you bring your bathing suit like Gina suggested?" he asked. Lately the temperature had been in the eighties.

"I did, but I don't know if I'll put it on. Going swimming at a wedding reception seems a little peculiar."

"Not peculiar, just out of the ordinary. Everything we do might be a little out of the ordinary. Did you ever think of that?"

"I don't know if that makes me more afraid or more excited!"

Shep's hand slid under her hair. "I don't want you to be afraid."

She moved her cheek against his thumb. "I'll try not to be."

The judge, who seemed in a hurry to return to his chambers, shook both their hands and congratulated them. He said a few words to Ryder and then made his way back to the courthouse.

Roy asked them, "Are you married now?"

Raina dropped her arm around his shoulders. "Yes, we're married now. Are you ready for a celebration?"

"That's a party, right?" Joey asked, apparently wanting to make sure.

"Yep, it's a party with a big cake."

Raina's mother came over to her and gave her a hug. "I wish you nothing but happiness," she murmured. But when Raina pulled back, she saw her mother looked worried.

"Thank you, Mom. I think I *will* be happy, once I get used to the idea of being married again."

"It won't be the same," her mother said with a shake of her head.

"No, it won't. I don't expect it to be. Maybe that's the secret."

Shep, standing beside Raina, obviously overheard. Her mother hesitated a moment, then patted Shep's arm. "Congratulations." She smiled at Manuel and held out her hands to him. "Will you come to me?"

The two-year-old gave a wide grin, babbled and then leaned into her.

"You're a friendly one," Sonya remarked.

Roy tugged on Manuel's foot, just to tease him,

then he asked Raina's mother, "Are you going to be our grandma?"

"I guess I will be," she answered, as if she hadn't thought about that. "What do *you* think about the idea?"

"I think it's a good idea. Do you bake cookies?"

Everyone standing there laughed, and after that, conversation seemed easier. Ryder was the only one who stood apart. He and Shep just seemed to be like oil and water, and Raina didn't know if there was anything she could do about that.

They were ready to walk to their cars when Raina saw the expression on Lily's face. She asked Shep to give her a minute, and went to her friend.

Lily's eyes were moist and her lip quivered.

"I can only imagine how hard this was for you," Raina said with her arm around her friend. "If you want to skip the reception, I'll understand."

"I know you said I didn't have to come, but I wanted to. This is an important day for you, and actually, I'm glad I'm here. Hearing you and Shep say your vows reminded me of my wedding day. We didn't have very many people there either, but it was the most wonderful day of my life and I don't ever want to forget that."

"You are one strong woman," Raina said.

Lily bumped her shoulder against Raina's. "I think we're both strong women. How are *you* feeling?"

"Like I just stepped onboard a rocket ship soaring to another planet."

Lily gave her a watery smile. "That's the way a wedding is supposed to feel. Now go on, go with your groom. I'll see you at Gina's."

As soon as Raina slipped into the chauffeur-driven

limo beside Shep—he had insisted they ride in style—he asked her, "Is Lily okay?"

"As okay as she can be. I just wish there was something more I could do to help her."

"You're helping her by being her friend." Shep's hand covered Raina's and they sat there for a moment, gazing straight ahead.

In the seat across from them, Roy said, "This is cool, but everyone else is going to beat us there, Dad. Shouldn't we go?"

"The bride and groom are supposed to arrive last," Shep said, joking. "We're the guests of honor."

"Us, too?" Joey asked.

"You, too. But since everyone else pulled away, I guess it's time." He knocked on the partition between them and the driver and nodded.

Raina heard Roy say to Joey, "I bet they're going to hold hands all the time, now that they said 'I do'."

She wondered to herself, would they hold hands? Would Shep be affectionate in the course of a day? What would happen tonight when they shared the same bed? *Would* they be sharing the same bed? In the flurry of getting their application at the courthouse, working, spending time with the kids, they hadn't asked or answered those questions.

But she'd be finding out some of the answers tonight.

When Raina saw what Gina had done to the pool area of her home with Logan, tears came to her eyes. With Shep beside her, she threw her arms around Gina and gave her a huge hug. "Thank you so much. We never expected anything like this."

White tables with turquoise umbrellas circled the pool. The flower arrangements on each table were the same as her bouquet—yellow roses and white gardenias. The scent of them on the breeze was heavenly. The buffet table held assorted hors d'oeuvres, crab puffs, chicken divan and prime rib for adults; pizza, chicken fingers and a crock of chili for anyone who preferred kid food.

Shep seemed a bit overwhelmed, too. He shook Logan's hand, clasped Gina's shoulder and said with heartfelt sincerity, "We'll never forget this."

"That's the idea," Gina said, teasing. "We want you indebted to us for a lifetime. That way you'll babysit Daniel whenever we need you."

Raina laughed. Gina and Logan had a wonderful nanny, Hannah, who was now rounding up the boys. After settling Manuel, along with Gina's and Logan's son, into high chairs, Raina noticed that her mother had joined Hannah and was introducing herself.

Shep bent to Raina. "Your mother's making a friend."

"She can't stay away from children. If nothing else, your boys will convince her to come out to the ranch. That is…if you want her to."

"She's your mother. Of course I want her to." He seemed disappointed in Raina that she would think differently.

"Mothers-in-law aren't always welcome. She might have suggestions."

Shep drew Raina away from the others. His hand still on her arm, he assured her, "I'll listen to whatever she has to say. That doesn't mean I'll do it. That doesn't mean *we'll* do it. But she'll be welcome, especially if she wants to give our kids attention and love."

"I'm sure I won't be able to keep her away once the baby's born. Do you think Eva will mind?"

"I think there'll be plenty for ten adults to do."

The tension that had suddenly cropped up between them dissipated. Raina realized the beginning of their marriage would seesaw like this until they were familiar with each other's quirks, sensitivities and pasts. She and Shep still had a lot to learn about each other. The question was, would he eventually be able to reveal his heart to her? She already knew each time she was with him, she was giving him a piece of hers.

"Uh-oh," she said to Shep in a low voice, watching Ryder stride toward them. "I don't like the look in his eyes."

"Easy, Raina. Give him a chance to get used to us together."

After Ryder approached the two of them, he said to Shep, "Nice reception. I imagine you could have thrown a bash like this if you'd wanted to."

Shep didn't seem to be ruffled. "Well, we couldn't refuse Gina and Logan's kind offer. Besides, Raina and I will throw a party for friends and family once she and I are more settled."

"Settled? You mean after the two of you get to know one another?"

"Ryder," Raina warned.

"Just stating the obvious," her brother said with a shrug. "This marriage was fast, and everyone knows it."

Squaring her shoulders, Raina assured him, "Everyone here does know I'm pregnant, Ryder. These are my friends."

"And where are Shep's friends?" Ryder asked.

Shep's face took on an unreadable expression, but Raina saw his jaw tighten. She took a step closer to him and laid her hand on his arm. He put his around her shoulders and she suddenly felt as if they stood as a couple against the world.

"I'm not sure why my friends are your concern," Shep said. "Besides, Raina and I decided to keep this small. There wasn't that much room around the gazebo," he remarked drily.

Ryder's eyes narrowed.

Although Shep wasn't showing it, Raina could feel the taut tension in his body. She would have to be the buffer until these two men could find some common ground. "Did you know Lily moved into the Victorian last week?"

Ryder cast a glance toward her bridesmaids. "You've really made friends since you came back to Sagebrush. I didn't know if you could fit back into small-town life."

"Once a Sagebrush girl, always a Sagebrush girl," she said, joking.

"Daddy! Daddy! Come see what we have to eat," Roy called to Shep.

"Have you met Shep's boys?" Raina asked her brother.

"No," he replied, looking over that way.

"Come on, I'll introduce you."

But before they could move away, Shep halted Ryder. "Wait."

Ryder swung around.

"Please don't tell them you're a police officer, at least not yet."

Ryder frowned. "Why shouldn't I? I'm proud of being a cop."

"I'm sure you are. But their parents were killed in an automobile accident. The police officer got to the house before the social worker did. He took them in the car to her office. Everything was handled badly."

After Ryder studied Shep for a few moments, he agreed. "Okay, I see your point." He headed toward the table where his mother was already seated with the boys.

Raina faced Shep. "I have a lot to learn about you. I didn't realize I have a lot to learn about the boys, too."

"When things come up, we'll deal with them. I don't think a crash course is going to work in a situation like this."

He was probably right. But just what would a crash course on Shep McGraw entail?

As he led her toward the kids, her stomach fluttered at the idea of finding out.

By 10:00 p.m., Roy, Joey and Manuel were all tucked in and sleeping. Raina had hugged Roy and asked Joey if it was okay to hug him, too. He'd grudgingly said yes, and she felt his hold grow a little tighter as she gave him what she hoped was the first of many bedtime comforts.

Now, however, she met Shep outside of Manuel's room. "Is he still sleeping soundly?" she asked.

"Being in the sun and dangling his toes in the pool tired him out."

After the luncheon at Gina's, many of the guests had left, including Raina's mother and brother. But Raina and Shep had changed into more casual clothes and watched the boys have fun in the pool as Logan acted as lifeguard. Raina had been super aware of Shep all afternoon. Since their glances had connected often, she suspected he'd been just as aware of her. Now, standing near his bed-room door, she felt unsure as to what to do next.

He ran his hand through his hair and shook his head. "I don't know how to play this, Raina. We got married today and should be having a honeymoon. The thing is—we're different than most married couples. I don't want to rush you into anything you don't want. I hung your clothes in my closet, but if you'd rather sleep in the guest bedroom, I'll understand."

"Do you want this to be a real marriage?" she asked, her voice a bit shaky.

He touched the back of his hand to her cheek. The feel of his taut, warm skin made her insides jump as he answered, "Hell, yes, I want this to be a real marriage."

She thought about their signed prenuptial agreement, their meeting with the caseworker and Carla Sumpter's admonition that Manuel's adoption would take longer. Now she pictured the gazebo, heard in her mind the vows she and Shep had exchanged. She considered the nine years she'd spent alone, the longing to be held again and most of all the child she was carrying.

"I want this to be a real marriage, too, starting tonight."

Shep came close enough to kiss her. Raina knew by now that he liked to start slow and ratchet up the passion. Was that a technique of his, or was that just his way with her? To her amazement, she wanted to be the only woman he thought about, the only woman who could arouse him to new heights of passion.

Touching his lips to hers, Shep reached between them and splayed his large hand over her midriff. With delib-erate slowness, he eased up her knit top, the tips of his fingers grazing her belly as he slid the material away.

His palm settled on her navel, as each of his fingers splayed across her stomach.

"It won't be long until we feel life here."

His voice was raspy, and she understood how much this baby meant to him. But what did *she* mean to him? Inside her mind, a question demanded to be asked—*Do you want me as much as this child?* But she couldn't let it out. The truth was, she was afraid of the answer.

She loved the feel of his hands protectively spread over their child, sensually spread across her skin. His cheek brushed hers as he kissed along her ear, as his tongue erotically played with her earlobe. Her knees started to buckle. She'd never felt such intense desire. Yet how could that be when she'd been married, in love with and loved by her husband for years?

That thought fled as Shep lifted her into his arms and carried her into his bedroom.

Shep set her on her feet by the bed, her arms still around his neck. He held her tightly against him. She could feel every nuance of their bodies connecting, her breasts pressed against his chest, his belt buckle against her belly, his erection pressing just where it was supposed to be.

"Do you want this as much as I do?" he asked.

*The marriage—or the sex they were about to have?* the devil on her shoulder demanded. Either way, at the moment, she wasn't sure it mattered. "I want it. I want *you.*"

He laughed. "Then maybe we can do it more than once. It *is* our wedding night, after all."

She suddenly worried about whether or not she could fulfill his needs.

The smile on his lips faded away. "I can tell what

you're thinking. This is about the two of us, Raina. You tell me what you want and need, and I'll tell you. We'll play, we'll explode, we'll compromise. I don't want you to do anything you don't want to do."

Right now, all she wanted was to be naked in that bed with Shep. Instead of telling him, she showed him. She slid her hands up the back of his head, nudged him down and kissed him as if it were the last kiss they'd ever share. Her boldness and desire lit the flame of his passion, and nothing went slow after that.

Shep undressed her with an abandon that she matched. After he slipped her shirt over her head and onto the floor, he unfastened her bra. Then he stood close again, letting her breasts touch his chest as he eased down her shorts. In the process, she pulled open the snaps on his shirt. Her lips at his collarbone, she kissed there and heard him groan as his palm slipped into her panties and down her backside. Each brush of his calloused fingers excited all her nerve endings. Her nipples were hard and she brushed them against his shirt. An electric spark shot from her breasts to her womb.

He shucked off his boots, jeans, briefs and shirt. She flipped her sandals to the side, and there they were, in his king-size bed, body to body, kissing, caressing, rushing toward fulfillment for both of them.

Suddenly a cry rent the air. Manuel's cry.

Shep went still and so did she.

"Bad dream?" she asked huskily.

Shep rested his jaw on top of her head. "We'll know in a second."

Another cry came. It was longer and louder. Shep didn't hesitate. He pulled away from her. "I'll be back," he mumbled hoarsely, and she knew he was still as aroused as she was. "Sometimes this can take a little while."

She could lie there waiting, or… "I'll come with you," she said, leaving the bed to find a nightgown in the closet. When he shot a questioning glance at her, she shrugged. "I'm his mother now."

Shep's slow grin was almost as arousing as a caress.

When Raina and Shep reached Manuel's room, he was standing in his crib, holding on to the rail tightly, his little face red and screwed up in a very upset expression.

When he saw Raina, he raised his arms to her.

She heard Shep grumble, "I guess a mom is more in demand than a dad this time of night."

She glanced at him over her shoulder. Bare-chested, in flannel jogging shorts with a drawstring below his navel, he looked as sexy as any man could.

"I'm a novelty," she said easily.

After a moment of considering that, Shep responded with, "I'll get him a drink of water."

After Shep left the room, she checked over Manuel. He quieted as soon as she took him in her arms, and she wondered if he'd had a bad dream. Did he remember anything of the neglect he'd experienced? Or was all of it an impression that could sometimes haunt him at night? She wanted to give him lots of love and only wonderful memories to dream about.

When Shep returned, they both held the glass as Manuel sipped.

Shep ran his thumb over the baby's forehead. "I think he had too much excitement today. He missed his nap."

Raina gave Manuel a comforting hug. He took another few sips of water and smiled at her.

After Shep took Manuel from Raina's arms, he carried him to the toy shelf and picked up a small stuffed dog. "How about this one?"

Eagerly, Manuel clutched the dog to himself and Shep settled his little boy in the crib where Manuel lay on his side clutching the dog, content once again.

"We'll see if that does it. At one of the adoption meetings, we had a session on children and sleep problems. I learned not to play with him when he wakes up like that, because then he expects it."

As Shep turned off the overhead light, leaving just the nightlight glowing, Raina saw that he tried to learn everything he could about raising his kids.

When he let her precede him through the door, she could feel his gaze on her as they returned to his bedroom. There he skimmed off his shorts and climbed into bed. Following his lead, she removed her nightgown.

His gaze followed her as she slid into bed. They were on separate sides of the bed when he asked, "Is the mood broken?"

"We'll both be listening for Manuel, to see if he's settled."

"That's not what I asked," he responded huskily.

Turning toward her husband, she suggested, "Kiss me and we'll find out."

Shep rolled toward her, reached for her, then tugged her to him. His lips came down on hers without the coaxing slowness she was used to, but at the moment, his possessive need seemed even better. She was intoxicated by his scent, tempted by his taste, excited by his arousal. As his tongue took the kiss to new heights, his hand slid between her thighs, his fingers pushed inside her and she discovered she was still aroused, still ready for him.

He tested, taunted and provoked, until she cried, "Shep, *now.*"

Moments later, Shep's body covered hers. He rose above her and spread her legs. Poised there, he slowly thrust into her, withdrew, then thrust harder. She clutched his shoulders, moaned, savored, rushed up to meet him, then unraveled with a cry that echoed in the room. Shep's body shuddered as his release followed hers.

Breathless, she held on to him, aware that this had been anything but sex for her. Somewhere between ministering to his kids and their wedding in the gazebo, she'd fallen in love with Shep McGraw. She knew he cared about their unborn child as much as he cared about his other sons. She knew that was the reason he'd married her. Hopefully, soon she'd find out if he was falling in love with *her,* too.

## Chapter Nine

Standing inside Shep's walk-in closet, Raina studied her wedding dress, hanging on the rod, the fringes swinging lower than the hems on her other dresses. She couldn't help touching the tulle on the hat on the shelf above the dress, remembering everything about her wedding day...including her passionate lovemaking with Shep that night.

They'd said their vows six days ago and she still wasn't sure where she stood in their marriage. They'd made love almost every night. Yet she suspected that Shep was holding back. He gave her physical pleasure and was attentive and considerate. But she knew in her soul he wasn't risking his innermost thoughts and feelings with her. He wasn't offering her the emotional intimacy she needed in this marriage.

Yes, they talked about the practical aspects of their lives—what the boys should eat for breakfast, how much time Eva should spend with Manuel outside, if they'd go on a trail ride when they both got home from work—day-to-day things. But nothing that led to more intimate knowledge about her husband. Raina had told him so much about herself. When her mother stopped over last weekend, she'd shared even more about Raina's childhood. But Raina realized she herself was holding some things back, too—things about her marriage to Clark.

With a sigh, she took a rust-colored tunic top and tan capris from hangers and quickly dressed. She'd gotten home late tonight. Now she just wanted to change into something comfortable, talk to her husband and play with the boys. It wouldn't be too long before it was time to get them ready for bed. She wished...

She couldn't even put into words what she wished for. More time with her husband? She'd had morning sickness today and she wanted to tell Shep about it. Maybe after the boys were asleep.

Barefoot, she went into the hall and would have gone downstairs, when she heard sounds from the boys' room.

She hurried down the hall and stood at their door. When she peeked in, she could see Joey was huddled on the bed, Roy sitting beside him. Pale-gray and tiger-striped kittens who'd outgrown the barn were asleep on the corner of Roy's bed. The other two and their mama had been cavorting in the playroom when she'd passed through.

Roy spotted her immediately, and he looked as if he didn't know what to do as Joey turned his face away, wiping away tears.

Crossing to Joey's bed, she stood beside him and laid her hand gently on his shoulder. "Hey! What's going on?"

He shook his head and wouldn't look up, so she turned to Roy. Although he was younger, he was always the more vocal of the two…the one who couldn't seem to keep anything bottled up inside.

"Come on," she said, coaxing. "I want to help."

"You can't tell Dad," Joey mumbled.

"That you're upset? He'd want to know. I can't keep secrets from your father, and you shouldn't, either."

Joey scooched over to make a place for her as she sat on the bed. She wasn't going anywhere until she found out what was going on. Even if they didn't want Shep to know, they had to at least tell *her*.

After a long silence, Roy blurted out, "Ben was mean to Joey. He stole his medal, the one Dad gave him. Our first dad."

Had she and Shep missed something so important as an absent St. Christopher's medal when they'd put Joey to bed?

"When did this happen?"

"Today," Roy said without hesitation. "But Ben's been mean for a long time. That's why Joey doesn't want to go to school."

That revelation came out in a rush, as if Roy had been holding it in for a long time. Shep had told her that his phone conference with Joey's teacher had revealed nothing. Joey still dragged his feet in the mornings, but got on the school bus every day…maybe because he knew Shep expected him to.

In spite of Joey's initial resistance, Raina scooted closer to him and wrapped her arm around his shoulders.

At first she thought he might pull away. But then he gave in to all the things that were troubling him and let her hold him as he cried.

She was wiping Joey's tears from his cheek when Shep appeared in the doorway. Before he entered the room, he started to say, "Raina, if you'd like something to eat—"

He stopped when he saw the three of them huddled on the bed.

Joey tucked his head more securely into Raina's shoulder and wouldn't look at his dad.

Roy leaned over and whispered to Raina, "Joey's afraid Dad will be mad because he didn't fight Ben."

Shep's expression grew troubled. His brows drew together, and his jaw seemed more sharply angled. But his voice was calm and gentle as he asked, "What's going on?"

Bending toward Joey, Raina whispered in his ear, "I understand about Ben. But you have to look your dad in the eye and tell him what's happening at school. That's the only way he can help."

Finally, Joey lifted his head, his big dark eyes swimming with tears. Swiping them away, he sniffed, and in a low voice, told Shep, "A boy at school stole my medal and stuffed it in his desk. He's mean. In the morning before school he comes to my locker and says you don't really want us. You just took us in so we could do chores for you. He says real parents are the only parents that count."

Raina could see Joey's words disturbed Shep deeply. Anger flared in his eyes, that someone could do this to his son.

"You're mad," Roy blurted out, seeing Shep's reaction. Kids were so good at reading adults, better than parents ever imagined.

As if he were counting to ten, Shep took in a breath, let it out, then beckoned to Joey. "Come here, son."

Pulling away from the eight-year-old, Raina patted him on the back, encouraging him.

Uneasily, Joey slid off the bed and stood before Shep, looking scared and lonely and altogether unsure of what was going to happen next.

As Shep crouched down to Joey so they were on eye level, he asked, "Is this why you didn't want to go to school?"

Joey nodded.

Shep put his hand on his boy's shoulder. "Yeah, I'm angry, but not at you. I'm mad that someone didn't see this happening. I'm also angry at myself that I didn't realize what was going on. Answer me something, Joey. Do you really believe that I wanted to adopt you and Roy so you could do chores?"

Joey didn't answer right away.

The nerve in Shep's jaw pulsed, but his gaze didn't leave his son's. "Do I do chores, too?"

Biting his lower lip, Joey thought about that, then answered, "Every day. You feed the horses. You fix the fence. You ride the horses. You even mow the field sometimes."

"That's right, and when I'm not here, what do I do?"

"You go to the lumberyard. You work on the computer and carry stuff from one place to the other—stuff people build houses with."

"That's right. That's my job. Right now, you don't have a job. You have school. That's sort of where you work. Chores are always part of life. On a ranch, I guess maybe there are more than if you live in a house in town. But I believe chores teach you and Roy about work. Do you understand that?"

Joey exchanged a look with Roy, then replied, "I understand."

"Good, now I want you to listen. I adopted you because I want to be your dad. I *am* your real parent now, and I'll be your dad forever." Shep pulled Joey into a hug. "I'll fix this, Joey. We'll get your medal back." Shep straightened and tipped up his son's chin. "Believe me?"

"Yes, sir."

Shep gave him a pat on the back. "Go on, now. Get ready for bed."

"Can you read to us?" Roy asked Raina.

"Get your pj's on and brush your teeth. Pick out a good book, then I'll be back." From the look on Shep's face, he was going to do something, and she wanted to know what it was. It wouldn't be good if he acted out of anger. But she knew he was probably mad enough to do that, although he'd put that aside when he was talking to Joey. Shep seemed to be able to compartmentalize his feelings, and she didn't know if that was good or bad.

Shep nodded to Manuel's room. Knowing Eva was with the baby downstairs, Raina went to the nursery. Once she was inside, Shep shut the door. Then he paced across the small space. "Why didn't someone see what was happening to him? Why didn't *I?*"

"You can't see everything, Shep. You can't be everything."

"That's a bunch of bull, Raina. I'm supposed to see these things. He had bellyaches and Dr. Rossi suspected something might be wrong at school."

"Or at home…or because of Manuel's adoption," she added, reminding him there had been lots of possibilities.

Shep shoved his hands into his pockets. "What else did Roy and Joey tell you? What else wouldn't they tell *me?*"

Going to her husband, Raina clasped his upper arm. "They respect you, Shep. They don't want you to be disappointed in them. The stakes are a lot higher with you than they are with me."

Pushing his fingers through his hair, Shep gazed at her face, searching it, looking for the truth. "What else did they say?"

"Joey was afraid you'd think he was a coward for not fighting this…Ben. Since the incident with the medal just happened today, it might still be in his desk."

"His name's Ben Raddigan. I saw the kid at the open house before school started. He's bigger than Joey, and I think he was kept back last year. I'm going to call his parents."

This time Raina gripped Shep's arm more firmly. "Maybe you should think about notifying the teacher, and let her handle it."

"Why deal with someone who can mess this up, when I can do it myself?"

Raina wasn't sure why, but Shep seemed to have a poor opinion of authority figures. When was he going to tell her about his childhood…his teenage years? His attitude now, the way he wanted to handle this situation, was probably rooted there.

She stepped into his space until their toes were touching, until their bodies were only a few inches from contact. That seemed to get his attention. "How does Joey's teacher want you to get in touch with her if you have to?"

"I can e-mail or phone her, but Raina, you don't get—"

"I do get that you want this settled quickly, but I really believe the way not to embarrass Joey and to produce the best outcome is to consult with his teacher and see what she suggests. Some schools have a policy about this."

"About bullies?"

"Yes. It's become a real problem, and teachers are trained to deal with it. So don't take for granted that she won't listen to you and understand your concerns. She listened when you spoke with her about Joey before, didn't she?"

Their gazes collided and Raina saw the turmoil in Shep. Apparently he was torn. He wanted to do what was best for Joey but wasn't absolutely sure what that was. Finally, he nodded.

"Yes, she did. Although apparently she didn't see what was happening. I'll call her. But I'm not letting this go any longer than it has to. I'll use the phone downstairs in my office. Do you mind getting Roy and Joey ready for bed?"

She was beginning to think of herself as not only "*a* mother" but as "*their* mother." Obviously, Shep wasn't thinking of her in that way yet. She guessed she imagined that at some point, she'd really leave. But she wasn't going anywhere.

"Don't ever think I mind taking care of the boys. I feel more like a mom every day, and I think they're starting to see me that way. We're going to be parents *together,* right? They're *all* ours."

After a short silence, he nodded. "I'd like to think they are." He dropped his arm around her and brought her in for a kiss, a short but resounding kiss that lit their desire in a way that might carry into bedtime.

Desire was wonderful and exciting and thrilling, but she wanted more than desire from Shep. She loved Shep McGraw, and if he couldn't learn to love her, her heart was going to be broken once more.

In the next half hour, Raina stayed with the boys upstairs and read to them. As she turned page after page of one of their favorite books, she sensed Joey glancing at her often. Finally he asked, "What's Dad gonna do?"

Closing the book, she told him honestly, "He's speaking with your teacher. We'll figure this out, honey. I promise."

"And she keeps her promises," Roy assured his brother.

"Yes, I do."

Boots sounded on the steps. Carrying Manuel, Shep brought the toddler into Roy and Joey's room to say good night. Raina looked up at him with questioning eyes, but his expression said they'd talk after all the little cowboys were in bed. So she gave Manuel a kiss and a hug, and helped Shep tuck in Joey and Roy. Usually she hugged Joey. But tonight, *he* hugged *her.*

With the house quiet, Shep led Raina to their room, checked the baby monitor, then closed the door. "I asked Eva to come in a little earlier in the morning. Mrs. Swenson suggested I bring Joey early tomorrow. She mentioned being pleased that you sent her the note about us being married."

"I meant to tell you I did that, but it just slipped my mind."

"I guess so, with work and the kids." He hesitated a moment, then added, "And us."

Although the subject was serious, heat shot through her when he looked at her like that. "Did she listen to you?"

"Actually, she did. She didn't think it would be a good idea for me to contact Ben's parents. She'd like to handle it differently, according to the school's policies. She said they're dealing with more than bullying here... with stealing, too. And she wants to handle that between the two boys first thing in the morning. I'm not sure exactly what she's going to do. The truth is, I don't like putting this in someone else's hands. But I want to do what's best for Joey, so we'll try it her way first."

"And if her way doesn't work, you'll come out with guns blazing?" Raina guessed, half teasing, half serious.

"If that's what it takes."

She knew he meant it, and she couldn't help but wonder if he'd fight for her the same way he'd fight for his kids.

Crossing to her, he wrapped his arms around her. "You were great tonight with Joey and Roy. In fact—"

"In fact?"

"In fact, I've got to admit I was a little jealous. For over a year and a half I've been trying to get them to trust me. Tonight they trusted you as if you'd been living here and taking care of them that long, too."

"Maybe it's because I'm a woman."

"I thought about that, and maybe that's part of it. But there's more, too. Something I'm missing."

"They respect you, Shep. They love you and they don't want to let you down. Joey thought you'd be mad at him. He had a lot more to risk in telling you."

"I want them to be able to tell me anything."

She suspected the boys were hesitant to talk to him about their emotions because Shep didn't talk about his. How could she say that without it sounding like a criticism? But she didn't even know if she was right. They really hadn't been living together long enough for her to know.

"You can't fight all their battles for them, and they probably know that even better than you."

"How I handle this tomorrow is important, isn't it?"

"Yes. But loving them every day is important, too, and that's what you've been doing."

After he searched her face, seeing that she meant her words, he smiled. "You know how to make a man feel ten feet tall."

"You mean you're not that tall?" she asked, joking.

He laughed and kissed her hard, pressed his tongue into her mouth, and she felt the world drop away. Soon he was cupping her bottom and her legs were around him and she couldn't remember what they'd been talking about.

Did she want him so badly because her hormones were in turmoil from her pregnancy? Or did she want him so badly because her love for him was growing deeper each day? She didn't know. She only knew that when he kissed her like this, nothing else mattered except the joining of their bodies, their mutual pleasure and the child inside of her, who she hoped would bring them closer together.

Right now their bodies were almost as close as they could get, their clothes the only impediments. But that soon changed, as Shep's hands grabbed fistfuls of her tunic top, trying to push it out of the way. She couldn't get to his belt buckle, not as long as he was holding her this tightly.

"I can't undress you unless you put me down," she said breathlessly as he broke away to kiss her neck and then her shoulder.

"If I put you down, we'll lose momentum," he growled.

"Momentum doesn't have anywhere to go with your jeans on."

She could feel his chest ripple with his chuckle as he set her gently on her feet. By the time she'd lifted her tunic over her head and pushed off her capris, he'd shucked off his jeans and briefs. Then he was holding her again, backing her up against the closet door, kissing her as if the world was going to end tonight and he'd never get a chance to do this again.

Raina didn't know where the intensity in Shep was coming from. But she didn't care, because it set her desire ablaze in a more spectacular way than it had before. She could hardly catch her breath as he held her hands above her head and pressed tightly against her. She intertwined her fingers with his, and held on for dear life as he teased her breasts with his chest hair and his tongue searched her mouth. They'd had sex before. They'd pleasured each other before. But never with this desperate intensity and need.

He wove his fingers into her hair, stroking it away from her face, kissing her cheek and her temple, and the pulse point at the base of her throat. Shep's pleasure giving was wonderful, but she wanted it to be mutual. She ran her hands down his sides, hesitated briefly on his hips and stretched her fingers to the front of him, to the most virile part of him. When she cupped him, he bowed his forehead against hers.

"You don't play fair," he grumbled. "And because

you don't, I'm going to have to show you what teasing a man will get you."

"Bring it on," she said, challenging flirtatiously.

His gaze crashed into hers, blue eyes on brown, his filled with enough heat to melt her. Melted or not, she didn't back down, didn't close her eyes, didn't shut him out.

"You're the strongest woman I've ever met," he growled.

"And you're one of the most generous men I've ever met, opening your house to the boys...and to me."

"Opening my house to you had nothing to do with generosity." His kisses started again.

Before she thought about what he'd said, he began touching her the way a woman only dreamed of being touched. The closet door supported her as he trailed kisses to her cleavage, then made her feel like the most adored woman on earth. He kissed her breasts all over. He touched them. He caressed them. When his mouth centered on her nipple, pulling and teasing and taunting, he made her so restless she could only move against his body, expressing without words what she wanted most.

"Not yet," he whispered under his breath more than once, as her right breast became the focus of his attention this time.

Raina was trembling, her body overloading on flaming sensations. Standing here with Shep was so different than leisurely lying in bed. It seemed to enunciate more clearly each kiss and caress, each tease of his tongue on her skin, each area he'd never touched before. She was an open book to him, letting him write where he pleased. He didn't miss a line or a page.

Before she knew what he was going to attempt to do, he knelt down before her and let his palms trail over her tummy…the place where their child lay. He was always reverent about that, and it was one of the reasons she trusted him so. But then his hands clasped her hips, his thumbs tracing slow erotic circles.

She thought her blood couldn't get any hotter, but she was wrong about that. When he gently scraped his nails over her backside, then moved his thumbs into the black hair that was fine and silky, she couldn't breathe.

"Shep, we can move to the bed."

"We can do this right here."

He lowered his head, touched his tongue to her most sensitive place and she let out a little cry.

"Don't try to keep it in, Raina. If I make you feel good, I want to know."

"The boys…"

"These old walls are thick."

His tongue touched her again, left a halo of heat and began a journey he intended to finish. She could only go along for the ride. The texture of his lips was searing hot as his tongue bathed her in an iridescent storm of excitement. She arched into him. He took more of her, and then the tip of his tongue sent her to heaven. She would have collapsed into his arms, but he rose to meet her, wrapped her securely in his embrace and carried her to the bed where she turned to him, eager to love him. But he stopped her by tucking her into the crook of his arm.

"Shep, what are you doing? I want to give you pleasure, too."

"I had my pleasure watching you."

"But you're still…"

"I'll settle down when you fall asleep on my shoulder. I always do."

"But—"

"Don't overanalyze, Raina."

"If you want—"

"I'll let you know what I want and when I want it. I want you to do the same. We'll learn each other's desires. It might just take a little time."

*And communication,* she thought. But she also worried about tonight and what had happened. Had he pleasured her so *he* was in control? In control of what? Their sex life? What happened in their marriage? Did he even realize that, by not accepting what she wanted to give him, he was preventing them from really becoming close? Was he trying to prove to himself that he didn't need her?

Shep had so many walls that she was having a difficult time figuring them all out—and she was beginning to wonder if he would ever let her break them down.

## Chapter Ten

"Is Raina going to be there?" Joey asked as Shep drove his son to school the next morning.

"No, she had appointments this morning. But I'm going to be there while you meet with Ben and your teacher. I'll be right outside the classroom door waiting, so you can tell me how it goes."

"Why can't you come in?"

"Mrs. Swenson thinks it's better if it's just her and you and Ben."

"But what if he…?"

Shep knew this was too important to say with half of his attention on the road and half of his attention on his son, so he pulled over to the shoulder. Turning to Joey, he laid his hand on his son's shoulder. "You don't know what Ben's going to say or do, but you do know what *you* can say and do."

"I don't know what to say." He looked scared.

Shep turned to look at Roy, too, who was sitting in the backseat, before he offered his advice. "I want you to both listen to me. You need to stand up for yourselves. Do you know what that means?"

"It means he should punch him," Roy mumbled.

"No, that's exactly what it *doesn't* mean. Always try to be respectful. Standing up for yourself means you tell the person who's done something wrong to you exactly how you feel."

"I'm not telling him I cried." Joey seemed horrified at the thought.

Shep almost smiled. "I can see this isn't easy. It's not easy for anybody. But you can tell him what that medal meant to you, who gave it to you, and why it's something you always want to keep. I'm not going to tell you what to say. You have to figure that out. Say the truth and what you feel. But do you understand where I'm going here?"

After staring out the windshield for a moment, Joey turned back to Shep. "So I could say something like— if he had a medal his dad gave him, he wouldn't want me to take it, would he?"

"That's right. You say the important truth that's inside here." He tapped Joey's chest.

Joey took a deep breath. "Okay, let's go."

Shep winked at Roy, put the truck in Drive, found his way into traffic again and headed for the school.

Shep's thoughts weren't just on Joey and what was about to happen to him. He couldn't stop thinking about Raina, either. He didn't know what had gotten into him last night. He seemed to want her more each time he was with her—not only want her, but claim her as his. The thing was, last night after he'd brought her to climax, he'd felt vulnerable afterward…like his soul had been ripped open and he couldn't sew it back together again. He knew he kept his guard up with everyone, except Cruz. Only the two of them understood what they'd gone through. Only the two of them knew the insecurities of being abandoned, the bravado of toughing through it, the need to succeed, the determination to wipe away everything that had gone before. Shep didn't open up with anyone else. It was too dangerous.

Yet with Raina, he found himself doing things he'd never done before, saying things he'd never said before. Marrying her had probably been an exceptionally foolish thing to do, yet she was the mother of his baby. Could she be a real mother to his sons, too? When their own child was born, would Raina be too busy for Joey and Roy and Manuel?

He didn't know.

*Say the truth and tell how you feel,* he'd told his son. Sometimes, as Joey would learn in the future, the truth was a little too much to tell, and protecting one's pride or heart or soul might be more important.

By the time Shep parked at the elementary school, took Roy to his classroom, then proceeded to Joey's, Joey looked less nervous and more determined. His teacher wore a serious expression and informed him Ben was already there. She'd make sure the boys were through before the other students started arriving.

"Are Ben's parents here?" Shep asked.

"No, they're not. His father said he'd stop in after school, and I hope he does."

Fifteen minutes later, Shep was pacing up and down outside the classroom, wondering why standing here waiting was harder than gentling a two-year-old colt. He'd taken off his hat and run his hand through his hair at least ten times by the time Raina came rushing up the hall. He couldn't name the feeling that filled his chest, but seeing her there felt better than making tons of money on a business deal, felt as good as a phone call from Cruz on Christmas, felt different than any feeling he'd had before. Yet the self-protective armor he'd kept in place for so many years kept his voice steady and his expression neutral.

"You came," he said simply.

She didn't look as if she knew exactly what to say, either. "I rearranged a few appointments."

Shep still felt a little caught up in what had happened last night, and he could see in her eyes that she was re-membering, too. They were newlyweds. Why should they be embarrassed by passion? But they weren't really newlyweds, were they? Not in the ordinary sense. They'd married for practicality's sake. A lifelong history of women coming and going had taught him that Raina could be gone just as quickly as she'd said "I do."

The door to the classroom suddenly opened and Joey stood there, his dark eyes big and wide as he clutched his St. Christopher medal in his hand. He rushed to Shep and said, "Mrs. Swenson made Ben clean out his desk. He still had it there. The chain's broken, but the medal's okay. Can we get a new chain?"

Shep crouched down. "Yes, we can get a new chain, a nice strong one that won't break."

"I told him what you said," Joey went on. "That he had no right to take my medal, that my dad had given it to me and he was dead and…" Joey looked up at Shep.

"It's okay," Shep said, encouraging him. "What else did you say?"

Glancing over at Raina, who'd come to stand beside him, Joey went on. "I told him that medal was supposed to keep me safe, and if there's any more trouble my new dad will take care of it."

Shep gave Joey a tight hug. "I'm real proud of you."

Joey looked up at Raina. "Will you take me to buy a chain? Dad doesn't like to shop."

With a smile only mothers could produce, she laid her hand on Joey's shoulder. "Of course I will." Then she leaned down and whispered in his ear, "I'm glad you told me. I won't make your dad go with me to the mall."

Joey laughed and glanced over his shoulder back into the classroom. "I'd better go in. The other kids will be coming soon."

As he turned to go, Raina said, "You have a good day."

Shep called, "See you later, cowboy."

Suddenly alone with Raina, Shep felt…nervous. That was crazy. He didn't get nervous around women, and he shouldn't be nervous about Raina when she was living under the same roof and sharing his bed.

What happened next really knocked him back on his heels. She turned away from him, tossed over her shoulder, "I'll be back," and took off down the hall. He would have thought she might have spotted Roy and was chasing after him, but he'd caught a glimpse of her face. It was pale, almost green.

He raced after her, stopping when he saw the word *girls* on the door. On top of that, kids started pouring in the front doors, swarming down the hall.

"Raina, are you in there? Are you okay?"

It seemed that minutes went by, though he supposed it was only seconds until her voice carried softly to him. "I'm fine. I'll be out in a minute."

That minute seemed to be a very long one, and kids looked up at him as they passed, some pointed, some giggled. He knew it was unusual for a man to be standing in front of the girls' bathroom.

Finally, when Raina came out, she didn't look much better than when she'd gone in. He took her arm, gripping her elbow. "What's going on?"

"Morning sickness. Or rather, Danish sickness. I should have known better. As long as I have a piece of toast in the morning and a little bit of juice, I'm fine. Somebody at the office had put out a tray of Danish, and my sweet tooth reared up. I don't think I even *had* a sweet tooth before I was pregnant."

He couldn't help but smile at her chagrin as they walked toward the school's entrance, then exited into the sunny October day. "Cravings are a part of pregnancy, aren't they?"

"I never believed it, but I guess they are."

Holding her arm as he was, he could feel her tremble. She looked really pale again. He was tempted to swing her up into his arms and carry her to his truck. Instead, he pointed to a bench under the shade of the building's overhang. She gratefully sank down and took a few deep breaths.

"This has happened before?" he asked.

"A few times. The first time was the day before our wedding. I thought I was just jittery. But Angie had made French toast, and I guess *that* didn't go down very well, either."

"Do you have a doctor's appointment soon?"

"In a couple of weeks."

He could suggest she go in sooner, but Raina was independent enough to make her own decisions. She wouldn't like it if he made them for her. But he was about to make one now, in spite of the consequences.

"I'm driving you to Lubbock, to your office."

"Shep, that's not necessary."

"I think it is. You're still pale and you don't seem all that steady. When I get back, I'll have Ed bring me out here to get your car."

"But I have to get home tonight."

"Give me a call when you're ready to leave, and I'll come pick you up."

"I can possibly hop a ride with Gina or Lily."

"Whatever you decide. I just don't want you taking any chances."

"I won't take chances. I'd never do anything to put this baby in harm's way. You know that, don't you?"

He studied her beautiful brown eyes and wanted to believe she was as loyal and kind and committed as she seemed. The thing was, if he believed it, he could be blindsided all the more easily.

Raina transferred the last of the chocolate macadamia nut cookies from the cookie sheet to the plate. She hoped Shep would like them.

It was almost 8:00 p.m. on Friday night and he wasn't home yet. Roy and Joey had gone to a sleepover at one of Joey's classmate's, who had a younger brother Roy's age. Shep had asked her if she minded putting Manuel to bed by herself so he could get caught up on some paperwork at the lumberyard.

No, she hadn't minded. But she did have to wonder if he didn't want to be alone with her. They hadn't made love since the night they'd both gone a little wild. He'd come to bed late the past two nights and she'd fallen asleep before he had. That bed seemed very big—and a bit lonely—when they were each on their own sides.

Two gray-and-black-striped kittens raced from under the table into the living room. She knew they'd probably end up on Roy's or Joey's bed.

Suddenly she heard the crunch of Shep's truck tires on the gravel drive. Her breath caught. She heard the engine go quiet, Shep's footfalls on the back stoop, the squeak of the screen door as he entered the kitchen, and she felt her heart race.

*Settle down,* she told herself. She was a married woman now, with a baby on the way. Still, her husband's smile could curl her toes.

Her husband. Was she even used to that term yet?

In the kitchen now, Shep breathed in the aroma of chocolate and butter and sugar. "Someone's been busy." He was staring at her curiously, wondering why she had baked cookies.

"Eva didn't have time today to make a treat for the weekend, so I thought I would."

He gestured to the plate she'd already fixed. "Are those for sampling?"

"Manuel's sound asleep. I thought maybe you'd like to get comfortable and go out on the front porch. It's such a beautiful night."

Through the kitchen window, they could both see the moonlit darkness stealing the last of dusk.

Shep was quiet for a while, then said, "Sure. I don't think the two of us have tried out the porch swing. We can put the baby monitor in the open window." He came closer to her, touched her turquoise earring with his forefinger, then grinned.

"Making out on a porch swing could be the perfect end to a long day."

"We can make out," she agreed. "And maybe…we can talk."

His expression changed. "Talk about…"

"I got a phone call from Mrs. Sumpter. I have an interview with a psychologist the week after next."

His focus entirely on her, he asked, "Are you worried about it?"

"Some. I just don't want anything to hold up the adoption. I know how important it is to you and Manuel."

"What are you concerned about besides that?"

"I'm worried that whoever interviews me will think we married too quickly and for the wrong reasons."

"And what will you say if he or she asks why you married me?"

It was on the tip of her tongue to blurt out "Because I love you," because that's what she'd tell the interviewer. But she didn't think Shep would accept that. It was too soon. Not only that, but a little voice in her mind whispered, *He hasn't told you what* he *feels.*

"I'll tell him or her that I want a family as much as you do, and you're a good man and I've always felt a…bond with you. We're having a baby, and I believe two parents are better than one."

"You've thought about this."

"Of course. I want to be prepared."

He wrapped his arm around her and brought her close for a kiss. Hoarsely, he said, "I'll change and be right down."

Ten minutes later they were sitting side by side on the porch swing, the dish of cookies on a table beside them accompanied by glasses of homemade lemonade. Before he'd come outside, he'd switched on the CD player in the living room. Trace Adkins sang "You're Gonna Miss This," and Raina knew it was so. Every moment was precious. Children grew up too fast and intimate moments were gone before you could catch them.

After all the passion they'd shared, Raina had thought sitting close together would seem natural. However, they both seemed off balance, and she supposed that was her fault. Shep didn't like heart-to-hearts, and that was really what she wanted to have with him.

He ate one of the chocolate cookies and offered her the plate. She shook her head.

"They're great," he said.

"Thanks."

After he finished another one, he gave her a considering look. "Morning sickness today?"

"On and off most of the day."

"Are you sure that's normal?"

"When I see Emily next week, I'll ask her."

"Are you sure about giving birth with a midwife? A hospital room with doctors around sounds better to me."

"I really believe a baby should come into the world with soft lights and lots of love surrounding him. You can be with me. The kids can even be around at the beginning of it. Emily won't take chances. If there's any problem, I'll go to the hospital and Jared Madison will take care of me."

"My stress meter will be off the charts," Shep muttered.

When the strains of the soft ballad floated through the open window, Raina suddenly stood, then held out her hand to him. "How about a dance? You can forget about your long day and the stress of my labor."

When he took her hand, the look in his eyes went from concerned to heated. Rising to his feet, he circled her with his arms. "Do you know how pretty you look tonight?"

She'd changed into a smocked, gauzy dress, the color she loved most—turquoise. She'd wanted to put on something soft and sexy, yet not too obviously so.

"When I'm away from my office, I like to look more…feminine."

He buried his nose in her hair and murmured against her ear, "You succeeded."

Instinctively, Raina wrapped her arms around Shep's neck, wanting to be as close as she possibly could to him, maybe closer than he wanted to become. Had it been a mistake to think that one day they could bare their hearts to each other completely?

With their bodies pressed together, their desire was obvious. Yet in some ways, she felt as if she had to take a step back from the physical aspect of their relationship to make the rest of it work.

The three-quarter moon cast its glow over the yard

around the porch. It was bright enough for Raina to see Shep's face as she leaned away, allowing a few inches between them.

"Tell me about your ex-fiancée," Raina requested.

Shep stilled. "Why would we want to talk about that at a time like this?"

"Because we're good in bed, Shep, but I want to feel close to you in other ways, too."

His shoulders stiffened and she thought he was going to drop his arms. But he didn't. He held her loosely. "What if I don't want to talk about her?"

She met his question head-on. "I'm not going to pull away or sulk, if that's what you think. But sometimes I still get the feeling that you think I won't stay. I just want to know more about her so it doesn't become a forbidden topic between us. I want to know *you*."

"You're in a funny mood tonight."

Maybe he was hoping she'd say "Just forget about it," but she wasn't going to do that. "How did you meet?" she asked, knowing she was prodding.

With a sigh, he answered, "On the golf course. There was a tournament for charity. She and I got paired up and it wasn't until after we broke up I found that she had asked to be my partner."

"I imagine a lot of women would have wanted to have been your partner."

"I think you're seeing it in a different way than I did. I never realized how manipulative she was. I think she was looking for someone with money to marry, and purposely went about it."

"Did *you* break off the engagement?"

"It was mutual. As soon as I started talking about returning to Texas to ranch and adopt kids, Belinda began getting cold. The day I bought Red Creek Ranch, she said goodbye. Apparently, when we got engaged she figured my money would buy fancy cars, a penthouse and servants."

"Were you living a different lifestyle in California?" She really couldn't imagine him anyplace but here.

"I had an office in Sacramento and a condo nearby. I had to wear suits a lot more often than I do now."

From his wry smile she could see he was much more comfortable with this conversation, rather than revealing his romantic past. But she wanted to know more.

"Can I ask you something without you getting angry?"

He narrowed his eyes. "Is that supposed to defuse it before it begins?"

"Maybe."

"Shoot," he replied with resignation.

"Why did you ask her to marry you?" Had he gotten engaged to *have* the family he'd never experienced?

After a silence that told her he was reluctant to reveal more, he replied, "You mean, what did I see in her that I liked? She was beautiful in a California, sun-drenched sort of way. Her parents adored her—they'd sacrificed for her education—and I thought that meant she would sacrifice for the people she loved. After all, she came from a good background."

The questions kept popping up in Raina's mind, and she didn't know how many more he'd tolerate. "How long did you date before you were engaged?"

Although his jaw tightened, he responded, "About four months. We were engaged another five months, but when I started talking about leaving California, I could see she had other plans. One night I asked if she ever wanted to have kids, and she blew up. That's when I saw a side of her she'd never shown to me before. In a temper, she said if I was thinking about moving to a hick town in Texas, I could move there alone. She would never allow her body to be changed forever by a child and she wouldn't be tied down with adopted ones, either. She wanted a lifestyle with maids and servants. She wasn't going to *be* one."

If Shep had really loved this woman, he must have been devastated. "That must have been *so* hard for you to hear."

"You could say that. I wondered how I'd been such a fool. So now do you understand why I don't like to talk about it?"

Without hesitation, she kissed him on the cheek and then laid her head on his shoulder. Shep was a private man, but he'd just revealed more than she'd ever expected.

They began swaying to the music, their bodies moving in unison once more.

This time Shep was the one to lean back. She looked up at him quizzically.

After he studied her for a verse of the song, he passed his hand down her back. "I could kiss you. I could pick you up and carry you upstairs and we could have a great time in bed. But I think all of this is coming from somewhere, and I want to know where."

With the fall of night, the air had grown cooler and she shivered. "I want us to be able to talk."

His voice was low and deep above her head. "You said that before. Why is it important?"

Now she was the one who had to be honest. "I've been thinking about my marriage to Clark."

"What kind of thinking have you been doing? Are you regretting—"

"No," she cut in. "I don't regret marrying you. I guess it's just…my marriage to Clark wasn't so perfect. Even though I was in med school, Clark really wanted us to have kids, and I did, too. I think I would have given up my career to be a mom."

Shep considered what she said. "So what happened? Why didn't you have children?"

"I couldn't get pregnant," she responded. "Med school was ferociously energy-consuming and Clark's schedule was erratic. I don't know what the problem was, but whatever it was, it was coming between us. We didn't talk about it. If there was just one thing I could change, that would be it. Whether the distance between us stemmed from my insecurities or his desire to have children, I don't know."

"It doesn't sound like you to let something like that go," Shep insisted.

"You're right. I was hoping to change things. I planned a second honeymoon, hoping that would help, but then—"

The pictures that had played over and over again on the TV screen were still so very blatant in her head. In spite of her best effort, her throat choked up and her eyes became moist as Shep held her. She let her tears fall. She wasn't sure where the sadness was coming from—from unfulfilled dreams and the loss of her husband, or from the closeness she and Clark could have had but didn't, because neither had made the effort or taken the risk.

The call of a night bird carried in the stillness as they stood on the porch, Shep stroking her back, thinking about all she'd said.

"I'm sorry," she murmured. "I don't know why I'm so…emotional. Being pregnant, I guess."

"That's not all," he decided, brushing her hair over her shoulders. "You got married a little over a week ago." Taking her face in his hands, he added, "You have a career and you're trying to be a ready-made mom. I think you should go on upstairs and get ready for bed. I'll make you a mug of hot cider and bring up some of those crackers you've been eating."

"Shep, this isn't what I intended."

"I know, but isn't our motto 'go with the flow'?" He gave her a smile that was meant to make her feel better, but it didn't. She could see the mood had been spoiled for both of them. She should have just let well enough alone. She should have settled for physical intimacy.

When Shep dropped his arms from around her, she stepped away.

Maybe talking was highly overrated. Possibly the next time, she'd just give in to the desire between them.

But was that the kind of marriage she wanted to have?

## Chapter Eleven

"**E**nough about me," Gina said on Sunday evening, the night before her wedding. Raina, Angie and Lily had invited her over for some girl talk before the big day. "You've learned every detail I can tell you about our honeymoon plans in Kauai. It came together so much more easily, once we decided to take along Daniel and Hannah."

Although Daniel was Logan's son, Gina already thought of him as hers. Raina knew the feeling. Her heart seemed to fill to top capacity when she thought about Roy and Joey and Manuel, about the closeness she felt to them and the closeness they were beginning to feel to her. Since Joey's revelations about the bully bothering him in school, he seemed to gravitate toward her more and was much more talkative. They'd gone shopping for a chain for his medal and he'd proudly shown it to Shep.

"We'll miss you for two weeks," Angie said. She picked up the glass of sparkling apple cider sitting on the table next to her on the patio of the Victorian. "To my sister, Gina, her soon-to-be husband, Logan, and their wonderful son, Daniel. All the happiness in the world."

Sitting close together on the outside furniture, all of the women clinked their glasses and drank their cider.

With the sun teetering on the horizon in a beautiful purple-and-pink West Texas sunset, Gina turned to Lily. "If tomorrow will be too difficult for you, I'll understand. If you want to sit out the bridal party, if you want to skip the wedding altogether, just say the word."

Slowly, Lily set down her glass and met their gazes, one by one. "I don't know what I would have done the past few weeks without all of you, and that's why I want to be part of your wedding tomorrow, Gina." She settled her hand on her stomach. "Knowing Troy's baby is here makes me feel less alone." She hesitated a moment, then went on. "Something happened today and I—" She cleared her throat. "I want to tell you about it. I received a letter in the mail from Troy— from one of his friends. He'd left it with him in case anything happened."

"Oh, Lily." Raina was quick to take her friend's hand.

"It's okay," Lily replied softly. "I cried all afternoon. That's why my eyes were puffy when I came in. I couldn't help but cry. He told me how much he loved me, how much the baby and I meant to him. He also said he took a precaution before he left. He asked Mitch Cortega to look after me if anything happened."

"You and Mitch are already friends," Raina pointed out. Mitch had always been a special friend to her and

Troy, because he'd served in Iraq and had also been a member of the Texas National Guard.

"Yes, he is a friend, and he's made going back to work easier. I always told Troy I didn't need anyone to look after me, and he just laughed at that. But it *is* true. I've got to stand on my own two feet, for my sake and the baby's."

"You can stand on your own two feet and still depend on your friends," Angie insisted.

Lily smiled a little. "I guess so. But I want you to understand, I'm going to focus on the positive. I'm going to remember all the love Troy and I shared and how much he would have loved our baby. Then I'm going to give this little one the best welcome into the world he or she could ever have."

Lily addressed Gina. "So I *will* be there tomorrow, walking down the aisle ahead of you, witnessing one of the happiest days of your life." She turned her attention to Raina. "So tell us what's going on with you."

"Can I ask you a question?"

"Anything," they all chorused.

"How long does it take for a man to open up, to share what he's been through in his life, to share what he's feeling now? I don't want to compare, but Clark was very different from Shep. At the beginning of our relationship, Clark was a talker. We spent hours on the phone when we first met, talking about everything. Now I just feel...that I'm trying to open doors Shep doesn't want opened...that he's still holding back."

"Your lives are busy," Lily pointed out. "And having three kids around doesn't give you a whole lot of time to talk, does it?"

"No, I guess not."

"So, how's your sex life?" Angie asked with a straight face.

Open-mouthed for a moment, Raina finally burst out laughing. "Are you saying that's a gauge?"

"It could be an indicator," Gina agreed.

Raina remembered the night when, in some respects, their lovemaking had been hotter than it had ever been. "When we're in bed, or not even," she added mischievously, "Shep makes me feel like the most loved woman in the world. But sometimes I wonder…"

"What do you wonder?" Gina asked, gently prodding.

"If all of it isn't duty on his part. He married me because of the baby. Maybe he's just making love to me because that's what a husband is supposed to do."

"Why did *you* marry *him?*" Lily asked.

"Because I love him," she admitted out loud.

"Then give it all time," Gina advised her. "After all, it took Logan and me fourteen years to get back together. Both you and Shep are adjusting to a whole new life. Let yourself settle into it."

But just how long should Raina give their adjustment period before she should really start to worry?

Shep didn't like feeling front and center, but Gina had insisted he sit in the pew with her brother. Since he was Raina's husband, Gina now considered him family, too.

At the altar, Gina and Logan knelt for their blessing before the priest. Shep's gaze reflexively drifted toward Raina, seated in the front pew with the other bridesmaids, her beauty in the candlelight almost socking him in the gut.

This ceremony tonight had been so much different than theirs. The century-old Catholic church had a hallowedness about it that the gazebo on the courthouse lawn couldn't match. A priest had directed Gina and Logan's vows, rather than a judge.

What was wrong with him? There were good reasons why he and Raina had married as they had—Raina's pregnancy, Manuel's adoption, an urgency he'd felt as much as she had. But this church wedding had shaken him up a bit, nudged him to again think about the questions Raina had been asking. He was sure there would be more to come. She insisted that's what emotional intimacy was all about.

When in his life had he been emotionally intimate with anyone? Was he going about this marriage all wrong? But how else could he go about it, knowing that her husband had been the kind of hero that Shep didn't believe he could compete with. Not with his background.

In the pew in front of him, Gina's mother held Daniel, who was getting restless. The eighteen-month-old saw his mom and dad up at the altar and he wanted to be with them. With this wedding, Gina, Logan and Daniel would truly become a family. He and Raina and the boys were a family. What would happen when the little one was born?

Shep had to admit he couldn't wait. He just didn't want Raina to feel overwhelmed, and he'd do whatever he had to to make sure she didn't. She'd had morning sickness again today. He was afraid she was doing too much with her practice and her new responsibilities. They had a meeting tomorrow night with the adoptive parents group. He'd insisted he could go alone, but she wanted to come, too.

They were a couple.

A happily married couple?

Music began to play and Shep stood, along with everyone else, as Gina and Logan walked down the aisle, their hands intertwined as they smiled at their family and friends. Shep recognized that they shared something that he and Raina hadn't found yet.

But then he and Raina had married for a different reason than Logan and Gina—a baby.

The guests left the church pew by pew. When Shep arrived in the vestibule, his gaze cut to his wife, who stood next to Angie in the receiving line. At first his attention was caught up in the guests congratulating the newlyweds and Logan holding his son. But as his gaze drifted back to Raina and he saw her sudden pallor, he realized something was wrong. As unobtrusively as possible, he edged behind the receiving line to her side.

"What's wrong?" he murmured, close to her ear.

"I'm having cramps. They started toward the end of the ceremony. I don't want to make a scene."

"A scene be damned. Let's do what you need to do." He touched Angie's arm. "Raina's not feeling well. We're going outside."

Angie's eyes were troubled. "Should I—"

"Don't alarm Gina," Shep said. "I'll handle this. Raina will leave a message on your cell phone if we leave."

Lily, who was speaking to somebody she knew, glanced over her shoulder. Raina clutched her arm and said, "I'll see you in a bit," and left with Shep, her hand on her midriff.

"Jared already left for the reception," she told Shep as they stepped outside.

"Do you want me to call him?"

"No, I will. My cell phone's in my purse in your truck."

"Have you ever had cramping like this before?"

She shook her head.

That was all he needed. He swung her up into his arms and carried her to his vehicle. By the time he climbed into the driver's seat, she was already calling Jared.

"Jared, it's Raina. I'm cramping. What should I do?" After another pause, she responded, "Are you sure?" She looked at Shep. "He wants me to meet him at the emergency room in Lubbock."

Shep's whole body was tight with tension and his heart was doing double time. "Whatever he thinks is best. We'll be there in ten minutes."

When she closed her phone, she said, "Jared warned you to drive safely."

"As if I'm going to do anything to put this pregnancy in jeopardy," he muttered. He backed out of the parking place and headed up the main street of Sagebrush while Raina called Angie.

Ten minutes later, he parked at the emergency room lot and carried Raina inside. She didn't protest, and that told him more than anything else that *she* was scared. The fact that *she* was scared almost panicked him.

Jared must have arrived just moments before them, as he was at the registration desk already, talking to the clerk. She recognized Raina. "Dr. Gibson…McGraw. I'll do this as quickly as I can."

Shep tapped his foot, unable to define all the turmoil raging inside of him, unable to express to Raina what the thought of losing their child did to him.

The three of them made a sight, standing there in

their wedding finery. Only a half hour ago, he'd been comparing his wedding to Gina and Logan's. Only a half hour ago, the possibility of losing his child hadn't entered his mind.

Finally Jared said to Shep, "Why don't you wait out here until I examine her and do an ultrasound. I'll send someone for you when we're through."

Shep wanted to be inside there with Raina, but he didn't say so. She was sitting in a wheelchair now, looking a little lost, and he just wanted to take her into his arms and tell her everything would be okay.

"Why don't I wheel her back? I'll wait outside the exam room, but I'll be right there."

Madison looked from one of them to the other, then agreed. "Okay, follow me." Shep took hold of Raina's wheelchair and pushed it, following Madison, remembering the night he'd brought Manuel to the emergency room, the night he and Raina had really connected.

By the time Jared beckoned Shep inside the cubicle, Shep had removed his suit jacket and opened two buttons of his shirt above his bolo tie. He didn't care how he looked. He only cared what was going on in that room.

Piercing Jared Madison with his hardest stare, he asked, "How's the baby?"

"From what I can tell, everything looks fine. A few cramps and a little spotting aren't necessarily anything to be alarmed about. But pregnancies are always in a state of flux. So I'd like Raina to take a couple of days, rest, put her feet up and just give her body a chance to adjust to everything that's going on."

"Physically, you mean?"

"Emotionally, too. She's had a lot of stress."

"Good stress," Raina interjected.

"Good stress is still stress, and you know that. Fortunately, you said you have a housekeeper to take care of the boys. Right now, take advantage of that," Jared suggested.

"Can she do steps, ride in the truck?"

"What I'd like is for Raina to rest through Thursday. Can you sleep downstairs for a few nights?"

"There's a guest bedroom downstairs, where Eva sometimes stays. Raina can sleep there," Shep informed him, his chest tight with worry about Raina and their child.

"Terrific. Call my office tomorrow morning and make an appointment for Friday."

"Can I drive?" Raina asked.

"I'll drive you to the appointment," Shep cut in. "There's no use taking any chances."

Raina's voice seemed a little thick as she responded, "All right."

With a compassionate expression, Jared glanced from Raina to Shep. "I know this is scary, but what happened tonight doesn't mean there will be any trouble. Let's just take this a day at a time." He patted Raina's shoulder. "If you have any more symptoms, or if the spotting gets worse, you call me immediately."

"I will," she assured him.

At the door, Jared said, "I'll send someone back to get you checked out."

After the obstetrician left the room, complete silence enveloped it. Crossing to his wife, Shep looked down at her. "How are you doing?"

"I'm okay. How about you?"

"Shaken up. The thought of losing this baby really threw me off balance."

"Me, too," she said, but she was searching his face, looking for something.

"What?" he asked.

She shook her head. "Never mind."

He was ready to pursue the question when a nurse came in, a sheaf of papers in her hand. He knew any further talking he and Raina wanted to do would have to wait. It seemed something more was troubling her than the possibility of losing their baby.

In the car, they seemed to be locked in their separate worlds, tied up by personal thoughts. Shep didn't know how to express his worry, didn't want to add stress to a tense situation, so he kept quiet. But she was quiet, too, which was unusual for her. Maybe she was just tired. It had been a long day. Maybe her body was trying to tell her she couldn't be a doctor and a mother, too. Was she trying to reconcile that thought?

Raina's cell phone rang and she fished it out of her purse. Opening it, she answered, "Hi, Gina. You should be throwing your bouquet about now…I know you were worried, but I'm okay. I have to rest for a few days, then Jared will examine me again…Okay, put her on…Hi, Lily. No, I don't need you to come over tomorrow. It will just be me and Eva and Manuel until the boys get home…Well, sure, if you want to visit, that's fine. A laptop is only good company for so long. Okay."

Shep thought Raina was going to close the phone, but then she said, "Hi, Angie. I know. This could be nothing to worry about. I promise I'll call you if I need anything. Thank you. I'll talk to you soon. Bye."

As Raina closed her phone, Shep glanced at her. "You've got good friends."

"They all want to help."

"The problem is, they can't."

"No, they can't," she agreed. "The only thing I can do is give this time."

Shep was not going to let Raina lift a finger for the next few days.

If she lost this baby…

He wouldn't even give the thought a home in his head.

Raina walked aimlessly around the house late Saturday afternoon, stopping to stroke two of the kittens who'd curled up on the wide windowsill. After a morning of the boys roughhousing and Manuel demanding attention, Shep had decided Raina needed a break. Eva had taken Manuel along with her to her cousin's to play with her children, and Shep had taken Joey and Roy with him to run errands. Shep had been very quiet since their scare at Gina's wedding. Raina was afraid the tension between them since then had to do with an underlying question. What if she had lost the baby?

For her, Manuel and Roy and Joey had become even more precious. Yesterday Jared had given her a clean bill of health. But Shep was treating her like a piece of delicate glass, and she was worried.

Her feelings for him had grown deeper each day. She so desperately wanted him to say, "No matter what happens with your pregnancy, it's you and me against the world. I love you."

Last night she'd slept upstairs in their bedroom. Shep had held her and given her a chaste good-night kiss. When she'd asked if something was bothering him, he told her not to worry about him. She should just concentrate on taking care of herself.

She *was* taking care of herself, but she wanted to take care of *him*, too. Why wouldn't he accept that?

When the phone rang, she realized how much she missed the chatter and laughter of the boys. She lifted the phone from the dock on the end table, recognizing Ryder's number on the small screen. She hadn't told him about the miscarriage scare. She hadn't wanted a…fuss.

"Hi, there, how are you? I haven't heard from you in a while," she said brightly.

"I've been busy," he responded gruffly. "Is Shep there?"

"Not right now. He drove into town. Why?"

"Because I need to talk to you."

"So talk."

"I'd like to do this face-to-face."

"Uh-oh. I smell a problem. What's going on, Ryder?"

"I told you, I want to talk to you in person. How long will he be gone?"

"He just left about fifteen minutes ago. He was driving into Lubbock to pick up some kind of equipment. I think he might stop to get the boys new sneakers, and they'll probably convince him they need ice cream. So I imagine he'll be gone at least an hour."

"Good, I'll be over in five minutes."

"Where are you?"

"I had to stop at the police station in Sagebrush, so I'll be there almost by the time you get to the door."

"Ryder, tell me what this is about."

"It's about your husband. I'll be there in five."

Raina couldn't even imagine what Ryder had to tell her. She didn't like the fact at all that he was acting mysterious about it. Could this have anything to do with that background check he'd warned her he was going to run? It shouldn't. She'd told him to forget about it.

By the time she gathered a few toys from the sofa in the living room, she heard a rap on the kitchen screen door.

"Come in," she called, wishing Ryder felt at home here, wishing he and Shep could become friends.

Seconds later, Ryder stood in the doorway, a sober expression on his face. He was dressed in street clothes—jeans and a snap-button shirt, and he was carrying a manila envelope.

Ryder glanced around. "It's quiet. Where's the baby?"

"Eva has Manuel. Shep decided I needed a break."

Ryder crossed to the sofa where she was seated and handed her the envelope. "Do you want to read it in private, or do you want me to tell you what's in it?"

"Why don't you tell me what this is all about." She tried to remain calm. But her hands were a little clammy, and she was suddenly afraid to open the envelope.

"I told you I was going to do a background check on McGraw."

"And I told you not to."

"Yeah, well, I don't always listen to you. And it's a good thing I didn't."

"What did you find out? That he has speeding tickets?" If she kept this light, maybe nothing serious would come of it.

"I didn't just want his paper trail. I wanted real information."

"And how do you get that?"

"Old-fashioned detective work. I had a couple of road blocks, though—retirement, vacations, that kind of thing."

"I don't understand what you were investigating."

"I know cops out there, Raina. They connected me with other cops. I finally found out where McGraw spent his teenage years—in Sandy Cove, California."

"He spent his childhood in a foster home, I know that."

"More than one foster home."

"That's not unusual."

"I suppose not, but I contacted a deputy in Sandy Cove. The retired chief of police hasn't answered my calls and that made me suspicious."

"Maybe he didn't have anything to tell you."

"Possibly. But the deputy did. He remembers the night that McGraw supposedly stole a truck, though there's nothing in black and white on file."

*"Supposedly?"*

"McGraw was fourteen when he spent the night in jail."

"A night in jail? He was just a boy!"

"He stole a truck, Raina."

"Supposedly," she repeated. "Why doesn't the deputy know for sure?"

"He wasn't on duty that night. He just heard about what happened through the rumor mill. The chief wouldn't talk about it. The foster family kicked McGraw out, and that's *not* a 'supposedly.'"

"Where did he go?"

"Conroy, the deputy, said he was sent to stay with a guy who took in troubled kids."

Closing her eyes, Raina tried to absorb that. She hated to admit to Ryder that she knew nothing about

Shep's early years. He still hadn't opened up to her about any of that.

"I've also looked into how McGraw made his money. I haven't found anything underhanded yet, but once a hoodlum, always a hoodlum."

"People can change! Boys grow into men."

"I don't believe people change, Raina. You know that. And boys who get into trouble usually turn into men who get into trouble."

"Shep is a wonderful father," she said hotly. "You have no right—"

Ryder held up his hand to cut her off. "I'm your big brother. I have the right to protect you. Do you know anything about Shep McGraw before he moved here?"

All she knew was that a woman had hurt him deeply. She wasn't about to tell Ryder about that. "I know some things."

"The bare minimum, I bet," Ryder muttered. "I just want you to be careful. I'm going to dig around some more. If I were you, I'd do the same—quietly—without letting him know about it."

"Ryder!"

Ignoring her scolding tone, he stood and handed her the envelope. "I can see I'm not going to get very far with you. These are my notes on everyone I talked to. I intend to reach that chief of police, whether he wants to talk to me or not. After I do, I'll be in touch."

She handed him back the envelope. "I don't want this."

He settled it on her lap once again. "Don't be stupid, Raina. You have a baby to protect." After he gave her shoulder a squeeze, he strode out of the house, leaving her in a world of turmoil. Ryder had just made her question everything she thought she knew about her husband. What exactly should she do now?

Shep checked the rearview mirror and saw Roy and Joey licking ice-cream cones. He had to smile, though he was definitely going to have a mess to clean up in the backseat. "Use your napkins," he warned them.

Shep's cell phone rang and he pushed a button to put the call on the truck's speaker. "Hey, Cruz. What are you up to?"

"Just checking to see if the groom is still as happy as he was the day he got married."

"Married life is good. We had a scare this week. We thought Raina might have a miscarriage, but everything seems to be okay now."

"That's great."

"You didn't just call to congratulate me again, did you?"

"You always could read me. I wanted to let you know someone has been asking questions."

"Questions about what?"

"About you. My ranch might be two hours north, but I have friends in Sandy Cove."

Just like Sagebrush, Sandy Cove was a town where gossip traveled in circles to as many people as it could find.

"What *about* me?"

"Background stuff, mostly. When you lived where, who you lived with, where you got your money."

"I see."

"Do you know who's looking into everything?" Cruz asked.

"I can make a good guess. Raina's brother's a cop.

He and I didn't take to each other too well, so I have a feeling he's fishing."

"He won't find anything."

"Not on paper. But what he finds out depends on who he talks to."

"Not many people can remember back that far."

"I hope you're right."

"I guess you haven't told Raina what happened when you were a kid?"

"I didn't see the point."

"Maybe there is one now. Maybe you should tell her before her brother does."

"Did anyone ever tell *you* you had some smarts?"

"Just a teenage rebel named Shep, who became my older brother."

"And Matt."

"Yeah, and Matt, too. We'll never be able to repay our debt to him."

"No, but we can pass along what he gave to us by helping other kids."

Shep knew they were both thinking about growing up on Matt's ranch, what they'd learned there, what they'd been given there.

Cruz interrupted his thoughts. "If you need a character reference, give me a call."

"Will do. Thanks, Cruz, for giving me a heads-up."

"Anytime."

When Shep ended the call, both Roy and Joey were still catching drips of ice cream with their tongues on their cones. But he felt as if he'd been thrust back in time. Now he had to decide when and how to tell Raina that he'd seen the inside of a jail.

## Chapter Twelve

As soon as Shep kissed Raina, he knew something was wrong. She didn't respond as she usually did. Afterward, her gaze didn't meet his—and she always looked him directly in the eye.

Granted, they hadn't been very physical the past week, not with the miscarriage scare, not with wondering what would happen if they lost the baby.

"Supper will be ready in about an hour," she told him as she turned away.

Shep had encouraged Joey and Roy to go upstairs and wash the ice cream from their hands and face. No time like the present to ask, "What's wrong?"

Good at reading people, he watched Raina do something she'd never done before.

She lied to him. "Nothing's wrong." She laid her

hand on her stomach. "I have a lot to think about, that's all. Did the boys have ice cream? Should I postpone supper another half hour?"

"Yes, they had ice cream," he answered, turmoil twisting his gut. This mundane conversation was driving him crazy. But he had to go slowly. "I brought you something," he said, hoping he was wrong about all of this, hoping she wasn't lying, hoping Ryder hadn't gotten to her.

Now she did swing around to face him. "What?"

He'd dropped the catalogues on the table when he came in. Now he picked them up and presented them to her. "I stopped at that furniture store in Lubbock that we passed a couple of times. I thought you might be interested in picking out what you want for the baby."

In the silence, there was that question between them again…the one he saw in her eyes. The one that echoed in his heart. *What would have happened if we had lost the baby?*

After she took the catalogue from him and paged through it, her eyes grew moist. "Oh, Shep. I don't know when I'll be comfortable ordering furniture, after what just happened."

He clasped her shoulders. "Hey, no pressure here. I just thought you could make a wish list."

That suggestion seemed to bring even more glistening anguish to her eyes. She murmured, "We have to talk."

"About?"

After a deep, shaky breath, she glanced toward the stairs.

"I don't even know how to begin," she said in a low

voice. "Ryder stopped by. He brought me some…information. Information about you."

Shep's body was strung tight, every nerve in it firing warning signals. "Did you *ask* him to get information?"

"No! In fact, after I told him I was pregnant he wanted to, and I told him not to."

"You knew this and you didn't tell me?"

"At that point, you and I hadn't made any decisions. I just told Ryder to forget it."

"And you really thought he'd do that?"

"I don't know. I didn't think it would matter. I didn't think he'd find anything. I trusted that you were who you seemed to be."

"And who was that, Raina?" Anger was starting to build, but he held it in, kept it locked up tight.

"You're a wonderful father, a business owner, and you seem to be a good person."

"Seem to be?" He must have let something escape in his voice, because she took a step away from him.

He dropped his hands to his sides. Damn it! Didn't he have a right to be angry? Didn't he have the right to believe she'd stand by him, not believe the first rumor that came along? Hadn't they said vows and made a commitment? Was she going to use this as an excuse to walk away?

"He's trying to protect me, Shep."

"Do you feel you *need* to be protected?"

The question seemed to sway between them, until she took hold of it and answered it. "He brought me an envelope. He gave me his notes concerning the people he'd talked to in Sandy Cove."

He could already feel her withdrawal and doubts.

"And just what did they have to say?" His tone was sarcastic, but he couldn't help it.

"Shep, this isn't easy for me. Ryder just called, came over and set it all down in front of me."

"What did he say, Raina?" Shep was having a difficult time pushing away a sense of betrayal.

"He told me you'd stolen a truck when you were fourteen, got thrown in jail and got kicked out of your foster home. He said you were sent to stay with someone who took in juveniles who got into trouble."

"And who did he get this information from?"

"A deputy. Burt Conroy. Are you saying it isn't true?"

Shep always tried to speak the truth. But sometimes the circumstances around it weren't black or white. "You know what, Raina? I'm not sure it matters if it's true or not. You've known me for months. You've watched me with my boys." He saw her wince when he called them *his,* but right now, they felt like *his,* not *theirs.* "You married me, said vows, said you'd be committed for a lifetime. So I have a question for *you.* Don't you trust your own judgment, even if you don't trust me?"

"Shep…" She reached out a hand to him, but he turned away, walked to the other side of the room, ran a hand through his hair and turned to face her once more.

"You want to know the truth? The truth is, I did steal a truck and I spent the night in jail. That's the truth."

Joey and Roy's laughter drifted down from upstairs. Shep ached so bad he couldn't stand here right now and watch the family he'd wanted to put together fall apart. Raina looked as if she was shocked at his blunt statement, as if she'd expected him to deny all of it. Maybe he shouldn't have told her in just that way, but after all, that *was* the bottom line.

He had to get out of here so he could think straight, so he could put it all in perspective. So he could decide what to do next.

"Will you be okay with Joey and Roy for a while? I think I need a little breathing space."

She looked as if she were about to burst into tears, and he wanted to do something about that, but he didn't know what. He couldn't change the past. He couldn't be somebody he wasn't. He certainly couldn't be the hero her first husband was, and that was probably the crux of the whole matter. That was probably the reason his marriage was going to fall apart.

"I'll be fine," she responded, pulling herself together. Shep could see she was hurting, too.

Yet he couldn't take on her pain. He was feeling too much of his own. When he went to the door, he called over his shoulder, "You have my cell phone number in case the boys need me."

Then he walked out and let the screen door slam behind him. Anger seemed to scald the back of his throat as he tried to figure out what hurt so bad. He was halfway into town when he realized the pain centered in his heart.

"I don't know if Shep's going to come home tonight," Raina said, confiding in Lily as she stood in the upstairs bathroom using her cell phone. Roy and Joey were downstairs in the playroom, with blankets covering the furniture as they played in their make-believe cave. They'd had a quiet supper without Shep. Roy and Joey asked where he'd gone, and she told them he had business to take care of. Even *they* knew that that was unusual on a Saturday night.

"Of course he'll come home," Lily reassured her. "Where's he going to go?"

"I don't know where he is."

"Then call him."

"He said he needed some space. Lily, what have I done? I *doubted* him."

"He told you he *did* steal the truck," her friend reminded her. Lily had pulled the whole story from her when Raina had called, looking for some support.

"Yes, he said he stole a truck. But something in the way he said it—I think there's a bigger story there. I don't think Ryder has it right, and I don't think he has all the information about it. I *do* know Shep. For just that little while this afternoon, Ryder put doubts in my head. With almost losing the baby, not knowing exactly how Shep feels about me, I'm in a rocky place. But I've known Shep ever since he started bringing his boys to me. I've watched him. He's gentle and caring with them. That can't be learned. It's innate. I just can't imagine a man with his nature being a wild, uncaring teenager. I've made a mess, Lily, and I don't know if he can ever forgive me. Maybe our marriage can't survive, even *with* the baby. Shep has good reason not to trust women, and I just gave him a reason not to trust me. He's been burned, and I burned him again."

"Raina, I want you to sit down and breathe. If you get totally stressed out it won't be good for you or the baby. Now come on. This is *one* argument. One bump. You can get over a bump."

"I don't know if Shep can."

"Have a little faith, will you?"

"I love him, Lily, but I don't know if he loves me."

"Have you told him?"

"No."

"Maybe you should. Maybe he needs to know just how much you have to lose, too. Do you want me to come over?"

Lily's presence would be comforting. They understood each other so well. But Raina wanted to be here alone when Shep came home...*if* Shep came home.

"Thanks so much for offering, but I need to wait for Shep and figure out what I'm going to say to him. I have to apologize in a way he understands—"

"If he loves you, 'I'm sorry' might be enough."

*If he loves you.*

Raina was almost afraid to hope.

Shep had switched on the lights in the outside, fenced-in area of the lumberyard. For the past hour he'd been moving two-by-fours from the supply area to a flatbed trailer to fill an order. He thought the activity would help. But like a broken wagon wheel thumping around and around and around, he couldn't get past his disappointment in Raina, or his anger at himself for giving in to the hope that things could be different.

He'd just hauled a few more boards onto his shoulder when the cell phone in his pocket rang. Could it be Raina? Did he want to talk to her now?

Setting down the lumber, he plucked the phone from his pocket and checked the caller ID. It was not Raina's number. It was a California number, a name he hadn't seen for a very long time—not since the night he'd spent in jail. Back then he'd spotted the name painted in black block letters on the door to the police station.

He answered, preparing himself for almost anything. "McGraw here."

"Hi, Shep, it's Chief Winston from Sandy Cove. Remember me?"

"You were definitely a memorable man in my life. I never forgot that night in jail."

"And you've held it against me ever since."

Shep sighed. "No, I let it go a long time back."

"That's good to hear. I'm calling to find out why Detective Ryder Greystone keeps calling me. I'm retired now. I took a vacation for a few weeks and didn't want to be bothered. But I had five messages from Detective Greystone. It seems he wants to know all about you and the night you spent in my jail. I have to ask, Shep. Are you in trouble of some kind?"

This man had seen Shep at his worst, when he was worried sick about Cruz and rebellious about everything that had happened with the Willets. There was no reason not to tell him the truth now.

"Greystone is investigating me because I married his sister fairly quickly. She's pregnant."

After an awkward silence, the former chief of police cleared his throat. "That's personal business. What's he trying to do, break you up?"

"Could be," Shep conceded.

After another pause, the chief finally said, "Even you don't know the real truth."

"What's that supposed to mean?"

After a momentary pause, the retired lawman continued. "The truth is, I had no choice but to put you in jail that night. If I hadn't done that, we would have had to officially give you a juvenile record, and I didn't want to. I knew the situation you were in with the Willets. I knew how careless they'd been with kids before you. I even reported them, but nothing got done. *I* was the one who called Matt Forester. We grew up together and I knew he had a good heart."

Matt had had more than a good heart. He'd taught Shep and Cruz about hard work, responsibility and getting a start in life. When he'd died, he'd left Cruz and Shep the ranch. Cruz had sold off some of it to give Shep his share. That ranch had gone a long way to making them both successful adults. Shep realized now that he'd had the wrong opinion of Chief Winston all these years. He'd thought the man had reveled in his position, that he'd thrown Shep in jail because he could. But now Shep recognized how the man had protected him, not just then, but for the future.

"You'd think a man would get smarter as he got older," Shep muttered.

"Are you talking about yourself or someone else?" the chief asked, joking.

"Why didn't you tell me you and Matt Forester were friends? Why did you let me think you just wanted to…punish me? I hated you when I was in that jail that night."

"I know you did. But I also knew you were a good kid, driving Cruz to the hospital the way you did. I guess I wanted to scare you a little, to make you see that there were rules and regulations, and you couldn't always go outside of them. I think it worked, for the most part. Matt kept me up-to-date on what was going on with you. After you moved to Texas, well, I have contacts there, too. So that's why, when a detective from Lubbock is trying to get in touch with me, I'm just not too eager to call him back. But I can, if you want me to set him straight."

Shep had grown up handling his own affairs, and that was exactly what he was going to do now. "I'm going to settle this from my end. Give me a couple of days. If he calls after that, tell him whatever you'd like."

"So what about his sister? Are you going to stay married to her?"

Shep had been sorely mistaken about the chief and his intentions. Because he'd misunderstood, his mule-headedness had categorized the chief in the wrong way. Now he realized he'd been just as mule-headed about Raina. Knowing who her first husband was, Shep had felt…unworthy.

Unworthy.

Because he'd been abandoned as a child? Over-looked for adoption? Been deserted by a selfish fiancée?

Looking at everything now, he saw clearly how unworthy he'd felt of Raina's love…as if he didn't deserve to *be* loved. He'd felt he had to compete with Clark Gibson.

Of course, he couldn't. He'd been so wrong not to pour out his past to her so she could look at it and maybe understand it. He hadn't told Raina about his troubled teenage years because of sheer pride. He didn't want her to think less of him because…

Because he loved her. His walls had broken down when he'd met her and she'd slipped inside his heart.

He'd tried to protect himself from loving her, but that hadn't worked, not one bit. He thought their physical attraction was why he wanted to be close to her, spend time with her, kiss her. Oh, sure, that might have started it all. But when he felt they might lose their baby, that she as well as the baby might be in some kind of danger, he should have admitted to himself that he loved her. He loved her with all his heart. If he'd admitted that, maybe she wouldn't have doubted him.

"Staying married to her is going to become my life's ambition. But I acted like an ass today, so I have some ground to cover first."

"Keep me informed," the chief said seriously.

Shep replied, just as seriously, "I will."

Then he went to work formulating a plan.

Raina had received the call from Shep around seven-thirty. He'd said, "We have to talk. Alone. I called Eva and she's going to bring Manuel home and stay with the boys. She should be there in about ten minutes. I'll pick you up in about fifteen, okay?"

Raina's mind had been racing. Her thoughts had screamed, *Don't decide anything without me. Give me time to let me tell you I love you.* But she hadn't wanted to say it over the phone. She wanted to look into those blue eyes of his and declare it with all the feeling in her heart.

So she simply said, "I'll be ready."

So now here they were, driving down the main street of Sagebrush, her husband tall and silent and looking troubled in the driver's seat.

"Are you okay?" he asked. "I don't want anything to happen—"

"With the baby," she finished for him in a low voice, not knowing if he was going to tell her they were finished, or if there was some way they could work through this together.

"The baby is one of the things we have to talk about," he said solemnly. "I reserved a room at the bed-and-breakfast over on Alamo Road. That way we can talk as long as we need to."

Talk about how to break up their marriage? Talk about how to explain to the kids? Talk about custody agreements and visitation arrangements? *Stop!* she warned herself, before she could make herself crazy.

The bed-and-breakfast was as old as Sagebrush. It had once housed dancing girls for the saloon down the street that had now been upgraded to a sports bar. The outside was stone and timber, refurbished as the inside had been. But Raina hardly paid attention to the tin roof covering the doorway, to the brass lamp and milk-glass shades in the foyer, to the mahogany desk where the hostess stood ready to check them in. Raina almost felt like telling her they had a whole lot of baggage that she just couldn't see.

They followed her up the staircase to a room on the second floor that was set apart from the others. Once she'd left and they were alone in the room, neither of them seemed to know what to do or say.

"Shep, I need to tell you—"

He took her hand and tugged her to the love seat. "Don't. Don't say anything yet, okay? I need to tell you some things. I should have done it long before now."

"The past doesn't matter to me, Shep."

"Well, it should." He sandwiched her hand between

both of his. "My dad and I were close. I followed him around everywhere he went and wanted to do anything he did. When he died, I sure didn't understand what had happened. My mother said something about heaven, and that that's where Dad was. That made about as much sense to me at four as when she told me we couldn't live in Texas anymore, and we ended up in California. California. Heaven. Maybe they were the same place. I was a mixed-up kid, and that didn't get any better when she left me in a shopping center and didn't come back. I was six."

Raina wanted to hold him. She wanted to kiss him. She wanted to love him. But he wasn't going to let her do that yet. He had to get this all out, and the only thing she could do was listen. She squeezed his hand.

"I became one of those kids who always had to be doing something, couldn't sit still for a minute. The foster homes I fell into just wanted a kid who would listen, not ask questions and not mouth back. So I got kicked from one to another, got angrier at the system and the adults who ran it."

It was easy for Raina to see that rebellious little boy who just wanted to be loved, but didn't know how to go about getting the love he wanted.

Shep continued, "When I was thirteen, I landed at the Willets' in Sandy Cove. But this time I lucked out. They already had taken in another foster child named Cruz, who was two years younger than me. It was as if no age difference even existed. We became brothers, in part because we knew the Willets didn't care about us. So we had to care about each other. They just wanted the money we brought in. They just wanted kids to do chores so they didn't have to. They liked to party, and they often went away and left us there alone. There wasn't anything unusual about it."

"But you were just kids. Didn't anybody check up on them?"

"They knew how to put on a good front. They knew caseworkers were overburdened. They knew we wouldn't say anything, because we had been kicked around often enough."

"Tell me the rest," she requested.

Shep stared across the room at a sepia-tinted painting of an old homestead. Finally, he shifted on the love seat and looked directly into her eyes. "They left us alone one weekend. I was fourteen and Cruz was twelve. He got sick. He had a fever before they left, but the day after they were gone, it spiked up to one hundred and four. I didn't know what to do. There was no one I could call, no hospital nearby. It was ten miles down the road in the next town. So I did what I knew how to do. I hot-wired the old truck they'd left behind and drove Cruz to the emergency room. I took him inside and told him to wait his turn and I'd be back for him later. He was scared, but he knew I couldn't stay or we'd both be in big trouble. The thing was, we never counted on one of the nurses getting the license plate number as I drove away. The authorities picked me up, waited for the Willets to get home, then all hell broke loose. The Willets claimed I was a troublemaker and it wasn't the first time I'd hot-wired the truck, so the chief of police put me in jail for the night."

"You were only fourteen! How could he do such a thing?"

"For all these years I wondered the same thing. I also didn't know how a rancher named Matt Forester came to find out about me and Cruz. He came to the jail and already had Cruz with him. He picked me up and drove us to his place, a huge ranch where he ran cattle and bred horses. That's where Cruz and I grew up, learning what was really right and wrong, what was work and what was play." He smiled a little, remembering.

"Is Mr. Forester still in California?"

"No. Matt died when I was in my early twenties. I had gotten my real-estate license and was trying to make a name for myself. Cruz had gone to college with every intention of becoming a veterinarian. But then Matt died and everything changed. Cruz decided he wanted to run the ranch. Since Matt left it to both of us, he sold off part of it to give me my stake. With that money, I bought real estate of my own, and a few years later turned it over for a nice profit." He blew out a breath. "Earlier today, Cruz called me to warn me someone was asking questions about me. Then tonight the chief of police, retired now, also called me to ask me who Ryder Greystone was. Apparently, he wanted a return call, but the chief didn't know if he should. That's when I learned that Matt Forester was one of his good friends. The chief had called him and told him two boys needed a home. All these years, I held a grudge against the chief and had a problem with authority figures. But he just threw me in jail that night to prevent the Willets from pressing charges and giving me a record. He thought it would also teach me to stay on the right side of the law."

Raina felt tears come to her eyes as she thought of

Shep as that little boy who'd lost his dad and then his mom, who'd been a teenager with no one to turn to except another boy whom he'd befriended and protected.

"Shep, I love you," she said, unable to hold in her feelings any longer. "And not because of what you told me tonight. That just confirms what I already knew. You're a noble man. You'd do anything for the people you love. It's obvious how much love you have to give—to your sons…to *our* sons. I do love you, if it's not too late to tell you that. I believe in you. I believe in *us*. Ryder just surprised me and rattled me this afternoon and threw me off balance. I'm so sorry I doubted you. If you can forgive me, I promise it will never happen again. I want to spend the rest of my life with you."

Shep didn't respond right away, and that made her nervous. But then a slow smile started at the corners of his lips and spread.

He took a small box from his pocket. "I just made it to the store before it closed. I know we didn't have a real engagement. You didn't have a real courtship."

When he opened the little black box, she gasped. It was a ring—a circle of diamonds.

"This is one of those eternity rings," he explained. "I'd like to put this on your finger as a sign that no matter what happens, we'll handle whatever it is together. It's also a promise that I'll court you for the rest of our lives. We're going to tear up that prenuptial agreement, too. What's mine is yours. I love you, Raina. My pride stood in the way of my admitting it. I couldn't see the best because I often thought about the worst—you leaving. Now I want to leave the worst behind and hold on to the future with you."

She gave him her hand. Gently, he slid the ring on her finger above her wedding band. "Perfect," he said.

"Perfect," she agreed, looking up into his eyes, letting him see everything that was in her heart.

Enfolding her in his arms, he kissed her. It was one of those shining kisses that lit their passion and seared their souls. The kiss was a coming together, a recommitment, a chance to start over the right way.

When he ended it, she clung to him, so in love she couldn't speak.

Shep pulled her onto his lap and held her in his arms. "When do you want to take a real honeymoon?"

"But the boys—"

"The boys will be fine for a couple of days without us." He settled his big hand on her tummy, "Once this baby's born, we'll hardly have time to breathe. How about three days' seclusion in Santa Fe or Taos?"

"As long as I'm with you, I don't care where we go." She could feel the chuckle in his chest as he kissed her temple.

"I'm so glad you feel that way."

"I'll feel that way for the rest of our lives."

When Shep kissed her again, she knew nothing could come between them. They were one, now and forever.

*Epilogue*

Raina crouched down next to the sofa, one arm around Joey, one arm around Roy.

"It's dark in here," Roy whispered in her ear.

"Only for a few more minutes."

Beside her on the sofa, Angie held Manuel. The toddler reached for Raina's hair and held on to it. "Mommy," he said quite clearly.

The light over the stove in the kitchen glowed softly, some of its illumination splaying into the living room. Raina reached over Roy's shoulder and patted Manuel's face. "Hey, sweet one. I know you're there."

For the past month, she'd truly become the happiest woman to walk the planet. She felt like a mom. She knew being a mother to three kids, and soon an infant, wouldn't be easy. Yet she also knew her husband loved her as much as she loved him. That gave her all the confidence in the world that she could handle anything... with a little help.

Lily, who was standing on the other side of Joey, said in a low voice, "I think he's coming. Get ready, everyone."

Lily had been a real trouper. Raina knew how difficult the past few months had been for her, how raw her grief was, yet how unbreakable her spirit seemed to be.

The kitchen door opened and shut. Shep's strong, deep voice called, "Raina?"

When he stepped into the living room, someone switched on the overhead light and everyone popped out of their hiding places.

"Surprise!" Roy and Joey called the loudest, running toward their father.

Grinning, Shep gave both of them a big hug. "What are you surprising me with?"

"A party," Roy answered gleefully.

Raina went to her cowboy, who looked a bit overwhelmed. "Happy birthday!"

Shep looked around at everyone, obviously speechless. His gaze fell on their friends—Logan, Gina and their son Daniel, Angie and Lily, Raina's mother and Ryder. When his gaze fell on Ryder, his eyebrows arched up. Ryder approached him and held out his hand for a shake. Shep firmly shook it.

With Raina standing right there, Ryder admitted, "I've never seen my sister happier, so I brought a present you might appreciate." He handed Shep a dark blue gift bag.

"Go ahead," Raina encouraged him. "Then we'll feed everyone ice cream and cake."

Shep dipped his hand into the bag and pulled out a branch.

"It's an olive branch," Ryder said. "I thought maybe we could start over."

"I'd like that," Shep told him sincerely, then caught Raina around the waist and gave her a hug. "Did you plan this?"

"No! Honestly, Ryder thought about it all on his own."

Joey pointed to a table that had been set up in the corner. "There's more presents over there."

"I see, but I think I have the best present I'll ever get right here."

"What's that?" Roy asked.

"Your mom, your new brother or sister and the three of you. I couldn't ask for anything more."

"I have a special present for you," Raina said, her hand caressing his jaw.

"But I have to wait until everyone's gone, right?" Shep asked wickedly.

She could feel a flush stain her cheeks. Their time in the bedroom was precious and passionate with the love and commitment and promise they shared every day. "If you blow out all the candles on your cake, you might get that wish," she said, teasing. "But no, I have another surprise. Come on out," she called toward the playroom.

Cruz Martinez emerged from the playroom and Shep's mouth dropped open. He was a striking man who wore a smile that practically spread from ear to ear. He was as tall as Shep and just as lean. As he embraced her husband, the affection and caring that the two of them shared was obvious.

Finally, Shep stepped back. "So I guess the two of you have met," he said, joking.

"We're already friends," Cruz told him. "I like your new wife. She knows how to throw a party."

Shep laughed out loud and Raina could hear the true happiness in that laughter.

"I'll be right back," he said to everyone, taking Raina's hand and pulling her through the doorway into the kitchen.

"They're going to kiss," Joey announced to everyone.

"What are you doing?" Raina asked Shep. "This is your party. We have guests."

"Thank you for going to so much trouble, for giving me a gift that means so much more than you can ever know."

"I know," she said softly, wrapping her arms around his neck.

Her cowboy bent his head and kissed her.

The round of applause from the living room just made them both hold tighter. They'd be spending a lifetime holding on tightly to each other, keeping promises and giving each other gifts they'd cherish always.

\* \* \* \* \*

0411/023b

# 2 FREE BOOKS
## AND A SURPRISE GIFT

We would like to take this opportunity to thank you for reading this Mills & Boon® book by offering you the chance to take TWO more specially selected books from the Cherish™ series absolutely FREE! We're also making this offer to introduce you to the benefits of the Mills & Boon® Book Club™—

- **FREE home delivery**
- **FREE gifts and competitions**
- **FREE monthly Newsletter**
- **Exclusive Mills & Boon Book Club offers**
- **Books available before they're in the shops**

Accepting these FREE books and gift places you under no obligation to buy, you may cancel at any time, even after receiving your free books. Simply complete your details below and return the entire page to the address below. You don't even need a stamp!

**YES** Please send me 2 free Cherish books and a surprise gift. I understand that unless you hear from me, I will receive 5 superb new stories every month, including two 2-in-1 books priced at £5.30 each, and a single book priced at £3.30, postage and packing free. I am under no obligation to purchase any books and may cancel my subscription at any time. The free books and gift will be mine to keep in any case.

Ms/Mrs/Miss/Mr _____ Initials _____

Surname _____

Address _____

_____

_____ Postcode _____

E-mail _____

Send this whole page to: Mills & Boon Book Club, Free Book Offer, FREEPOST NAT 10298, Richmond, TW9 1BR